DECEIT and other CONVENIENCES

CONVENIENCES

LOVE AND WAR ON WALL STREET

DECEIT and other CONVENIENCES

LOVE AND WAR ON WALL STREET

a novel by Alex Adelson

THE WINDESSA PRESS

DECEIT and other CONVENIENCES
Copyright 2014 Alex Adelson

www.deceitandotherconveniences.com

This book is a work of fiction. Any references to historical events, real people, or real places are used fictitiously. Other names, characters, places, and events are products of the author's imagination, and any resemblance to actual events or places or persons, living or dead, is entirely coincidental.

The Windessa Press
Alex Adelson
P.O. Box 145
Andes, NY 13731
U.S.A.

www.windessapress.com

ISBN-13: 978-0692239568 (The Windessa Press)
ISBN-10: 0692239561

Dedicated to Margie, my wife...
as sweet as it can be.

CONTENTS

If heaven exists, it's not overpopulated.

PART 1 PRACTICE

CHAPTER 1 THE OBLIGATION

The embers that house memories are never without pain or without pleasure. Time heals, but at best the memory of the pain that became scar tissue remains as scattered segments of what we are. He recalled the feelings and some were a bit rough, but then again he was who he had always been ... approximately.

Garrett Carlssen grew up in the town of Millsport located on the banks of the Susquehanna River. His Grandfather, Father and Uncle were in the auto parts business. They had become modestly prosperous after World War II which had provided the means for an education for him, his brother, and his sister. His brother went into the family business and his sister married a dentist after a short career in marketing. Garrett became a physicist.

Garrett Carlssen was a kid who, like most kids, crossed bridges because he had to. Sometimes it was quite scary, but generally not that hard. Usually Mom, Pop, a friend, Grandma, Grandpa, or somebody would be there to reassure him or hold his hand. As Garrett grew up he had to learn to cross them by himself. He ultimately came to realize the most difficult bridges to traverse were relationships. They could, and most often did, evoke those familiar feelings: terrors, boredom, pain, pleasure, and at times, sheer delight. Some relationships contained every one of them.

Jersey Smart, like his name, was a very smart, exceptional engineer, some even said a visionary. He was the head of a very promising company that was beginning to show significant signs of success. The commercial world had discovered the power of electronic data capture and identification technology. The Company made the electronic gadgets that detect the information resident in such venues as retail barcodes, QR codes, radio tags, etc. and send that information to computers. The technology serves as precision 'eyes' for the computers that report commercial events such as shopping, sales, and inventory management – avoiding the numerous mistakes that people make entering data on keyboards. Further, the data is captured and delivered at incredibly faster speeds. The same technology is also used in retail to prevent pilfering.

Some Wall Street firms were beginning to pay attention to the industry in general and its potential for significant growth. One of them, through an initial public offering, had recently raised money for the Company.

Jersey and Garrett and three other veterans of a NASA think tank had started the Company three times before they had gotten it right. They currently occupied a 40,000 square foot building in Northern Westchester and employed over 200 employees

Garrett and Jersey were in a waiting room located in a Westchester County hospital. Westchester is a bedroom community north of New York City. An employee of theirs had been taken to the hospital because of an emergency.

"Damn it!" Garrett growled, "You can't pull this kind of crap on Scully!" Jersey simply looked away, seemingly peering out the waiting room window at the evening expressway traffic. Garrett knew better. Jersey Smart wasn't looking at anything. He was crafting a good retort. These two had been at this point many times over the years and the conversation was about to get louder. They had known each other for fifteen years as scientists, at times buddies, and eventually, business partners. But in so many ways neither had gotten to know the other, really. Anne Mills would eventually change so much of that.

Scully Paterson had come to the Company from a Division of General Technologies, where he was highly valued as a manufacturing manager.

Pristinimatic Technologies, Inc., or "PT Boat," was the name that Jersey insisted on calling the Company. Eventually, almost everybody else working at the Company did the same. It became the company nickname. As time went on the "boat" part was dropped and it became simply "PT." It really was a silly homage to the old World War II high speed patrol boat which was featured or appeared in some very successful Hollywood movies of the 40's, 50's, and 60's that Jersey loved to watch on the cable channels. Much to Jersey's delight, PTPB had become their market symbol on the stock market. "PT" had a lot of things right about it; great technology, excellent patent protection, aggressive and effective marketing, but, on the other hand, lousy manufacturing capability. Thirty percent of the stuff they made they rejected and would have to rework or throw it out. Fortunately, their high mark-up selling prices were saving them for the moment. Everybody knew this couldn't continue. They needed a first class manufacturing manager.

Jersey had come to know Scully Paterson by accident. This happened at a technology symposium in Albany and he fell in love. He came back from his trip raving about Scully. "This guy will solve our manufacturing problems. This is a guy with the right stuff," he loudly announced, proclaimed, and decreed.

Garrett had heard this kind of refrain before - many times. Sometimes Jersey was right, and sometimes he was wrong.

Scully had a great job where he was, and was not interested in leaving General Technology for emerging "PT." But Jersey was determined and started the courtship. It eventually led to a very fat signing bonus, and a very fat salary, a generous stock option agreement, and moving expenses. Scully, with a push from his wife, accepted. There was one little caveat that showed up at the contract signing. Scully had to last six months on the job or no signing bonus or stock options. Jersey had it inserted at the last moment - the morning of the signing, unbeknownst to Scully's lawyer. He found out about it at the same time his lawyer did. Influencing matters was a house that a Westchester real estate salesman under guidance from Jersey had found for Scully. It was way above anything Scully had ever lived in or owned. Further, it was located in the best neighborhood a kid from South Philly had ever dreamed of – all of this carefully and quietly engineered by Jersey.

Scully was clearly off his turf and didn't listen to his lawyer's protest at the signing. A warm wind was at his back and he had been seduced. This also included his wife and kids. They too were excited and anxious to move on with their new luxury lifestyle. Although Scully's wife didn't come from South Philly, she came from a small Pennsylvania coal town which was a very close second to Scully's old Philadelphia neighborhood's impoverishment.

Actually things went fairly well for Scully on the manufacturing floor, but there was constant badgering and clubbing from Jersey, a form of abuse that Jersey had been honing and perfecting since he had become CEO. As the Company grew it became worse. Any time he could, he was in Scully's face. The other partners pleaded with Jersey to layoff, but to no avail. Nobody really understood why Jersey was doing it.

Garrett recognized an emerging pattern, whatever Jersey fell in love with he eventually needed to abuse. It didn't matter if it was a pen, a car, a secretary, or a lover – that was the new Jersey. Throughout the many years Garrett had worked with Jersey he could always be difficult, but never abusive.

Garrett had had a number of screaming sessions with Jersey about Scully - sometimes in the office, sometimes on the phone late at night. Once when Garrett was in Belgium and Jersey was in Japan, Jersey called Garrett at two o'clock in the morning and they spent an hour and a half arguing about Jersey's behavior towards Scully. As usual it was a waste of time.

Things went on this way until the last day of the end of the sixth month contract trial period. At three thirty in the afternoon Scully, working in his office, had a heart attack, and not being dead, was taken to the St. Frances Memorial Hospital Cardiac Intensive Care Unit.

Garrett, who lived in New York City, was returning from a business meeting in Connecticut. As he walked into his lower 5th Avenue apartment, he was greeted by his teenage daughter's sarcastic announcement that he was to call Jersey immediately – "an emergency." Call Jersey on his cell phone.

Not bad, he thought. *Better than usual.* Such messages were often reported the next day or not reported at all. "Emergency messages" happened all the time with Jersey, and Garrett thought little of it, but he always responded.

He began, "Hello Jersey, what's happening?"

"Get your ass up here; we've got a big problem!" barked Jersey.

"What are you talking about?" asked Garrett.

"I'm at the St. Frances Memorial Hospital in Westchester – third floor waiting room," retorted Jersey. Then click.

Jesus Christ, thought Garrett, *What in the hell is going on?*

He tried Jersey's cell phone several times and got nothing. *Vintage Jersey*, he thought. He called Brian Goldberg, one of the other partners, who had always been the calmest, but who was not home or at the office and he too was not answering his cell phone. Garrett looked at his phone to see if there were any

3

relevant messages. There was none. In fifteen minutes, he was in the car and on his way to the expressway trying to remember where the Hospital was located. Finally, after several tries on the phone and fumbling with his GPS he managed to get directions.

Forty-five minutes later he arrived in the waiting room to be greeted by Jersey with, "That son-of-a-bitch has had a heart attack."

"What son-of-a-bitch are you talking about?" asked an alarmed Garrett.

"Scully!" replied Jersey.

"Oh my god! What kind of condition is he in?" asked Garrett.

"Shitty," responded Jersey. "We've got a problem. If he lives past midnight, he or his wife gets his contract package bonus – all $400,000 worth and the damn options as well. But if he dies before midnight we only owe the wife the rest of this year's salary."

"Jeeeesus, what do you want to do, kill him?" scowled Garrett.

"No, I want to fire him!"

"You what?" exclaimed a shocked Garrett. Pausing for a moment, then with a big exhale, "The guy is fighting for his life and you want to fire him now. You could kill him doing that."

"I don't think so. I got Bill Amstead - remember the cardiac guy who invested $200,000, two years ago - treating him. He's reassured me that he's so doped up, nothing will happen. And he'll put some extra stuff in him to make sure," explained an unflinching Jersey.

"Jersey, this guy has really improved our manufacturing problems. You stood on your head to get him. You acted like Paul selling Jesus to the multitudes. You really convinced us and the Board, that he was perfect for the job when you were trying to hire him. Scully, in your opinion, was the best man available for the job in the whole wide world, and now, you want to fire him. I don't get it," answered a perplexed Garrett.

"I want him out and I don't want to pay him the contract obligation," responded Jersey. "If I fire him I don't have to."

"Armstead is really going along with this shit?" asked Garrett.

"You bet!" replied Jersey.

Garrett stared at Jersey with genuine anger and a familiar exasperation, "I can't stop you, but I'm not going to be any goddamn part of it. How in the hell can you do anything like this? Your buddy Amstead must be a real piece of garbage to go along with it. Jersey, this is really wrong, you'll end up regretting it."

"No, I won't,," replied a calm Jersey.

"I don't see how you can say that," stated Garrett.

Jersey replied calmly, "It's my nature."

And that was that.

CHAPTER 2 ANNE MILLS

Scully got fired. He didn't die. In fact, he made an excellent recovery, sued "PT," got a small settlement, and disappeared.

Anne Mills grew up in Central Pennsylvania in a town called Millsport. Whether the town was started by the Mills family was never entirely clear but the Mills certainly owned a lot of it. Anne was the daughter of a Judge, who dropped dead one night after eating too much. He had spent much of his life overeating. He had been warned over and over about the risk and eventually, the risk showed up.

Anne was ten at the time, and with the death of her father lost her only protection against her three older brothers and abusive Mother. The Judge really loved only three things in this world – Anne, food and his dog. The three brothers spent much of their time tormenting and demeaning fat little Anne. They were just plain mean. Mother Mills, a very attractive woman from Charleston, South Carolina, came to the marriage complete with a set of social airs and a collection of venomous social attitudes and nonsense. Her salt and pepper colored hair was always worn in an upswept Victorian fashion that was rather out of step in central Pennsylvania for the time and place.

She was often heard to say, "The world would be in better order if people would stay in the class they were born to." She liked her good looking boys but was not fond of girls, particularly her overweight daughter, Anne.

Garrett Carlssen had grown up in the same town and was a contemporary of one of the Mills boys. He went to the same elementary school, and on rare occasions, was in the Mills house, briefly. He wasn't really welcome, and he knew it. He was Jewish and the Mills house was not a welcoming stop as measured by Mother Mills' social metrics. But, after playing sandlot sports that included one of the Mills boy's even Jewish kids get thirsty and water was available at the nearby Mills house. He knew of Anne, had occasionally glimpsed her in school, but had never spoken to her. She always seemed to retreat, hiding in all the shadows and dark corners so available in the large Tudor dwelling the Mills called their home.

Anne Mills was highly intelligent and excelled in her school work. She made it to Smith and the University of Pennsylvania's Wharton School of Business for a Master's in Business Administration. She eventually found a home on Wall Street. She had risen to an important VP position in her firm and had made herself quite prosperous. Socially, she still hid in the shadows and corners. After leaving Millsport and spending twelve years on "The Street", she was no longer fat. She was respected and feared by her contemporaries. Nobody really liked her in her work circle, but being liked is not important on Wall Street.

5

Socially there was almost nothing but an unexpected relationship with an old deli owner and, her two cats were fond of her.

Anne Mills had developed a taste for the kill, and that stood her well in the particular jungle she had chosen to exercise her skills.

CHAPTER 3 GOING TO A CHURCH

As "PT" prospered it needed capital, lots of capital, and the kind of capital that only big Wall Street firms could raise. The partners had started the Company during the early 80's and being basically technocrats and secondarily businessmen, they had gotten used to giving up too much equity to their investors.

Garrett and Jersey entered the hallowed church-like building on lower Broadway that housed one of the legendary investment banks of Wall Street. They were entering the Ashton, Copper, and Smith offices - ACS - to present their case for a hundred million dollar stock offering. ACS had been around since the early 1900's. It was a classic "white shoe" firm that had been run by the finest families of New York and Connecticut, but times change, and now was run by two guys well outside of that social circle, one an Italian named Joseph Taglafferri and the other, an Arab named Ibrahim Sahid. The white shoes had been replaced by $300 jeans, and high fashion power sunglasses.

After the security check, they went up to the fortieth floor to meet with one Charles Cowen. As they exited the elevator, they were amazed to see a waiting room big enough to play a full court basketball game in. It would also accommodate, at the same time, three to four hundred fans as well as a hotdog and beer stand to boot. They were further amazed by the art collection dominating all of the walls of this elaborate edifice - stuff, very valuable stuff that could just as well have been hanging on the walls of the Met. They were greeted immediately by a polite and well-dressed young woman sitting in the waiting room at a magnificent French Colonial desk who told them Mr. Cowen would be with them in a few minutes and offered them a beverage in the meantime. Garrett sat down on a big stuffed couch twisting, shifting, and sliding around to find a comfortable position. But, as usual, he never found a sweet spot in this kind of environment. Meanwhile, Jersey was taking a tour of, and mentally inventorying, the entire art collection hanging on the walls of the room. When he finished his survey he sat down next to Garrett and commented, "I'll bet there are thirty to forty million bucks on these walls."

In a few minutes a secretary appeared, introduced herself, and escorted them to a conference room.

"Christ," said Jersey, "the furniture alone in this room is worth more than my house."

"Chill out Jersey," whispered Garrett.

They spent the next half hour talking about the problems of the new Mets line-up, a girl Jersey was dating, Garrett's new sailboat, and looking at New York Harbor through the view from the conference room windows.

7

A half hour later in walked Charles Cowen. If he was over thirty, it wasn't by much. He came with a male assistant who was much younger. They both opened files and the assistant activated his laptop.

Cowen spoke, "We have reviewed your numbers and the business plan. It doesn't meet with our standards. Further, we don't like your market model and organizational structure. And also, your personnel do not meet our standards."

An amazed Jersey asked, "Where does that leave us?"

Cowen replied with a slight smile, "Obviously, nowhere. Are there any other questions?" Cowen asked.

Garrett, not able to resist, asked, "How'd you like the colors we used for the business plan?"

Cowen ignoring Garrett stood up, his assistant following, and walked out with "Have a nice day."

The secretary returned for the purpose of escorting them to the elevator.

Jersey walking down the hall pouted, "Let's steal a painting, on second thought, let's kidnap our escort."

The escort smiling said, "Sorry gentleman, hope the rest of your day is better."

As they were exiting the building, a pissed-off Garrett asked, "Why the hell did they drag us down here?" Then answering his own question, "Because they can ... fucking Wall Street!"

CHAPTER 4 TIDINGS FROM ENGLAND AND WESTWARD HO

Two weeks later Jersey and Garrett were in Belgium visiting a potential product engineering service provider for the purpose of designing a much easier product family to manufacture than the current generation.

Pristinimatic Technologies was very good at technology but weak when it came to designing a product that could be easily manufactured. They needed help, and the five months and one hour short of six months that Scully had provided, reaffirmed that fact. One of "PT" investors was a very wealthy Belgian and had introduced them to a Belgian Government Institution that was formed after World War II to help rebuild that country. The institute had done their job well, and they were looking now to provide services for industry throughout the world. The Belgian investor said they would be very generous in extending credit to get involved with an American Company. The meetings went well and a deal was struck.

The night before they were to return to the U.S., Jersey picked up a message at the Hotel Desk from where they had been staying. It was from a Mr. Thomas Tidings, the Managing Director of the UK division of Glen Hills Equities of Palo Alto, California, who requested he be called at "Mr. Smart's earliest convenience."

Jersey immediately responded.

Tidings stated that his firm was extremely interested in Pristinimatic Technologies and wanted to meet as soon as possible to discuss a hundred million dollar financing deal. Further, he was willing to fly into Belgium from London the very next morning for discussions.

Jersey called him immediately and began the conversation by asking, "How'd you find out about us?"

Thomas Tidings responded, "My dear fellow, that's our business. Are you interested?"

"Sure, give me a minute please I want to talk to my Partner." He muted his cell phone.

Before Jersey could say anything, Garrett, who had heard the conversation said, "Jersey, I know the firm from my Solotex days. Glen Hills is very big and has access to the kind of bread we are looking for. What have we got to lose? Tell him we'll meet him at the Brussels Airport as early as he can get there. We're due to fly back at one twenty tomorrow afternoon. That should give us adequate time for both parties to know if they and we want to go forward."

That worked for Tidings and they were scheduled to meet at seven thirty in a small breakfast restaurant that served the best smoked salmon and croissants in the EU according to Jersey.

"Maybe our luck is changing," sighed Jersey.

"We'll see," good-nighted Garrett as they were ascending the elevator to their rooms for the evening.

The next morning they were busily engaged with Thomas Tidings as Jersey was finishing his third round of smoked salmon.

Tidings was a well-dressed good looking man complete with goatee, in his early fifties, who oozed that special kind of East Indian Tea Company British charm that masked any representation of real feelings and character. By eleven o'clock, they had outlined a deal and agreed to an informal, non-binding memo of understanding and signed a mutual non-disclosure agreement – in reality, it meant nothing. Tidings would set up a meeting in Palo Alto in the next week or two with the senior partners of the firm and *get the project going*. He advised bringing all the Pristinimatic decision makers to the meeting as well as legal counsel. As soon as Jersey and Garrett returned, they would overnight all financial details, plans, and a host of other material to both the Palo Alto and UK offices.

They flew back on schedule and put all agreed upon details into action. Waiting for them in New York was a long communication from Tidings, which included an extended list of actions, and the appointed day and time for the meeting in Palo Alto. Tidings would meet them there.

All this had to be accomplished in eight days and they were excited. Jersey and Garrett went full throttle with every resource available, working, pushing, and even stretching the long hours. There were many conversations with Thomas Tidings. They made it, and five "PT" people arrived in Palo Alto on the appointed day fully prepared. Jersey, Garrett, Brian, one of their Directors, and Mike Metcalf - a very expensive NY corporate attorney - were in the Glen Hills Equities waiting room at the appointed time.

Almost immediately they were escorted into a very brightly lit conference room that was composed of glass and stainless steel and a view of an atrium that contained objects also made of glass and stainless steel, objects that required no watering, feeding, or trimming – only occasional dusting and cleaning.

Sitting around the table were four young people. The woman sitting at the head introduced herself as Rose Haas, Senior Analyst - the next three had lesser titles.

Jersey introduced the Pristinimatic team and asked, "Where is a projector we can use for the slide show deck we prepared for this meeting?"

Rose Hass responded, "She was unaware there was to be same."

"Ohhhh," responded Jersey, "and where is Thomas Tidings?"

Rose Haas casually replied, "I don't know, he is no longer with the firm."

A bewildered Jersey asked, "What? When did that happen?"

Rose Haas matter-of-factly answered, "That's confidential. You have thirty minutes, please proceed if you wish."

They proceeded, knowing it was a waste of time. As it ended there also were no exclamations, interest, or apologies. They were dismissed.

The Glen Hills debacle was temporarily submerged in alcohol and weed. Nobody ever found out what happened to Tidings. Glen Hills Equities was interchangeable with Dante's Inferno and a pile of shit as far as "PT" management was concerned

CHAPTER 5 INTRODUCTION

A thoroughly depressed and frustrated crew returned to New York the next day. They had been totally screwed by the investment establishment as far as they were concerned. There was initially an "I can't believe anybody could be that rotten" and ultimate resignation to "That's the way it is, get over it!"

An unexpected call was announced by the Pristinimatic receptionist to Jersey's assistant. It was a Ms. Anne Mills of Ashton, Copper, and Smith, wishing to talk to Jersey.

"What's an Anne Mills? Find out before I take the call," was his response. Their recent experience at ACS did not conjure up any warm feelings towards that firm to say the least.

"She just said it was important, and that she was important, and it was in your best interest to take the call," she relayed.

"Give it to Garrett," ordered Jersey.

Garrett was buzzed and informed of the call by Jersey's assistant.

He began with, "Hello, this is Garrett Carlssen; I'm a senior partner in the firm and COO. Jersey's occupied. How can I help you?"

"You probably can't," Anne Mills responded coldly. "I'm not used to dealing with 'lessors'."

"Neither am I," barked Garrett and hung up.

He was thinking to himself, *those people at ACS are the most arrogant bastards I've ever come across - screw'em!*

Within a minute, the phone rang again and the Secretary announced Anne Mills was on the phone again. Curious as hell, Garrett picked up the call, "Garrett Carlssen here."

"That hang up was unacceptable, Mr. Carlssen," an obviously very annoyed Anne Mills delivered coldly. "I expect a person in your position to behave professionally!"

Garrett started to respond defensively, but decided to change his tune a bit and replied with a bit of sarcasm and irony, "If you can manage to deal with a lesser person - would you please inform me why you are calling?"

There was a moment of silence and then Anne Mills conceded, "I have been looking at the materials you supplied our Company and spending some time understanding your emerging industry. I would like to learn more."

"Let me be up front with you, Ms. Mills – Is that correct; your name?" Garrett asked.

"Yes, that's my name," Anne Mills answered.

"We have been to your office and had a meeting with one Charles Cowen. He rejected us, lock, stock, and barrel. But, we liked your art."

12

"What are you talking about?" asked a slightly bewildered Anne Mills.

"The art in that cathedral you refer to as a waiting room," retorted Garrett.

"Oh, I get it," responded Anne Mills. "Can we please get past your brilliant repartee, and get on with business?"

"Look, Ms. Mills, your Mr. Cowen let all the air out of the 'Pristinimatic tire' and made it imminently clear that your Company didn't like, or approve of anything about us. That included, if I remember correctly, our market model, organization, and – we really loved this one - our personnel didn't meet your standards. We didn't like Mr. Cowen either. So what's the purpose of this call?" and Garrett went silent.

After a pause, Anne Mills answered, "I am thoroughly aware of Charles Cowen's appraisal. Please understand I generally agree with him, but there's a 'but.' I have examined your competition quite thoroughly, and have come to the conclusion they are worse. In general, the entire industry is populated and organized in and around either incompetence or at best, mediocrity. Mr. Carlssen, in other words, your Company, in my opinion, is the best of the worst; you know the cleanest pair of socks in the dirty wash hamper."

"That's got to be the lowest form of a compliment I have ever experienced. So, Ms. Mills, where do we go from here with the least of the dirty socks?" croaked Garrett.

Anne Mills, ignoring Garrett continued, "I believe your industry is going to be a big industry with a profound effect on how the entire world does business. Consequently I would like to explore the possibility of ACS getting involved with your Company."

"That's interesting, I just can't wait, and oh ... what about Cowen?" Garrett asked.

"That's not any concern of yours. Shall we move on?"

"Oh, I get it, the Emperor has no clothes," sneered Garrett.

CHAPTER 6 ANNE, TECHNOLOGY, AND UNCLE COW

A meeting began two days later at the Pristinimatic offices in Westchester near White Plains, NY.

Anne Mills showed up with a small, slim elderly gentleman with a shaved head named Bob Roberts. She introduced him as a senior analyst. For some reason, Garrett thought there was more to him than that. Time would prove he was right. On the other side of the table leading the "PT" group was Jersey, backed up by Garrett and Brian Goldberg, the quiet, calm, and most technically proficient partner. Actually he was one of the most stoic people that Garrett had ever known. Garrett had been acquainted with Brian for years and had even gotten to know his whacky family background as well as meeting some of them over time. Brian and Garrett had become acquainted at the NASA think tank having worked on joint projects. Jersey also knew Brian from NASA, but there was no interest in friendship. Jersey never paid any attention to Brian's personality. Brian was an extremely creative engineer, and that's all Jersey really cared about.

Anne Mills was a forty-two year old woman, tall – maybe five foot ten – with a patrician's face and a very carefully coiffed head of brunette hair – not one hair out of place. Her complexion was unusually fair and smooth. She wore a plain, and Garrett assumed, expensive business suit that deliberately hid her femininity. Garrett couldn't tell if she wore make-up or not. She was a fine looking woman and would even be a better looking woman if only she would smile once in a while. Ann Mills exuded coldness. Not someone you would like to have a drink with, not even a tuna fish sandwich if you were hungry. She seemed to be composed of hardness and intelligence. *Where were they going to go with her, or more to the point, where was she taking them?* Garrett shuddered, he had no idea. It occurred to him that they were suddenly being carried along by an alien wind. Anne Mills and Bob Roberts were there, at least on the surface, to get to know the Company well enough to initiate the process of possibly raising a hundred million dollars. Garrett sensed – what he liked to refer to as that 'click at the back of your head' informing you of impending trouble. If you ignore it, it eventually will come back to bite you. They, the "PT" group, were in a forest without a compass or a map, and didn't have the slightest idea of where they should go. On that happy note, the meeting commenced.

After the usual introductions, background presentations, slide show, and financial reviews, Anne Mills suggested she and Roberts be given a tour of the facility. Garrett was better than Jersey at this kind of exercise and led the way.

An hour later they were back in the meeting room and Roberts began with, "Why do you think you will succeed?"

Jersey carried on for a good ten minutes delivering his usual sermon. It was very good and there were no further questions on that subject.

Then Anne asked something quite meaningful, "What is the purpose of your technology?"

Garrett answered, "We're in the business of giving precise eyes to computers. The mistakes associated with manually entering data into computers before our technology existed were notorious. Our technology reduces those errors to almost nothing."

"Very good," responded Anne, "That's the best explanation I've come across."

Jersey took back the lead and a discussion of a plethora of details ensued. This began to bore Garrett and his mind began to wander to his youth. It was Anne Mills that seemed to be a catalyst for these thoughts. It occurred to him that her name was somewhere in his past. He remembered that Judge Mills had a fat little daughter named Anne. *So what?* He didn't have the slightest idea where this Anne Mills came from. He stared at her face to see if she looked like any of the Mills' he could remember. It was all very vague.

He pictured the imposing Susquehanna River that flowed through the town in central Pennsylvania where he had been raised. It was a beautiful river that divided the Appalachian Mountains from the mountains of the north and the vast forests of that area. The river was the final home of many creeks that contributed to its flow and, on occasion, great turbulence. The river ran most of the time gently but after heavy winter snowfalls and fast spring thaws, the town would, on such occasions, become flooded with great overflows of water and with the water mud. When the floods came, a few people would die and some would lose their homes or businesses or both. But it was life by the Susquehanna and it was accepted. It had been that way since the town had been started over two hundred years before.

Fortunes were made back then, cutting the great virgin forests of this region. It was done without mercy or forethought. It was called "wildcatting." When a mountain was sheared of all its timber, it looked like the top of the head of a new marine recruit. It was a pathetic and sad sight. Pictures of the cropped mountains could be seen in all their nakedness in old photos, proudly displayed in the town museum. It was the shearing of these mountains that accelerated and intensified the floods. Without the great forests, there was nothing to slow down the melting snows. Many families had benefitted from this industry, now gone, and formed a wealthy society that ruled the town even to the present day. The Mills were one of those families. They were, in fact, one of the originals.

Garrett's mind wandered to one of the Susquehanna tributaries, Chimney Creek Run. It fed the great river with miserly flows most of the time. But on occasion, it would deluge the river with violent unrestricted volumes of water with no organized direction. The devastation could be unimaginable. Most of the time the creek was gentle, it ran over and around fields of rocks, occasionally pouring over small cliffs, and wandered lazily through many gorges providing beautiful trout habitats and swimming holes. These were special places visited by teenagers on hot summer days and evenings, ripe with opportunities to discover one another.

He remembered hiking far up the Chimney to where it began its journey from the great plateau formed by the Allegheny Front and the odd formation known as High Slope Rocks. The rocks were an overwhelming outcrop that looked like it was about to fall but apparently had remained stable for eons. The formation acted as an open gate that provided the means for the Chimney Creek to begin its trek downhill, eventually flowing into the Susquehanna River.

Garrett also remembered that hikes into this territory had provided him, occasionally under very special circumstances, the privilege of getting to know the normally unknowable Pennsylvania Hillbillies, and one in particular, Uncle Cow Eisenbrewer. What a different sort of human being he was compared to the company he was currently keeping. The experience of Uncle Cow had, as Garrett's life unfolded, defined his definition of contentment. Somehow that old man was always there providing a metric for the measurement of some of his values.

The Pennsylvania Hillbillies were of old English, German, and some Irish stock, and not ever discussed, runaway slaves. The English and the Germans came from the old world almost a century and three quarters before, fleeing everything unpleasant in their European homes. The Irish were running away from the brutal labors of the Eire Canal. The runaway slaves started arriving during and just after the end of the Civil War. Some of them managed to stay and, oddly, successfully integrated with the original group. They all had found a place in these mountains where they could hide and live by their own rules. They didn't pay or collect any taxes, purchase any licenses, serve in any wars, or abide by any gaming laws. They killed any game available when they were hungry or preparing for winter. No game wardens or federal agents enforced any laws in their mountain forests. There was a time when the regulators tried, but they had either given up or never really were willing to make the effort – It was just too damn dangerous and not that big a pie! They existed as unrecognized tenants in the great mountain preserves of North Central Pennsylvania and carved out a life style from the grit of nature. They had no concept of assimilation. They made a highly desired alcohol beverage from wild crab apples. They didn't call it moonshine, they called it Applejack. They traded and/or sold it to the "city" people who were only too anxious to obtain it. Every once in a while the Feds would intercept a trade and jail a person or two, but had given up on really stopping them many years ago. The trade was necessary for their "needs". These were things that were essential for their existence such as gun powder, sulfur, and salt, things impossible or very difficult to make or find in the mountains. They were still hunting with ball and black powder during Garrett's youth. They were considered, correctly, very unfriendly and dangerous. The two counties these folks inhabited are still the sparsest populated region on the east side of the Mississippi, and amazingly, only 200 miles from New York City.

Uncle Cow came into Garrett's life through a friend he often went hiking with during his teenage years, Gary Eisenbrewer.

Gary Eisenbrewer was somehow related to Uncle Cow. Garrett never got the relationship straight, but it didn't matter. Gary simply announced one late spring day, "I'm going hiking way up the Chimney, not too far from Falls End. Gonna' visit my Uncle Cow. Wanna' come along?"

"Whose Uncle Cow?" asked Garrett?

"My Uncle," replied Gary.

"He lives up in the mountains near Fall's End?" inquired a suspicious Garrett.

"Yep, he's one of those Englishtown Hillbillies," announced Gary, cutting off any further suspicious inquiries.

Englishtown Hillbillies was the name these folks, or somebody, had given them many years ago, and that's the name that stuck. Falls End was a spectacular place where a small river with waterfalls ran straight into an underground cavern. Garrett had never seen it, but had heard about it and the Englishtown Hillbillies many times.

"Aren't they dangerous?" asked Garrett.

"Well, yes and no, it depends," replied Gary. "If they know you and you're related to them, some of them can be real nice. If they don't know you, they're not so friendly. Don't worry, I've been there many times and I'm welcome, very welcome."

"Will we be close enough to Falls End to go have a look?" asked Garrett.

"Probably, if the weather is good," replied Gary. "My old man will drive us up to Buck Horn Corners where we can hike in, and then he'll pick us up Sunday. You'll like Uncle Cow, he's a real nice old man, and he tells great stories."

"Ok, I've got to get permission from my parents. Let you know tonight," confirmed Garrett.

"Just tell your parents were going to Buck Horn Corners and let it go at that," advised Gary.

Garrett had hiked a lot with Gary. The family was very nice, and Mr. and Mrs. Eisenbrewer were always very warm to Garrett which was not the norm for a Jewish kid in Millsport. The Country Club, the Eating Clubs, the Women's Clubs, the Masons were all restricted – no Jews, Negroes, dogs, etc. were welcome.

Gary was one of his few real buddies.

They were delivered to Buck Horn Corners by Gary's father on Tuesday at eight in the morning. He dropped them off by a bridge running over the Chimney where they began their trek into the mountains. They followed the

Chimney Creek for over four hours, eventually veering off into the woods as they began to follow a footpath up a thickly wooded mountain slope. The foliage was so dense they could see nothing of the mountain they were climbing. They only knew that they were on a mountain by the steepness of the seemingly never ending path and the sweat they were generating. Finally, they reached the mountain top and slowly descended into a series of steep hills and steep valleys.

It took much of the rest of the day for them to reach a very crude, but strong looking cabin that had been built deeply into the side of one of those steep hills. It had an attached front deck without any railing that sat on long posts – tree trunks with the bark still on - that were anchored to natural outcrops in the hillside. It was about a hundred feet above a rapidly flowing run, and overlooked a narrow valley. The run had over time carved out a very deep narrow gorge which dominated and defined the landscape. On one side of the cabin was a crude set of steps that zigzagged their way up from the run to the cabin deck. It was quite spectacular. The climb up the steps was nerve racking, the un-railed deck terrifying, and the cabin wonderful.

The run water raced so hard and the steepness of the gorge, with its many rock outcrops and waterfalls, amplified the noise of the rushing water to a level that required raising one's voice to be understood - even to people just nearby. They climbed up the narrow steps that were mostly rock but occasionally mud to reach the cabin. Gary, without knocking, opened the cabin door - knocking would be a waste of time with the noise level – and peered inside. Nobody was home. "Let's wander down to the stream and see if we can find Uncle Cow," announced Gary.

Back down they went and worked their way down the wandering stream. Soon they spotted Uncle Cow sitting on a toilet seat that was fastened to an old five gallon paint pail. Garrett was immediately taken aback. Then, as he realized the old man had not dropped his pants one inch, he became quite amused at the purpose of the toilet seat. He could feel an irresistible smile on his face forming and he couldn't stop it as he realized what the real purpose was for the contraption. It had nothing to do with a bathroom. It was Uncle Cow's fishing chair. He caught them, spread his legs, and put them in the bucket, and closed his legs. The only way out was through Uncle Cow. In the meantime the fish remained fresh swimming around in the pail in good clean stream water.

Uncle Cow was a slim white bearded man about six feet tall. His beard was like a big fluff of cotton candy that grew down from his ears and ended somewhere about a foot below his chin. He wore a pair of glasses that were taped together at the center, with another pair sticking out of one of his coverall jean's pockets. He was wearing a very faded baseball cap with a beat-up Bugs-Bunny pin attached to one side and a pencil trapped between his ear and the cap rim on the other side.

As they approached Uncle Cow spotted Gary, "Who ya' got with you Gary?"

Gary answered, "A friend of mine, his name is Garrett Carlssen."

"A pleasure to meet ya' boy," responded Uncle Cow. "Have ya' two come to stay with me awhile?"

They both nodded yes.

Suddenly in the middle of his reflection Garrett was interrupted by Jersey with a question. "Can you remember what Persament, LMT – that guy Sterling-Smith from England – was offering us last year?"

Garrett was startled at being interrupted during his mind trip to Pennsylvania, as well as being asked to answer the question that Jersey was requesting. After collecting himself for a bit he realized that Jersey was passing the buck. Jersey couldn't figure a way out, so he was putting it on Garrett.

Garrett thought a moment, looking straight at Anne Mills and stated, "Yes."

"Well?" Anne waited.

Looking at Jersey, trying to hide his disgust, "Please remember we agreed with him not to reveal any of the details."

"Oh yeah, we shook hands on it," responded Garrett knowing damn well he was making it up. And since Sterling-Smith had recently died there would be no way of checking. It appeared that one of his many enemies had dispatched him to the great eternity. The matter was still under investigation according to the BBC.

Again, looking at Jersey, Garrett thought, *that's the best I can do under the circumstances.*

Anne did not pursue the matter and the discussion went to other matters leaving Garrett to return to Pennsylvania and Uncle Cow.

The two boys were sitting at an old stained table made of thick roughly unfinished oak planks, strong enough to support very heavy things, enjoying a dinner that had been prepared by Uncle Cow. It was different than what Garrett was used to. It consisted of extremely thick slices of cured bacon and ham cut from large chunks of same. The meats were hanging by ropes from the ceiling rafters covered with some kind of cloth. Uncle Cow simply sliced the dinner from the sides of the hanging meat with a very big, very sharp knife that was also hanging by a longer rope from the ceiling. The ceiling also contained other hanging meats that included smoked venison, and a few more hams and bacons, and some things Garrett could not identify, and all together gave the cabin a delicatessen odor that made the boys hungry. The meat had been put into a big cast iron pan with what he assumed was lard. Then some potatoes and onions were added and all the ingredients well fried on a wood stove. When finished to Uncle Cow's requirements – well browned edges - the meat was served with some fresh apples and slightly hard cider and a side of store bought sliced white bread that was sort of toasted by frying it on the stove top. On the side was something that Uncle Cow called butter that definitely was not butter. The boys found it all very delicious. Garrett wondered where the 'store bought' sliced white bread came from but decided not to ask.

Later Garrett and Gary were sitting out on the porch floor and the old man was sitting on a beat-up rocker, all watching the valley flooding with shadow as the sun disappeared.

"I take it you two boys have known each other for some time?" Uncle Cow asked.

They nodded *yes*.

"How's your old man doing since he's become a man of the legal trade?" asked Uncle Cow.

Gene Eisenbrewer, Gary's father, had pulled himself up from years of laboring in a local steel plant by attending night school and eventually attending a law school. He had recently passed the bar.

Gary responded, "He's beginning to get some clients."

"I respect your old man, he's climbed a hard road including that damn war," stated Uncle Cow, "That couldn't of been easy, no sir! Tell me boy," looking at Garrett, "Wachtya' aimin' to be when you grow up?"

Garrett answered quickly, "A scientist. Can I ask you a question?"

Uncle Cow cut him off, "You wanna' know about my name, that's it, isn't it boy?"

Garrett nodded yes with a big guilty smile.

"I guess I gotta' tell it once again," Uncle Cow complained with a sigh. "It started when I was born. I was the eleventh son born to my parents. My Mother was gettin' tired of sons and wanted a daughter. She was so sure that I was gonna' be a girl she chose the name Gladys before I was actually born. She was real good at sewin' and she sewed the name Gladys on all the baby clothes for her little girl that was about to be me. Well I come along, and I ain't no girl. That didn't stop Ma.

"Even if he ain't a she, he's still gonna' be called Gladys," commanded Ma.

"It was pink for me the whole way. Of course, bein' a baby, I didn't know no better. Everybody just called me Gladys and I just answered to Gladys. I didn't think a lick about it until I got to some schoolin' from other kids. It was pretty rough for a while. We grew up farmin' and huntin' in these parts, and when I was old enough my Pa assigned me my first serious farm chore. We kept a few milk cows and I was to herd them cows into the barn for milkin', and then take them out after milkin'. My brothers started callin' me the cowboy. For some darn reason, I insisted on being called the cowman. Somehow that stuck and somewhere along the way the 'man' part got dropped, and I was called just plain Cow. I liked Cow a whole lot better than Gladys. As I met new people I told them my name was Cow, short for Cowman. I became G. Cowman Eisenbrewer. It stuck real good until I met my wife. She didn't like the idea of bein' married to a man named Cow. On the other hand, she had no problem with Gladys. That's how it is, and still is with some of her relatives even though she's gone. I'm gettin' sleepy. Gary knows where you'll be sleepin'. I'll see you two tomorrow morning, goodnight," and off went Uncle Cow.

20

The business meeting came to an end with the preparation of a mutually agreed action list. They were waiting for copies to be brought in. The lists arrived and were distributed. Everybody got up and shook hands and began to leave. Garrett looked over at Anne as their eyes glanced at each other briefly and whispered, "Are you from a town in north central Pennsylvania? Millsport?"

She, almost invisibly, nodded *yes*.

CHAPTER 7 ACS AND THE DEAL

Alan DeSocio carefully entered Bob Roberts' executive office on the top floor of the ACS building.

Bob Roberts was really Robert Copper Robertson, the only old money partner connection that remained at ACS. He detested the current executives who controlled and ran ACS, Taglaferri and Sahid and along with all the young Ivy-league "financial trash" that made up ACS, but he still enjoyed the game – apparently he was addicted. He had managed to remain with the Company during the takeover that eliminated the old guard. Further, he was permitted to attend Board meetings as a condition of the Change in Control contract, even though he was not a Board member and therefore, could not vote. His family still had a minority ownership in ACS, enough that the new majority, on occasion, had to deal with them.

Robert Copper Robertson was at heart and training a patrician who was quite sure of his superiority. There were those that might say he was also a racist and a bigot, and they would be quite right, but he was currently keeping those views to himself. The point was, there was no point. They - the "old money" people - were no longer in charge, at least at ACS. His role at the Company was generally quiet, but economically quite successful. He worked on deals of his choice, and had a fair amount of freedom to manage them anyway he preferred. He made money for the firm and the amount was more than adequate to maintain his position. Most of Wall Street was not, or at best barely aware that he existed. He insisted on the "Bob Roberts" thing to the outside world and avoided any kind of publicity. At the bottom of this ruse was a feeling of profound shame and frustration that the originating families were no longer in charge. Although, he was no fan of Anne Mills he respected her capabilities even though she was a woman - at least she had the proper breeding. She had brought the Pristinimatic idea to him and it appealed.

Alan DeSocio was an experienced analyst who had been with the Company for over twenty years. He was one of the few researchers that the old pro trusted. *God save me from these ivy-league plebeians. Arrogance is good provided you have something to be arrogant about,* Bob Roberts often thought.

After DeSocio presented his research to Robert Copper Robertson, Robertson scanned it and then asked Anne to join them.

Bob Roberts began, "The Pristinimatic boys have made some mistakes in their capitalization planning. They've given too much of the Company away. That's the easy part. The tough part is the way it's spread. I think, in fact, they are well aware of their problem and have hired a very smart lawyer from Harkson, Merit. His name is Mike Levins. I've been across the table from him several times and I know he is very, very good. His game is a mixture of humor and low level repartee. He'll easily loll the opposition into thinking they are way ahead of him when it's quite the other way around. Most people are very unimpressed with him until they realize they are the prey, not the hunter. We are smart enough to beat him, but we must remain aware of our opponent's capabilities and his unique style at all times. In fact I believe it will be great fun to beat him on this deal."

"Anne, how are your negotiations with Photo Symbology going?" Robertson asked.

"Gale is ready to move," she answered.

James Gale was the Chairman and CEO of Photo Symbology, Inc., Pristinimatic's main competitor. Photo Symbology was another, but smaller, aggressive company in the same business. They lacked the superior technology that Pristinimatic had developed. Photo Symbology was very good at marketing. Jersey Smart and James Gale knew and despised one another. One might say they were very unfriendly competitors.

Jersey was a New York City kid that had attended Bronx High School of Science and had gained his education, including his PhD in Electrical Engineering, from city institutions on scholarships. He came from a lower class East Bronx neighborhood and a dysfunctional family environment which included a junkie uncle, an angry father that worked as a laborer in the meat markets of lower Manhattan, a pretty and smart sister who became a hooker, and a certifiable mentally ill mother.

Jersey was a wiry tough street kid who wore horn rimmed glasses because he was 'near sighted as hell'. Somewhere around the age of twelve or thirteen he discovered a brilliant propensity for math and an interest in science. His intellectual life and career path took a direction. He was a Neanderthal socially and never grew out of it, or cared to. He and Gale had first gotten to know each other at technical symposiums presenting peer reviewed papers.

Gale was a graduate of the University of Michigan and from a wealthy Detroit Grosse Point family. He also earned his Master's in Electrical Engineering from the same school. He too, had grown up in a dysfunctional family with a mother who was on her fourth husband and a father who had worked his way through a long list of mistresses. James Gale, an only child, was also a very good scientist and, also, a social Neanderthal. They were amazingly alike but with very different styles created by different ends of the social machinery. It was inevitable they could not and would not be friends. It would always be personal with these two.

Anne outlined the plan with facts, figures, charts, etc., "Regarding Pristinimatic, there are two classes of stock, as you know, a common public company practice - one class with more voting power than the other. The first, is the Class A stock. It has a voting power of one vote per share and is what the public owns. The other, the Class B stock, has a voting power of two votes per share."

She continued, "It comes down to this, the Pristinimatic partners, the founders of the Company, own 23 ½% of the Company, but because their stock is Class B, they have double the voting power giving them 47% of the votes. It's how the Fords still control Ford Motor. When they were raising money to start the Company, Jersey Smart convinced a physician friend of his, a Bill Amstead along with two of Amstead's friends, to invest in the Company. They received Class B stock also. Today that comes to 3 ¼% ownership but because of the 2 for 1 voting power, they have 6 ½% of the voting power.

Amstead and his friends agreed to give the partners a voting trust agreement.

> **Voting Trust** - A legal trust created to combine the voting power of certain shareholders and transfer that voting power to a third party. The stocks in the agreement retain the individual legal title of the contributing stock holders, and therefore, the stock remains in each contributing stockholder's name for financial purposes – hopefully, financial gain.

It was not possible to give it to the partners as a group because of the way the Company was organized; therefore, it had to be granted to one partner. The partners chose to give the trust agreement to Brian Goldberg, their Chief Technical Officer. This was done at the insistence of all the other partners and particularly encouraged by Garrett Carlssen, the Chief Operations Officer, and the Company lawyer because they felt Brian would always be the fairest member of the group if a dispute arose and the voting power created by the voting trust. Jersey Smart, the Chief Executive Officer, would never qualify as being fair, or nice. Jersey didn't like it, but he had to go along with it if he wanted the deal. That added an additional 6 ½% to the partners 47% voting power giving them as a group a total voting block of 53 ½%. In other words they have control, but thin control. Brian with his shares, plus the voting trust from the Amstead group gives him more votes than anyone of the group and that is where we could have an advantage and break the founder's group control. The group has always voted together."

What Anne and Bob Roberts had in mind was to merge Photo Symbology with Pristinimatic. The merged companies would, in aggregate, become worth approximately two hundred million dollars on paper. Then having accomplished that step, ACS would raise one hundred million dollars from the public markets by selling 33% of the then merged companies. This would increase the total value of the new merged entity to three hundred million. This deal when presented to the public would be quite appealing for it would probably raise the combined Company's share price by 2 to 3 times as compared to their current combined values.

As presented to the Pristinimatic insiders, Gale would leave Photo Symbology and Jersey would head the new Company. They assumed Jersey

Smart would adore the idea. What Anne and Robertson – Bob Roberts - were really planning was getting rid of Jersey, as well as Garrett. This would occur at the last moment as the Merger was closing, installing Gale and some other handpicked executives in their place.

In particular, they did not like Jersey because of his demeanor, class, and style. They realized he would be impossible to control, and he wasn't one of their "kinds" of management types. Anne gave him high marks for his visionary capabilities. But Roberts would have none of it. Garrett was also out because he also was not a member of their 'club'. Roberts also objected to the long relationship he had with Jersey. "That kind of loyalty could be a problem someday," stated Bob Roberts.

Roberts put it succinctly, "We're grafting our kind of apples on to this tree and I do not want any hybrids that are not of our making!"

What had to be accomplished was a break in the insider group vote along with rounding up a portion of the public votes. They believed they knew how to accomplish this. They had done it before, quite successfully. The prize would be, once the deal had been completed, an aggregate of 8 ½ million dollars in their pockets, along with options totaling four percent of the merged Companies. Over half would go to ACS and the remaining would be split 40/60 between Anne and Bob Roberts. Not a bad day's pay!

Anne had convinced Roberts, backed up by Alan DeSocio's analytical work that the industry these two companies were focused on would grow quickly and become quite important.

The games were about to begin.

CHAPTER 8 GREENWICH VILLAGE

Garrett was returning to Manhattan after a day's work thinking about what they had, in principle, agreed to the past week with ACS. It struck him, once again, that he didn't like anybody he had met at ACS, with maybe the exception of the woman who escorted them to the meeting rooms. It wasn't a matter of something like *...maybe I should give them a little time and try to be more tolerant.* "Eh, eh," he said out loud, "Forget the tolerant stuff, I just don't like those people. They radiate what they are, a group of perfect sons-of-bitches!"

Garrett lived on lower Fifth Avenue with his teen age daughter Sallie Kate, a junior in High School. They lived a half a block from Eighth Street in Greenwich Village in an apartment Garrett had occupied for all the years he had been in New York.

He remembered the day he had left Millsport on a Gray Hound Bus and traveled the two hundred miles to New York City with two duffel bags and a back pack. With his formal education over and the money he had saved from a six month job in a steel plant he was on his way to the adventures of living in Greenwich Village and, hopefully, a career in science. It was amazing what happened. He had always been sure it was beginners luck.

He got off the bus in the Port Authority Bus Terminal of New York and asked somebody how to get to Greenwich Village, "Take the subway to Eighth Street and you're there."

He did, and as he came out of the Subway Kiosk he spotted a big sign over a store front advertising "Rentals".

He went in and said he needed a place to rent. A fat and friendly middle aged guy who was sitting at a dingy desk said, "It's your lucky day kid, I got something for one hundred and eighty-seven bucks a month on Fifth Avenue. Can you swing it?"

"Yeh, sure," Garrett replied.

The apartment was in an old, kind of beat-up building across from some of the fanciest real-estate in the City. The apartment was rough but it had the supreme attribute of being rent controlled. It was on the ninth floor of a ten story building serviced by a very shaky elevator. It had the high ceilings of an earlier age, a long hallway big enough to be called a third room, three way exposures, a fireplace that didn't work, two fair sized rooms, and a beat-up, but workable bathroom. The tenth floor was only a half-finished floor with one apartment that led out to the building roof to what was euphemistically known as "tar beach". "Tar beach" privileges were extended to the apartment. The apartment came with well used couches that were also beds and a couple of rickety chairs. The kitchen had a counter for eating and a couple of grimy stools. He took it.

Over the years the building had become a co-operative, gotten restored, and Garrett ultimately took the entire floor and completely remodeled it several times. During this period he had met and married a girl from the City, had Sallie Kate, and found his wife in bed one day with a guy from Paris. The usual messy divorce proceeded and he won, to his surprise, custody of Sallie Kate who was five at the time. The wife moved to Paris, where she remained to this day, still with the guy from Paris. Sallie Kate visited with her Mother in the summer, and they spoke on the phone often. For some reason Garrett never understood, the wife never returned to the States again, or at least, never returned to visit her daughter. Garrett and his former wife talked from time to time about matters concerning Sallie Kate, and it was always just business. Garrett had never really forgiven her for the betrayal, but with time his anger mitigated – at least the edge was off. On the other hand, she didn't seem to care a squat for what she had done or what Garrett felt. Shit happens, life goes on.

Sallie Kate, on the other hand, was a great experience, fun, and an enormous satisfaction for Garrett. He really liked bringing her up. They were Father and Daughter and good friends and, as far as he was concerned, the best thing he had ever accomplished. Now that she was in the full flower of her teenage years she could be a pain-in-the-ass from time to time, but the radio psychology shows he often listened to in his car, re-assured him that it was normal and to be expected. So be it, and more important, he got it.

CHAPTER 9 TROUBLE IN THE NEIGHBORHOOD

Garrett and Sallie Kate went to a small Italian restaurant for dinner. It was located only a few blocks from where they lived. They were very frequent customers and treated it as an extension of their home. Garrett had found the place as soon as he had arrived in New York and had never stopped going there. He and Sallie Kate knew the owners and everybody who worked there. They knew all the staff gossip and their lives and histories including the proprietor and his wife and children, and in turn, the restaurant folks knew the same regarding Garrett and Sallie Kate.

On the way back home walking through Washington Square Park with Sallie Kate, his mind drifted unexpectedly to Anne Mills.

Anne Mills, I'll be damned, I guess she was the fat little girl I used to see at the Mills house. After all these years I've got that damn family in my head again. Once again a Mills is making me uncomfortable. I wonder what the hell Anne Mills and Bob Roberts are up to?

Garrett once again drifted back to Anne Mills. Then he remembered something he had completely forgotten. It was during his years at college and it was Christmas vacation and he was home in Millsport. Things had changed and he was now invited to parties that would not have welcomed him five or six years earlier. He was attending a busy party filled with college types and other young adults that were held one after another in the days between Christmas and New Year's. They were basically attended by the same crowd, but every day it was at a different house and different folks were paying for the food and booze. He was standing with some people when a tall attractive girl walked in with some friends. She caught his attention and he asked, "Who's that?"

Some one answered, "Anne Mills."

"You're kidding," he exclaimed. Then he remembered thinking, *the fat little kid isn't fat anymore. Damn patricians, they're never nice and they seem to always end up being good looking. God, she's very good looking,* he thought. *But then again they usually ruin it with bad marriages and too much booze.* Then he thought further with a bit of guilt, *you intolerant bastard, you don't even know her.* It was odd that after all these years he remembered the thoughts of that moment exactly as it had happened. Ironically, he now knew her just well enough to know he was probably right about her a long time ago ...but, then again ... maybe not. *If I remember correctly and I do, I actually played with the idea of asking her out for a date. That impulse lasted for few minutes. Then I never got up the nerve, and she probably would have told me to take a hike. Oh well.*

This keyed off some other memories - *all the many layers that make us who we are.* He remembered the big palatial Mills house on Green Tree Drive with its Tudor design, manicured lawn, and the big formal iron fence with woven filigree decorations. In another part of town where his Uncle Morris and Aunt Ida lived was another big, but quite different house that also had a lawn and fence. It was an old Victorian house that had had several architecturally odd additions attached to it over the years. The additions hardly blended with the original Victorian template. He had spent many hours of his youth in that house. Then he remembered his Grandparents house located in another town hundreds of miles from Millsport, and it too was a Victorian, also with an iron fence, but with a strict observance to its architectural heritage both inside and outside. Whatever he was, or had become, those houses and the people who occupied them or passed through them were part of the fabric that composed Garrett Carlssen. Then he remembered an event that he was involved in with his Grandfather and it brought a big smile to his face.

Garrett was, maybe 10 or 11 years old, and he remembered his visits with Grandma Kate and Grandpa Charlie. Ahh, life with Grandpa Charlie was magic for a kid. He still remembered Grandpa Charlie's hugs, the constant smell of his pipe, and even the touch of his cheeks with the ever present slight stubble. There were no fancy razors in that day and the close shave enjoyed with today's technology just didn't exist. *Now, there was a man who could tell tales, make you laugh, and think up all kinds of mischief, the kind a kid adored.*

Grandma and Grandpa Carlssen lived in a small town on the banks of the Alleghany River. Charlie had become a prosperous Victorian who began from very humble means and never forgot it. Grandpa Charlie was an old time Republican who thought Teddy Roosevelt was the best there ever was. Charlie was convinced that Teddy's cousin FDR, the New Deal President, would probably end up ruining the country. But things were never quite that bad if the Pirates were playing good baseball.

Garrett thought he was one helleva' Grandfather. He loved the old man dearly and the old man returned the feelings. He still remembered, as it just happened yesterday, his Grandfather whispering into his ear on his deathbed kissing him goodbye, "You're the best of them, kid. Don't forget it." He died later that night. Garrett, these many years later, could still feel the loss, and the love. He always tried to give that same love to his daughter, and he did.

Grandma Kate Carlssen was a small gentle sweet woman who's every feature was round. There were no sharp edges to her body or personality. Charlie loved her dearly and was always bringing her flowers or some token of his feeling for her. Garrett remembered, when as a little boy, he would watch Charlie, then well into his seventies, pursue her around the kitchen to give her a kiss. She would laugh with embarrassment and try to push him away. "Not in front of the children, Charlie." But somehow Charlie always got his kiss.

Garrett and Sallie Kate arrived at their building. The doorman greeted them and gave Garrett a package that had been delivered earlier. It was a preliminary prospectus of the deal from ACS. He took it into his office and spent the better part of an hour reviewing it. After reading it, he laughed to himself, *it never fails. These kind of business documents always contain things that were never agreed too or discussed. Now, as sure as the sun rises, the lawyers put that stuff there and we will have to spend hours, perhaps days* negotiating their removal. *Indeed, the world is filled with deceit and other conveniences, particularly, on Wall Street.* He decided to lie down on the couch, close his eyes, and take a catnap. As the pleasantness of the nap began to caress him he began remembering one of Grandpa Charlie's adventures that he was very much a part of.

It was the Fourth of July week and he had been sent to visit his Grandparents for two weeks. He always looked forward to these stays with Grandpa Charlie and Grandma Kate. Garrett had been put on a train going to Pittsburgh under the care of a Conductor. Garrett's Mother was well known by both the Station Master and the train Conductors on the Pennsylvania line that ran through Millsport because she travelled it often to visit her sisters who were spread throughout the State. Their familiarity with Mother was based on a bad habit of Mother's that they were all quite familiar with. She was almost always late arriving at the train station and would call ahead and ask them to hold the train. What was amazing, they did. She knew the Station Master because he was a customer of the family business and knew most of the Conductors by their first names. She would engage them in conversation about their families, their work difficulties, and railroad gossip. She was amazingly good at that. When she put Garrett on the train and turned him over to the Conductor she would always leave him with a lunch of egg salad sandwiches and very important, a treat for the Conductor - which was every time, well received. When he arrived in Pittsburgh the Conductor would put him on another train turning him over to yet, another Conductor. That train would eventually take him to his Grandparents town where he would be met by Grandpa.

In the neighborhood where Grandma and Grandpa lived there was a neighbor whose proper name Garrett couldn't recall, but he was generally known as Scrags. Living in the same neighborhood with Scrags was Dr. Levering Wyatt, MD. Doc Wyatt was almost everybody's doctor in the town. He was the same age as Grandpa. They had known each other all their lives. The Doc was a silver haired slightly overweight man who wore pinch nose glasses. He was a man who smiled a lot and had a reassuring way about him. Doc Wyatt and Grandpa were very good friends. They played in a poker game with three other friends every Wednesday night that was held in the second floor office of Grandpa's scrap iron yard. It included some kind of whisky and something to eat that had been prepared by Grandma. This game had been played for over 50 years and the only way it would end, was when the players got too sick to play or died.

The week that Garrett arrived, big trouble was brewing. It seems about ten years before, the small town where Grandma and Grandpa lived had decided to get modern and install sewers. Before that everybody used outhouses. As a result of this progress the residents installed toilets in their houses and all was well – well almost all was well. Doc Wyatt and Scrags lived right next to each other. The trouble stemmed from the fact that Scrags, who could well afford it, refused to install a toilet and continued using the outhouse. Doc Wyatt's house was also his office. On hot summer days, in particular, Scrag's outhouse would start warming up, spreading its fragrance throughout the neighborhood. Doc Wyatt's office being right next door was at ground zero. Over the years Doc Wyatt and many of the neighbors asked, begged, even offered to pay, to get rid of that damned outhouse. Scrags, for some reason, wouldn't budge. It had come before the town council a number of times and there wasn't a thing that they could do.

It was the day before the 4th of July and Grandpa and Doc Wyatt were on the ever present swing located on Grandpa's front porch. Garrett was in the middle just listening.

Doc Wyatt started, "Charlie that damned outhouse was really cooking yesterday and my patients were complaining. I tell you, I never get used to it. What makes that man tic, I'd like to know. Even when we offered to pay for the john and the installation he wouldn't budge."

Grandpa Charlie answered with one of his favorite expressions, "Levering, how many times do I have to tell you he's a real 'goddamnit'. That's the way 'goddamnits' are. There are no explanations how they got that way, they just are that way. Do you remember Orly Simpson who played for the Pirates? Now there was a well-known 'goddamnit'. Pie Traynor used to go nuts trying to manage Simpson, even in the dugout, because he would never keep his mouth shut, and never did. He had the worst mouth in the league and it caused many a fight. He got on base more times because he would get hit. That was easily more times than he would hit. Pie knew he was a true 'goddamnit' and a good infielder, but eventually he had to get rid of him just to bring some peace on the field."

Grandpa suddenly stopped talking and got a slight smile on his face, and then he changed the subject.

Next morning Grandpa Charlie approached Garrett with a question, "Do you know what tomorrow is?"

Garrett replied, "its Monday, Grandpa."

"It surely is," responded Grandpa Charlie, "but more important, it's the 4th of July – our country's birthday!"

"Grandpa, I know that," responded Garrett.

Grandpa Charlie continued, "On the 4th of July we celebrate. We'll go and watch the parade downtown. Then we'll go to a picnic and set off some firecrackers and something else. When you finish breakfast I'll be in the garage and I'll show you something."

Ten minutes later Garrett entered the garage through a side door. Grandpa Charlie kept his new Pontiac Bonneville carefully protected and shined in his garage whenever he wasn't using the car. Garrett loved just to look at it, and admire the fact that Grandpa Charlie had such a slick car.

Grandpa Charlie was sitting on a stool in front of his work bench which was located at the rear of the garage and, of course, biting on his ever present pipe that was not lit and for good reason. Next to him on the work bench was a small brass cannon. It had cast iron wheels attached to a wooden carriage. Next to it was a large can that was labeled Black Powder, a roll of toilet paper, and some little green straw like things, about two inches long. Garrett guessed they were some kind of fuses. Also on the bench was a carton filled with big firecrackers. The cannon was about a foot long. The muzzle was about an inch and half in diameter that got bigger towards the back where the chamber was located. Garrett was amazed, and thought it was one of the neatest things he had ever seen.

Garrett asked, "Grandpa, are we going to shoot off that cannon?"

Grandpa answered, "Yes, tomorrow of course, on the 4th of July. We'll go down to the river after the picnic and make a whole lot of noise."

So the next day arrived and they attended a parade that included a lot of veterans from the World War II and a few from World War I. After the parade they went to a huge picnic in the town park complete with band music. At about four-o-clock Garret and Grandpa drove Grandma home, picked up the cannon, the cannon supplies, and the fire crackers and drove to the top of a bank beside the Allegheny River. Soon the cannon, supplies, and firecrackers were in place and Grandpa Charlie showed Garrett how much black powder explosive to use and how to load the powder explosive into the cannon bore. Next he showed him how to make and place the toilet paper wadding that held the explosive in place. Finally, at the rear of the cannon there was a small hole that led into the chamber where the explosive resided. This, as he explained, was where the fuse was inserted. Grandpa carefully explained that it had to be pushed all the way in so that it was in contact with the black powder explosive and packed very tight.

"Well," said Grandpa, "it's time to shoot the cannon, Garrett."

He handed Garrett a match with instructions to light the fuse and immediately step several paces back behind the cannon. He did as he was told and in a second or two the noisiest bang he had ever heard went off. He was amazed how loud the cannon noise was. The two of them spent the next hour setting off the cannon and when it would be too hot, set off the firecrackers. Eventually they gathered a small audience. Garrett always thought it was one of the best times of his youth. Finally they were down to a handful of firecrackers and they were out of black powder and the cannon had become much too hot to continue. They had poured river water on it from time to time to keep it cool but they had passed that point and had to stop. Garret was about to set off the last few firecrackers when Grandpa stopped him.

"Garrett, no more," instructed Grandpa Charlie, "I want to save them."

Garrett had had his fill and so did Grandpa. They spent the next hour waiting for the cannon to cool down enough so they could pick it up and put it back in the car. They watched the river, tracked occasional boats passing, listened to the noise of other celebrants, and chatted as the sun began to settle towards the hills on the other side of the river. Finally, they packed up and went back to Grandpa's house where Grandma had a light dinner waiting. After dinner Grandpa tuned on a Pirates game on his black and white RCA television set. Garrett sat next to his Grandfather listening to him as he commented on the game as it unfolded. This was where Garrett really learned baseball. It was well into the evening now and Grandpa asked Garrett if he would like some ice-cream?

"Sure!" replied Garrett.

Grandpa announced to Grandma that they were going to the ice-cream parlor down the block and would she like some also. She thanked them, but wasn't interested.

Off they went. They ate their cones and were returning when Grandpa walked past his house. He looked at Garrett and announced, "I have a little chore that I would like to attend to."

With a Cheshire grin on his face he pulled six three inch long fire crackers out of his pocket. These were the firecrackers that had not been ignited at the end of their cannon festivity. From his other pocket he pulled out some cord and then he sat down on the curb underneath a corner street light and proceeded to tie the six firecrackers into a bundle. From inside his suit pocket he pulled out six fuses, each about a foot long. Then he carefully removed each of the short fuses from the firecrackers and inserted in their place, the long fuses. When he finished doing that he twisted the six fuses together and bundled them by wrapping them around with some of the cord.

Garrett was wide eyed and could not imagine what was going on, but whatever it was it was going to make a very loud noise.

Grandpa then walked up to the next block past Doc Wyatt's office and turned left at the corner. Then he, with Garrett following, turned into the ally and walked quietly past a few houses, then stopped. Grandpa put his finger to his lips – no talking. And a breeze floated by carrying the unmistakable smell of an outhouse. It was then, that Garrett realized they were at the rear of Scrag's property. Garrett suddenly realized that Grandpa was going to scare the hell out of Scrag with his firecracker bomb.

Grandpa whispered to Garrett to stay where he was and be very quiet. Then Grandpa disappeared into Scrag's vegetable garden. A few minutes went by and suddenly Grandpa returned grabbing Garrett's hand and they scurried down the alley. Those firecrackers went off with an unbelievable bang. Of course, the whole neighborhood was awakened and people came out their houses to see what was going on. You could hear "What in tarnation happened? What in the sam hell was that noise?" and so on. Grandpa slowed down and proceeded to walk down the alley to the other end. They turned and shortly turned again back to the street they had come from to get to Scrag's house. All the neighbors were out and gathering by Scrag's and somebody began to laugh. Then they heard somebody say, "I'll be god damned if somebody didn't blow up Scrag's outhouse." At this time the cops arrived and followed by a fire truck.

The outhouse was collapsed and laying on its side. The toilet seat was splintered into many pieces and the lower contents were spread in a rather neat circle around the base of what was left. The smell was an interesting mixture of gun powder and Scrag's daily contribution to his outhouse.

By now Chief Macelhenny was bringing order to the highly amused crowd. Scrags, mad as hell, was standing next to and hollering at the Chief. Finally, the Chief had had enough and told Scrags to shut up.

The Chief then said, loud enough for everybody to hear, "Scrags, you've been acting like a total jackass, stinking up the neighborhood for many years. Somebody or somebodies have had enough, and blew your damn outhouse up. We offered to connect you to the sewer for nothin' and even buy you a toilet. Now I'm suggesting that you finally do it, and Scrags I'm not going to treat this as a crime, but more of a public service. Further, considering the outhouses' present condition I'm recommending to the Town Council that it be condemned and the land that it was built on condemned – no further use be allowed for an outhouse. Do we understand each other?"

Scrags looked straight at the Chief for a minute with anger pouring from his eyes, then took a deep breath, shrugged his shoulders, and said a quiet "OK."

Grandpa and Garrett walked back home and Garrett couldn't stop laughing. Sallie Kate looked at her Father who was laughing, "Dad what's so funny?"

Whenever he thought of that incident he would laugh, sometimes it would last for minutes – so he told her about Grandpa Charlie and the outhouse affair and she laughed.

CHAPTER 10 REASSURANCES

Robert Cooper Robertson was meeting with CEO Joseph Taglafferri explaining the Pristinimatic situation. "Anne has come up with a good plan to accomplish the idea we chatted about last week. If it works, and I am quite confident it will work, we will make eight and a half million minimum and a four percent equity share through options, and your wife's "nephew", James Gale, gets the catbird seat. I hope he's up to it. I've met him and frankly I didn't see anything very special."

"Oh," replied Joe, "You didn't look close enough. He's a very ambitious bastard who will fit very nicely into our plans. Take my word for it. He's our kind of management."

"If you say so," conceded Bob begrudgingly.

Joe Taglaferri looked out the window at New York harbor chewing a mouth full of bubble gum, a habit from his youth that he still clung to. Joe Taglaferri was an Ivy League business school graduate, who earlier in his life had wanted a professional baseball career. He was an excellent catcher and made it as far as Triple-A ball, but ruined his knee so badly skiing one winter, it became impossible. Business, Wall Street business, was the choice of his very ambitious Mother, and he turned out to be very good at it. With a bit of a smirk he asked, "Who are you guys gonna' kill this time?"

An annoyed Robertson answered, "Two of the founders and an extremely good engineer named Brian Goldberg."

"Will we lose him?" asked Joe.

Robertson replied, "No, we are just trying to bust up the founding group. They have always been tight, always voting as a unit, but Anne has found a way to bust them up, I assure you."

"I assume employing her usual pleasantries," Joe said.

"Do you really want to know?" Robertson asked.

Shaking his head with a firm no, Joe Taglaferri responded, "Please, I don't want any details. Just assure me that there's absolutely no crime being considered."

Robertson spoke carefully, "Joe, it's not necessary. Anne always finds a way to walk through the legal mine fields. Anne may not be very nice, but she's no fool and would never take those kinds of chances."

Joe blew a bubble, it popped, and with that, the project was officially underway.

CHAPTER 11 BRIAN AND YVETTE

It was 10:05pm and Brian Goldberg was sitting in his home in an overstuffed living room chair. His legs were off the floor and crossed tightly working on an anagram. Puzzles, math challenges, anagrams, and the like were Brian's favorite pastime activities along with gardening. He was very good at these kinds of things and never tired of them. There was rococo music playing in the background and Yvette Goldberg was on the couch reading a book. The house was very quiet because there were no children. Except for an occasional dog noise, by one of their two sleeping Great Danes, nothing else interfered with the apparent serenity. Brian stopped and stared at his wife's voluptuous breasts in her tight sweater.

Five years ago Brian Goldberg had done something he had never done before. He went to a strip club outside of Philadelphia in an area called Cherry Hill. It was an impulsive and somehow, a frightening adventure. He was never quite capable of explaining to himself how he came to do it.

He nervously entered the club and sat down at a small table. He was enmeshed in the garish haze of smoke, the disruptive glare of colored lights, the odors of alcoholic beverages, and a collection of unseemly aspects of human behavior.

He watched a pole dancer for the first time ever.

A waitress appeared in costume bending over to expose her femininity and asked what he would like to drink. He ordered a beer. He was embarrassed and physically, very uncomfortable. It occurred to him that this place was, perhaps in odd ways, similar in appearance and feeling to what Dante described as he was being led through Purgatory. In fact he realized he was slightly disoriented. This was, indeed, an unexpected place for Brian Goldberg to be. The waitress returned with his drink and served it with another purposeful view of what the patrons came and paid for. He drank and watched and ordered again and watched more. Eventually the unencumbered sensuality of the place began to occupy his brain and body. But above all, was the fourth dancer. She was a brunette by the name of Tara according to the announcer. Brian was struck by the carnal power of her body. She was as appealing as any he ever had imagined. She was gifted in both bosom and thigh. Her face was Roman classic, and before she exited he had seen all of her. Another drink and the intensity of the experience overwhelmed him. He had to leave. He could no longer endure all the stimulation and the unfamiliar awakenings.

Leaving made him sad and lonely. He remembered Tarrytown and his Mother and Father. John Goldberg was a physician who hated his contemporaries, his office, his nurse, his hospital, his patients and on and on,

36

and all the things that were the assemblage of his profession. He always remembered his father sitting back in a chair with his right hand raised to the top of his forehead working one side or another, pulling at a hair, always one hair, and carefully and ultimately removing it from its root. After he had completed this exercise he would examine it carefully and then cast it aside. Then he would go at it again with another hair. This would go on for hours, whether he was reading, talking, or watching television. He did that until he was seventy years old and bald, and then, he died. His father was the only man he ever knew or heard of, who made himself bald by pulling each hair on his head out one at a time. Brian often thought that his father was doing something like Samson. The point being simply when all his hair was gone he had lost all his strength and therefore was compelled to die – a very unusual suicide.

His Mother, a very attractive woman, was a social worker, a socialist, a weaver, and a woman prone to extramarital affairs. His parents fought constantly and their three children learned to be invisible. Brian disappeared the most and was best at it. Now as a grown man he continued to practice the art.

Brian Goldberg was very smart and became an Electrical Engineer with a Masters from MIT. Garrett had met him at the NASA think tank that both Jersey and Garrett worked for and invited him to help form Pristinimatic. Brian saw an opportunity and quickly accepted.

One week after he had visited the strip club he was thinking about the dancer, Tara. This went on for weeks, he became obsessed with her. He went back to Cherry Hill every weekend. He eventually got the nerve to stuff five dollar bills into her cleavage.

The unexpected happens only because, it is unexpected.

Brian, months later, was traveling to Washington on business and was sitting in an Amtrak Coach that stopped to pick up passengers in Philadelphia. A young woman, dressed in jeans and a sweater with a back pack fastened to her shoulders, sat down in one of the only unoccupied seats in the car. It turned out to be right next to Brian. Brian immediately knew it was Tara. She looked at him and laughed softly, "I know you, and I guess you know me rather intimately."

Her real name was Yvette Carbone and she came from a family that lived in the Washington, DC area. The family thought Yvette was going to Temple University at night and working as a waitress in the daytime to pay for college.

Brian married the lush Yvette six difficult months later. The difficulties were a result of his inherent social discomforts, his inexperience with women, Yvette's defenses, the oddness of them as a couple, and his many awkward persuasive efforts to convince her to marry him. On their honeymoon he discovered that Yvette had no interest in sex whatsoever. She was faithful, kept an orderly and clean house, provided him with excellent cuisine, trained two well behaved dogs, and presented a very sensual woman to look at and admire.

37

There would never be children, and sadly for Brian there would never be any intimacy.

CHAPTER 12 HOLLIDAY TIME

The date arrived when Anne Mills could no longer put off the yearly shopping task and the agony of finding Mother Mills a birthday present. This was not an easy task because Mother Mills was very, very difficult to please, particularly if you were her daughter. In fact Anne could never really remember buying anything that pleased her. It really came down to choosing a gift that would mildly displease her as opposed to extremely displeasing her. *Oh well*, she thought.

Mrs. Mills, a woman well up in her years but still with the posture of a Marine recruit, lived in Charleston, South Carolina during the cold months and back in Millsport for the warm months. She still occupied the Tudor house where Anne had grown up. She still wore her now completely gray hair in an upswept Victorian bun, the very same way she always had. She still did not like her daughter, and her daughter returned the feeling, but proper behavior and appropriate familial obligations must be followed. Mother Mills expected nothing less. Christmas, Thanksgiving, and Fourth-of-July were also required commitments. Her three brothers and their families were also always present. The third brother, August, who had always been nice to her in a small ways, was theoretically a recovering alcoholic and was also currently recovering from a bad auto accident. He, of all her brothers, was never really comfortable tormenting fat little Anne as her other two brothers did. She was too easy a target and he was well aware of his Mother's attitude towards her. He had always felt guilty, but said nothing. Anne who would never know of that guilt, felt August was at heart a nice person who was in great pain.

The trip to Millsport was something she always chose to drive rather than fly even though it was over two hundred and fifty miles from New York City. The choice was based on the longer it took to get there the less time she would have to stay there. Leaving Millsport by car also relieved her from dependence upon airline schedules and the vagaries of air travel.

Her Mother greeted her with, "Have you found any prospects for a husband or is there something wrong with you that you haven't told me?"

"Mother, I'm not gay!" she answered disparagingly.

"Then, why no husband?" she demanded.

"I'm not interested," she quietly replied. *The usual fine start to our little visit*, she thought. Changing the subject, she asked, "Have my brothers arrived?"

"Yes, Grahm and Webster are at the Country Club playing golf. I imagine August is having a drink in the Clubhouse bar, and the families are at the club pool," she answered.

"Why aren't you with them?" asked Anne.

"Since the minorities have penetrated the membership, I have no interest," she explained. "We still have clubs in Charleston that are properly run."

Anne looked at her Mother and smiled, "You still hang on to the idea that people should know their proper place."

"Indeed!" Mother Mills proclaimed. She went on, "We'd have a better Country, if they did."

Anne raised her hands in a gesture to stop, "Mother, I'm going up to my room to take a shower and a little nap. I'm tired from the drive. See you at dinner."

The house had its usual depressing effect on Anne. She thought, why *ever, do I keep coming back here? I guess, I'm just like a well-trained dog.* She unpacked, undressed, and went into the shower. She thought about seeing her brothers in a few hours and it made her uncomfortable like it always did. In fact, she dreaded those first moments.

Grahm had become a Judge in the Virginia Courts following his father's path, using his family's and his wife's connections to pave the way. His wife, an attractive but shrinking personality from the Washington, D.C. area, had produced three children, twin girls and a boy. Grahm was still the same mean bastard he had always been and his family was a reflection of his handiwork.

Webster had veered into retail in Western Pennsylvania having, with a partner, developed a small chain of hardware stores that serviced small towns. He had married a very nice woman from that area who came without a pedigree. Webster had grown out of his meanness, but revealed little at the family gatherings, still being led on those occasions by the dominating Grahm. Mother Mills could command his presence, and he always jumped. They had one child, a very bright young man named Peter who was about to enter Carnegie-Mellon to study physics. August had married a quiet woman from a small town in upstate New York and they had one child – a boy. August had become a lawyer and developed a modest practice in that same town.

The families returned and got ready for dinner. Dinner was served at six fifteen sharp. The family gathered on time and as seven-o-clock approached, tea and coffee were served. The children had had their dessert and had been dismissed, even Webster's seventeen year old, Peter. Mother Mills had something she wanted to announce.

She began, "I have recently spent some time considering my estate. In doing so, I have considered each of your positions in life. I will be very frank. Anne, I do not approve of your lifestyle and I don't think you have been honest with me. You are very difficult, you were that way as a child and, in my opinion, and nothing has changed. Webster, you have followed the path of a merchant, and were born to better. I am as you know, disappointed in that choice."

"August," she continued, "you are a small town lawyer with a plain wife and an equally plain child. You have no ambition and you drink much too much."

Looking appreciatively at Grahm, "You, above all, have followed the family path, employed the tools handed you, and, therefore, behaved the most responsibly. You have built your career and family upon the efforts of the generations who preceded you. Therefore, I have decided to leave one half of my estate to you. Regarding the other half, it will be in a trust which will be managed by you, Grahm.

Grahm will be directed to dispense certain amounts to the three of you under certain conditions. Anne, you will receive nothing unless you marry and have at least one child. Webster, you only will be eligible to receive a meaningful portion as Grahm judges it, when and if your boy follows the path I would have wanted you to follow. August, the same goes for you. Grahm will be the final arbiter of whether these conditions have been met. If any of you fail to comply with my carefully thought out requirements over a seven year period following my death, the remainder will go to Grahm's children in equal amounts. We are talking about a lot of money, a fortune that can trace its roots back to the formation of this Country." Mother Mills was finished.

Grahm Mills looked at his Mother and speaking softly and nodding, "Thank you for your confidence in me."

Webster Mills said nothing, reached out for his wife's hand, got up, and left. August looked at his Mother and said, "Did you have to take it out on my son? I understand how you feel about me, but my son is faultless. Never mind, I'll be leaving."

Anne Mills looked at her Mother and raised her voice coldly, "I understand your attitude towards me, but how can you do that to Webster and August? Webster has a fine wife, a talented kid, and has made a good life in the hardware business. August has settled down and lives a modest, but respectable life as a small town lawyer. He's got his drinking under control. Not everybody can be a star as you define it."

She hesitated for a few moments then moving closer to her Mother continued, "Mother, you're a witch, and you always were. Keep your damn money if it is so important to you. Grahm will never give as much as a nickel to Webster or August under any circumstances. He'll keep it all. You're a relic, a dinosaur from another age. You have no love in you, and ... you deserve no love. I'll be leaving for New York within the hour," and out she went.

Mother Mills, unmoved by Anne's outburst, looked at Grahm and his wife and remarked, "There's always been something unnatural about her ... too bad."

Grahm nodded in agreement.

As Anne drove back to New York City, she was amazed at her outburst. In forty-two years she had never once spoken to her Mother that way. As she was driving she kept thinking, *what a mean set of conditions Mother has put together for the estate, something out of a really bad movie.* Anne really didn't need the money, in fact, she had never seriously thought about the estate. She wasn't sorry for

41

her outburst, *that's the first time in my life that I actually was honest with her about my feelings.*

Her mind drifted to Pristinimatic and Garrett Carlssen. *Why am I thinking about Garrett Carlssen ... I guess it's the Millsport thing?*

CHAPTER 13 CLUES

Something was bothering Brian Goldberg. Garrett picked it up immediately upon entering the room, *Mr. Stoic, didn't seem so stoic.* They were at a technology meeting and Jersey was holding forth. Meetings with Jersey were always in a set pattern. Jersey was always late, very late. Then he would make an entrance carrying on about his perceptions and thoughts regarding the subject of the meeting as if he'd been there from the beginning of the meeting, precisely on time, even though the group was well into their discussion. It struck Garrett for the umpteenth time that a discussion with Jersey wasn't really a discussion but a lecture and/or an argument. Jersey was very smart and could fake an unending series of positions without the need for honesty or logic. He was quick, as quick as any bullshitter Garrett had ever known. Not knowing the answer was irrelevant to Jersey. He'd find a way to make one up and convince everybody he was right. He could begin a sentence with "absolutely yes" and end it with "absolutely no." This combination of attributes made everybody a little crazy. But, make no mistake about it; he was a visionary in his field, and one hell of a salesman.

Brian saw through all of it, but had never said anything, ever. Jersey was carrying on about a quality control issue that was affecting the production yield when, seemingly from nowhere, Brian angrily hurled an outburst at Jersey, "Jersey, that's dishonest. There isn't a word of truth in what you're saying." Then louder, "It's total bullshit!"

Jersey was almost knocked off his chair with Brian's outburst along with everybody else. He turned his head towards Brian and started to say something, then said nothing.

Then to put icing on the cake, Brian stood up and said, "I'm out of here, I've got better things to do for this Company then listen to your petty nonsense." And out he went.

Garrett looked at Jersey, "What the hell was that all about?"

Jersey replied as if this had happened many times before, "He probably had a fight with his wife."

"No way," Garrett responded. "They don't fight. I know what I'm talking about. Something is wrong."

"Ok, what's wrong?" asked Jersey.

"I don't have the slightest idea ... then again, maybe it's just your bullshit," sneered Garrett with a slight smile. "Have you ever considered coming to a meeting on time or apologizing for being late?

"Nope," answered Jersey.

CHAPTER 14 HUBRIS

Anne Mills had just returned from Robertson's office where they had gone over the agenda for a meeting with Jersey and Garrett. Anne found herself uncharacteristically anxious about the meeting and she hadn't a clue why.

This would be the first time that Jersey and Garrett would return to the "money gallery in the sky," as Jersey had nicknamed it. They arrived on schedule and were soon greeted by the woman who had escorted them from their unpleasant meeting with Charles Cowen a few weeks earlier. *I wonder how welcome we really are*, Garrett thought.

"Gentlemen, you're back I see. Welcome to ACS." Then quietly, staring at both of them, and with a bit of a grin, "We're obnoxious but quite effective. Have a good meeting." Then, "Would you like a beverage?" as she was seating them in a conference room. They gestured no thank you, and she left.

"Hmmm?" said Garrett wondering to Jersey.

Jersey shrugged his shoulders.

Anne came in with an assistant who was carrying a laptop. Bob Roberts appeared almost simultaneously with no assistant. A detailed review of the Pristinimatic business plan began. As the meeting progressed, Garrett kept looking at Anne and wondering about her. *I wonder how she got to here from Millsport. I'm not surprised how damn tough and cold she is coming from that Mills family.* Then out of nowhere, *I wonder if she's married.* He looked at her left hand. *Nothing! Maybe she's divorced.* He looked out the window at the Hudson and the Port of New York. It was a gloomy day with the bottom of the clouds hovering very close to the floor where they were sitting. His eyes turned and looked at Anne very closely studying her fine features. He saw that everything was in its place and not one hair was where it didn't belong.

Anne had finally finished speaking and Bob Roberts took over. Anne had noticed Garrett staring at her while she was speaking and it made her uncomfortable. *I remember that kid coming around to play with August. He never said anything but occasionally he would ask for a glass of water. Mother couldn't stand him. I wasn't sure why at the time. I guess it was because he was of 'the Hebrew faith,' as Mother referred to him.*

Garrett surfaced from his reverie realizing he was obsessing a bit too much about Anne Mills and his Millsport history. After all, he was there for business and not day dreaming about his past. He returned to paying attention to the business dialog and realized that Act One of the meeting was over. Lots of information had been exchanged with a smattering of commentary. It was time to start Act Two, the terms of the engagement. Garrett thought of one of his old mentors, a very senior vice president from one of America's largest and most successful pharmaceutical companies and of his wise advice.

"Business is a game, but a very serious game. Like any game it has rules and structure and you must be a player in the game. Only players can win or can lose."

Now it was Anne's turn to take control of the conversation and she began to describe the deal with its components and requirements.

It occurred to Garrett that the hundred million would probably cost the inside group control. This came as no surprise, but there was a surprise, one hell of a surprise. Anne announced the plans for a Merger with their competitor, Photo Symbology, Inc. Before Anne could explain any of the details, Jersey reacted.

"What in the hell are you guys talking about?" he asked trying to contain himself and keep it polite.

Bob and I, along with our analyst, believe that putting the two Companies together would be the basis for market domination. Your Company is, without a doubt, superior at technology and Photo Symbology is extremely good at marketing. You have a slight upper hand today with market share based on your technology, but as the market matures over the next three years, good marketing will overcome your technical advantage and Photo Symbology will dominate. This Merger makes real sense and we believe our investors will agree through their pocketbooks," Anne calmly explained.

Jersey was shaken. He had no idea a Merger was in the works, nor did Garrett.

"And who's going to run this new company – the -Merger?" Jersey asked slowly and angrily.

Without hesitation Anne answered, "You, of course."

Garrett quickly spoke out, "You never mentioned this possibility to us. This is a significant difference from what we thought we were coming here for. Give Jersey and me some time to think this over and we have to talk about this with our other partners. We'll go out for coffee and discuss this between ourselves, or we can end the meeting now and pick it up later in the week. On second thought let's do this later in the week if that's all right with you Jersey? Have you prepared a pro forma covering the Merger?"

"Yes, of course." She handed a package to Garrett.

Jersey nodded yes, and out they went finding their own way to the elevator.

Neither Jersey nor Garrett said a thing until they were in Jersey's car heading back to the office in Westchester. "What the sam hell is she up to?" asked a very emotional Jersey.

"You mean her and Bob Roberts. They're up to a Merger. It makes sense to me. In fact, it's a very good idea in my opinion. But old buddy, I believe in my gut that there's more stuff in the recipe for this cake then we know. I don't know what it is, but I can smell it, and I don't like the smell. We need to get Levin's into the game, now!"

"Bullshit, let's get away from these tricky bastards now. I'll call them tomorrow and tell them we're not interested," Jersey ordered.

"As my daughter would say, chill out. Let's quietly think about it for a day and calmly talk this over with everybody. Remember, we do need the money. Let me remind you, Wall Street is not known for its sensitivity, politeness, or tact. The next firm won't be any better. Our job is to figure out what they're really up to. Remember it always is a game," Garrett finished responding.

"You and your 'business is a game' ideas," Jersey barked. Then he thought for a while , ...“OK".

CHAPTER 15 SWEET SIXTEEN

Anne and Robert Copper Robertson - aka Bob Roberts - were in the ACS executive dining room having coffee.

"You were quite right about Jersey Smart," said Robertson. "He went off like a Jack-in-a-Box. On the other hand, Carlssen was cool. Did you expect that?"

"I didn't know what to expect from him. But I now understand that his role as the calmer personality is important to Jersey, and Jersey, apparently listens, at least some of the time. I don't think that Carlssen is really that calm but is better controlled. He could be a bigger problem ultimately. I've learned that Brian Goldberg likes him and respects him. Brian, according to my sources, merely tolerates Jersey. These are early impressions, so consider these opinions as hip shots. We have to get to know Carlssen better. I think I have a very clear picture of Brian."

"Speaking of Brian Goldberg, how's the 'Brian Goldberg' project coming along?" asked Robertson.

"The first bee sting was delivered last week,"

"And the next," asked Robertson.

"I have work to do there. I'm confident the next step will succeed if I can successfully accomplish the next piece of my plan. Two things have to occur. I have to successfully finish my work and they have to agree to the Merger," Anne informed him.

"Do you know how the first sting worked," Robertson asked.

"No, not really. Don't worry. The process is cumulative."

"Don't tell me what you're up to, just tell me when it is done successfully," ordered Robertson.

Robertson left for a meeting and Anne's thoughts drifted back to Millsport and her clash with Mother Mills. *I always knew she never loved me, and it always hurt ... the almost incurable wound that a parent can inflict upon a child.*

Daddy, why did you have to die? She repeated these thoughts like a merry-go-round, over and over again — they really never went away. She remembered herself as a little girl looking out the window of her bedroom at a small vacation trailer being pulled by an old truck slowly passing by and wishing she was in the trailer. The Mills house, as she remembered it, was always dark and cold. When she thought of that trailer, she could see everything about and around it. All was black or shades of gray except a funny little window in the rear of the trailer that was lit with some kind of warm yellow light that seemed to reach out and somehow touch Anne. It was that same warm yellow that became her favorite color. She wasn't sure it really ever happened, but nevertheless it became a dream and a reverie that she had repeated and repeated.

Then her thoughts turned. She remembered getting ready for her sixteenth birthday and her 'coming out' party at the country club. A necessary ritual that was one of Mother Mills protocols of life. Anne had no friends other than an alcoholic instructor at a riding academy that she had attended since she was eight years old and a cleaning woman who had been part of the Mills household for years. The party her Mother had arranged was what would be expected of a Mills 'coming out' affair. Anne, who had nothing but dread regarding this event, was being trained, coiffed, and drilled according to Mother Mills regimen. Anne despised every aspect of it. Mother Mills even sent her to a dancing school to learn how to waltz properly. All the choices were Mother Mills, nothing was Anne's, or would ever be.

The evening arrived and off they went to the country club. Anne remembered sitting next to Mother Mills as they were being driven to the beautiful clubhouse with its perfect landscaping and parking lot filled with glistening cars arranged in perfect rows. There was an air of expectation, and she could see wisps of formally dressed guests through the windows of the country club ballroom as their car approached the entrance. They were greeted by the doorman who was really a college boy working there for the summer. She recognized him, but didn't really know him.

Mother Mills, once they were past the front door, quickly ushered her up a stairway for a last minute 'once over' before they made the required grand entrance down the central stairway at the front of the ballroom. Anne looked at herself in a mirror. She saw a fat Anne, although not as fat as she once had been, and there was something else that really shocked her. The fact that she really hadn't noticed it up to now was a puzzle, for it had been there all along. It was her hair style. It was exactly like her Mother's. In fact, everything she was wearing and doing was her Mother's style. She suddenly felt like an antique, something from somewhere else at some other time. She knew that she didn't belong in that time, and she also knew that she didn't belong at the country club, let alone for a coming out party. But the worst of it was the realization that her Mother was in complete control. Her descending the staircase with the band playing her introduction theme was an excruciating march through an alien crowd where she could find no comfort nor embrace any rhythm. The evening was filled with dancing with boys she didn't know and didn't care to know. She was greeted and embraced by people she either didn't know or if she did, felt no affection for or interest in them. The evening was the longest three hours she had ever endured. She could, all these years later, still feel the agony of that party as it slowly and agonizingly unwound. She endured. The party ran its course and then it finally ended.

At the conclusion of the festivities, she and Mother Mills were driven back to their house.

As they walked in Anne asked weakly, "Was it all right?"

Mother Mills stopped walking and turned towards Anne. She hesitated for a minute looking at Anne, and then turned to stare at a living room portrait of herself as a younger woman. "I was a classic debutant ... and I'm afraid you're not, and surely, will never be.

CHAPTER 16 PROBLEMS AND LESSONS OF CHILDHOOD

Jersey called an after-hours meeting with Garrett, Brian, Ivan, and Minor; the founders of Pristinimatic. Ivan Rokov was a brilliant Russian trained Electronic Engineer. He was a Jew who had left Mother Russia in one of those few periods when the "door was open". He had immigrated to Israel to get away from Russian anti-Semitism, the rot that plagued that country insidiously for so long, and was so enthusiastically embraced by so many of his non-Jewish colleagues. He had answered an ad placed by NASA in the Jerusalem Times and was quickly offered a job at the same "think tank" where Jersey and Garrett were employed.

Ivan was tall and rather good looking with beautiful – the ladies working in the office would say – bedroom eyes. He liked the ladies and they liked him. He smoked, as Jersey constantly proclaimed, "those god awful stinking Russian cigarettes." The odor always informed everybody when Ivan was there or had recently been there. He was given to Russian understatement and traditional Russian conservatism. When referring to the Russian government, he would quietly say with his heavy Russian accent and a slight smile, "You must always realize that these governing people are not really very nice." (Translation: "They are, every one of them, complete fucking bastards.") Then he would add a quotation from a Russian poet, "Russia can't be understood with your mind." Then he would smile.

Minor Brown was from San Antonio, Texas. Minor was trained as an Electronic Engineer but was, at heart and soul, a marketer. Five feet ten with a mop of curly blond hair, he was married to a tall Texan with blue eyes, blond hair, and a loud personality. Minor was anything but minor - one of those people who, when entering a room full of people, everybody almost instantly knew he was there. Garrett was always suggesting that politics would be a perfect profession for him to pursue. Minor's only, but constant response was, "I hate politicians."

Garrett's constant retort was, "Then be a new kind of politician, one that you won't hate."

Minor always responded, "It isn't possible. The profession is made for people that naturally like to be hateful. And besides, I don't like lookin' in a mirror that often."

Jersey proceeded to lay out for the group what had occurred and that 'we' – Jersey and Garrett - had decided to immediately terminate the meeting with ACS because of the Merger talk and bring it "here" for discussion. Before

51

responding, he wanted to hear from everybody. It didn't take long to understand that everybody wanted the negotiation to continue, that was everybody but Brian who said nothing. Eventually, Jersey asked Brian for his thoughts.

Brian told the group the following: "When I joined this Company I was convinced that we had a good idea and the proper team to execute that idea. I thought that between Jersey and Garrett we would have the appropriate leadership. Now you tell us that these Wall Street people want to raise the money we are seeking, but also want us to join with our main competitor in the form of a Merger. If I understand you guys correctly, they're telling us that our greatest strength is our technology and our competitor's greatest strength is their marketing capability. And finally, Jersey will lead the 'new' Company. That certainly implies that James Gale, the CEO of our competitor will be demoted or fired. Do I have it right?" Brian asked.

"Yes, I think so," answered Jersey.

Brian continued, "It all sounds very nice except I don't believe it. I know Photo Symbology extremely well, as all of you do. They're second rate across the board compared to us. Period! The Merger has another purpose and it isn't for the reasons you stated if you are telling us the truth. Are you Jersey?"

"Go to hell Brian ... of course I'm telling the truth," Jersey angrily responded.

Garrett interrupted, "I don't know what this 'telling the truth' stuff is, but Brian, you've got a point. You're right, Photo Symbology is second rate. Do you have any ideas of what they might be up to?"

Brian shook his head no.

It occurred to Garrett that, *Anne Mills must be the key to this. This is her play, I'm sure. I don't think its Bob Roberts, but it has to be Anne who cooked up whatever is cooking.*

Garrett continued, "I've thought about this quite carefully and I'm in favor of continuing. It's this simple; we really need the money if we are to grow. Further guys, remember, we've been trying to raise this money for a while and have fallen on our faces continuously. If we're going to proceed with this idea, we need to engage our best corporate legal mind - that's Mike Levins. Also, we've got to spend some time understanding Anne Mills and Bob Roberts. We need to do some serious due diligence. They sure know a hell-of-lot about us. We're acting like amateurs and we're in a big time game. Hey guys, we're chasing one hundred million dollars," he reminded everybody and finished.

Everybody agreed but Brian, who just made a placating gesture, and the meeting broke up. As Jersey and Garrett were walking back to their offices Jersey asked, "Do you have any idea what's bothering Brian?"

Garrett looking at Jersey, shaking his head negatively, "But something is. I respect Brian and I trust his instincts, but we need the money. We must be very careful."

52

Garrett walked into his office and sat down in his desk chair. Then he started thinking about how to deal with Anne Mills. *I'm sure I'm right about her; she's the brains behind the deal. Roberts is a Company administrator, a manager, there's no creativity in him.* He continued to ponder about Anne Mills and he was suddenly remembering exactly what Anne Mills looked like when he was a kid and would see her in her house - the fat little girl with a pretty, but lonely face. He also remembered Mother Mills and exactly what she looked like – cold, distant, and disapproving. That woman frightened him. He always remembered feeling something unpleasant ... then it came back to him. He would have trouble breathing in that house, and it got worse if Anne's Mother was nearby. He recalled that he would actually have to remember to breathe, and how to breathe. It was the sensation of suffocation, like asthma.

It was a cold winter day with fresh snow everywhere and he was in school - it was either third or fourth grade. The kids were all talking about Judge Mills dropping dead. Everybody assumed it was a heart attack. According to the kids, it happened as he was walking his dog after supper. The Judge had apparently died in the woods next to the school – a place that Garrett and most of his classmates were very familiar with. The Judge had been found lying in the freshly fallen snow with his dog tethered to his body by the leash. It was the first time Garrett realized that Daddies could die when their kids were young, as opposed to the appropriate time – that being, when they were old. It scared him and he remembered dreaming about it often as a child.

It continued to be the main topic of conversation at recess. Miss Miller, his homeroom teacher, had suggested to the class that they take up a collection and send flowers to the Mills family. He wondered why the Judge's family should get flowers. There had been other people that died and she had never made that suggestion before. One of his classmates had died from polio last fall and another family had perished in a house fire. He wondered what was so special about the Judge.

At about the same time that Garrett was having his reverie; Anne Mills was getting ready to leave the office and started thinking about Garrett Carlssen. *It's funny*, she thought, *that after all these years Millsport stuff is in my business life. Somehow Garrett Carlssen reminds me of all those feelings - ahhhhh, the joys of Millsport. Even my fight with my Mother seems to be part of what's going on. My Mother really overstepped this time. That's bullshit;* Anne said to herself, *she has always overstepped everything.* Her mind jumped to the ridiculous. *I should marry that Jew and have a kid. That'll meet mother's conditions.* She began to laugh a little. Then, she reminded herself, *Grahm would tell me to stick it. Get your mind back to the project,* but she kept wandering back to Millsport. She remembered the Monday after her coming out party and remembered Mary Barton and Eleanor what's-her-name coming over to her in the high school cafeteria. The two girls, who rarely spoke to her sat down opposite Anne.

"Hi, Anne," Eleanor what's-her-name said. We heard about your coming out party? Have a good time?"

Anne shrugged her shoulders.

"You didn't do so well, we hear. A stupid dress your Mommy made you wear, your Mommy's hair style, you can't hardly dance, and the only boys that danced with you were the ones forced to by their parents," and on and on.

The worst part for Anne was that it was true and there was nothing she could do about it. She remembered running to the girl's room and crying. She could still feel the hurt as if it happened yesterday. Those girls did not leave her alone for the next couple of weeks. They continued to remind her and anybody who was interested in any details or gossip concerning Anne's coming out party. She became the subject of mockery and verbal abuse. For some reason, it gained momentum and the abuse increased. They gave her the name "Sorry Anne, the loser" and it stuck.

Anne had been a quiet student. She had no friends and hardly ever spoke to anyone, but was a very good student. Most of her classmates were quite aware of that, and the fact that she came from a very wealthy family. Why those two girls picked her out, she would never quite understand.

Anne's professional style began, as a result, of that incident. It was during this unpleasant experience that she began to use her exceptional intelligence to find a way to stop their tormenting her. She spent several weeks trying to figure a way to end it. It occurred to her that if she could find a way to put them on the defensive about something very personal, they wouldn't have time to focus on her. It would have to do with something that they would never connect to her. She put a lot of time into figuring out a way to accomplish the task. Just thinking about it made her feel better. She was no longer helpless. Maybe even, no longer a victim. For the first time in her life she was fighting back. *Think, think, think - see how others had successfully accomplished such tasks,* she thought. In the end, she chose a very nasty move right out of a famous novel. This would be the prototype for the kind of methods that would serve her throughout her career. She was learning how to fight, and if required, fight dirty. An ancient Chinese General once advised, always begin a campaign by attacking the softest part of the belly. The idea she chose came from a famous play she had recently read," Mary and Eleanor were always together, they were buddies. She would somehow start a rumor that they were lesbians. She would never say anything but somehow find a way to engineer the rumor without it being connected to her.

In the end, it was so easy to accomplish. The ease and simplicity of her attack surprised her. This was a lesson she would not forget. It was tactical, and it was the way the military created and used misinformation. Small towns, gullible teenagers, the instabilities of becoming an adult, were perfect soil to plant the poison seed. It came down to a simple "love note" on the school bulletin board.

The first thing she did was watch Eleanor and look for an opportunity to get a sample of her handwriting. That turned out to be quite simple. Eleanor had written something in class and threw it into a waste basket. Anne retrieved

54

it and used that to learn how to imitate her handwriting. The second thing she did was make up a simple love note to Mary. Again, she researched to find a lesbian "love note" in literature and imitated it. Then, the third thing she did was to crumple up the note and step on it to "weather" it - make it look worn and dirty. The fourth and final thing was to get to school early one morning when no one was around and post it on the school bulletin board. It worked like a charm and created a terrible few months for the two girls. Eventually, the story burned out and things became reasonably normal again. The girls were too involved with their own problem to bother with Anne. She had found an effective method – a convenient deceit - for accomplishing certain tasks, and now it was Pristinimatic's turn.

CHAPTER 17 HOUSEKEEPING WITH YVETTE

Yvette Goldberg having finished her list of chores for the day was preparing dinner. She was pleased with herself. Everything was in its place and everything she had on her list was accomplished. There was order and Brian would soon be home to enjoy one of her carefully prepared meals. As seven o'clock arrived, in came Brian. They exchanged the usual ceremonial kiss, Brian took off his jacket and tie and sat down to dinner.

After a few minutes into dinner he asked Yvette, "How was your day?"

"Fine, nothing special," she answered. I went to the supermarket and deli, picked up some stuff from the cleaners, and got the house in order. Oh, I watched that TV show we talked about. Brian, I found that jam you wanted. I had to go to the internet to find it. The price was outrageous."

Brian thought, *I wonder if I should pursue this business about the note*. It bothered him a lot. But it didn't make any sense - the note from the "observer."

It was under a memo in his "inbox". It was just nothing more than a scrap of paper. But Brian Goldberg was a careful man who paid attention to details. Like all things in Brian's world everything was checked and put in its proper place and in its proper order. So he examined the note.

"Things are changing and your wife is part of it." It was signed, "Observer."

This was the second note that he had received from the "Observer." Several days before an email had arrived with the message "Things are changing, be very careful." And, it too was signed, "Observer."

He remembered the unpleasantness that swept over him like a cold fog after the Jersey's meeting. He was not happy. He had never ever really trusted Jersey. The reason he had joined the team was because of Garrett. Garrett was the only person he really trusted. He had to admit to himself that the first note from the "Observer" had troubled him a lot, but the second note burned him. His instincts told him Jersey was up to something and the meeting only made it worse. *That damn Jersey was not telling us everything* – he was sure of that. In fact, he had to admit something further – he was very angry with Jersey. He couldn't really say why.

Yvette offered him coffee. He nodded yes. She got up and turned towards the kitchen. He was struck, once again, by her lines and textures, her moves and gestures. Visually perfect, he thought. *She's mine, everything she is, but she's incomplete. I love her, god how I love her. She gives me everything I need, but what I need most. What a goddamn conundrum I've made of my life.*

56

He started to talk about the "Observer's" notes, then, thought better of it. Getting to sleep would be more difficult than usual.

CHAPTER 18 PLANS AND REMEMBERENCES

It was a beautiful spring Saturday. The cats were sunning themselves on the bright side of her balcony.

She found herself thinking about Garrett Carlssen when, she told herself, *I should be thinking about the Pristinimatic/Photo Symbology deal.* She had learned the general details of his life; where he went to school, whom he had married and divorced, his teenage daughter, his work history, his relationship with Jersey, and a list of random facts which made up so many pieces of his life. Although his relationship with Jersey was often combative, they were definitely committed partners who had found a successful way to work together. She was also satisfied with her original appraisal concerning the partners.

She once again went over the details. The partners voted as a block with each partner having equal voting power with the exception of Brian, who had a larger voting share by group consent, as a result of the voting trust. The whole maneuver required simple majority consent of the Pristinimatic stockholders. This would occur at a special stockholders meeting that would be arranged specifically for the purpose of approving the transaction before the Merger could occur. This would include, as part of the approval process, the all-important caveats required by Pristinimatic management as a condition of voting for the Merger. At the top of this list was who exactly would be the management team. Who would be the CEO, COO, Board members, etc.? Thus, as planned by Anne, if the inside voting control group could be fractured - meaning breaking Brian away from the group and voting with ACS - then, with his votes in combination with the outside votes ACS had collected, ACS would be in control. They then could achieve their ultimate goals, the Merger and new management.

Anne had become quite convinced that the potential chink in the inside voting bloc was Brian Goldberg. Everything, in her opinion, pointed to Brian. The extensive investigation of Brian had revealed an obsessive man living in a delicately balanced personal world. In the laboratory, he was in control, king, confident, and ready. At home, he carefully worked his way through an emotional minefield. He was merely a visitor, not an occupant. *Perfect,* she thought.

She was now satisfied with the strategy she had chosen to undermine the Pristinimatic board. She was sure it would work. Having set the table and arranging the menu, it was time for the main course. This would be a formal offer and she would have it ready for Bob Roberts by Thursday. He, in turn, would bring it to Joseph and Ibrahim for final approval.

If this one works, my girl, they've got to make me a senior partner, she thought, *If not, I'll go somewhere else. I think this is almost my eighth year here. It could be my time.* Her mind switched to the next "Observer" note. Past experience convinced her it should get the job done.

Again, Anne drifted. To her surprise a small memory surfaced out of seemingly nowhere. It involved Garrett. She remembered hearing that Garrett played on the high school golf team and, therefore, had to practice at the only real golf course in the town, and occasionally play school matches at the country club. She never really saw him, but his name came up as gossip because he was the first Jewish person that was ever allowed on the golf course. Many members were quite angry over his presence. He wasn't allowed in the clubhouse or the locker room but still, he was on the course almost every day during the high school golfing season. She remembered her Mother and some of the club members complaining to the officers that if you let that "kike" on the course it won't be too long before one of them finds a way to join the club. Anne laughed to herself because it was true. The Jews eventually were allowed to join. It wasn't because the members got nicer, they just needed more money to expand and upgrade the facility. *Always follow the money,* she thought. *Country clubs, Wall Street, they're all the same.* Then she thought to herself, *it's about time I put my mother's Jew thing away with so much of her other poisons.*

This lovely Saturday found the Brian Goldberg's working in their yard with many plantings and transplanting some plants from their neat little green house that was attached to the rear of their house. Both Goldberg's were passionate gardeners. It was here that they were at their best as man and wife. They shared equally the pleasure and delight of growing things. Both Brian and Yvette always looked forward to these times. Brian would always get depressed when their gardening day ended. They would clean up and shower and he would see Yvette at her most intimate. On occasion, she would ask him to hook her bra as she was dressing and he would be overcome with the wanting. Then things would revert to their normal existence.

Garrett Carlssen had just delivered Sallie Kate to one of her friends for the weekend and was heading for an upscale supermarket located in the East Village. Garrett liked good food and cooking was his revered hobby. As he was checking out of the store, it occurred to him for the umpteenth time that ACS had it in mind to gain control of the Company in order to pull off what they were suggesting. As long as we stay together we're all right, but if we get into a fight among us, we could be in trouble. He thought over each of the partners in his head and could find nobody who would betray the group. We've got to *get Mike Levins involved,* he reminded himself. *I'll talk to Jersey first thing Monday.*

Garrett began unexpectedly to review the many double crosses and betrayals he had observed or been involved in during his lifetime. How naïve he had been so many times. He knew the signs better than he used to, but still was no expert and never would be. He found himself replaying some of them in the theater of his head.

One involved an Uncle that lived in the same town where his alma mater was located. He remembered responding to a request from that Uncle and getting a dozen fraternity brothers to go to work for the gentleman one weekend. They were to help his Uncle to move his hardware store. When it was over the Uncle refused to pay the crew because he said they didn't work hard enough. They were really pissed at Garrett and were merciless about it for months. He didn't blame them. It took him six months to square that obligation. He never ever had anything to do with that Uncle again.

His mind continued surfing the past and it was his cousin's turn. Mark Jason Smith was Garrett's cousin by marriage. He was a pretty screwed up character. His parents could never abide by the fact that Mark was gay. The odd part about Mark is that he never consummated his lifestyle, only announced it everywhere. Upon this declaration, his parents declared him persona non grata and put him out to pasture with a trust fund which provided him with food, shelter, and a reasonable set of luxuries for life. After his formal education in English literature had been completed, he settled in Greenwich Village and found his way to running around with an arty set of interior decorators and their coterie. His contribution was a constant flow of clever social commentary and biting humor which bruised, but never entirely drew blood, which was quite entertaining to the group. He was welcomed but found no, nor sought any romance. Garrett thought of him as a successful, but unpaid entertainer. Several years ago he had become extremely depressed and attempted suicide. The event was followed by intense psychotherapy.

Garrett and Sallie Kate were avid sailors and they, at that time, had a thirty-two foot ketch that they kept on Long Island Sound. Summer weekends were dedicated to sailing. Garrett got it into his head to invite Mark to join them for the summer. The weekends on the Sound with Sallie Kate whom Mark always showed affection for seemed like good therapy to aid in his recovery. It worked.

At the end of the summer, rather impulsively, Garrett asked Mark if he would like to come to work for Pristinimatic as a "point man" in Public Relations. Mark accepted and did rather well at it. About ten months into the job they were setting up for a tour of west coast brokerages and money manager houses. Garrett objected quite strongly to the schedule Mark had arranged. It led to a conflict that resulted in an unpleasant disagreement. This led to a series of similar disagreements. One day, several weeks after the last fight, Garrett received a call from one of the outside board members. It seems that Mark had gone to the board member and bitterly complained about Garrett and his sheer lack of talent to hold the position he held in the Company and on and on. Garrett was quite embarrassed and humiliated. He had no choice but to fire Mark, and that is what he did.

He realized, as he was checking out with this groceries, that he had chosen every item in his cart without thinking about any of them.

60

CHAPTER 19 JELLY BEANS

The Pristinimatic executive team met every Monday morning first thing to discuss the Company events of the past week and the actions required for the new week. This took place at a large conference table that was directly connected to Jersey's desk. This was quite convenient because anybody at the conference table had a clear view of all three of Jersey's large computer screens. Jersey's desk was usually cluttered with papers, a coffee cup or two, some Company pictures, occasionally a picture of the current girlfriend, assorted business souvenirs, a big ash tray, and several jars of jelly beans. Everybody liked Jersey's jelly beans.

With everybody assembled, Garrett, who generally made up the meeting agenda, began reviewing the past week's list and the list going forward. Soon they were through with the past and had completed reviewing the action list for the new week. It went faster than usual because everybody was anxious to discuss ACS, the potential Merger, and, of course, all that green money that was going to be raised. There was definitely an aura of greed in the air.

Jersey began, "The ACS deal seems to be quite real, but they've tied the deal to our merging with our unpleasant competitor, Photo Symbology, Inc. There is nobody in this room who knows anything about Mergers and what that really can mean for us, including me. I spoke with Mike Levins this morning, our best lawyer for this purpose, and he will get involved immediately. The ACS representative we are dealing with is one tough cookie - a real bitch. Her name is Anne Mills. She's very smart and arrogant as hell. I get the impression she can suck information out of anybody like a leech sucking somebody's blood in a swamp. I don't want anybody in this room except Garrett and me talking to her."

Jersey continued, "On another subject let me be up front with you guys and remind you of my feelings about Photo Symbology's boss, Jim Gale. I can't stand that son-of-a-bitch. They told me Gale will be out and I'll run the show. We'll see."

"Garrett stays where he is and the same for everyone else. This is a chance for all of us to get a lot of money, but we've got to be very, very careful. In the meantime, we've got to run this business better than we have been doing. If the deal falls apart, we are still here and we've got clients to satisfy and payrolls to meet. That's it, any questions?"

A discussion ensued that was filled with basically unanswered questions. As usual in these meetings, coffee was being devoured and the jelly beans were starting to be consumed. Then something happened.

As Jersey was passing one of the jelly bean jars to Brian, the jar slipped out of his hand and fell to the floor spilling jelly beans all over the place. Brian, always first to volunteer in an emergency, immediately got off his chair, down onto his knees, and started picking up the jelly beans. Some of the others policed the carpet at the far end of the conference table. As Brian was almost finished he noticed a small photo lying on the carpet just under Jersey's desk. Without really thinking – he was listening to the chatter and wisecracks regarding Jersey's sloppiness - he reached for the photo intending to put it back on Jersey's desk. Still down on his knees under the table he looked at the photo. He was startled!

It was a picture of Yvette. She was wearing a tight blouse. He stared at the photo for a few seconds and turned it over. There was something written on the back. Although it was hard to read, he was able to make it out - "Enjoyed every minute." He looked at it to see if it was his wife's handwriting. It seemed to be, but it had been written with a very light pencil and was hard to see in the dim light under the table. Still on his knees, he put it in his shirt pocket. He was deluged with so many bad feelings he couldn't navigate.

Why was that photo in Jersey's office? That question swirled in his head like a storm. He was in a dark place – shattered.

Why did I ever marry her? Why? Why? The answer is simple, I couldn't help it.

The jelly beans were gathered and disposed of. The meeting ended. Brian left the room saying nothing.

CHAPTER 20 DANCING WITH ANNE

Garrett was on his way to ACS in a cab working its way down the West Side Drive. Looking out the window, he was fascinated by the appearance of the Hudson River on this very windy day. The water seemed to be boiling. It reminded him of what sudden squalls could do so quickly on Long Island Sound. Such storms would occasionally do that to the River above the dam outside of Millsport. They could even disturb the creeks where he had spent time in his youth hiking, swimming, fishing, and meeting and chasing girls. Over the years of that young time, there were parties and gatherings to attend to. They were held in summer cabins that were usually alongside friendly banks adjoining the creeks that fed the Susquehanna. They were somehow always a bit remote and exciting. The bright days, with the coming of the night, would fuse into the privacy of the shadows of the evening and the panoply of the night stars. Young people would build fires, drink and smoke too much, and perhaps, find each other in those shadows. Then he remembered Anne Mills at one of those times.

Memories are playbacks of events in our history, and some events are more indelible than others. We never remember in continuous sequences, but rather those chapters that were powerful enough to always become available. We often, unexpectedly, retrieve them as scripts from the past, sometimes as pain, and sometimes as pleasure. They represent both pain and pleasure. We retrieve them for all kinds of reasons, comprehension, fear, survival, amusement, passion, or the result of something like indigestion. They can be of the most pleasant or most horrific aspects of our lives – a plethora of all our emotions. In the complex nature of what we are, we can edit, exaggerate, deceive, or recall, and on occasion, even remember events as they actually occurred. We come with no metrics to measure their value or intensity. And in the end, we fear that they will be lost.

It was a Saturday evening at the Piperberg cabin on the Chimney Creek, and Dan Piperberg, Jr. had invited a bunch of kids, and predictably, a bunch more had also come. There was beer, chips, pretzels, hot dogs and hamburgers and more beer and young people everywhere. There was music playing and couples were dancing on the cabin porch.

Garrett, who was now in his junior year at college, was with some of his male acquaintances at the other end of the porch playing the "brilliant" game of who could take the hardest punch in the stomach with a beer can. The beer can wasn't thrown at your opponent, but held in the attacker's fist and punched

64

directly into the opponent's stomach. The winner was the last man standing. The result the next morning would be painful black and blue marks on one's abdomen. Remembering as an adult, he had to admit then and now, what an incredibly stupid game it was. But in the context of the world he was trying to be part of at that time in his life, it was simply the price of admission, and he was good at it.

He had been at the game for some time when he spotted a new girl walking reservedly with some people, "Who's the tall chick?"

Somebody answered, "Anne Mills."

Garrett thought, *Jesus, the fat little kid has grown up. Not bad, not bad at all.* He remembered that he was struck hard by her demeanor, the way she carried herself, and something he could not identify, but was powerfully drawn to.

He left the game and got a beer. Then he finally followed her inside the cabin, found where she was, and watched her. After a few minutes, he decided to take a chance and crossed the room and asked her to dance. She casually nodded all right with a tone of indifference, said nothing, and they walked out to the porch and lightly held each other in the way that defined a slow dance. They said nothing and they both looked away from one another. Garrett felt an excitement that he could not understand or deny. He felt the texture and movement of her waist as he so gently embraced her. He became aware of the details of her hand as he gently supported her. They barely touched elsewhere, but there was contact. He finally said, "Do you know who I am?"

"No," as she shook her head indifferently.

"I'm Garrett Carlssen. I used to play with your brothers when I was a kid," he informed her.

"Oh, you're the Jewish kid who lived down the block," she replied. "I remember."

"That's me," Garrett said thinking, *this is not going anywhere good.*

Anne looked him directly for the first time, "I think I recognize you now."

Garrett without thinking blurted out, "I would not ever have recognized you." Then suddenly, "I'm sorry, but you really have changed."

Much to Garrett's surprise Anne asked, "Do you like the change?"

Garrett fired back, nodding his head, "You bet!"

Then abruptly before the music had completely finished playing she smiled, stopped dancing, and announced, "You dance well, thank you."

Garrett gently pulled her back. To his surprise there was no resistance, "One more, please." Their dance became more intimate. Somehow he felt the measure of her body and he believed she was feeling the same. The music ended and without either of them saying anything they smiled at each other, then turned and left as if exiting from something neither of them could deal with.

Garrett remembered just how deeply he felt at that moment, both physically and emotionally. There was even an element of embarrassment, although no one was watching. *Do you have to be watched to be embarrassed?* He asked himself. He remembered the power of the attraction and at the same time he remembered feelings of despair and rejection. It was a moment of helplessness. He was out of bounds – he'd wandered into forbidden territory - so did she. Those feelings stayed with him long after that evening. They eventually mitigated and the adventures of youth were, for the most part, forgotten and life went on. Anne's obtuse reappearance had unexpectedly brought that evening back, back into sharp focus. *Amazing,* he thought, *I'm still obsessed with the evening I danced with Anne Mills as if it happened yesterday.*

The cab stopped abruptly as they arrived at ACS.

Anne and Garrett were in one of the conference rooms going over an agenda that included both Pristinimatic's and the ACS' requirements which, of course, included Photo Symbology. Each point was literally being positioned for negotiation. Although nothing had been agreed to in writing, things were really being agreed to through the subtle business tools of body language and repartee', and conversely, issues that were not being accepted were being made quite clear. All in all it was going well, but the hard issues of dilution, control, and some other sticky issues of the Merger had only glazed the surface. Then again, nothing else was really expected at this point in the negotiation.

As the meeting proceeded, Garrett was intermittently distracted by the thoughts that had surfaced during his cab ride. Out of nowhere, and as a surprise to him, he looked at Anne and asked, "Do you remember the time I danced with you at Dan Piperberg's cabin?"

She looked at him and replied with an impatient frown, "Probably."

"What kind of answer is that?"

"We're here to talk business, not about growing up in Millsport."

"Not so fast, I really want to know," he demanded.

"Why?"

He wasn't sure he wanted to tell her, but he did, "I'll be completely frank, we had a very pleasant, in fact, intense is the word, two dances together and then we parted. For some reason, it bothered me a lot at the time," and then he laughed. Then looking straight at Anne, he rather sentimentally stated, "I guess, I consider that it has always been some sort of unfinished business."

"That was a long time ago and we were kids. Let it go," she advised.

"I guess you're right," he replied. *It occurred to him that he had just given her a significant negotiating advantage. Nothing personal should ever be revealed. What in the hell were you thinking,* he lambasted himself. *I better get out of here now and regroup. What is this lady doing to me? Grow up! This is now and you're not a kid at a party at Chimney Creek.*

CHAPTER 21 MARRIAGE PROBLEMS

Brian Goldberg was sipping a cup of coffee in his office. He opened his desk drawer and looked at the picture of Yvette and the writing on the back once again. It had been more than a week since he picked up the picture from under Jersey's desk. He had said nothing to anybody. To quote an expression of his father's, an expression the old man had used often, "It's eating my liver." His structured work habits were out of sync. His normally stoic temper was short, and he found himself barking at his employees. He had been unusually quiet at home. Even Saturday in the garden with Yvette was tense. He really didn't know what to do but, he knew he would eventually have to do something. He could not live this way.

Garrett walked in and asked, "Hey Brian, wanna' get some lunch?"

Brian at first hesitated then it occurred to him that Garrett might be able to help. He always felt Garrett could be counted on to be honest and could keep his mouth shut. Brian had no close friends, but Garrett was as close as anyone. "Yes, I'll join you," he responded.

They chose a Chinese restaurant a few blocks from their office. After they finished eating Garrett looked at Brian and said, "You look terrible, what the hell's wrong?"

"Is it that obvious? " Brian asked. "How long have we known each other?"

Garrett responded, "Twelve, maybe fourteen years. Come to think of it, we both started at NASA the same year. It's longer. Why?"

Brian twisted and smiled a smile that is not really a smile, but in essence, an upside down frown. Looking down he began to explain, "Something happened that really has me screwed up," then a long hesitation.

"Garrett, you know me better than anybody around here. You know I'm a very private person. I don't like to talk about me to anyone. I haven't slept much in the past week. This has got to be just between you and me. Can you promise that?"

Garrett carefully nodded his head yes and continued with his reassurance, "You know I can keep my mouth shut. I don't know what's going on, but you really seem fucked up, old buddy. If I can help, I'll be glad to."

Brian stared at Garrett and continued, "At last week's Monday meeting, if you remember, the jelly beans spilled onto the floor where we were sitting. Jersey dropped them as he was passing them around. Also, if you remember I got down to help pick up the mess. They went all over the place. I was the one who cleaned up under the conference table next to Jersey's desk. They were everywhere. Jersey, as usual, didn't do a thing to help clean up the mess he made."

"So, where are you going with this?" murmured Garrett.

"As I was picking up the damn jelly beans I discovered a small photo lying on the floor under the table." He stopped at that point.

"A photo? Was there something special about the photo?"

Brian took a deep breath, "Yes, it was a picture of Yvette."

"That's odd, so?" questioned Garrett.

Brian continued, "She was in a sexy pose ...wearing a tight blouse. There was some writing on the back of the picture."

"Writing? What kind of writing? What did it say?" asked a surprised Garrett.

An obviously pained Brian responded, "It said, 'I enjoyed every minute.'"

"Ohhh, my god, are you having some marriage problems?" asked Garrett. "I've been there." Then he regretted having said that.

"Well, we have a funny relationship, Yvette and me" explained Brian. Then Brian pushed his chair back and stood up. "Garrett, I can't do this. Let's get back to the office. Sorry."

Garrett, driving back to the office in silence, was beginning to get upset realizing that something was very wrong. *What is a sexy picture of Brian's wife doing under Jersey's desk?* He thought. It stirred up all kinds of screwy ideas in Garrett's head. Garrett knew damn well that Jersey was capable of some terrible things, particularly where woman were concerned. He recalled the Scully Patterson affair, but screwing around with Brian's wife was a stretch. Jersey always put business first and Brian was the Company's most creative and best disciplined engineer. *It didn't fit,* he reasoned. *Brian's a mess and he's too goddamned up tight to deal with this. I remember when I caught my wife in bed with her buddy. I couldn't see straight for months. I don't know if I would ever have gotten my act together if I didn't have Sallie Kate. Brian has no kids. I hardly know his wife. Weird, we've never even had dinner together. On the other hand, Brian's no fun. He generally says nothing at all. But still I like him, I really like and respect him. I know how good an engineer and honorable human being he is, but socially he's a washout. I've got a feeling this is just the beginning of some god awful mess. Shit happens.*

He parked the car and both men walked back into their offices.

Garrett sat down and the phone rang. Yvette Goldberg of all people was on the line. *Oh, Christ* thought Garrett. "Hello Yvette. This is a surprise. What can I do for you?" That was the best he could think of ...basically nothing.

"Garrett are you available to come to dinner this Saturday?" asked Yvette.

"Ehh, yes, I'd be glad to," answered a very surprised Garrett.

"Seven o'clock, looking forward to it. See you then. Bye," and she was gone.

Well, I guess I no longer will be able to say I've never had dinner with Brian and Yvette, he said to himself. *What in god's name is she up to?* One thing was for sure, he was not looking forward to Saturday evening with the Goldberg's.

68

CHAPTER 22 A LOVING BROTHER

"Are you finished with your, ah ... Pristinimatic moves? Is it enough to get the job done?" Bob Roberts asked with a raised eyebrow.

"I really don't know. We have to be a little patient. We probably have Mr. Goldberg very upset. His being upset should have an effect on the rest of the management, I would imagine. If I'm right, we have created tension and worry beyond the usual feelings associated with change. It should start to play out in our favor soon. You know Bob, it's quite a game," she finished.

"You really enjoy this combat, don't you?" asked a slightly amused Bob Roberts.

She, surprisingly, hesitated, "I think I do."

"Are we having some second thoughts?" he asked with a smile on his face.

"No!" she declared, but she was wondering why it wasn't feeling as good as it usually did. She had been playing these games for years. "They have no idea what we're up to. It seems they've brought in a guy from Harkson Merit, to help them. I don't know him, but our lawyers do. They say he's very good. His name is Mike Levins."

"Get to know him. Get your researcher busy. There's too much at stake to be careless," Bob ordered.

"I already have," she responded. "The hardest part will be handling Jersey. He's not stupid and he can be very rough. I've learned a lot about him and he can be a ruthless bastard. I also think he has the potential to be very dishonest."

"You mean he's one of us," Bob laughed teasingly. Something he rarely did.

Anne laughed back, but it was forced. Oddly for her, she was uncomfortable.

The plan that Anne had put together was to break the unity of the five founders of Pristinimatic. The old 'divide and conquer' move. In a showdown vote, if the Pristinimatic group didn't vote together as a block, the gentlemen – the founding group - will have lost their inside slim majority. That would leave a path open for ACS to impose their plan on the Merger. Because of the arrangement the founding partners had made with Brian Goldberg regarding the voting trust, he controlled the single largest voting bloc. If Brian were so manipulated by anger, betrayal, whatever, and, as a result, chose not to vote with the group, the remaining group vote would be reduced to well less than 50%, resulting in a clear loss of control.

Therefore, the key was breaking Brian from the group to achieve that goal. Also, they had every reason now to believe that they had had their clients purchase enough Pristinimatic stock, that when combined with the stock that

Brian Goldberg controlled, would give ACS explicit control of the Merger. These are the kinds of deals that brokers often persuade their clients to go along with. In return, the clients are usually are given preferences on the new stock purchases and sales. They, in turn, expect the clients that purchased a particular stock (in this case Pristinimatic) to vote the way they have advised. It works out successfully this way, quite often.

"Well, I guess it's just a matter of time and we'll know whether you've done it or not," Bob Roberts speculated. "Does Jersey suspect anything regarding his future?"

"No, no way!" responded Anne. "God forbid if he found out at this time. Not good, but he won't know that before the stockholders meeting unless I tell him."

A surprised Bob Roberts blurted out, "Why would you do that?"

"I haven't the slightest idea," smiled Anne and got up and left, returning to her office.

She sat at her desk wondering what she meant about not telling Jersey, *I remember another time when I didn't tell.*

She didn't want to, but she thought of Grahm, her older brother. The brother who was always a sharp stick pointed at her eye. She always shivered either mentally or physically, when she thought of Grahm. She had good reason.

She was eleven; she remembered living in the shadows of her home and how she had learned not to be seen, avoiding being heard, always quiet, very quiet, avoiding and avoiding whatever had to be avoided, but always watching and watching. Then there was that evening when mother was visiting friends and Grahm was out. It was safe, she could relax, there were no dangers, but it didn't work out that way.

It was peculiar how she learned about the beginning of Grahm's evening. She only knew about the ending of Grahm's evening as a witness.

Small towns really never keep secrets. There is always noise and gossip. And woven within the chaos of these streams are events and thoughts, and some of these are secrets, but secrets are only secret if they remain small separate islands of knowledge. People do not generally live their lives in small separate islands of knowledge. People live with other people. And time always seems to undo all such separations of knowledge.

Grahm Mills was seventeen and driving an old souped-up Ford. It was a Saturday night and he and some friends were drinking at a dive outside of town called the Black Horse Tavern. They were trying to flirt with and maybe score with women that were, for the most part, at least twice their age.

The Black Horse was a place that attracted many types, but particularly people who worked second rate jobs when they worked. They drank too much sometimes, or sometimes, always. Their cars, trucks, or motorcycles, like them, were used and worn. Reliability was an evasive attribute for these folks. They drifted through their lives often with a pained carelessness. Many were plagued

71

by a burden of rage and its constant companion, a melancholy pain because of their inability to change their lives for the better. The joy of living, so often avoided them as they arose and faced each day. Saturday nights at the Black Horse was, hopefully, their best time of the week. Perhaps, something good might occur.

The women who attended those weekend nights were the counterparts to the men and their lifestyle. Some were married, some were not, and some were something else. The music was the best and most honest part of the Black Horse - Country, Waylon, Elvis, and Patsy. The lights in these places were scattered patches of neon red, yellow, blue, and green, and a smattering of dirty dull white light bulbs. There were always dark spaces where intimacies could occur or on occasion, force. It was a harsh honky-tonk world where the smells of beer, liquor, smoke, and cheap perfume were ever present. Body odors were often present, as a result, of some island of human activity. The bathroom floors and walls were stained and the stalls adorned with graffiti expressing latent desires, telephone numbers, and on occasion, political statements. Moderation was generally out of place.

Grahm and his friends entered that world because they could get served even though some were clearly underage. They believed places like the Black Hoarse promised them the forbidden, the exciting, and the opportunity to satisfy and prove something that made them men. Most of it was really a simple distortion of reality and foolishness that so often invades the brains of teenage boy/men. In truth, mostly the only thing they could really depend on was getting drunk on cheap booze. On occasion, they would become involved with or be a witness to things that they had no business seeing or being part of.

On this particular occasion, the boys had been drinking for about two hours when Grahm decided to make a move. Grahm was a big, good looking, six foot two specimen with a mop of curly blond hair. He had been watching a very buxom woman dressed in a peasant skirt and low cut blouse playing darts with some of her girlfriends. They were drinking boiler-makers and eating pretzels that they dipped in very peppery hot mustard – a Pennsylvania specialty of that era. They were very noisy and very drunk. The women were hard, drearily pretty, and worn. Grahm inserted himself into their party by buying a round of drinks for all. He was immediately welcomed and he joined in the dart competition. He gradually focused in on the lady of choice and she was responding. Eventually, he asked her to dance and she responded enthusiastically. By the time Patsy Cline had finished her second song the two were locked together as if they had been intimate for years. As they separated to return to the dart game, Grahm saw a troubled look suddenly appear on his new partner's face. She was looking at a heavy set man standing near the dart board.

"Oh shit, that's my fucking husband," she murmured.

The husband pulled out the darts from the dart board. Clutching five of them in one hand, and holding one in the other hand, he proceeded to holler

72

at the top of his lungs, looking straight at her, "You fucking bitch, I'm gonna' kill you and your fucking boyfriend."

He began throwing the darts across the dance floor at them. He threw as hard and as fast as he could. The first few missed Grahm and the wife along with the crowd behind them. Everybody was sent ducking and/or running for cover, but the last one found its mark straight into his wife's left breast. To Grahm's surprise she didn't scream, she just looked down at the dart projecting from her chest and the beginning of a patch of spreading blood. Slowly and deliberately she pulled it out. The dart was buried in her ample breast by at least a good inch. Then, with the blood profusely covering much of her blouse she started walking towards her husband. The whole place suddenly got very quiet, even somebody had turned off the music. With everyone watching, she turned for a moment and looking at Grahm, ordered, "Stay the fuck out of this kid!" Then she announced to everyone, "This bastard can't get it up anymore. How about that, Weilly, you prick? You were never good at anything but being pissed off or getting drunk and you fucked like a girl."

They were now standing face to face glaring at each other. Weilly's fists were clutched and he began to punch his wife in the jaw but was met with an uppercut in his belly. The wife, with her arm at her side, was holding the dart in her fist with the point projecting towards his abdomen. She was ready, and as Weilly started to punch she struck, driving the point of the dart straight into his belly, He screamed, covering his belly with his hands, and sunk down onto the floor.

She stood over him, "I hope you die you no good worthless bastard!"

The bouncers appeared and grabbed the woman. One of them said, "Somebody, call the cops and an ambulance."

Then the owner appeared and ordered everybody to leave. "None of you want to be here when the cops arrive! Believe me! I'll take care of it. Get outa' here, now!" Almost everybody quickly obeyed, including Grahm and his buddies.

Grahm and company got into the car and Grahm suggested they go someplace else for the evening. His friends were not interested. "Are you crazy, Grahm? That's enough bad shit for one evening. I've never seen anything like that before and I don't want to see something like that again; that was terrible. Jesus, that woman is one tough cookie."

"You got to admit that bastard got what was coming to him. It was terrific."

One of the guys replied, "Grahm, you're sick!"

Their evening was over.

Grahm dropped the boys off and started for home. It was still early.

At the same time, Anne was taking their dog out for his last walk around the block for the evening. Most dogs in Millsport were in charge of their evening walks as well as for all their walks, requiring no one to accompany them. Mother Mills didn't believe that was proper, so their dog was always walked at the end of a leash. As Anne was rounding the corner about a full block from her house, Grahm was speedily driving down the same street. He was quite drunk and noticeably weaving a bit.

Anne saw who it was immediately and Grahm saw her. On the opposite corner was another dog doing his business. The dog, Jeeves, a standard Poodle, belonged to Sheila Feld, another eleven year old girl who adored her pet. The Feld's were also a prominent family in the town. Even Mother Mills approved of them. Dr. Feld was head of surgery at the local hospital.

As Grahm was staring at his sister he weaved drunkenly to his left heading right for her and then avoiding disaster, jerked to his right. The maneuver was too far towards the other corner and he hit the curb where Jeeves was frozen in the moment. The dog was instantly obliterated under the right tire of his car. There was no howling or crying, just a crunch. Grahm speeded up and disappeared around the corner of the next block.

Anne, quite upset, ran over to check Jeeves. As she approached, she saw what was left of the dog and she began to cry. There was nothing to do. She went home and went to bed. She couldn't sleep; she kept reliving that awful scene.

About a half hour later her door opened and in walked Grahm. He smelled of cigarettes and liquor. He sat down on her bed. He stared at the wall for a few minutes. Then he turned, facing her and grabbed her by her shoulders and pushed her violently down against her bed, squeezing her as hard as he could. "Anne, you fat little shit, never, never tell anybody about what you saw, or I swear, I'll make your life miserable, and I promise ... to hurt you! You know me well enough to know I mean it." Then he slapped her hard across her face and left.

She believed him. Oh god, how she believed him. She was scared, terribly scared. She never told anybody about that night. She was destined to re-live it, or scattered wisps of it, many times in her dreams or in those elusive moments, not quite a dream, that some call twilight. She always carried a feeling of ambivalence concerning her guilt. It was simply survival. She was torn between exposing Grahm and protecting herself. And at this point in her life he still scared her.

It was two days later and she was outside working in her Mother's garden planting tulip bulbs – 150 tulip bulbs, each planted three inches deep. This was a required task imposed by Mother that was beyond dispute. Actually, Anne liked gardening and this was one of the few things her Mother imposed that she enjoyed.

A garbage truck pulled up in front of her house on the other side of the fence from where she was working. Two men got out of the truck and sat down on the running board and began eating lunch. They did not see Anne because of the thick ivy vines covering the iron fence next to where she was working. The vines precluded their view. Anne could hear them talking quite clearly. One of the men was recounting what had happened Saturday night at the Black Horse. He'd been there when all hell broke loose between Weilly Klinger and

74

his crazy wife and some big teenage kid. In fact, the kid had been playing darts and dancing with Klinger's wife. That set Klinger off. He saw and heard the whole damn thing.

At first it was quite an interesting tale but as the man went on with detail after detail, it didn't take Ann long to understand who the big kid was.

CHAPTER 23 DINNER AT THE GOLDBERGS

Brian was sitting in his home pretending to be reading the paper. He was trying to find a way to ask his wife about Jersey. He had been mentally squirming for almost the better part of an hour looking for an opening and couldn't find an approach. The whole thing was eating him up, but he was in emotional territory that he just plain didn't know how to handle. He had tried to bury it and just forget about it many times since the business meeting last Monday, but to no avail. One way or another he had to confront her and get some kind of explanation. It was driving him crazy. It was almost seven o'clock and Garrett was due to arrive for dinner. Yvette had been busy preparing the house and the food and herself for the past six hours, at least. Whatever had gotten into her to invite Garrett was a complete puzzle. He had asked her why she did it and got, "It seemed like a good idea," for an answer.

Sure enough, the doorbell rang at a minute or two after the appointed hour and there was Garrett with a bottle of wine in one hand and a bouquet of flowers in the other. Both Brian and Yvette greeted him and everybody was really quite uncomfortable. They all seemed embarrassed. It just came down to this, the Goldberg's never entertained and Garrett was never their guest. Nobody was ever their guest. The normal social landscape of their existence had been altered for the moment and like so many things in life, it takes the desire and some practice to become both good as well as comfortable at it.

Garrett realized that in the years he had known Brian, although he had been by his house many times to pick him up, he had never ever passed through the front door of that home. *What in the hell am I doing here*, he thought to himself. Yvette offered him a drink, a Gin and Tonic, and he enthusiastically responded, "That sounds great."

She nodded with a smile and disappeared into the kitchen. Brian was already drinking some kind of cocktail, which in itself was unusual. He had never seen Brian drink anything but a beer, or once in a while, a Manhattan, and always very, very slowly.

Yvette returned with a very tall glass filled to the brim with the Gin and Tonic. *Excellent*, he thought, *I'm thirsty as hell and I probably need to get a little buzz on to get through this evening.*

Yvette brought in some hors d'oeuvres and they were caught in the moment looking at one another, not knowing what to say. Finally, Yvette started some small talk about the weather and its effect on their gardening. Garrett started swallowing the drink enthusiastically, hoping for a quick numbing. The irrelevant conversation continued and Garrett had finished his drink in record time and had requested another. The second drink was also ingested quickly. The booze hit home with an un-expected bang, and he found himself getting more intoxicated by the moment.

It began to occur to him, m*aybe too much too fast. Oh shit, the horse had been let out of the barn much too quickly. Asshole, I wonder where this evening is really going*, he pondered in his new found and unexpected stupor. Garrett was not really much of a drinker. He was what was euphemistically known as a cheap drunk. It didn't take much and he couldn't really handle it when he got there. Things moved rather quickly and Yvette served dinner. By this time, Garrett was so stoned he couldn't eat anything. He was quite embarrassed.

He had to come up with something. Then he got the brilliant idea to take some action which might mitigate his present stupor. He admitted he had consumed too much alcohol too quickly and he thought he could improve things if he could be dismissed from dinner for a few minutes and take a walk outside. The theory he was selling himself was based on metabolism. He would not walk, but rather go for a run and the strenuous exercise would speed up his system's metabolism thereby removing the extreme effects of the alcohol that was currently screwing up his brain. The Goldberg's were astonished and immediately gave him permission to go for his "walk." Garrett got up and unsteadily went outside, took off his sport jacket and, hanging it on a nearby bush, and took off on his run.

It was a warm evening and in a very short time Garrett was ringing wet from a well-earned sweat. He found himself even more inebriated as the run continued. He began to think, *I wonder if this is going to kill me.* He found himself running through a park he had never been in, admiring the beauty of the landscaping, when he was suddenly confronted with an enormous need to throw up. He stopped and expelled the relevant contents as his body demanded. Then he looked for a water fountain to flush out the unpleasant taste that remained in his mouth. Eventually, he succeeded in his search. He spotted a drinking fountain. The fountain came with a group of noisy teenagers hanging about it. They were busy passing around a bottle of some kind of liquor. As he was about to wash out his mouth the fragrance of their alcohol hit his nose and once again, he had to throw up. They were amused. The best he could utter was, "Hey guys cut me some slack. I don't feel so well."

He actually felt a little better and started to walk back towards the Goldberg's. There was no more run left in him.

Yvette was looking at the clock; it was now nearly an hour that had passed since Garrett had gone for his "walk." She looked at Brian quizzically, "Maybe you should go out and try to find him. Something might have happened to him."

Then the doorbell rang. Brian opened the door and there was a now disheveled and smelly Garrett. Before either of them could say anything, Garrett began with a profuse apology for his behavior which ended with a declaration of never doing anything like it again. Then he said it was probably best that he go home, clean up, and get some badly needed sleep. Brian, judging his condition, immediately declared that he was not fit to drive anywhere. He led Garrett to a couch and said, "Go to sleep here for a while until you are sober enough to drive. Then, you can go home."

He accepted the couch suggestion readily. But before he settled down Brian informed him, with profuse apologies, that Yvette had never made a Gin and Tonic before. She had, unfortunately, mixed up the proportion of the Gin to the Tonic. That was where the trouble had originated. I'm very sorry, but we have inadvertently poisoned you."

Garrett chuckled for a moment and almost immediately fell asleep.

Yvette and Brian started cleaning up, washing, polishing, in great detail and a couple of hours passed. They said practically nothing to each other. As Brian was walking into the kitchen for the seventh or eighth time he suddenly burst out with, "Why did I find a picture of you underneath Jersey's desk last Monday?"

"What?" she responded incredulously?

"Don't lie to me, Yvette!" ordered Brian quite uncharacteristically.

Yvette replied with some anger of her own, "Whatever are you talking about, Brian?"

Brian was suddenly overcome with the pain of guilt and a wave of insecurity. Sheepishly he reported, "I found a picture of you underneath Jersey's desk at last Monday morning's meeting."

Yvette twisted a bit, turned, and took a deep breath, then shaking her head negatively and staring intently at her husband, "You're saying you found a picture of me underneath Jersey Smart's desk at a meeting last week? What in heaven's name were you doing underneath Jersey's desk? I don't get it."

Brian hesitated, not quite knowing how to conduct his interrogation or succinctly explain the circumstances of his discovery, finally answered, "Jersey spilled a bunch of jelly beans on the floor during a meeting and I got down on my knees to help pick them up."

"So jelly beans led to my picture. Jesus, where are you going with this, Brian?" demanded Yvette.

Brian slowly painted the picture for Yvette. He did it as completely as he could with all that he could convey and with all he could feel. He was met with an overwhelming rush of sadness. For the first time in his life as an adult, that he could remember, he broke down in an unexpected and uncontrollable rush of tears.

"I don't know. I really don't know who you are." Then it got more intense and he began to sob in a way he had never even known even as a child. Yvette was paralyzed with this bewildering scene.

Finally, he regained some composure. He was totally embarrassed; his cheeks as red as a beet. Yvette was paralyzed. Then he said, "You know how I really feel about you, and I know how you really feel about me. I received half

78

a loaf when we married and that had to be enough." But shaking his head said, "I have accepted that, but I don't know how to deal with betrayal."

Yvette, in a fury, threw the pan she had been holding down to the kitchen floor, chipping a piece of the floor tile that flew across the room bouncing off the wall scattering in many pieces. She hurried out of the kitchen and ran up the stairs. The next thing that was heard was a door slamming. Then it was very quiet. Yvette sat down on the edge of her bed for a long time staring at nothing. Slowly the anger dissolved into sadness.

Brian walked back into the living room with an unopened six pack and removed one can and opened it, guzzling it down with an uncharacteristic gulp and a burp. He immediately went to work on a second can. He pitched the empty across the room at the sleeping Garrett. Garrett quickly stirred, opened his eyes, "Thanks pal, I was up. I heard you two going at it in the kitchen. You all right?"

"No," Brian responded. "Did you hear what I said to Yvette?"

"Something about a picture?"

"Yeah, that's right. It's that picture of my wife. There's a lot more to it that I can't talk about."

Garrett hesitatingly asked, "Do you think Jersey's fooling around with Yvette?"

"I don't know what's going on, but it's not that simple."

"You sober enough to drive home?"

"Strangely enough, it's all gone."

"Go home, I've got a lot of thinking to do."

"Ok," and a concerned Garrett left.

CHAPTER 24 SATURDAY IN THE PARK

Garrett rose up Saturday morning with - to his surprise – no after effects from dinner at Brian's. He made some tea and thought about the strange happenings of last night. He was embarrassed, but more, he was apprehensive. There was something very wrong at the Goldberg's and he somehow affected or accelerated the situation with his getting drunk and ruining the dinner or some damn thing. Whatever it was, it somehow changed whatever was planned. He really didn't know.

The picture, what the hell was the picture all about? He pondered. *I've never seen Brian like the Brian I saw last night. What's Jersey got to do with it?* Garrett was uneasy with all that was happening at the office. Brian's behavior pushed him from apprehensive to honest-to-god worry. *Too many things are happening at once. The ACS deal. Why can't we just raise the money and forget the Merger? This is one hell of a way to begin a relaxing weekend,* he thought disgustingly.

Staring up at him intensely was Molly. She was accustomed to patiently waiting until Garrett had his morning coffee then it was her turn for the morning walk into Washington Square Park. Garrett looked down at Molly, "OK lady, it's your turn." Off they went.

It was a beautiful day as Molly was sniffing her way through the Park. She stopped every few minutes and would start pointing at something. Garrett was always amused because he could never see what she was pointing at. *She was a German Short Hair Pointer, and Garrett guessed pointers have to point even if they are pointing at nothing.* In all fairness, she had never been trained as a hunter. Molly was a New York City apartment dog and her job was to be a sweet family companion, and she excelled at that. The closest he had ever come to seeing one of her targets was a June bug crawling up a tree.

After taking Molly for her morning constitutional, Garrett decided that the best way to spend the day would be a good bike ride. Perhaps he would work his way up to Central Park and do the whole Park from top to bottom. He hadn't done it in a while and this seemed to be a perfect day for such an excursion.

As he and Molly returned, a sleepy Sallie Kate greeted him with a morning grunt as he entered their apartment. "I'm going to go for a bike ride in the Park, honey. How about joining me?"

She shook her head no, "I have a date with Laura and Jason and one of his friends. We're going to go down to the Battery. They want to go to see the

Statue of Liberty, would you believe? I suppose as a true New York citizen I should see it once in my life. Besides, the friend is supposed to be cute."

"When will you be home?" Garrett asked. "We might have a dinner date with your Aunt Jean"

"Do I have to go?" she protested. "She's a crazy old lady who always tells me how I should live my life, how I should dress, how I should improve my posture, and on and on."

"She also loves you very much," reminded Garrett. "I admit she's a bit crazy, perhaps a better word is eccentric. But between her giving you advice and telling fascinating stories of the life she's led, she is a woman who is extraordinarily well read and cultured. You won't meet many like her ever, and I think you'll someday hold dear the snippets of her life she has shared with you. C'mon, admit it, it's always fun."

"All right Dad, what time do you want me to be ready?" Sallie Kate asked.

"Six-thirty, we're going to Brooklyn Heights to something your Aunt is raving about. It's called the "Dark Enclave." I can't begin to imagine what kind of cuisine that name implies. But if your Aunt picked it, I'll bet the food is good."

Garrett dressed for his bike ride and off he went up Fifth Avenue. He entered the Park around noon. The Park was in full bloom and bursting with a crop of new growth. The special color of spring green was everywhere along with young flowers of every color - the spectrum was complete. This was one of those years when nothing was brown or burnt. It was the season of renewal and everything that was growing was producing something interesting and/or delightful.

People were everywhere, including clusters of kids and parents. This tapestry was filled with bikers, runners, walkers, dogs, baby strollers, sunbathers, and baseball and soccer games. From time to time, the soft fragrances of the young flowers further improved the experience of being there. Violets wiggled their way between rocks and even invaded some cracks in the sidewalks. Dandelions seemed to grow on the lawns where they wanted to, tenaciously defying the gardener's careful plans.

Garrett followed the bike path North passing people sitting on benches reading, feeding birds or squirrels, staring at others, some staring at nothing with sad faces, some listening to music through ear buds, and on occasion, sleeping, and of course, lovers, loving. The day was filled with the excitement of rebirth that a rich spring is all about. Then the brilliance of the sun reflecting off the many colored Mylar balloons the park seemed to attract, somehow shattered this symphony.

Finally, Garrett stopped at a fountain to take a much needed drink. At the same time, a little dog was being chased by a little girl who was giggling and screaming with delight at her quest. Not far behind was a daddy running after her who, as he approached the fountain with his eyes on his daughter's trail and not where he was going, ran right into a puddle that had collected near where

Garrett was standing. He slipped and down he went hard with water flying everywhere. Garrett ducked and cursed, and then realizing the guy may be hurt. He immediately went over to check him.

Garrett asked, "Hey fella, are you all right?"

"I think so," as he slowly got up and shook off the fall. "I think I'm going to be a bit sore tomorrow." He quickly started to look around for his daughter.

Just as this happened a woman, seeing what had occurred, took upon herself to run after the little girl and caught her and brought her back to her father.

"I believe this belongs to you," the woman said.

"Thank you very much for bringing Violet back. Thank you, thank you," he proclaimed.

Garrett looked at the woman. The woman's back was facing Garrett. He hadn't paid any attention to her. He had been entirely focused on the father and his little girl. The woman slowly turned around. It was Anne Mills.

They were both surprised and a little embarrassed. Garrett could feel his face heat up. Anne was a bit shaken. The two protagonists were not on their normal turfs.

"Anne Mills, I presume," spoke Garrett.

"Anne Mills, you presume correctly," she replied.

The only thing a reticent Garrett could think of was, "What are you doing here?"

She replied somewhat defensively "I live across the street. It's a beautiful day and I came out to enjoy the park and do some reading. What are you doing here?"

Garrett softened his tone, "The same as you, enjoying a beautiful day in the park, but on a bike." Then with a bit of hesitation and rather spontaneously Garrett suggested, "Anne let's put the business away and let me buy you a hot dog or a coke and catch up on Millsport gossip."

"God, not that!" she barked. Then to her surprise and Garrett's relief she said cheerfully, "But I'd like the hot dog and the coke ... I accept." Anne was now walking beside Garrett, who was pushing his bike along, then asked, "Where do you live?"

"The Village, Fifth Avenue and Eighth Street; I've been in that building ever since I came to New York. I walked up out of the subway straight into a rental office the day I arrived in the city and rented a place in that building. Got married and divorced in that building. But best of all had my daughter Sallie Kate living in that building, and still do. It's a great neighborhood," proclaimed Garrett.

"You have custody?" asked Anne.

"Most of the time," replied Garrett. "Sallie Kate visits her Mother in Paris for about a month every summer."

"We do live complicated lives," stated Anne.

"You married?"

Anne shook her head no, "Never got a proposal I wanted."

"Do you ever go back to Millsport?"

"Once in a while, there are certain 'official' occasions that are required by my Mother. But it's all become very unpleasant recently. To tell the truth, it has always been unpleasant, but more than usual lately," explained Anne with some surprise that she was sharing this with Garrett. *My god*, she thought, *He probably has relatives in Millsport and could tell them about my personal business.*

Garrett immediately read Anne's concern, "Anne, I promise on scout's honor not to tell anybody ever." He waited to see if she believed him. Apparently she did. "Your Mother's still alive?"

"Strong and kicking as ever," replied Anne. "She's the same old force she's always been. Do you really remember her?"

"I was a little kid when I was in your house. To tell you the truth she scared me. I don't think she liked me. To be quite frank, I'm Jewish and I don't think she liked Jews. She never said anything, but when you were growing up in Millsport in those days, you could always kind of tell."

Anne wasn't rather sure if she should confirm the obvious, but she thought, *oh well, what the hell!* "You got it right. She's a very prejudiced lady. She's from the South, the real old South. She's still fighting the civil war. It's peculiar how those things in that generation don't go away."

"How are your brothers?" inquired Garrett.

"The youngest, August, is doing fine. He's a lawyer in a small town in upstate New York. Webster is maybe all right when he's not around Grahm, my older brother. Webster runs a small chain of hardware stores in small towns in western Pennsylvania. Grahm is a lawyer and a judge in Virginia. They're all married with children," reported Anne.

For some reason Garrett blurted out, "I never liked Grahm, he was a mean son-of-bitch. I hope you're not too offended"

Anne, smiling slightly, turned her head towards Garrett, "No problem there. I agree with you about Grahm."

"Anne, what about you? How did you get into the Wall Street business?"

"Studied business as an undergraduate and went on to Wharton for my MBA. When I graduated, I was offered a job on Wall Street at Hendricks and Company and eventually ended up at ACS and have been there ever since. That was almost eight years ago" answered Anne.

"You like it?"

"I love the combat,"

"I think I get that," shaking his head and smiling. "We're breaking the ground rules – no more business."

"Fair enough," replied a smiling Anne.

They spotted a hot dog vendor and Garrett bought the dogs and drinks. They sat down on a nearby bench. Garrett excused himself to make a call to his daughter.

Anne was thinking about Grahm. *She had a bad history with her older brother. There had been many bad moments with him. The recent episode with Grahm and Mother Mills was awful, but at the end of the day it was predictable. She knew both of them only too well. She was just the sister, an extra piece that really didn't fit. But damn it, it always hurt.* She stared at the beautiful blooms in a nearby flower bed and her mind wandered. *Grahm,* she thought, *you are the worst of my family. My Mother is a very close second or maybe an equivalent. Daddy, why did you have to die? She remembered once again about Grahm and his brutality.* Then she told herself, *it's too beautiful a day to think about those things. Stop it!* She ordered herself. But she couldn't.

She was seventeen, almost eighteen, home from college. The fat little girl was gone and she had become a young woman, a freshman in college. She was a very smart student and beginning to feel a trickle of confidence for the first time in her life. Yes, she had gotten accepted to a very good school because she had very good grades, but the acceptance was really more about who her family was. The new thinner young woman was attractive and a few boys were trying to date her. But the truth was she was frightened. She was not really prepared for an intense college social life but she could carry on what she referred to as a "social life". In truth she felt she was second rate at the woman thing at best. But she was smart and was able to apply her mind in school. She realized she could excel academically and that felt good. She focused for the first time in her life and chose a path. Anne Mills would learn the way of the business world and would find her way to some kind of success and independence - the hell with being the bell-of-the-ball. She could never be that. She didn't have the 'right stuff'. Her Mother had made that quite clear.

It was four-o'clock in the afternoon and she had just returned from a run. She was coming out of the shower and there was a knock on the door. "Just a moment, I'm not dressed."

Grahm didn't wait. She was completely nude as he entered. "I'll be god dammed that's a nice set of tits."

She was terrified and grabbed the bed spread and covered herself. "Get out of here, I'll call Mother!" she screamed.

"Call anybody you want, it won't help," he informed her. "Mother and the maid went out."

"Grahm, please get out here," she pleaded. He didn't. Ten minutes later she was no longer a virgin.

Grahm looked at her and hissed, "This is between you and me. If you ever tell anybody I'll punish you forever. Do you understand me?"

She nodded her head that she understood. He left. Anne went over to a full length mirror and saw a bruised body, a cut lip, an eye beginning to swell and a trickle of blood on her thigh. She was mentally numb. There were no thoughts, only the sound of her breathing reached her consciousness. She sat at the edge of the bed for over an hour and slowly a rage began to build from somewhere deep. *Daddy, where are you? I have been compromised for life and there's nothing I can do.* She took a very long shower and went to bed and slept until ten-thirty the next day. She was very sore but the eye turned out not to be too bad. She answered any questions about her appearance by blaming it on a running accident.

The trauma became bearable in about a week, but the wounds were always there. She never told anybody. Her logistics, whenever Grahm was near, were never to be in a position to be caught alone with him under any circumstances. She, these many years later, shuttered at the thought of him and that afternoon. Grahm never said anything and she only exuded quiet hate towards him.

"My god woman, what's wrong?" asked a curious Garrett. "You look like something terrible happened."

Much to Anne's surprise she answered, "I was thinking about something very unpleasant that happened a long time ago."

"What?" asked Garrett.

She bowed her head, and nodded no, "Please, It's something I don't want to talk about."

"Talk can help," said Garrett.

Surprisingly she replied, "Maybe some other time." Then it occurred to her, *why ever would I say such a thing to Garrett Carlssen?* Her mind quickly flashed to the days and hours she had fantasized about an act of revenge. But she reminded herself, *I know how to fight in business, but I don't know how to fight Grahm. Never did, never will.*

"OK, some other time," he responded.

She remained quiet for some time and her mood slowly changed. Garrett sensed every bit of it. Finally thinking it might be safe he asked, "Want to go to the Museum and see the "Can Man Survive?" exhibit. "I hear it's terrific," suggested Garrett.

She nodded, yes and off they went. They spent the afternoon together enjoying the museum and it was quickly five-thirty. Garrett then, with some hesitation, asked, "When I called my daughter before, I found out that a dinner engagement my daughter and I were supposed to be having with an Aunt of mine had been cancelled. She's a wonderful whacky old lady who is incredibly amusing to be with. I get a real kick out of her. My daughter has made plans of her own and I wonder if I could talk you into dinner? We'll go back to our homes and freshen up, take a shower, or whatever, and I'll pick up around eight-o'clock."

"It was a very nice afternoon, Garrett, but we have business dealings to complete and I don't think that's a very good idea," she answered.

Garrett pushed, "Look, we aren't kids. What's happening between our companies is a business deal. There's nothing personal."

He thought to himself, *sure, your hoping there's nothing personal.* "Don't think of it as a date. I would just like the company of an interesting person for dinner. Think about it this way; who likes to eat alone on a Saturday night? I haven't done this for so long I can't think of what to say next. Please? What kind of food do you like?"

Anne laughed, "Alright, but it must be a secret between you and me. I like Spanish."

CHAPTER 25 DINNER AT EIGHT

Garrett arrived at eight-o'clock at Anne's apartment building. He asked the Doorman to inform her that he was in the lobby. In a few minutes she came out of the elevator to greet him and discovered he wasn't alone.

"I'd like you to meet my daughter, Sallie Kate Carlssen," he proudly announced. Standing before her was an attractive fifteen year old brunette with the greenest eyes she had ever seen. Sallie Kate was not bubbling over with enthusiasm to be there with her Dad and his 'date'. But circumstances had forced Garrett to take her or call off the dinner.

"I tried to call you about Sallie Kate joining us but your phones are not listed and I neglected to get a phone number," he informed her. "I'm hungry and we have reservations at the Old Sevilla Fonda in the Village for eight-thirty. Let's go and we'll grab a cab."

As they were riding in the cab, Garrett flashed back to Millsport just after he had graduated from college. Times had changed at the Country Club and under certain circumstances he was allowed to attend. He had a date with a girl to go to the club for the July Summer Ball. Her name was Martha and she was very tall. When dancing they were eye to eye and somehow that always made him feel out of balance. She was the daughter of the guy who ran the steel plant that he was working at for the summer. They had become friends in High School and remained so. There was no romance on Garrett's side but Martha definitely had a thing for him. He really didn't want to go, but Martha talked him into it.

This was the first time he had ever entered the club house which was quite beautiful in a pre-World War II way. Although few people noticed him, he felt as if he had a Star of David attached to his dinner jacket, circa World War II, and couldn't have been more conspicuous or uncomfortable. As he sat down at their assigned table he remembered spotting the Mill's table and seeing Grahm. *There was nothing more to think about, he was in the wrong place at the wrong time*, he thought. *How in the hell can I get out of here and do it quickly?*

Martha picked up on it immediately. "Garrett, screw those bastards!" she ordered with a mouthful of distain and at the same time asking a waiter for a round of drinks. "They think their excrements don't stink. The truth is it stinks worse than most."

It didn't help, Garrett still wanted out. But he was committed to Martha and the evening was to wear on.

The cab hit a pot hole and jerked him back to the present. *What am I doing with Anne Mills? This is crazy. What have I imposed on Sallie Kate?* He felt as if he had lost control of something. *Was this business or something else that was motivating*

87

him? It's just going out to dinner. Don't make so much out of it. Then it hit him, *these are Millsport feelings, the kind I left that town to get away from, those many years ago.*

They arrived at the restaurant and were seated. Sallie Kate started the conversation, "You have some business with my Dad, don't you?"

"Yes," replied Anne.

Sallie went on, "My Dad says that you're a very tough business woman to work with. Is that true?"

Garrett was ready to crawl under the table with that proclamation. He knew she was mad at being forced to go out with him, but this was way over the line. Garrett really had no choice when he learned that Sallie Kate was very upset at what had happened to her that afternoon with her friend and the boy that she was supposed to meet and go to the Statue of Liberty with. It seems that the boy was very aggressive with Sallie Kate and she had gotten very angry with him. Her friend did not defend her and the three of them deserted her at the Battery, calling her a wimp. Sallie Kate took the subway back home and Garrett came back to the apartment to find a tearful daughter. An hour of talking, and no way to contact Anne Mills, had created the threesome. It was then, that he realized that her phones were not listed and he stupidly had neglected to get a phone number.

"Jesus, Sallie Kate, you're out of line," barked Garrett.

Curiously and with a bit of irony Anne asked, "Do you always discuss your business affairs with your daughter?"

"Not usually," responded Garrett, "But my daughter hears many of my phone conversations. Looking directly at Sallie Kate, "And she's being very inconsiderate and impolite because she had an unpleasant experience this afternoon with one of her friends and is taking it out on us. I apologize on behalf of both of us."

Sallie Kate apparently wasn't finished, "You didn't answer me, is it true you're not easy to deal with? You're a real pain, right?"

Anne looked at her for a long minute. She thought, my, *my you've managed to ruin what promised to be a pleasant evening.* Then, feeling that the horse was out of the barn anyhow, she replied, "I have a reputation for being very tough and have been difficult to deal with on occasion. Young lady, it's expected and required in that part of the business world I deal with – Wall Street."

Sallie Kate continued, "Why is it expected that you have to act so tough?"

"Oh Christ, Sallie let it go!" pleaded a frustrated Garrett. Then he thought, *I wonder where she really wants to take this.* Then Garrett, in a perverse sort of way decided to sit back and see where it would go. *The evening is screwed up and I don't have the slightest Idea how to fix it,* he thought. *Well ladies, go at it.*

Anne had never been in a confrontation like this before. She had had many experiences in the business world and had learned well how to handle any opponent in that milieu, but a teen age kid driven by all those hormones was a challenge that she was not in the least prepared to handle. As crazy as it might be, she found herself liking Sallie Kate - quite the opposite of what she expected. She decided to answer Sallie Kate directly, "It's the woman thing. Wall Street has traditionally been a man's world. Men are very tough on each other in that highly competitive world. Almost nobody is particularly nice. If a woman wants in, she has to go one better to be successful. It's really that simple."

Sallie Kate was not satisfied, "So that's the reason, your reason for being ... a very tough person."

Anne hesitated, smiling softly answered, "I think you mean bitch. I really hadn't thought about it in those terms, but that's the reason. Why are you so interested in my behavior?"

Sallie Kate hadn't expected the question but she was quick with a reply, "I want to know who my Dad is dating."

"We aren't dating! We were just having dinner together. We accidently met in the park this afternoon and spent a few hours together chatting. We actually kept business out of it. Your Dad suggested, since neither of us had any plans, that we have dinner together. That was very nice on his part. It was only a pleasant interlude and there is no possible way we could ever date," responded Anne.

"Why not?" demanded Sallie Kate.

"We are just representing each other's companies in a business arrangement. We would have never met for any other reason, let alone-dated," responded Anne.

"Don't you know each other from Millsport?" asked Sallie Kate.

"Hardly," responded Anne. "We knew who each other were but I don't think we ever said anything other than, 'Hi'. No, that's not completely true, we once danced together, but I don't remember any conversation before or after."

"Well you have said more than 'Hi' today and any way you want to cut it, it's a date. So stop pretending," insisted Sallie Kate. "I think you like each other."

At that, nobody knew what to say. The silence continued for a bit then Anne spoke, "Garrett, I think this has turned out to be a really bad idea. I'm no longer hungry. Let's pretend it never happened. I'll see you at the Wednesday meeting. It was interesting meeting you Sallie Kate. Sorry you had a bad afternoon." She got up, said goodnight, and left.

Garrett just shook his head at his daughter, took a deep breath, and announced, "Let's order, I'm hungry."

Anne left the restaurant and hailed a cab. As she was being driven up town she was simply overcome with some remorse. *I really wanted to have that dinner and continue with the evening. Maybe I acted hastily. The kid got to me, but I find myself liking her.*

CHAPTER 26   A MEETING, MEMORIES, AND A POST CARD

Jersey was headed to the City for a meeting. Anne and Bob Roberts had requested this encounter – it was only to be between the three of them. He had been strongly advised by Anne, not to inform anybody about it. Jersey loved the idea of intrigue, so he had no problem complying. It reminded him of the many intrigues in his life; the way he had fooled his Father from stopping him from getting a college education; the way he had suckered Annette Greico into a relationship and eventually marriage – that hadn't worked out too well in the end; and the way he had gotten rid of his first partner. That started him thinking about his Father – not a good subject - a nightmare.

The old man was a bastard, even when I was a little kid, he thought. *He always seemed on the verge of rage.* Abraham Smart worked as a teamster in the show business industry. He either drove a truck or loaded a truck that delivered scenery to and from the New York theatrical district and its boroughs. He was physically a very powerful man as well as an extremely good looking man. He ran his house with an iron fist that was richly flavored with meanness. Dealing with him could be a challenge when just passing mashed potatoes. Getting permission to go out and play ball was a major struggle. If it wasn't done just right, he would become threatening or explode. Physical and mental insults were always part of the menu. The blows were never soft. It was never safe. That was the life for a kid whose father was Abraham Smart. Jersey had two sisters: Ida and Susan. They both had been damaged by their father and their lives were sufficiently screwed up as a result. They would probably always be in too much pain to enjoy normal lives. Jersey helped them financially but kept his distance otherwise.

Jersey recalled a particularly painful moment when Ida was caught by Abraham kissing a boy goodnight on one of her few dates. It was a simple kiss on the doorstep. Abraham was waiting inside by the doorway and burst open the door as the kiss had begun. He grabbed Ida by the arm and ordered the boy to never again come anywhere near the house or his daughter again. He then pulled her into the house, slammed the door and slapped her face and body repeatedly. As he was administering each blow he repeatedly insulted her, by calling her a whore and a Jezebel. *God, how he used those biblical metaphors, to impose his punishments,* Jersey thought. Poor Ida was sent to her room hurting in the full grasp as an innocent teenager. She was made to remain confined in that room for several days. Jersey had become convinced over the years that she had never really left that room after the incident. She barely functioned in a menial job in an insurance office. Susan, who was very pretty, became obese and worked in the garment industry. Her one enjoyment in life was to become a sports fan. She belonged to the New York Ranger Fan Club and drank and ate too much. She hadn't seen her parents in years.

Jersey's Mother was a very attractive woman when she married Abraham. Abraham was a decorated World War II veteran. As their marriage progressed she became completely dominated by him. Their relationship was a complete mystery to Jersey, a mystery he had no intention of solving. As the years went by his Mother seemed to fade away into complete obscurity. It was as if she was on film and was experiencing a fade out that spanned years. She progressed from beautiful, to plain, to insignificant. Jersey would think of her as almost transparent. He couldn't recall any thing she voiced or did that was not laced with her husband's desires, thoughts, tastes, and opinions. She was a Mother that neither imposed, nor protected – at best an echo.

Abraham had decided that his son would follow in his footsteps into the union and enjoy the benefits and security of being a teamster. His son had another idea. Jersey was very smart and was an exceptional student. Abraham had no appreciation or any pride in Jersey's scholastic ability. In fact Abraham despised the educated class. He was a product of an underclass that had inherited a hate of the educated and wealthy. He rejected the idea of a social meritocracy having any value in the real world. "You can't ever trust them. They always look down on us," he was often heard to complain. Abraham's view of life and the plan he had for his son was completely rejected by Jersey. He was not about to let any of that happen to him.

In the spring of the year before he graduated high school he was offered a scholastic scholarship. It was a dedicated chair scholarship fund for promising young technical students at NYU. It was lot of money for the time and a perfect opportunity for a paid education that Jersey could never afford, and therefore was anxious to accept. He didn't tell his father about it before he concocted a scheme to gain his Father's permission. He carefully planned and rehearsed a strategy the old man would buy - total bullshit.

He started by asking Abraham to introduce him to the union. Meet the boys and get to understand the turf. Abraham complied. After several weeks of this he finally told Abraham about the scholarship. Abraham, as expected, reacted with disapproval and his usual anger. "They'll screw you over boy, and you'll end up with nothing," he proclaimed.

Jersey came back with a different idea, "I'll accept their money, get my room and board, go to a class once in a while and wait to get thrown out. Screw'em. Meanwhile I start as an apprentice teamster, and I'm out of the house and off your back."

He looked at his Father for a reaction. It was a bit screwy and not totally believable, but he was appealing to his father's malice. It might work. Malice won and he got permission. To this day he was amazed that he pulled that off.

Jersey excelled at school. He was, by the middle of his freshman year, recognized as someone special. He was noticed by the academic staff for his exceptional theoretical talents and became a pet of one very famous professor, but a cruel PhD, Dr. Gerhard Milde, known over the world for his work in the emerging field of advanced semi-conductor technology. Being one of Milde's pets came with a price. Jersey could be called at any moment, from anywhere, at any time to perform a personal favor for the 'good' doctor. That could mean anything from driving the doctor somewhere, to delivering and picking up his laundry or spending a weekend cleaning up and painting his garage. Jersey was after more scholarship money and wanted to get a PhD. He was convinced that if he stayed on the right side of Milde, and was willing to perform the appointed tasks as well as endure the verbal abuse - which never ended - the money and degrees would come. When the doctorate process began, it was Milde who became his Supervising Overseer and the personal obligations became even worse. It took seven long years to pull it off.

When Jersey's Father became aware of his son's real intensions he severed his relationship with Jersey permanently which included his Mother. He called him a lying betrayer, a Cain, and wished him the same curse. None of it came as a surprise to Jersey. But in spite of this he managed to keep quiet contact with his sisters, and they with him. They reported that the old man had gotten worse as he had gotten older. One day they reported that their Mother had passed away. They didn't really know what was wrong with her. Jersey always believed she just gave up living and it was the old man's doing. Living with him had sucked out all the joy and desire for any existence what-so-ever.

Jersey had parked the car and was now entering Anne Mills' office under the guidance of the usual talky escort. He found Anne and Bob Roberts at a table drinking coffee. They greeted him but didn't offer him any coffee. That bothered him.

The conference began.

"We are ready to present you with a term sheet – the financial details of the deal," Roberts Announced. "If you are OK with it, we can proceed." He handed a copy to Jersey and he spent the next few minutes looking it over.

After digesting the document Jersey responded, "It looks OK to me, but Mike Levins will have to look it over and approve. But what's not written here is what I'd like to review with you folks once again - the Merger and who gets to run it. You have informed me quite clearly that in return for my co-operation, I get what I want. Let me be blunt. As you know I have done what you want. Therefore, I get to run the Merger and Jim Gale is out. Anne has made it clear that that was the price of the deal. Once again I'll say it; I get to be the head of the Merger – no ifs, ands, or buts. More succinctly, in return for my helping you break up our voting bloc – and we are assuming the maneuver will work - Brian will vote with you and not the group. Is that correct?"

Roberts nodded yes.

"Can you assure me that you have enough outside votes from the market along with Brian's votes to achieve that control?"

"Yes, absolutely," answered Roberts.

"Have your partners agreed to back the deal as of this point?" asked Anne.

"Yes, provided Levins approves of this Term Sheet," responded Jersey. "It boils down to this. Right now we control the votes through our arrangement with the partners. You will not do the deal – no hundred mil, no Merger – if you don't control. But in return for that control we get the money and I am the head of the Merger. Do I have that absolutely correct?"

Roberts answered, "My god, yes!"

"Once again I'm asking - why do you need control?" Jersey demanded.

Roberts responded, "It's simple. As Anne has informed you before, we and our surrogates have purchased a lot of your stock. They will have all acted on our say so, therefore voting the way we have advised. They depend on us to make sure this works. You might do a lousy job and have to be replaced. Our being in control is the insurance they depend on."

Jersey had nothing further. He had made his deal with the devil and was ready to proceed, "Let's get on with it."

Anne and Roberts were satisfied. The rest of the meeting was spent going over details.

On the way home in the car Jersey wondered if he had covered all the possibilities and wasn't missing anything. Brian seemed to be well on his way to breaking with the partners. *This is big, if I can pull it off,* he thought to himself.

Once again his mind drifted off and he thought of the Old Man and something he hadn't thought about in years. He was a freshman in College and found himself in a money crunch. He decided just this one time he'd try to ask his Father for a loan. Instead of asking directly in person or over the phone, which in either case never ever went well, he wrote a letter to Abraham carefully explaining his predicament and how he would repay the loan that included a repayment schedule and significant interest. A week later he received a post card. The message was simple, "You will find the money you requested enclosed within. It was signed, "Your, Father".

That still stung.

PART 2 THE GAME

CHAPTER 27 BREAKFAST

It was 5:30 in the morning when Anne awoke. She turned and pulled the sheet over her head and found herself squirming. Thoughts began to pour out of her brain like water from a spinning lawn sprayer. It was like a quick series of scenes in a movie trailer, each thought jumped front and center and she would start focusing and before she could deal with it, a new thought would appear. Sleep became impossible. She tried to meditate with no success. This was something new for her. She had spent so many years of her life focused on specific tasks, all of them with her usual discipline. She tried to concentrate on office matters, but she couldn't even make that work. This went on for an hour and nothing changed. She decided the only rational thing to do was get up, shower, and get something to eat. It was now around six and she looked in the 'frig' and found nothing that appealed. She decided to go to the neighborhood deli she frequented so often. She was sure it was open, and out she went.

The Enchanted Bagel was a typical New York City deli-restaurant. The owner was over seventy and most of the crew was from somewhere in Central America. Sam the boss and owner, who had been feeding Anne for over ten years, greeted her.

"Good morning Anne. Whatever brings you in here this early in the morning?" he kindly asked.

"I couldn't sleep."

"I see ... coffee?" Sam asked.

Anne nodded yes.

Sam came back with two cups of coffee, one for Anne and one for him. "Got problems at the office or with a boyfriend?"

Anne who was not the most communicative and gregarious person in the world, for some reason, had developed a relationship with this old deli owner, Sam Axinov. They had somehow become friends and amazingly, best friends. She liked his food and his warmth, and his intelligence. Slowly she had gotten to know him over many years and had learned a little of his history. He was a German Jew, who, as very young man, had survived a concentration camp. Life and luck had taken him from Europe to Mexico where he found work in a hotel in Mexico City. He spent five years starting with busing and washing dishes to working in the kitchen as a cook. He learned the food business, Spanish, and eventually English. There he met a New York girl on vacation and ended up marrying her, had three children, and with help from her two brothers opened up the Enchanted Bagel Deli. He explained that he had lived two complete lives. The first was terrible. The second was perfect.

Anne Mills, the small town provincial, for some unexplained reason, had connected with Sam, the Jewish deli man who was living his second complete life, but now, unfortunately as a widower. Sam's wife had died several years ago. Sam was the only person she had ever confided with openly, honest conversations with somebody for the first time in her life. Sam had figured her out early in their relationship, but never brought it up, and he truly had affection for her.

"So what's the trouble, young lady?" Sam inquired.

"I'm not that young, Sam. I don't know. I guess I'm not sure. Sam, I'm a very successful investment banker and I'm in the middle of a deal that's going to make me and my firm a great deal of money, but it doesn't feel right." stated Anne pensively.

"Hmmm, is your conscience bothering you?" Sam asked casually.

"No, that's not it. I'm doing what I always do. But still it doesn't feel right." Anne restated. "This has never happened to me before. Sam, I'm smart, and arrogant, and a bitch in a man's world, and that's what I have to be to win. But I'm not dishonest. I generally win by outsmarting my opponents, and often my co-workers. The deal I'm working on has the usual complications and it's like any battle. You make careful plans and the battle begins, and the unexpected happens, and you adjust."

"Hmmm ... so what you do is wage war," stated Sam. "I thought you were a businesswoman. You call yourself an investment banker, but I think you are something else.

"What are you talking about?"

"You sound to me like a warrior, a soldier."

Anne laughed, "Hardly."

"If you aren't a soldier you sure talk like one," responded Sam. "Plans, battles, the unexpected; this is soldier talk, not business talk. Anne you are a soldier, and I suspect you have been one for a long time. Soldiers hurt and kill people. They don't do nice things. I know."

"I've never killed anybody," Anne protested.

"Have you ever hurt anybody?" quickly asked Sam.

Anne was silent.

"There are all kinds of ways to hurt and kill. Killing can be just parts of people, not the whole person," instructed Sam.

"From time to time people get hurt in business," said Anne. "It can't be helped. It's part of the turf."

Sam looked at Anne directly and sighed, "Maybe, you're getting tired of being a soldier. Most soldiers get very tired of being soldiers after a while, especially if they experience real combat."

They sat in silence.

Finally, "Enough for now, what would you like for breakfast?" asked Sam.

"Surprise me Sam," declared Anne smiling.

96

Breakfast was very good and she felt better. She took her morning run, showered, and left for the office. It was quite early and she decided to walk for a while before catching a cab. *So he thinks I'm a soldier. Maybe I am. A damn good one*, she thought. Her attention turned to the next step of the deal.

CHAPTER 28 MONDAY MORNING

It was Monday morning and Garrett arrived at the office a few minutes early and ran into Brian at the coffee maker. "Greetings, old buddy," was the first thing out of his mouth. Brian looked at him expressionlessly, then frowned, shook his head, and walked away saying nothing. Garrett thought to himself, *that wasn't exactly an appropriate greeting, you jerk.*

Garrett went to his office. Jersey had planted himself in Garrett's desk chair and was smoking a cigarette. Jersey smoked a cigarette four or five times a year. *This wasn't good.*

"Good morning Garrett," Jersey muttered. "I heard you had dinner at Brian's house Friday evening."

"Yeh," responded Garrett.

"How was dinner?"

"I really don't really know. I got ripped accidentally."

"Oh, and how in the hell did you do that?" responded a suspicious Jersey.

"Yvette made me a few Gin and Tonics. Something she had apparently never made before and somehow mixed up the proportion of the tonic to the gin. I was very thirsty from working out and the day was very warm. I gulped two of them down like I'd been on a desert for a week. It hit me like a hammer in probably ten minutes or less and I was off to the races," informed Garrett. "Jesus, I was drunk! Who told you I was at Brian's for dinner?"

"Brian. Since when has Brian been sociable? I've never been invited to Brian's for dinner." exclaimed Jersey

"Neither have I."

"C'mon, Garrett, why do you think you were invited?" insisted Jersey.

"It has something to do with some picture that was on the floor under your desk."

"What are you talking about?" demanded Jersey.

"Remember when you spilled the jelly beans at last week's meeting?

"Yeah!" replied Jersey.

"Apparently when Brian was crawling around under your desk cleaning up the jelly bean mess, he found some kind of picture," informed Garrett. "That's all I really can say. You've got to talk to Brian for any other information. Leave me out of it. It's not any of my business."

Much to Garrett's surprise Jersey nodded in agreement. Then it occurred to him that Jersey might know what was going on. Then, Jersey changed the subject.

"I spoke with our lawyer this morning. He's been in touch with ACS. He had a little surprise for us. Guess who Bob Roberts is?"

"Who?"

"Robert Cooper Robertson," announced Jersey.

"What' a Robert Cooper Robertson?"

The son of one of the founding families of ACS - Ashton, Cooper, and Smith," answered Jersey.

"Hmmm, why do you think he insists on being Bob Roberts, just another Wall Street player?" asked Garrett.

"I haven't the slightest idea. But one thing's for sure, he's more important than he's presenting himself," commented Jersey.

"Maybe he's not a partner," reflected Garrett. "The firm is currently run by an Italian and an Arab."

"I'll ask Mike to find out more about him," responded Jersey.

"Moving on, we've got to start counting votes, for the deal," said Jersey, changing the subject.

"What's the problem, we've got control?"

"No problem, let's just start counting votes," stated Jersey. "Tomorrow we're meeting with Mills and Roberts."

"Oh ... I didn't know that. When was that scheduled?" asked a surprised Garrett.

"Last week, I forgot to tell you. Here's the term sheet and a copy of the proposed contract," handing them to Garrett. "Read them and be ready for tomorrow's meeting."

"For Christ's sake, that's a lot to digest in twenty-four hours. When did you get this material?" asked a very annoyed Garrett.

"Friday, last thing," informed Jersey, who was lying.

"Why and the hell didn't you give me a copy to read over the weekend?" demanded Garrett.

"I wanted to read it first."

"This is bullshit. I know you Jersey. You didn't want me to see it before you had a chance to read and make a change if necessary. You were afraid that there was something in it that you didn't want me to see or something like that. What in blazes is going on?" demanded Garrett.

"Nothing, absolutely nothing; read it and be ready for the meeting tomorrow and leave your paranoia at home." Then Jersey got up and began to leave.

As he was exiting Garrett's office, Garrett asked, "Where in hell are we meeting?"

Stopping and turning his head towards Garrett nodding his head with a slight smile, "At ACS."

"Oh shit," Garrett whispered.

CHAPTER 29 COFFEE

Anne Mills was at her desk reading the latest version of the contract. Sitting in her office with her was Bob Roberts doing the same. They had been at it for over two hours. They had made some changes and many side notes. They still had more to do. Anne felt the need for a break and to get some coffee. "Bob, I'm going for coffee, you want some?" she asked. He nodded yes.

Anne walked out to the little kitchen and found there was no coffee waiting. She rinsed the coffee maker and put up a new pot. As she was waiting for the coffee to brew she looked out on lower Manhattan and the Hudson River. From that high position, the sun glistened off the rippled water surface making Anne squint.

I'm a soldier, Sam said. *What a crazy thing to say. I don't see myself as a soldier, but Sam said I do everything a soldier does therefore he insisted that I'm a soldier. If that's true .. then I'm a good soldier, a very competent soldier. Tomorrow we meet with Jersey Smart and Garrett Carlssen and it's my job to win. Does that prove I'm a soldier? I can't believe I'm buying this. Stop it! Get on with your business. I wish Garrett Carlssen weren't part of this deal. I want nothing to do with Millsport anymore. Damn it! The sooner we get this done, the better.* Anne purposely drifted to escape the uncomfortable feelings she was experiencing. She remembered another uncomfortable feeling when she was twelve or was it eleven.

Mother Mills ran the house according to rules that were implied, but never spoken. Somehow, you just knew. When you did something wrong, you felt it. Maybe it was her body english or small changes in her eyes or maybe it was the tension in the muscles of her face. Nothing ever obvious, but it was always there – and entirely clear. Anne realized at this moment how carefully and often she would watch her Mother's face. She looked for signs of safety or danger. *I was always scared. God*, she thought, *I was always tense. What's Garrett Carlssen have to do with this? Why does he conjure up those old feelings? He had nothing to do with me or my upbringing. I guess it's just because he's from Millsport.*

The thoughts kept coming, *I remember waking up in the middle of the night. I had wet my bed. I started crying and turned on the light. There was blood on the sheet, not urine. I screamed and began sobbing. Mother Mills finally came in and looked at the stained sheet.*

"Stop your crying, you've probably got the curse," she said. *She ordered me to take off my stained panties.* "Spread your legs and let me look," she further ordered.

I did as I was told. I felt so embarrassed. I was humiliated. She never warned me about the curse.

"Yes, it's a curse," she proclaimed. "You won't die. She left the room and came back with a box of Kotex. Use these like diapers and put on a fresh pair

100

of panties. Read the instructions. Clean up your bed and change the sheet. Go back to sleep. You'll stop bleeding in a few days," she stated. *That was all she ever spoke to me about menstruating and being a woman. I went to the library a week later and researched the subject. That was the total sex education Mother granted me.*

The coffee was ready.

CHAPTER 30 LAYING OUT THE NUMBERS AND THE DREAMS

Tuesday morning began with thunderstorms. A slightly wet Jersey met a slightly wet Garrett in the lobby of the ACS building. They had some breakfast at a deli located across the street from ACS and discussed their strategy and what they didn't like. So far, nothing too ominous but ... be careful.

At 9:30, they had arrived at the infamous lobby and announced to the receptionist that they were there to meet with Anne Mills and Bob Roberts who were expecting them. In a few minutes the familiar escort arrived with a smile, handshakes, and an offer for coffee. She took them to a conference room. One wall was all windows and had a spectacular view of the Hudson and the New Jersey horizon. They could see thunderheads and scattered concentrations of rain. Occasionally they would see lightning and hear distant thunder. All too often, the thunder and lightning would be much too close. It was quite a show. After unpacking they continued to watch.

Anne Mills and Bob Roberts arrived a few minutes later and greeted them, but they too were distracted by the storms and all four gathered and watched it for a few minutes.

Garrett standing next to Anne felt compelled to turn slightly towards her as if hiding, to look at her eyes. She felt his gaze. Only slightly turning her head, her eyes met his. There was a nearer lightning flash that made them both blink and they quickly turned their eyes back to the storms. It was a strong distraction for both of them. They weren't there for exploring personal feelings; they were there for business purposes.

Anne brought herself back to the reason for the meeting, "Gentlemen, let's get started."

Garrett was still feeling Anne's presence and had to look at Anne. They exchanged brief glances again. There was definitely something happening between them.

The meeting finally began.

Anne began with outlining the deal, "It is agreed that ACS will be the lead agency for the syndicate, raising $100,000,000. Further, we will place 40% of the offering within our brokerage. We have had preliminary talks with some peer groups who have verbally agreed to join the syndicate and have assured us they can and will complete the deal. As soon as we are able to give them a "red herring" they will join officially."

Red Herring – A "red Herring" is a preliminary prospectus that is filed with the SEC describing a new issue of stock containing details and prospects of the company. It does not state the stock price or issue size. It is known as a "red herring" because it contains a passage in red that states that the company is not attempting to sell its shares before the registration is approved by the SEC.

Anne got up from the table and unfolded a white board on the wall that was directly in front of the conference table and began to speak, "I know everybody here understands what I'm about to describe, but to make sure we all are understanding the deal I'm going to walk you all through it. First let us consider the capitalization. The way Pristinimatic is capitalized is with two classes of stock. Class A has a voting power of one vote per share and that class is what the public owns. Class B, has a voting power of two votes per share. The inside control group owns 23.5% of the Company because they, and only they, with a few exceptions, hold Class B stock. Since the Class B stock has twice the voting power - two votes per share - they have voting power of double their financial ownership - 23½% x 2 - giving them 47% of the vote. Added to the 47% are Bill Amstead and two other early investors - Jersey's doctor friend and two of his buddies who own collectively 3¼%. This is also Class B stock with twice the voting power adding up to 6½% of the votes. Adding that voting power to the partners 47% gives the insiders 53½% of the votes, or in other words, voting control of the Company. Dr. Amsted and his buddies have given a voting trust to Brian Goldberg. As you all know this was done at the insistence of all the partners with, as I've understood it, some protest and resistance from you, Jersey.

Jersey winced a bit with this. He thought, *how the hell did she find that out?*

"Brian was chosen because every one of the partners – ultimately including you, Jersey – felt that Brian would always be the most objective and fair partner if a dispute were to arise. All the partners have always voted together. There never have been any exceptions."

Then she focused on the numbers, "Pristinimatic has issued approximately 16,000,000 shares, and as of this morning the Pristinimatic stock was selling for $8.33/share. Multiplying 16MM shares by $8.33/share translates into a total share value of $133,000,000. Photo Symbology is selling this morning for $5.55/share with 15,500,000 shares issued. Multiplying by that the share price brings their value to approximately $85,000,000. Both Companies are profitable. Combining each Company's current market value translates to approximately into $218,000,000, but we believe that we can get the Street to go along with a $300,000,000 value based on the merged companies increased strength at every level - management, technology, marketing, and combined market share value. Using these values the Merger ownership would breakdown into the following new stock distribution percentages: Pristinimatic – 61% and Photo Symbology – 39%."

Anne continued for another forty-five minutes on the technical details and what would be the final selling price of the stock to the public.

"Both Companies are growing at approximately 15% per year. Therefore, let us assume that the combined profits for the new Company will be in the neighborhood of $10,000,000 or $0.33/share for their first full year together as the new merged company."

She continued speaking about historical, projected and comparable price-earnings ratios, etc. explaining and justifying the rationale for a very rich share price in the near future and said, "ACS is committed to raising $100,000,000 by selling 33% of the new Company – the new merged companies, the Merger. We further believe that this deal, when presented to the public and trading, will be quite appealing because the two most competitive and leading companies will now be one company in this fast emerging market and the new company can be the 800lb. Gorilla in their industry. The new company will only have one class of stock – one share equals one vote. That covers the deal capitalization and values. Any questions?" asked Anne.

For the next hour, there was a discussion regarding details and justification of the details that Anne had presented. Then it was Anne's turn again.

Anne began, "The next step is for the Pristinimatic Board to meet and agree to the deal and then present it to the stockholders for their approval. Photo Symbology must do the same. Before any of this can take place the two companies must meet and finish their due diligence. We are well aware that both of you know a great deal about each other. These meetings, since you are competitors, will be tricky, but they must proceed. We have already had a meeting with Photo Symbology and have walked them through the deal. They have informed us that they are ready to proceed. Gale has agreed to leave Photo Symbology and Jersey will head the new Company. There are significant things to work out; the make-up of the new Board, where the corporate headquarters will reside, and a host of other items. I will give you an action list at the end of the meeting."

At this point Jersey interrupted, "Why has Gale agreed to go so fast? I know him, there's got to be some damn good reason."

"The reason is approximately $16,000,000," answered Anne. He owns around 12% of his Company. We agreed to buy 15% of his stock at the closing and will sell the rest over the following two years at market without commission. He'll walk away with a little over $2,000,000 the first day."

"Ohhhh," murmured Jersey. "That easy?" and he shrugged his shoulders. "What if I walked away, what would you do for me?"

"Nothing, we're providing the accommodation to get the deal we want," replied Anne.

Jersey said nothing further. Anne smiled to herself. She thought, *You're not hard to read. That's just one of the reasons why we don't want you.*

The Meeting was over and everybody left.

Anne looked over at Bob Roberts, "What do you think?" This was not like Anne to ask such a question.

Roberts immediately responded, "My, my Anne, the ultimate field General daring to show a little uncertainty."

Anne flinched at that. It was a combination of revealing herself and the military reference. Leaning on her elbows and rubbing her forehead, "I admit there's something about this deal that bothers me, Bob."

"Well, what?" demanded Roberts.

"I don't know," said Anne shaking her head. "You've been doing this all your life, Bob. Why do you do it?"

"I was born to it and I do it well," replied Roberts.

"That's it, that's all?" asked Anne.

Roberts got up and looked out the window. Then he turned, "I've worked with you for over seven years, Anne, and I've never heard you ask a personal question. What's going on?"

"I don't know anything that is going on, but honestly answer my question," demanded Anne.

"Oh, one has to do something, and this is what I do," replied Bob Roberts and walked out of Anne's office. He walked over to his office and closed the door. He sat down behind his desk and remembered Kingdom Ashton.

Kingdom Ashton was in his fifties, a handsome, tall man with a carefully trimmed mustache who always wore a very carefully tailored Brooks Brothers pinstripe suit. He smoked very good cigars and drank very good scotch. He lived on Fifth Avenue and had a Country home by the seashore in Connecticut. Robert Cooper Robertson was then a young man learning to be a Wall Street Trader for the firm he was born to, and Kingdom Ashton, who was in charge, was his teacher. Robertson had graduated from Harvard Business School and had spent several years learning the ACS business, and now Ashton was teaching him the culture.

They were in Kingdom Ashton's office, which was a large room that consisted of French provincial furniture, an exquisite hand carved desk and table to match, a vast and thick oriental carpet, a carefully stocked bar, and several traditional American West paintings by Alfred Miller and a small Frederic Remington sculpture. Two chairs had been arranged facing each other in front of the desk – one for Kingdom and one for young Robertson.

He began, "I've called you in because I feel you are ready to take up your responsibilities as a fully-fledged member of the firm. Robert, your obligation to the firm is each and every day to make money for the firm. You will do whatever is necessary to fulfill that obligation. Nothing, nothing else is more important. It's that simple. Don't ever worry about who loses if they are not part of the firm. There are no shades of grays, only black and white, or should I say red and green. You are to pursue green. That's what you owe your firm. That is our power and always has been our power. All the men who succeeded that had come before you understood that and lived by that obligation. That is why we are so successful today. That, if you understand your obligation, will be your success. This is to be before any personal obligations and any allegiance to god and country. You will learn, and life will teach you, that you can never depend on a lover, god, or your country, only your firm. If you don't believe that and can't live by that, you don't belong here and you're not one of us. We are surrounded by enemies. The politicians are easily bought. You'll be surprised how cheap.

The street is filled with trash. They come from every place on the planet. They're Irish, Italians, Jews, and worse. Now we can see the beginning of the coming of Blacks, Latinos, Arabs, and Orientals. Their people were the losers of the world and always will be. They are nothing more than transients, temporary squatters. They were either brought to this country as laborers or servants or came here to steal what is ours. We come from the good classes of Europe. Our forebears were granted proprietary estates by royalty in the seventeen hundreds and these lower classes have, over two and half centuries, stolen much of it away. Now they are trying to own Wall Street. They will never own us. Never trust them. Never befriend them. Hurt them and destroy them when you can. They are your enemy. Your power, your firm's power is money, and men like you who are dedicated to these truths. If this is acceptable, you are the firm and the firm will always be you. I will never ask you this again, nor will I discuss this with you again. Do you understand your obligation? Are you one of us?" with that question Kingdom Ashton was finished.

Robert Cooper Robertson quickly replied, "Yes." He was brought up to believe these fundamentals.

It hadn't all quite worked out that way, the firm was now run by an Italian and an Arab and Robert Cooper Robertson was tolerated. Kingdom Ashton had long been dead, but Wall Street was still filled with thousands who embraced many of his values. It just wasn't the exclusive club that Kingdom Ashton had in mind.

CHAPTER 31 THE VOTE

Brian came home at his usual time. He had received an email that day from Yvette. It had arrived a few minutes before he was leaving the office.

It simply said, "I'm leaving. Yvette."

As he slowly put the key into the lock to open the front door, he heard the clicks of the lock tumblers, something he had never paid any attention to before. In a bizarre way, they were the tiny sounds of a fanfare announcing the house was empty – something was missing. Then he realized the house was no longer a home. Actually this did not surprise Brian. Somewhere deep he had always thought he would eventually lose her and now, it had happened. It was a loss that had something in common with his feelings about death.

I'm a cliché, I'm a damn moth and she was the damn flame. I know it was me that caused her to leave. I'm an expert on electrons, circuits, and systems, but when it comes to people, I don't know much. I tried hard with Yvette, but the truth is, I really didn't know what to do.

He went into the kitchen, which was meticulously neat and spotlessly clean as always. He put up some water for tea. *She always kept everything in this house, and the yard for that matter, pristine. Nothing was ever dirty for long and nothing was ever out of its place for long, except Yvette and me. It was like … if we kept it that way, we were safe. At least I liked to think we were safe. But I guess all that was an illusion. I was a member of a partnership based on some kind of pretense. The only thing we really had together that was real was the gardens and the dogs. They were not enough.* For the first time in his life that he remembered he cried. He cried for a long time and then it passed.

Then the question, *How did Jersey get involved with my wife?*

He was in a rage regarding Jersey. It was the rage that impotence breeds. He dug his nails into his palm until it hurt, and then pounded his hands repeatedly onto the kitchen table until some blood appeared. He stopped and took a deep breath and at that moment the tea kettle started playing its tune. He made his tea and sat down at the kitchen table. He spoke out loud angrily, "Jersey you are scum. I've always known that you were scum, but I thought I was safe because you needed me for my engineering skills. How bloody naïve I've been!"

It was time to eat, but he wasn't hungry. He saw his life as soiled. *What could he do?* He thought. *Nothing, there was nothing, not a damn thing he could do.* And that was how he spent the evening.

The next morning Brian went to work at the usual time. He said nothing about Yvette to anybody. Jersey had scheduled a meeting for ten o'clock to discuss the Merger and relate the results of the previous day's meeting with ACS. The partners were gathered in Jersey's office.

Jersey recited the essentials of the deal and then went on, "I want to caution every one of you not to speak of the Merger or any of the financing details in any way to anyone. If you do not keep silent, you could ruin the deal and bring the SEC down on us. We are a public Company and don't ever forget that. If we violate the rules they can impose severe fines and/or criminal charges on the Company along with the individuals responsible, and, of course, stop the deal from happening." The meeting ended.

The notifications were sent to the stockholders and the allotted time the SEC requires. It was finally the morning of the Stockholders meeting and a crowd was gathering at the Royal Inn Ball Room in Manhattan. It had been retained by the Company yearly for the annual stockholders meeting and now, for the first time, a special stockholders meeting was being held in this familiar place. Jersey, Garrett and the rest of the Board were in an adjacent room preparing for the meeting. They had gone over all the details and were prepared. Jersey would conduct most of the meeting. Garrett, who was Secretary of the Corporation, had little to do other than count the votes and report the results to the Board and the stockholders. Having finished the prep, Garrett was sitting by a window drinking coffee. He was thinking about an unexpected occurrence with Anne Mills. It wasn't a planned meeting but ...

Garrett had gone to ACS to meet with some of the team who were working on the deal to negotiate a long list of minor issues, but nevertheless had to be agreed upon. The meeting had gone on for several hours but was finally completed successfully. The meeting went right through lunch time to midafternoon and Garrett was hungry and in the mood for a hot cup of tea. He was escorted to the ACS cafeteria and left on his own. It would have to do. For all practical purposes, the ACS cafeteria was closed but there were vending machines and the makings of a cup of nondescript tea. Again, it would have to do. He found a cold carefully wrapped tuna fish sandwich waiting to be chosen in one of the vending machines. He was half way through his tuna fish sandwich when Anne Mills entered the room. They saw each other immediately.

Damn, he thought to himself, *every time I see her it affects me. I get uncomfortable, but it is also like the same feeling I had when encountering a new girl I was attracted to at a party, a school prom, or whatever.* He stared at her admiring the way she carried herself. *That takes schooling. Almost like training horses - Dressage. Old buddy, you better keep that one to yourself.* "Hello Anne," he almost whispered, "I've have been meeting with some of your team for the past several hours to go over a list of the minor points of the deal that .." He stopped. "Of course you know that."

She nodded yes. "There's one point they agreed to that I don't."

"Oh, and what is that?"

"The new company logo," she stated, "I want a logo that doesn't indicate the combining of the two Companies. I think that both your Company's names are ridiculous. You need something new."

"You don't like our Company name? It's a play on an old William F. Buckley word meaning not spoiled, uncorrupted, or polluted ...pure, pure as the driven snow. It's probably an adjective that he made up from the word pristine. I'll miss it, but it's no deal breaker. Jersey won't be happy but don't worry, we'll yield."

"Good," she smiled, "How's your daughter ...Sallie Kate?"

Garrett was surprised, "She's fine. I'm surprised you want to bring up Sallie Kate. She was rather unpleasant the night we had our ...'date.' In fact, I would use the word impolite and I wouldn't be exaggerating. But it was interesting. Other than dinner it was a really fine day we had together. It was a shame you missed a meal, the paella was great. Sallie Kate calmed down and eventually she told me to send her apologies to you for her behavior. This is the first chance we've been alone for me to convey her message."

"Tell her I accept," declared Anne, "Actually, I really liked her. That's an interesting child you've raised. I must admit she did, indeed, read me correctly."

Garrett raised his hands in submission, "Let's not go there, we've got a deal to finish."

"I agree, let's never go there again," reinforced Anne with a cold wave of her hand and left the room.

Damn, that woman could be cold, he felt the chill. *She was almost human for a moment and then quickly closed the door.* And then he thought, *growing up in the Mills house couldn't have been very pleasant - Millsport and its feudal layers and ways. But she's really good to look at and there's something else ... but looking's all you can do.* He laughed to himself. It was the first time he admitted that he was attracted to Anne Mills. It was just like the time when he danced with her *at the Piperberg cabin.* He shrugged his shoulders and shook his head and then thought, *Get back on point, you're here to do a deal and absolutely nothing else.* Then just as quick his mind drifted back to the very pleasant afternoon they spent together.

Jersey appeared and interrupted, "It's time for the meeting, let's go."

The room had more people in it than Garrett expected. It was full and there were even people standing. ACS was represented by Anne, Roberts, and two legal types. Everybody representing the Company took their seats behind a long table and Jersey began his remarks. He went on for a half hour. A Q&A session followed. There were many questions asked by the audience. Between Jersey, Garrett, the Company lawyer, and the Board, they were answered. Finally, there was nothing more to be asked. It was time to vote. Ushers collected the votes from the stockholders and all proxies were delivered. Then the count took place including Brian Goldberg's angry opposition.

CHAPTER 32 A CHANGE AND AMUSEMENT

Jersey was at his desk cleaning it out. Almost everything else had been packed in appropriate cartons and this would be his last day. Across the hall, Garrett was doing the same. It was very unpleasant.

Garrett finished and walked over into Jersey's office and found him staring at nothing.

"We built this place. We did a damn good job, and somehow, we got screwed," sadly commented Garrett.

"What do mean 'somehow'? What's the mystery? Brian got pissed off and did us in. He thinks I was screwing his wife. I can't imagine getting close to that cold bitch. What he saw in her is beyond me, but then again it's Brian, and who in the hell ever knew or knows what Brian was or is thinking. I'll admit she is very pretty, a piece of ass to look at, but an iceberg. Shit. Has she been heard from?"

"Jersey, whatever happened between those two is something you and I will probably never know. I know one thing, and that is the damn picture he found under your desk started the whole thing. Are you sure you don't know where it came from, maybe a little idea?" sneered Garrett.

"Fuck you buddy," quietly returned Jersey.

"Want some coffee?" asked Garrett. They walked to the cafeteria. It was almost empty. "What are you going to do now that you don't have a day job?"

"I suppose I'll take a vacation, go somewhere and get myself together. We still have a big stake in this place. With Jim Gale at the head of our new Company, the stock could be in trouble very soon. But I've got to hand it to him, he pulled it off, and I never had the slightest hint it was coming. He had it wired through ACS all the time. But then again, if Brian hadn't jumped ship and voted against us, it never would have happened," declared Jersey.

"It was the picture, that damn picture," sighed Garrett. "You sure you don't have any idea?"

"Nope!" replied Jersey.

Garrett said his 'goodbyes,' walked out of the building, and took one last look at where he had spent so much time, and waved goodbye to nobody. As he was driving home to the city, he began to remember a few other times that had made him feel so rotten. He told himself he was performing an exercise in remembering how he had successfully dealt with such bad moments before. Then an amusing past occurrence surfaced.

Brandon Helder was a fat middle-aged bully who had made a great fortune exploiting other people's ideas. He ran, what is called intellectual property transfer company. It involved inventors, their companies, and third party companies. Generally, inventors who created ideas that became significant patents and, therefore, the basis for a company, so often could not find adequate financing to monetize them successfully. In desperation, they would go to companies that were run by the likes of Brandon Helder.

The Brandon Helder's of this world that performed these services, or rather their companies were known as patent trolls. Brandon's Company was where an inventor went, when there was no other choice. Brandon did not generally invest in the inventor's companies, but there were occasional exceptions. The way he most often became involved with an inventor would be to take over the inventor's intellectual property only. His business was to transfer the ownership of the invention or inventions to a third party for royalties that would be divided using the Brandon Helder formula. It was quite complex, but it ultimately resulted in the inventor getting screwed, with only about 5 to 6% of the royalties actually going to him or her, if ever, and only after all of Holder's expenses had been repaid and certain profits had been reached. This was predicated upon the invention being a great success. A modest success would usually leave the inventor with nothing. Most of the royalties eventually went to Brandon. Brandon was fond of saying "inventors are people who make other people a lot of money."

Garrett had become involved with Brandon through a member of his Board. Well before Garrett became involved with Pristinimatic, he had started a Company based on an idea he had devised for micro control systems for use in calculator and computer systems. The Company, though very small, had quickly become successful and had a need to raise capital. He had gone through one cycle of public financing and was about to start another when a Board member introduced him to Brandon, who was interested in investing in Garrett's Company.

The Board member who had made the introduction was a man who had helped him through the tough business of getting the Company started and they had developed a real friendship. His name was Ken Kassen, and he was smart, well read, cultured, and a nice human being. The introduction to Brandon was the only mistake Ken had ever made in their relationship. Brandon eventually made a sizable investment and became a member of the Board.

A year went by and the business flourished. No matter how good things went, Brandon would create some kind of conflict at the monthly Board meetings. When he was opposed in a business argument, no matter how reasonable and logical it was, he would become angrier and angrier. This would be accompanied by his becoming redder and redder in the face and neck which would then lead to a physical crescendo. With the full passion of a denied child and the reach of a concert conductor, he would stand up, flailing his arms, fingers pointing, screaming his opposition, and then finish with a complete pirouette. There were six other members of the Board, who couldn't quite believe what they were seeing when this display occurred the first few times. But he was very rich and a significant investor. They tolerated it and kept their mouths shut.

Garrett and his Managing Director, Alan, were actually astounded the first time they saw Brandon's display. But they soon became used to it, and in some bizarre way found it amusing. It became a sort of joke between them. Before each Board meeting, they would try to predict the subject that would be the basis for the outburst and the inevitable pirouette. In fact, after a while, they started betting on what would make it happen. The loser would buy lunch. About eighteen months into the Brandon relationship Alan came trotting into Garrett's office with an idea.

"Garrett," he said, "next week at the Board meeting we will be introducing the potential Xander Corp. relationship. Brandon hates their management and said so at the last board meeting. We've made some real progress with Xander and I believe all the Board members with the exception of Brandon are in favor of the deal. He's gonna' go nuts if we vote to accept the deal."

"I know that," stated Garrett, "We're just going to stand against him and let the chips fall where they may. You have something in mind?"

"Yeah," responded Alan with a big smile. "I think we've got the ammunition to get old fat Brandon to do a double pirouette. Wanna' bet?"

Garrett started laughing, "You might have something there. I'll tell you what I'll do. If you get your double, I treat you and Jane to a steak dinner at that place you love in Cos Cob." They shook hands.

The Board meeting started at 9:00am promptly. They worked their way to lunch - sandwiches, coffee, and soft drinks served at the meeting table. About 1:45pm the Xander discussion began. The discussion progressed for about an hour. Brandon Helder raised one objection after another as he got angrier and angrier. About a quarter to three he did his first stand up and a vintage pirouette. Garrett looked at Alan and nodded - no success. The discussion got hotter causing the second stand up and another vintage pirouette. Garrett looked at Alan again and nodded slightly again - no success. Alan looked back and wrote a small note he passed to Garrett. "Have some faith, it isn't over!"

Garrett wrote back, "It isn't gonna' happen." Finally, Garrett called for a motion to vote in favor or reject the Xander deal. He quickly got a second, and asked if there was any further discussion. Brandon got up and walked to the front of the room and held forth for 15 to 20 minutes on the subject.

After he had finished Ken spoke, "I listened to you very carefully, Brandon, and I've listened to you all day. And I've come to the conclusion the whole thing is personal and does not have a damn thing to do with business. I'm going to vote in favor of the deal."

Garrett asked if anybody else wanted to speak and it was quiet. He then asked for a vote. It came out six in favor one against. At that point, Brandon

112

in a tirade began to attack everybody and it became very personal. After insultingly his away around the table, and it was ugly, he reached an ever higher plain shouting, "You're a bunch of idiots who couldn't tell the difference between ... "And as he was at the top of his aria he stood up with arms flailing and pointing at nothing and he did his pirouette but instead of stopping, he kept going and executed a second pirouette, then sat down.

Everybody at the table was shocked at Brandon's display except Alan and Garrett, who were trying their damnedest not to laugh. Within seconds, they were out of control with tears coming down their cheeks and almost falling off their chairs. The entire Board was looking at them incredulously, including Brandon. This had gone on for almost five minutes before they got control of themselves. In the meantime, Brandon got up and left, slamming the door almost off its hinges.

Eventually, Garrett and Alan confessed their bet.

The Board wasn't amused.

CHAPTER 33 SEDUCTION

Some days later Garrett got a call from Brandon. The tone of the call was as if nothing had ever happened at the Board meeting. Brandon invited Garrett to join him for dinner at the very exclusive Harbor Club the following week. "There are some things I should like to discuss with you concerning the future of the Company," explained Brandon.

Oh shit, Garrett thought, *what's Brandon up to now? No choice, I've got to go.*

As time went by, Garrett became more agitated over the meeting. He discussed it with Ken. The only thing he could surmise was that Brandon was up to something unpleasant, but there was no way he could find out except going to the meeting.

He arrived at the downtown address of the infamous Harbor Club. The building was an almost perfect example of a Stanford White turn of the Century building. The entrance was decorated with elaborate filigree and carved door hardware all polished daily. Hanging out from the upper porch balcony, were a series of flags gently waving in the early evening breeze. As he approached the door, a uniformed doorman opened the great door and he was immediately met by another uniformed person. "May I help you sir?"

It was quite clear he would not be allowed to go any further without a proper invitation or credentials. "I'm here to meet Brandon Helder."

The uniformed person looked in a book, "Ahh Mr. Carlssen?"

Garrett nodded yes.

"I will have you escorted to your table. Mr. Helder called and asked us to tell you he would be a bit late, perhaps as much as fifteen minutes, depending on the traffic," he informed Garrett. He pressed a button attached to the inner door buttress, and in a few seconds a formally attired man appeared, "Please follow me, sir. Have you ever been to the Harbor Club?"

"No," replied Garrett.

"Would you like to see our famous ship display room, sir?"

"My host will be late, why not?"

They went up a very beautiful broad and curving staircase to the second floor. From the top of the steps, he could view the entire lobby. It was quite an amazing display of complex designs with an incredible mix of materials and colors that only great wealth could afford – the Victorian inability to resist extravagance. Almost all the wood was hand carved, and every wall was embellished with magnificent wood framed panels that included beautiful oil paintings of that era. The subjects were of ships, yachts, and boat people. The floor was a maze of Roman tiles celebrating the myths and legends of the sea.

The great chandeliers hanging from the ceiling were intricate groups of lamp styles inspired by 18th and 19th century nautical themes. Garrett was impressed.

Garrett was ushered into the ship model room which was filled with perfect models of steamships, sailing ships, yachts, and some boat oddities that were unfamiliar to him. Most were inside glass enclosures with some larger models hanging from the ceiling. The room was huge. It contained, what Garrett guessed was easily, several hundred models. Each model was carefully lit with one or more spotlights that went on automatically as you approached it. On the walls and columns were a collection of marine objects. One could spend days in the room and not see the whole collection. After about 15 minutes he was escorted to an elevator which brought him to the fifth floor – the dining room. Another formally attired man took him to the table where Brandon Helder was waiting.

"Good evening, Garrett," said Brandon. "Are you impressed with our club's collection?"

"It's fascinating. I've never seen anything quite like it," replied Garrett.

"Wait until you taste the cuisine," advised Brandon. "There's nothing better in the City."

For the next hour and a half they ate a magnificent dinner complemented with a superb wine. The conversation wandered from politics to business, and then to sports. There was no mention, not even a hint, of the recent Board meeting. With dinner finished Brandon asked, "Do you smoke cigars?"

"On occasion, if they are very good and mild," replied Garrett.

"Then follow me."

And with that he led Garrett to the elevator which took them up one more floor to an elaborately decorated hallway filled with more nautical paraphernalia. At the end was a very large glassed in portico with a magnificent view of the lower end of Manhattan. The room had a large bar running most of the width of the building and a large collection of overstuffed leather bound chairs in small groupings. Next to each chair was a small table. Each table contained a candled lantern designed after 19th century port and starboard stern lights along with various smoking implements such as cigar cutters, lighters, and ashtrays. Each table also contained a fresh water thermos, an ice bucket, a selection of mineral waters, and several glasses. To complete the room, the floor of the portico, which now was completely glassed in, was a series of terraced levels, each providing an unimpeded panorama of the lower metropolis and the New York harbor. It was a clear night that at this moment provided a breathtaking view of all the nautical and land activities in and around the harbor. It was an extravagant series of random sparkling lights and occasional patterned wavy images in every color imaginable. The water was only visible where it embraced a multitude of reflections from the thousands of light sources a great city could provide on such a pristine night. The room was only lit with the low light of the candled nautical table lamps. It was secure, quiet, inviting, and comfortable, and very, very rich. It provided a feeling of anonymity and privacy. It was clear that this was no accident; it had been very carefully designed to achieve these attributes. As they took their places Garrett experienced two things; the visual effect was breathtaking, and the extravagance was overwhelming.

Garrett observed that Brandon Helder's chair was just that - Brandon Helder's chair - it had a highly polished brass plate fastened to the side with his name clearly engraved.

Quickly, two formally attired waiters came over to them. One poured the water of choice and the other requested what kind of after dinner drink would be desired. As they left to attend to the drink order, another gentleman came with a magnificent selection of cigars. He announced that if requested, complete descriptions of the genealogy and pedigree of each cigar label being offered could be presented. Garrett was fascinated. He had been to some of the city's best cigar bars from time to time, and had even been a guest at one of the most exclusive cigar clubs in Chicago. But this place was in a class all by itself.

With their drinks poured and their cigars lit, and the small talk over, Brandon asked, looking out on the harbor with a curl of smoke rising from his cigar, "How would you like to join our club?"

Garrett hadn't expected this. "Brandon, I think it's way above my pay grade."

"Not necessarily," answered Brandon. "It certainly was for me, when I was your age. But with time and success, that changed." He turned and looked directly at Garrett. It could ... be the same for you."

Garrett said nothing for a while, then finally asked, "Brandon, there is no such thing as a free lunch. What do you want?"

Brandon began, "You are a very smart technologist and very creative, but you need to learn many things about business. You're a neophyte. One of your most significant problems is your business advisor, Ken Kassen. He is a child, a trust child who thinks he knows, but I assure you he's incompetent. I want you to get rid of him. You have that power, you have the vote, and I can't do it without your co-operation. This is hard for you I know, but as a businessman with obligations to your stockholders, you have no choice. If you can do this successfully, and I've brought you here to show you what can be yours, this indeed will be yours. That will be all I have to say on the subject."

There were some more discussions on other Company subjects as the two smoked their cigars and sipped their after dinner drinks. It was a superbly pleasant experience. It ended an hour later with, "I will let you know, Brandon."

Garrett never did. He never was invited to join the Harbor Club. His friendship with Ken Kassen endured to the day that Ken unexpectedly died a few months later.

He now knew how tempting the apple must have been to Eve.

CHAPTER 34 A HIKING SURPRISE

With the deal finally consummated, Anne took some time off.

Anne Mills had just come off a day's hike in the mountains. She was at a favorite resort of hers in Wyoming. She changed into a bathing suit and went outside to the hotel's marvelous heated pool to warm and soothe her tired muscles.

From the pool looking up, the mountains appeared to be so close they could almost be touched from either side of the pool, an illusion reinforced by the setting sun as it carved great sharp shadows on the trees, rocky outcrops, cliffs and chutes. There still was some snow clinging to the bases of the outcrops where the steep mountains provided shelter from the sun. She felt a calm that rarely was her companion.

A waiter came by offering some kind of sweet mixed drink. She sipped the drink relaxing her tired muscles in the caress of the warmed water. This beautiful place translated into quiet dinners and very little nightlife. It suited Anne perfectly. She knew no one other than the hotel owner and a few guides, and that was fine.

The owner appeared at that moment and looking around spotted Anne. He walked over to her and handed her a cell phone.

"Anne, I hate to do this, but you're needed back here immediately," Bob Roberts exclaimed.

"Why, damn it, why?" demanded Anne.

"The Pristinimatic/Photo Symbology deal is in trouble," replied Bob Roberts. "It appears that Brian Goldberg has destroyed all the important Pristinimatic Software and he is nowhere to be found. Put it this way, if we can't put Humpty Dumpty back together again the deal will be in a real jam and there's gonna' be one hell of a lawsuit to contend with, and, of course, we can kiss our bonuses goodbye."

"This deal was closed, what happened that you're not telling me?" asked Anne.

"I honestly know nothing else. Remember, the deal has a six month period before we have a full release. They can bring us in, and you can bet they will. Brian did it, that's all I know. And apparently he knew exactly what he was doing. Their management thinks he did it from an outside location. They think, and they claim to have found some evidence that some kind of virus, or equivalent destructive device, was planted in the servers that he could trigger when he chose to, remotely," explained Bob Roberts. "Whatever it was, was planted in their main servers as well as their remote back-up and emergency servers. It has screwed up everything, everything! We've got a mess and we need you, now! "

She chartered a private jet that evening and was ready for work as the office opened the next day. She walked into Bob Robert's office exactly at nine o'clock. *Vintage Anne*, Bob Roberts thought as she sat down with her laptop open, ready to take notes.

"Give me all you know and start from the beginning," requested Anne.

They spent the next two hours going over detail after detail and it opened no doors to a solution.

Anne then suggested, "What are they saying about re-creating the lost records? Have they brought in some software security specialists to see if they can restore the software?"

"Yes, but so far no luck," continued Bob Roberts. "They've retained the best firm in Silicon Valley to make the repair, or whatever, to get them and us out of this mess. The only thing I've heard is that the experts from the firm say the guy who did this was 'terrific' - their term. I guess the difference between a safecracker and a safe opener is almost non-existent. At the professional level, they're all the same. Both make a lot of money if they can open the safe. On the other hand, only one of them has to pay taxes. It's simply a matter of one professional respecting the work of another professional."

"OK, OK, but what about recreating the records? There must be a lot of paper records around," suggested Anne.

Bob Roberts answered, "There is, but that creates more problems. First, it will take several months and a lot of costly work by an accounting firm to recreate the records which could end up outside our six months release period. Second, they want us to help pay for it. Third, once this hits the street the stock will tank, and the SEC will be all over us. Fourth, our friends from Photo Symbology feel that they've been cheated on the deal and want to renegotiate the terms, to use their word –'significantly.' They certainly don't intend to give back the money we raised. Is that enough?"

"What's legal have to say about this mess?"

"It's a mess," responded Bob Roberts. "It could severely damage the firm. Perhaps, put us under."

"That's nonsense Bob. Hurt us, yes. Put us out of business – that's silly," insisted Anne.

Bob Roberts ignored Anne and continued. "Joe and Ibrahim are furious, to say the least. They've threatened me in every way possible. You and I have been accused of incompetent judgment. If this problem isn't fixed to their satisfaction, they have explicitly stated that they will sue and hound us, to our dying day, and on and on. I believe them. At the very least, we're through on the street. I've seen Joe lose his temper many times, but I've never seen Ibrahim lose his cool, even once. He did yesterday. It was downright frightening."

"Cool down Bob," advised Anne. "This is Wall Street. We've made a lot of money for this firm and the Street knows it. Even if we are fired and get some bad publicity, sooner or later someone will hire us. They'll want us for our many, many wins, and will take a chance on losses. It's simple math. You do ten deals, lose some, but you still end up with so much from the wins the losses are tolerated. Even Joe and Ibrahim might reconsider in the end. It's just about money and absolutely nothing else."

"My god, you are even more cynical than me," declared Bob Roberts.

"Coming from you that's a compliment," retorted Anne. "The best thing to solve the problem is for the safecrackers to be successful. While that is happening, the next best way to end this mess is to find Brian and make a deal. I'm assuming he knows how to restore the software he corrupted. There are two things that must be done immediately. First, nobody tells anybody! And second, buy some time! We've got some leverage and we've got to use it. I need some time to study and re-familiarize myself with the contract and the SEC documents. Who's working on this from our law firm?"

"Nobody really, at this time," answered Bob Roberts. "Two of their senior partners have started, but nobody has taken the lead. Anne, this just happened two days ago."

"Then get those two senior partners focused and moving at light speed," demanded Anne. With that, she got up and left and headed into her office where she spent the next twenty-four hours.

CHAPTER 35 A VACATION AND AN ENLISTMENT

Brian Goldberg was on a bike, pedaling his way around an island in the South Pacific. He was in Easter Island, an Island 2350 miles from its owner, the country of Chile. He had no real plans. He was just drifting, trying to reassemble his life. He had decided quite impulsively, at least for the present, to exit the life he had been leading and do something quite different and disappear for a while. No explanations, no goodbyes. When he made this decision, he discussed this with nobody and he had no idea where he was going or what he would do. The evening he walked out of the Company he accidentally watched a travel piece on TV about Easter Island with its ancient Papa Nui mysteries. *Why not?* He thought. *It was very far away and looked very interesting.* With that, he decided that was where he would go. The next day he paid all his bills online for a year in advance with a small note explaining he would be traveling. Went to the bank and withdrew a lot of money. Then called his accountant and explained that he would be gone and asked him to quickly approximate his taxes. This was followed by transferring enough cash to easily cover the obligation and signing the required papers. He then went to a shopping center and bought some clothes for biking and a very good backpack. The next day he was on a plane to the Chile mainland, and then on to Easter Island. Maybe he could figure out a new life, and at least compartmentalize Yvette.

Garrett was in his apartment working on an idea that he'd been thinking about for some time that could possibly be his re-entry into the technical business world. He was at the beginning of putting together a business plan and happened to be working on a pro forma when he received a call from Mike Levins.

"Hi Garrett," he started. "How ya' doin'?"

"Is that you Mike?"

"Yep, your friendly shyster," responded Mike Levins.

"What in sam hell are you calling me for?" asked Garrett with a nervous laugh.

"Something has come up that you may be able to help with. No questions, I don't want to talk about this over a phone. Can we meet in the next couple of hours ...preferably at your place" asked Mike.

"Yeh, sure. You know where I live – fifth and eighth."

"Good, I'll see you in two hours," and he hung up.

In a little less than two hours, Garrett was informed by the doorman of his building that he had a visitor, a Mr. Levins. "Send him up," Garrett responding to the intercom.

"Well Mike, what in blazes brings you here on this fine day?" queried Garrett. "Would you like something to eat or drink?"

"Booze, no, eat yes. I haven't had a thing to eat all day," replied Mike.

"C'mon in the kitchen and I'll make you a sandwich."

As Mike was eating his sandwich and drinking some ice tea Garrett spoke, "I can't believe what you're saying about Brian. It doesn't fit. I've known him for many years, Brian Goldberg deliberately screwing up 'Torpedo', or worse.

"Whoa! 'Torpedo'? What's that?"

"That's what we call our software. We even have a little logo for the system. We like giving all projects names. Some are a bit silly I admit, but everybody likes 'Torpedo'. Brian Goldberg gave it that name and he would never hurt 'Torpedo on purpose, destroying his baby and Company data - no way. Walking out and telling nobody he was quitting, I guess I can buy that. He really was shaken to his core when his wife, Yvette, left. He never liked or trusted Jersey, and I know Jim Gale has never warmed his heart."

It was Mike's turn, "Look, the guy leaves, disappears and two days later all hell breaks loose. Who is clever enough to know how to pull this stunt off? Who's very depressed and really big time pissed off? Brian Goldberg, that's who, it fits!"

Now it was Garrett's turn again, "It fits too well, in my opinion. It's too obvious. I'm telling you, I know Brian. There's nobody else there who does. I even knew his family. He's a guy with great integrity. This isn't his style. He also would be shooting himself in his financial foot by destroying the Company. No, damn it, there's another explanation. The leaving part, I'll admit is a bit out of character, but under the circumstances he may have concluded that it would be the only way he could get out. I can understand why he would have wanted to get out, better yet, why he needed to get out. That guy has been through hell."

"Your being quite generous, considering that his voting against you guys provided the means for getting you and Jersey kicked out," retorted Mike.

"Look Mike, sure I was furious, but as time has gone by I'm not in any way convinced as to what really happened except I got my ass kicked out of the Company. The Company I helped to build from day one," revealed Garrett. "It doesn't add up. I know Jersey can be a shit, but the picture thing under Jersey's desk, that's just too convenient. Jersey swears he never had anything to do with Yvette and I know that Jersey can lie with the best of them. I'll concede that there's a very small possibility that Jersey could make a move on Yvette, she's a very good looking woman and sexy as hell to fantasize about, but Yvette cooperating, that's more than a stretch. Jersey is the last kind of guy she would want to have anything, and I mean anything, to do with.

Yvette is strange, in many ways, but I think there was a real tie to Brian, something she desperately needed. I'm guessing Brian has always been so insecure socially and never thought he deserved Yvette. You had to know his family and his upbringing to understand just how immature he was as a husband, or a mate. They were some screwy combination, but it worked in some odd way. Were they happy, probably not very happy, but, they were as good as it could get for those two. Look, I'm hip-shooting, but what I know of Brian is not that far off. I'll admit when it comes to Yvette, I'm depending on Brian's indirect remarks over the many years I've known him. On the other hand, I may be full of shit."

Mike walked across the kitchen looking out the window with his hands behind his back. "You've a great view of the park from here. How'd you ever find this place?" asked Mike.

"Pure dumb beginners luck," replied Garrett. "That's a tale for another day. What do you want from me? I have no idea where Brian is. In fact I haven't spoken with him since the day I was dismissed, and if I'd seen him that day, it wasn't to kiss him goodbye."

"I didn't think you would really know anything when I came up here. It was worth a try but, I've got an agenda. What I really want is two things. One, I want you involved in solving this problem. You're my bridge between business and technology. I don't trust any of Gale's people to get it right, or more to the point, to tell the truth. I don't really know them, but I know you and I trust you. I want you looking over their shoulders and the California software guys they hired

Garrett interrupted, "What makes you think they will let me in? At the very least they will see me as the enemy."

"Don't worry about that, they have no choice. They announced the problem before the release, so technically, 'we' who are representing the 'late Pristinimatic Corporation' are still in charge. They want a fix. We want a fix. I, as lead council for the Pristinimatic interests, have chosen you to represent Pristinimatic as the technical advisor, and that is that," stated Mike quite emphatically.

"Ye gods, what a mess! I suppose there's no way I can turn you down, unless I'm willing to shoot myself in the foot. I still have a lot of stock in the new Company and you, of course, knew that when you came up here," sighed Garrett. "How long do you think this will take? Oh yes, you said there were two things you wanted me to do. What's the second?"

Answering the first question, "Not too long."; Continuing, "If we can't overcome this problem quickly - like in a few days - that will lead to a very long ugly legal procedure. That's an entirely different can of worms. If this can't be resolved in a very short period of time we will have to announce it publically and inform the SEC. Let's put that aside for the moment and focus on the current problem."

"Hold on Mike, I don't want to go near any SEC violations, period," clearly stated Garrett.

"We have some time to make sure this is what we think it is and not some damn mistake. Even under the toughest rules we have to be sure what we think has occurred, has really occurred. If we act too soon, before we really are sure, we could inflict terrible damage on the Company, and subsequently the stockholders. We would have made the move based on bad information, and therefore subject to a liability. I know it's tricky, there are no clean straight lines in business, and there is always that element of gray."

Your function is only to advise me and, of course, the former Pristinimatic folks - that's you and Jersey, and the other partners. For all we really know at this time there might be nothing wrong except some bad information."

"You really sound like a goddamned lawyer," stated Garrett. "Can you look me in the eye and guarantee me, I'm not at risk?"

"I am a damn good lawyer and the answer is yes, providing you keep an excellent paper trail and give us, particularly me, your honest appraisal or anything else that you think is relevant, as it might become relevant, or is becoming relevant," stated Mike. "Regarding the other purpose of my visit, I admit it is a bit stickier."

"Well?" inquired Garrett.

"This involves ACS," stated Mike.

"They were informed almost immediately, and I'm sure they have started with their defensive strategy which will be very ugly for us, if I know them. In fact, they were making noises about hiring me, but I am already committed to any remaining Pristinimatic business. Jersey got me involved immediately after he found out what was happening." Mike took a deep breath, "We need you to be our contact with Anne Mills and Bob Roberts."

"Oh shit, why me?" pleaded Garrett.

"Jersey is convinced you had and have the best rapport with Mills," replied Mike. "Apparently nobody had any rapport with Roberts."

"Nobody had a good rapport with Anne Mills either," insisted Garrett.

"That might be the truth, but everyone we discussed this with is convinced yours was still the best. They think it has something to do with both of you coming from the same town in Pennsylvania, and that you evidently knew each other as kids."

"So you want me to be the Ambassador. Keep the wolves at bay, or something like that?" stated a very annoyed Garrett.

"Yep!" replied Mike. "You know her better than anyone else. So, what do ya' say, buddy? Are we gonna' have to beg you?" Mike laughed at this point. "You don't have any choice, and you know it. Foot shooting is painful."

After Mike Levins left Garrett was filled with all kind of thoughts. *Brian Goldberg, a very weird guy, but a good guy. I'm damn sure of that. I'd bet money on that. Come to think of it, I'm betting a lot of money on that.* He laughed to himself. *Damn it, I really don't want to get mixed up with ACS again. They were difficult and it never really ever felt good. Then there's Anne Mills and once again, the Mills curse and all those uncomfortable feelings. So I'll get to meet with Anne Mills again. Here goes the Millsport thing again. It's funny how often I think about her. Is this all because we lived in the same neighborhood? I feel like a pinball machine on 'tilt'*

CHAPTER 36 A MEETING

Two days later Jim Gale met with a very tough New York cop who had left the police force years ago and set up a detective agency that had become quite successful. His clients were not the usual divorce clients, angry wives or husbands, victims of embezzlement or robberies, et al, but Wall Street Banks, Hedge Funds, Venture Capitalists, and Corporations. It was all about corporate and business information. He called it business intelligence. His agency crossed many lines of legality, but his clients weren't too fussy about that or the ethics of his service. His offices looked like a rich lawyer's suite and his employees were a group of use-to-be or retired cops and computer geeks. Sean O'Ryan was a bit of a celebrity in the big Apple. He was a short heavyset man, crude in speech and body gestures, but he was very entertaining. Some of the local talk shows and talking heads had him as a regular guest. He knew the town and he knew where a lot of the bodies were buried and he was very good at acquiring the kind of information his clients sought.

Jim Gale, with the approval of his board, had decided to retain Sean O'Ryan's services to find out who had corrupted the software and to locate the villain. After signing a retainer contract and forking over a starting down payment of $50,000, he was in the third hour of discussing all the events that had led up to the 'crime'.

Sean O'Ryan had listened intently along with one of his assistants who were taking careful notes. He sat back in his well-appointed desk chair smoking his ever-present Cuban and spoke. "Well Jim, I've listened to your tale of woe. And I've been thinking that you tell an interesting tale, but, to be perfectly frank, it doesn't add up. You sure you're telling me the whole fuckin' story. You're about to spend a lot of bread having me and my boys chasing your problem, and if you haven't told me the whole story, your Company will be wasting a shit load of money. What in the fuck are you holding back? If you want to stop this bullshit right now, I'll give you your money back and we'll pretend this never happened."

Jim Gale became very uncomfortable. He thought, *this old cop is smarter than I thought*. He got up and walked over to the window looking out at the Brooklyn Bridge and thought for a few minutes if he should continue with this hard ass old bastard. Then, again, how in the devil could he go back to the board and tell them what O'Ryan had said. He went back to his chair and leaning forward, took a deep breath. "Sean, what I'm about to tell you guys has got to stay in this room. Can we agree to this?" asked Jim.

"Absolutely", replied Sean, "but that don't mean I accept the case. What the fuck did you leave out of your little tale? Don't leave nothin' ... nothin' out now"

"I had a deal with ACS." stated Jim.

"So, what kind of deal?"

"They guaranteed they would make the Merger come out in my favor. Going back to the beginning of the deal, Pristinimatic had control - that is voting control. They were a bigger Company than our Company. They had more market share. The whole idea of the Merger was ACS's idea. They were the people who put the idea in both Companies heads. Let me go further, they really liked Pristinimatic's technology and marketing skills, but they didn't like their leaders. I'm talking about their CEO and COO."

"Why?" asked Sean.

"To be perfectly frank, pedigree."

O'Ryan chuckled and shook his head in disgust, "You fuckin' guys never learn. So what was the deal?"

"A riff would be created within the very united Pristinimatic partner group. They had always voted together, thus giving them control. The riff would be the something that would break up that voting group. The partners had a form of stock that gave them double voting power. One guy in particular, a Brian Goldberg, had more voting power than anybody else in the group. There also were some original outside investors that agreed to give them a voting trust to help maintain their control. Because of the way their Company was organized one member of the group had to hold the trust. This Brian guy was considered the most fair and trustworthy so he was chosen to hold the voting trust power. One of the ACS people found a way to break Brian away from the group and therefore, the votes he controlled. It came down to this, by combining Goldberg's votes with votes from third party investors, people that had purchased Pristinimatic stock on the public market as a result of ACS's recommendation, would give ACS the power to control the outcome of the Merger. That's how I got to be the head of the Merger. That's how the new Board of the Merger was able to fire the management team of Pristinimatic. The Merger Board was for the most part appointed by ACS and accepted the ACS recommendation to dismiss the Pristinimatic management team. The management team names are Jersey Smart, the former CEO and Garrett Carlssen, the former COO.

"That's interesting. Now tell me how did they break this Brian guy away from the group and don't leave out the fucking details?" ordered Sean.

"Somehow, they got a hold of a picture of Goldberg's wife. It had some message on it that suggested she was having an affair with Jersey Smart, the Pristinimatic CEO. I don't really know much about Brian Goldberg, but that he's a very odd guy. I've been told that he never had much to do with women. Not gay, but extremely shy and introverted. His wife, who is very hot to look at, somehow hooked up with Brian and they married. They were never social and lived a very isolated existence. The affair absolutely blew Goldberg apart from Jersey Smart. Out of anger, I guess, he broke from the group and voted with us. Consequently the group lost their voting power, and then all the pieces fell our way.

"How did this guy Brian get the picture?" asked Sean.

"It had something to do with a meeting in Jersey's office where Brian accidentally found the picture," responded Jim. "I really don't know the exact facts. Nobody was about to tell me those details."

"Do you know who the mechanic was at ACS?"

"Mechanic?" queried Jim.

"Who was responsible for cooking up the picture bit, or better, who thought up this cute little scheme?" responded Sean.

"I don't know. I really don't know, but there are a lot of people at ACS that could be responsible," replied Jim.

"Something like that has to be carefully researched and planned," Sean went on. "Somebody had to find out a lot about the parties involved. My instincts tell me that there never was an affair. The whole thing was a crock of shit that this Goldberg bought hook, line, and sinker. What happened to the wife?"

"She disappeared, I'm told," answered Jim.

"Fuckin' Wall Street," sighed Sean shaking his head. "I guess it was a pretty damn good plan. It worked. So who really gives a shit about who fucked up the software? You guys got what you wanted. Fix it and move on."

"They, or Brian, or somebody screwed us. We'll take a big hit on the stock price and it will take months to recreate the lost software. We want compensated for all this trouble. We want more ownership," stated Jim Gale.

"So if we can find out who the bad guy is for sure, you got leverage - big time - to get your pound of flesh. That it?" asked Sean.

"Yes," confirmed Jim quietly.

"What if it turns out to be one of your guys?"

"I don't believe that's possible."

"Oh, it's possible," stated Sean. "I've seen all kinds of monkey business since I've been in this business. I suggest you think about this for a day or two and then we'll talk. I'll give you your money back if you don't want us to proceed. No hard feelings."

Even though, Jim was ready to proceed, he accepted Sean's advice. "All right, I'll think about it and call you tomorrow. I don't think I'm going to back away."

Jim Gale shook hands with Sean and his assistant and then left.

Sean O'Ryan looked over at his assistant, "We still don't know the whole goddamned story."

His assistant nodded in agreement.

CHAPTER 37 ANOTHER MEETING

Jim Gale was meeting with his Board, which included, by invitation, Bob Roberts. The discussion had gone on for two hours and it became apparent that Gale and company were looking to take advantage of the new circumstances and significantly improve their ownership position. The stance they were taking was that they had been torpedoed by a former Pristinimatic employee, Brian Goldberg, who was now the Merger's new Chief Technology Officer (CTO), certainly one that they were depending on to help them with the transition and the Company's future. He had been sold to them as the master engineer of Pristinimatic. Instead, he turned out to be some kind of crazy-man bent on destroying the new Company.

The deal that they had signed onto, which was approximately forty-five percent of ownership for the former Photo Symbology stockholders and fifty-five for Pristinimatic, had to change. They were asking for sixty-seven percent for them and thirty-three for Pristinimatic.

Roberts made it very clear that if this information, or the new deal they just had described to him, were to hit Wall Street before an acceptable resolution was achieved, the value of the new Company stock would crash and the SEC would be all over them.

Gale didn't seem to care. "Since they had the best products and lots of money it would pass and the stock would recover and eventually we would be a better Company."

Good sense and common sense were nowhere to be found as far as Roberts was concerned. As usual, greed was dominating the day. Roberts returned to ACS in time to meet with the two managing partners, Joseph Taglaferri and Ibrahim Sahid, and Anne. He reported the events of the meeting. They talked about several solutions, none of which, after examination, were probable or even possible. Then Ibrahim asked Anne to recount the entire process from beginning to end.

As she worked her way through his request, he kept asking very pointed questions and taking copious notes. This went on for a very long time. Anne, the ever confident Anne, was starting to feel a bit nervous. *When will he have heard enough?* She thought. Then he stopped and suggested everyone get some coffee or tea before continuing.

"Where's he going with this," she whispered to Bob Roberts in the hallway on the way to the refreshments.

"He's interrogating you."

"You're saying I'm like a prisoner. Is that what you mean?"

Then the conversation she had with Sam Axinov suddenly was in her thoughts and it once again disturbed her. *Sam said I was a soldier and now I'm being interrogated like a captured soldier.* She didn't like the implication. *Sam said soldiers kill people. I haven't killed anybody.*

They were back at the managing partner's office. Ibrahim Sahid, sitting up even straighter than his usual military bearing, asked, "Anne why do you think this happened?"

Anne really didn't have an answer, only a suspicion, "I'm not sure."

Ibrahim continued, "You said you were not sure. That means to me that you have some idea, perhaps an incorrect idea, but nevertheless an idea of what might have caused this. Anne, please share it with us."

The 'please' was an order, not a polite request, Anne understood. "Brian Goldberg became infuriated at Jersey Smart because he thought that Jersey was having an affair with his wife. Brian and his wife had some kind of fight and she left, in fact, she disappeared. As you know, Brian voted with our faction destroying the Pristinimatic voting majority bloc. We got what we wanted and I guess Brian eventually needed more retaliation than the outcome of the vote."

"Why did Brian think his wife was having an affair with Jersey?" pointedly asked Ibrahim.

"I'm not completely sure."

"For crying out loud woman, answer the question!" Ibrahim demanded.

This was the first time she ever heard him raise his voice and it disturbed her. It reminded her of Grahm. She could sense ruthlessness in Ibrahim that was similar to her brother, and she always was afraid of Grahm. She answered quickly, "Brian found a picture on the floor under Jersey's desk during a meeting. The picture implied that there was a relationship between Brian's wife and Jersey."

"Ohhhhh," hummed Ibrahim. "How bloody convenient."

Ibrahim Sahid was, amongst other things, a graduate of the London School of Economics and his hobby was reading mystery books and solving mathematical puzzles. The interrogation was right up his alley. "How did the picture get under the desk?"

The room was suddenly loud with silence. Anne thought, *you wanted the job done successfully, always successfully. Get the money, we don't care who gets hurt as long as it's not us and we get the money. You're very careful not to ever know exactly how it is accomplished, you son-of-a bitch. You rotten sons-of-bitches! Well, now you're going to know.*

"I talked Jersey into doing it," informed Anne. "And why would Jersey do such a thing?" inquired Ibrahim.

"To make sure that Jim Gale would be eliminated from the new Company and Jersey would be head of the Company. He knew before Brian Goldberg's defection that he had the votes to control certain aspects of the Merger, but not enough to dominate. In exchange for his co-operation, we guaranteed he would be given the CEO position in the Merger. In order to accomplish that, he would need the votes that we controlled to insure the outcome. So he was the one who provided the means. That's how we got the outcome you wanted."

"What a bloody snake," Joseph Taglaferri piped in.

"Not really, Joe" commented Ibrahim. "It's just corporate business. And further, it was you Anne, who provided the means. Jersey was merely your tool."

"I'm curious, why were you so sure it would work?" asked Ibrahim.

"I spent time researching Brian Goldberg, a lot of time in fact, and I came to understand his insecurities, and an obvious path that would take advantage of his weakness - his relationship with his wife," replied Anne. "Sure, it was always possible that it could have gone wrong, but it didn't. It worked just as I had planned it. The result was what you all demanded," stated Anne coldly.

"Those two guys, Jersey Smart and Garrett Carlssen, must be quite angry with the result, but there's nothing they can do about it," stated Ibrahim. "Interesting, Jersey can say nothing because he was a co-operating partner in the ... maneuver. On the other hand, Garrett Carlssen really doesn't know anything other than Brian's actions, as a result, of his seeing the photo. He has no idea who arranged everything. Is that correct Anne?"

"Yes, as far as I know it appears that way," confirmed Anne.

"There are a lot of moving parts to this situation and somehow, perhaps using your 'black' talents, Anne, we can mitigate, no, eliminate our problem," commented Ibrahim. "Please understand that a satisfactory outcome to the problem is not what happens to the Merger but that we get to keep our fees and reputation and have no unmanageable interchanges with the SEC. Joe and I will need the weekend to consider the situation and what we should do that will be best for the Company. Both of you be here at seven-thirty Monday morning. This meeting is over."

The two of them walked down the hallway together, and when they arrived at Bob Roberts' office, he turned and looked at Anne and smiled, "As I have said many times before, business is a game, a very serious game, but none the less a game, and sometimes Anne, a very dangerous game." With that, he turned and entered his office and closed the door. Anne felt a cold wind where there was none.

CHAPTER 38 AND STILL ANOTHER MEETING

It was a beautiful Saturday morning and Garrett had been planning a bicycle ride up along the East River with Sallie Kate but instead Garrett picked up his cell phone and went to Anne Mill's contact information. He looked at it for a few minutes thinking about Anne. *I don't want to do this! Damn it!* Finally, he selected it, but he didn't push the send button. He reviewed it in a sort of scientific way - *I am a scientist for Christ's sake.* He continued to think about the many ambivalent feelings he had experienced since he had become involved with her. It was a full spectrum from old unpleasant to a new catalog of feelings that included frustrations, anger and, he had to admit, some very pleasant. He'd really enjoyed the afternoon in the park. He finally pushed the send button.

They decided to meet in neutral territory which turned out to be the café in the Museum of Modern Art - a most pleasant place. Garrett was tense, unusually tense for such an occasion. He had come early and ordered a cappuccino that he had no interest in. Anne Mills came walking in looking every bit the woman that Garrett saw her as. *Damn it*, he thought, *she's one fine looking woman. Hey, you're not here to admire her, you're here on business.*

"Hello, Anne," he spoke. "How you've been?"

"Oh, just ducky," returned Anne. She sat down and immediately signaled the waiter. "I'll have one of those - nodding in the direction of Garrett's cappuccino - and some water."

"Well Garrett, it appears that we are here to see if we can find a way out of this mess. Got any ideas?" she asked.

Garrett responded, "Anne, how in the hell did this ever happen? It doesn't make sense, I know Brian Goldberg better than anyone else at the Company. He wouldn't do what everybody is accusing him of, no way. It's just not consistent with his character. Whatever Brian is, he's a person of integrity."

"But, what about his disappearance?" queried Anne. "Things go wrong and immediately he's nowhere to be found."

"Anne, I buy the disappearance, but not from a crime, perhaps from the way everything in his life crashed. Think about it, he finds, or suspects, his wife has cheated. The guy she has cheated with is his partner. She never even defends herself and immediately disappears. He no longer trusts his relationship with his life partner, or even his business partners, including me. His home life and his way of life are gone. Poof, nothing!! This all happens in a very short period of time. His business life is completely changed. He has no friends. And he's, above all, Brian Goldberg."

"What do you mean, he's Brian Goldberg?" he inquired.

"Brian came from a screwed up family. I have spent time with all of them. He hardly ever dated or had any kind of social life. He always has had, one thing going for him; he's a brilliant engineer, creative, and a person of great intellectual honesty. Frankly, I think he just ran away. The whole thing became too much for him. He no longer liked or trusted anybody, including me. It was time to run, or more to the point, make a change. There was no way that could occur in the new Company. As they say, 'he flew the coop.' Not so unrealistic under the circumstances. Even Ben Franklin 'flew the coop' from England to become a dedicated revolutionary after trying the opposite for fifteen years. Kinda' the same deal, he was betrayed and humiliated and he couldn't trust his friends any longer."

"You really believe that's what happened?" she asked.

"Look Anne, I don't really know what happened, but my instincts are screaming that the dirty work is not of Brian's doing. And in most of my life when I ignored my instincts I've been wrong. I'm going with my instincts."

"Then, if you're correct, somebody else, or even more than one person could be involved," declared Anne.

"That's what I believe. I don't know anybody from the old Pristinimatic crew that would be motivated to pull a stunt like this. It could do nothing but hurt them financially. There's always the possibility that there's a nut in our midst. Then you can throw logic and motivation out the window."

They considered a plethora of possibilities, but eventually agreed that all they were doing was fishing for what amounted to useless speculations.

Finally, Garrett suggested that they approach the problem logically and try to review what had occurred chronologically. Garrett set up a chart on the back of the paper place mat that came with the cappuccino. Soon they had a set of events placed in the proper time order. Garrett then suggested they look for tipping points.

Anne knew damn well when the tipping point occurred because she engineered it - the now infamous meeting in Jersey's office when the photo had been discovered by Brian. "We should try to associate tipping points with people beginning with Brian, of course."

"I agree, whether I like it or not," acknowledged Garrett. This was when Brian's wife, Yvette, left. They once again both agreed. The third was Brian's surprise vote. That was the killer. Once again they both agreed. And so it went for the next hour.

They had now consumed their way through two more cappuccinos and some cookies and a couple of bottles of water when Garrett, almost to his own surprise, asked, "It's getting quite late and I'm hungry for some real food, how about some dinner?"

Anne looked at him, "That didn't work out so well the last time, did it?"

Garrett responded, "No, but that was then, this is now. We're on the same side this time ... c'mon."

132

"How will your daughter ...Sallie Kate, if I remember her name correctly, like this?" asked Anne.

"It's not a problem, she really liked you. As you know, the next day she asked me to apologize to you for her rudeness. Anne, we really had a nice time that afternoon. It only went badly because we got caught up with a teenager's conflict that had absolutely nothing to do with you or me. Let's move on to a nice dinner. We will call it a business dinner meeting and not a date, how about it?" suggested Garrett.

"I accepted her apology the last time you brought it up. Please tell her I liked her too. I hope I'm not making a mistake. Let's go to dinner. You can call it whatever you want," replied Anne.

Garrett made a call for a reservation at an informal, delightful little French restaurant he often visited in the village and off they went.

It was nearing nine-o'clock and they had finished dinner. They were sipping a treat, rare liquor that came from Northern France that neither of them had ever heard of. It was a fitting finish to a superb meal served to them both carefully and tactfully by the waiter as directed by the proprietor, Henri. Garrett had gotten to know Henri over the years he had lived in the village and the many meals he had enjoyed in Henri's restaurant. When Henri brought over the liquor bottle, he brought three glasses. He joined them for a few minutes and chatted. Actually, Henri wanted to know who Garrett's date was. It had been a long time since Garrett had been to dinner with a "date." He got a warm introduction but not too much information.

Anne and Garrett spent much of the dinner relating their work histories over the last fifteen years. They left Millsport out of the conversation, and were having a very good time. When they left, they started walking towards Washington Square. Garrett said, "I keep my car in a garage about a block from here. I'll drive you home."

"Don't be silly Garrett, I'll grab a cab," declared Anne.

"I want to be silly," he looked intensely at Anne. "I want to drive you home."

"Are you sure?"

He nodded a very definite yes. She smiled and shrugged her shoulders. Garrett felt good. A kind of good he hadn't felt for a long time. They picked up the car and drove uptown towards Anne's apartment. They said almost nothing during the trip. Garrett pulled up to the entrance of Anne's building and stopped the car."

Anne spoke, "This turned out to be a much better day than I would have expected. We didn't solve any of the Merger mystery, but we'll keep working on it. Thank you. The meal was wonderful."

Garrett spoke, looking very directly, almost penetratingly, at Anne, "This was delightful. I'll call you first thing Monday morning." Then he stopped and looked out the window and slowly turned back taking an unexpected deep breath. He held out his hand to shake Anne's hand goodnight. Suddenly there was an intense connection that filled the space between them. Garrett took Anne's outreached hand and gently brought it up to his lips and grazed it with a kiss, then without thinking he embraced her. Then to both of their surprises they exchanged a kiss and then parted. He smiled warmly. Anne just stared at him, her expression was pensive, almost sad, and then she turned away.

They both sat quietly for a minute or two. Finally, Anne spoke, "I've got to go upstairs and I've got to go to bed, I have an early morning obligation."

"I know."

"What do you mean?" asked Anne a bit disturbed.

"That it's time for you for you to go upstairs."

They said nothing else. Anne opened the door and left. She disappeared into the lobby and never looked back. Garrett left. As Garrett drove back to the Village, he kept wondering where that exchange came from. It conjured up feelings of kissing a girl on a first date as a teenager. He laughed at his feelings and then thought, *Anne Mills, ridiculous.*

CHAPTER 39 RECESS

Garrett had spent much of the rest of the weekend going back and forth between his encounter with Anne and contemplating the puzzle Mike Levins had saddled him with.

What a crazy mess the whole thing turned out to be, a thought that kept erupting. It plagued him during the day, during the night, and managed to invade his sleep. *There are a lot of players in this game - Brian, Yvette, Gale, Jersey, Anne, Roberts, and who the hell else I don't know about, and, I guess, me. At least I know about me. I know what I didn't do.* It didn't help.

The Pristinimatic cast had been in the conference room in Mike Levin's office for several hours agonizing on how to handle their problem and trying to figure out why it had gone wrong and who was the bad guy. Jersey led the discussion trying too subtly to direct it away from him. Everyone was aware of the "picture event" in Jersey's office, but Jersey was swearing to anyone who would listen that he never had any affair with Yvette. While few believed him, Garrett did. Over and over, he was convinced that Jersey was the last person on earth that Yvette would be attracted to. He wasn't quite sure why he believed it without any doubt, but he was thoroughly convinced he was right.

Garrett had reported on his meeting with Anne and explained that during their long conversation on Monday they had continued with their "scientific approach" and had only come up with one murky possibility - If Brian was not the culprit, it had to be from Gale's group. They had something big to gain and were making no bones about it. But the problem was that it was at one hell of a price. There was too much risk.

On and on it went and Garrett's mind began to drift to Anne Mills, Millsport, and an old child acquaintance, Pete Andersen. Even though he was eleven years old at the time, he could still remember feelings of anger and humiliation. Then he thought, *Why does Anne key off all these old memories? She's like a pin in that old balloon that contains my good, bad, and pedestrian history. As soon as she gets in my head it opens the past and scatters so many feelings that I thought I had put to sleep long ago. Hey old Pete Andersen... why didn't you tell the truth?* Then Garrett replayed the event - an old movie for sure - but one that still bothered him.

It was sixth grade and it was a beautiful spring day. It was recess and Garrett and two of his classmates were sitting near the baseball field when a different Ann - Ann Young - came walking by with her friend Mary. Pete Andersen, a tall skinny son of a local doctor, and his close buddy Rich Hall stood up and blocked this Ann's path. He and Rich immediately started teasing Ann Young, who was probably the prettiest girl in the sixth grade, "that she knew all about sex." That was all that was ever said and it probably only lasted for a minute no more. Then Ann and her friend were gone. Nothing, but innocent adolescent teasing, but this was in another time in a small, provincial town, where the social rules were very clear, and where Ann's father ran an important factory that employed a lot of people.

The next day, just after school had begun, the three boys were called down to the principal's office. Sitting next to the Principal was Ann's father, Mr. Young. What followed was an accusation of sexual malfeasance. Pete and Richard admitted to teasing, but that was all. Garrett protested that he had not said a thing, nor in any way had he been part of the "crime." Ann's father called him a liar. He then advised that the two boys who had admitted their "crime" be given modest punishments. The Principal suggested that they be turned over to their homeroom teachers, who knew them well, for modest and appropriate discipline actions. Concerning "the Hebrew boy," he, the Principal, would deal with him directly.

Anne's father was satisfied and parted with, "You little bastard, don't you ever go near or speak to my daughter again." Garrett never did.

The Principal beat Garrett with a paddle after the school day was over. Further, he was to report to the Principal's office every day at the two recesses and write "I will never be disobedient again to girls." This was to be done five thousand times, and five thousand times it was. At the end of the punishment, which took over a month and a half to complete, Garrett received another paddling, and then was sent on his way. Every kid in the school knew about it, or so it seemed to Garrett. For better or worse, he gained a reputation from that day on as a "fast" boy with the girls, beware!" There were girls who would not even dance with him throughout his high school days because of his reputation. On the other hand, there were girls who wanted to dance with him because of his reputation. *Oh well, you take the good with the bad.*

CHAPTER 40 DIGGING

Jersey Smart was standing at the window of his living room looking out at Long Island Sound from his house in Cos Cob. Jersey was a worried man. If it ever came out that it was he who had accepted the deal with Anne and ACS to plant the photograph, he would be in trouble – big trouble. That would lead to all kinds of unpleasant things. There would be lawsuits followed by terrible publicity. Who would want to have anything to do with him in business knowing what he had done. He needed the current investigation to continue being pointed towards the 'guilty' party; that being, of course, the villain who had corrupted 'Torpedo' – Brian Goldberg. As long as Brian was considered the bad guy most people would believe and accept the obvious motive - Brian's anger over Jersey's betrayal with his wife. The photo incident would be the whole story, the revelation that caused Brian to ruin the 'Torpedo' software. That would be enough to keep any suspicions from him. At least that's what Jersey hoped.

Jim Gale would be another problem. Gale wanted more, and he would dig in deeper to gain greater advantage. A cold thought surfaced. *What if ACS told him exactly what podium had happened? I could ask Anne Mills,* he thought. *On second thought, that bitch wouldn't tell me squat. She fucked me over good, and there isn't a damn thing I can do about it.* He was overcome with a familiar rage. Finally, he steadied himself. He took a very deep breath and thought, *keep your mind on the end game. I've got to fix it. I brought this on myself, whatever was I thinking?* Then he chuckled to himself, *money and power.*

He moved from the window of his living room and went into his home office. He poured himself a drink and spent the next hour trying to come up with a move that would keep him out of trouble. Each thought came down to Jim Gale. He had to find a way to keep Gale at bay. He needed information about Gale. Information that could be used to stop Gale; that meant one of those organizations, guys who specialized in dirt, people dirt. He made a decision that would be his next move.

The next day, Jersey called a contact he had on Wall Street and asked for a recommendation of a person or organization that could supply him with 'significant' information about an individual he was dealing with. His contact recommended, ironically, the same people that Jim Gale had met with, Mr. Sean O'Ryan's organization. He made the call and ended up on the phone with O'Ryan. An appointment was scheduled for the following day.

The issue of conflict of interest on O'Ryan's part never entered his mind for a moment. In fact, once he realized who Jersey was, he saw it as an opportunity to gather information he was after for his other client Jim Gale, cheaply. He was amused by his good luck. Unsolicited information was walking in right through his front door and it was costing him nothing and perhaps, another source of money from the same situation – two birds for one stone at double the profit.

The next day after signing a contract and forking over a down payment retainer Jersey was in the second hour of discussing all his edited versions of the events that had led up to the 'crime.' The same assistant who had taken the Jim Gale notes was doing the same with Jersey.

"I need this as fast as possible," stated Jersey.

"What do you have in mind?" asked Sean.

"By the end of the week," replied Jersey.

"Hmmmm," pondered Sean. He sat back in his well-appointed desk chair smoking his ever-present Cuban. "Well Jersey, I've listened to your story and I think we can gather the information you require in the time you require. You're sure you're telling us all that we should know. The kind of stuff you're looking for requires us knowing all the facts you can supply us with. In other words, we can be more effective in the shortest time if we are amply informed. Please understand that the information will be expensive. Having it so quickly will make it even more expensive. Please reassure us, you're prepared to pay for it. Do we understand each other?"

Jersey was a bit unnerved by Sean's speech and could feel the costs getting out of hand, but on the other hand he had to do something to neutralize Jim Gale. "What kind of money are we talking about? I've already given you $25,000. How much more do you guys have in mind?"

Sean carefully tapped his cigar on the large ashtray located on his desk, breaking off a good half inch of ash and leaned over towards Jersey, "You need it fast and precise. That means I'll have to put several of my best on it immediately. Think of a minimum of another $25,000.

"Jesus, that's $50,000 total," protested Jersey. "Fast information is very costly around here, I see."

"Look," stated Sean, "The kind of information you want is not in a telephone book. We have to do a lot of digging to get what you want. We can stop now and I'll give you your money back and that will be the end of it - yes or no?"

"You're sure you can get the information I need?" asked an uncomfortable Jersey.

"We're the best in the business," stated Sean. "Nobody is better! If it's there, we'll get it."

Jersey stood up, "I've got to go to the bathroom."

"First room on the right, help yourself," replied Sean.

Jersey, as both Sean and his assistant, were quite aware, was just buying some 'getting- ready-to-put-up-the-cash-time.'

After Jersey left the room they huddled by Sean's desk. "Do you think he'll split for the cash?" The assistant asked.

138

"Absolutely!" Sean answered. "He's in some kind of deep shit he hasn't told us about. He didn't hesitate to sign the contract or plunk over the 25 G's. He's just spending a little time getting used to the idea."

About ten minutes later Jersey returned.

"Have you made a decision?" asked Sean.

"Well... yes, but what if you find nothing?" asked Jersey.

"Then there is nothing," responded Sean. "Same work goes into finding nothing as finding something."

"I'm screwed financially, either way," stated Jersey.

Sean responded, "Think of it this way, you will now have real facts to base your decisions on as opposed to rumors and bullshit. That's what you're paying for."

Jersey took a deep breath and nodded yes, "Go ahead, I'll pay, but $50,000 is the top, right?"

"Yes," responded Sean. "It could come in lower."

Sure, Jersey thought to himself, *and I believe in the good fairy*. He should have believed in the good fairy because ultimately the bill came in for less than he expected.

"Well, now that that is settled, I have a few questions. You talked about how this whole mess started with the software failure and there was some kind of picture that got the craziness going. That picture caused the chief technical guy to go ape shit, and eventually it was he who caused the software failure. Do I have that right?" asked Sean.

"Yes," replied Jersey.

"And it got him so pissed off he broke away from your voting bloc, right?" persisted Sean.

Jersey nodded yes.

"What was it exactly about that goddamned picture that got him so pissed off?"

"It suggested that I was having an affair with his wife."

"Well, were you?" demanded Sean.

"No fucking way. She was very pretty and very sexy to look at, but a stainless steel lady, a total deep freeze," stated Jersey. "She was about the coldest bitch I ever met. You didn't have to know her very well to figure that out."

Jersey continued, "Somehow, they - ACS - got a hold of the picture ... maybe they created it. You know that's quite possible with today's technology. Anyhow, it was a picture of his wife with some message on it that suggested she was having an affair with me. Although I've known the CTO for many years, I really don't know that much personally about him other than he is a very odd guy. I've been told that he never had much to do with women, and was shy and introverted. His wife, who is very hot to look at, somehow hooked up with him and they married. They were never social and lived a very isolated existence. The supposed affair absolutely blew Goldberg, the CTO, apart from me and our group. I assume he hates me now. For some reason everybody else on the team was on his shit list by then, and consequently all the pieces fell the way ACS wanted them to."

"How did this guy Brian get the picture? Was it sent to him?" asked Sean.

Jersey replied, "No, he found it in my office."

"Oh, what the hell was he doin' there?" asked a surprised Sean. "Was he rooting around your office because he suspected that you were screwin' his wife?"

"No, for Christ's sake, nothing like that!" exclaimed Jersey. "All the partners were having a meeting in my office about the details of the Merger," Jersey stopped.

"Well, and ... " coaxed Sean

"He found the picture on the floor under my office meeting table," answered Jersey.

"How in hell did he get under the table to find the picture? Are you telling me, that people having meetings in your office regularly go under your conference table?" asked Sean sarcastically as he rolled his eyes in the direction of his assistant and chuckled to himself.

"Jelly Beans," replied Jersey.

"Jelly Beans?"

"Yes Jelly Beans," confirmed Jersey. "I always have a few jars of Jelly Beans in my office. I love Jelly Beans. I always put them out for meetings. I, on purpose, "accidentally" knocked the jar over during the meeting. Brian was the kind of guy who would quickly help someone clean up a mess, and he was the first one under the desk gathering the spilled Jelly Beans. That's where he found the picture."

"That's interesting. And just how did the damn picture get their?" queried Sean knowing damn well what the answer was.

"I put it there," confirmed Jersey. "That was the price."

"Cute, real cute! As it turned out they screwed you and they knew, there wasn't a damn thing you can or could do about it. They made you an accessory to the crime and all this without compensation. Oh, I love it. Another Wall Street tale of sensitivity and good will," announced Sean shaking his head. "I've seen and heard a lot of Wall Street crap in my day, but this one is right up there, a 'beaut'. I wonder how they could be so sure it would work. Somebody must have done a lot of homework. But, of course you always need Lady Luck on your side. They were lucky, and well you were not. We'll talk to each day at five."

Jersey left.

The assistant said to Sean, "I wonder what he hasn't told us."

Sean replied, "It don't matter at this time."

CHAPTER 41 REPORT AND EXECUTE

Jersey received a call from Sean O'Ryan at the middle of the day only three days after he had retained him. "Come to my office. I have a full report. I don't think it's in your best interest for me to email it to you. This is for security reasons."

Jersey arrived in the afternoon at O'Ryan's office, listened to his report, and then spent several hours alone in the conference room trying to decide how to use the information he had just bought for a lot of money.

Was it worth what he had paid for it? Only time would tell. Was it enough to get the result he needed? At the end of the day he would have loved to completely destroy Jim Gale, but that was unrealistic and really unnecessary. He would settle for stopping him from exposing his – Jersey's - actions in the deal. That was first and foremost. It probably would keep Jim Gale from getting more of the deal, or at least reduce his mightiest ambitions a tad. *Then life would go on. Did he, Jersey have enough on Jim to get that effect? Jersey* wondered.

Gale's bad marriage was one thing. His fooling around was another thing, but the possible gay stuff was perhaps dynamite, or was it? This was a new age and so many things that used to matter didn't matter as much anymore. Maybe the best way to handle this would be a trial balloon, a hint, and see what would happen. It was becoming quite obvious he, Jersey, didn't possess any kind of magic bullet.

The more he thought about the stunt with the picture and Brian, the more he realized the real tactician behind that maneuver was probably Anne Mills. Bob Roberts was not anything more than a manager, no creativity. It was she who determined and planned the moves of the game they were playing and he - Jersey - had been nothing more than a sacrificial rook on her chessboard. It really pissed him off. He never saw it coming. Then he began to play with the idea of contacting her and disclosing his information about Gale. Let the mastermind, Mills, figure out the next move. Anne and her gang would not want to see this mess get worse. He played with this idea for a while and finally decided that it really wouldn't be such a good move. Prudently, he decided he would like to discuss this with Sean O'Ryan.

He had been in O'Ryan's conference room for almost two hours going over all his thoughts. He wanted to hear O'Ryan's thoughts. O'Ryan and his assistant entered the room with a, "What do ya' think of what we found?"

Jersey responded, "I was thinking of bringing ACS into this. They will not want this to get worse. They could be drawn into it at the potential of great expense and pain. Tell me your thoughts."

O'Ryan thought for a while as he paced around the room occasionally puffing on his cigar. Finally, O'Ryan stopped and spoke. "Has it occurred to you that Mills and her buddies will never want to do anything with you? They promised you that you would be king and fucked you big time. They've thrown you away, get it? Gale always was their man and I'm sure they know all about him and his bad habits. What we found out is probably some of their reserve ammunition for the future to be used to manipulate Gale. The real target to get what you want is Gale and his relationship with ACS, the organization. You might not like Gale, but the real sons-of-bitches in this deal are the 'Wall Streeters'- ACS. This is their game and we don't have the slightest idea of what they're really up to, except they're always dedicated to making a lot of money. The path to getting control of this is finding out who screwed up the software and what they really thought it would accomplish. ACS was probably at the bottom of the whole damn scheme from day one. Gale was just another fuckin' pawn. If we can find that out, we may be able to throw a bomb in the middle of their plans. Do you want to continue, it's expensive?" and O'Ryan was finished.

"I'll think about it," he replied as he got up to leave. Later that evening Jersey made a phone call to Garrett. Jersey had decided it was in his best interest to point at ACS and Anne's participation as a fundamental aspect of their problems. It was a further deflection move on his part.

CHAPTER 42 ANOTHER DATE

Garrett had, independently, also believed that ACS was part of the problem, and if that was true, how did Anne fit in? He called Anne Mills for another meeting. They were obligated to meet and continue with their attempt to figure out who was responsible for corrupting 'Torpedo.' Garrett called her and set up an appointment later that afternoon. They agreed to meet once again at the Museum of Modern Art's outdoor café. Garrett arrived very early and spent the time trying not to think about the meeting by reading a book that was really boring him. *What was he meeting her for? If ACS was part of this mess, their meetings were a charade and he was somehow being manipulated. Damn it,* he kept repeating to himself. By the time she arrived he was beginning to become quite upset at this ever more growing possibility.

Anne showed up promptly at the scheduled time, *of course.* "Hello Anne."

She nodded and said nothing. A waiter immediately came over and she ordered her usual water and espresso. "Got any new ideas?" asked Anne.

"Not a damn one!" growled Garrett.

Suddenly Garrett could not contain himself, "Damn it Anne, I am beginning to believe that you or your Company, or both of you, are somehow behind this whole mess."

A startled Anne said nothing.

"C'mon Anne, you folks have had it your way, what's left? Do you have to squeeze some more out of us?' demanded Garrett.

There was a long silence.

"Jesus, it's time to come clean!" again demanded Garrett.

Anne looked straight at Garrett, "We have nothing, nothing to do with the present situation."

Anne got up, reached into her purse and took out a ten dollar bill and carefully laid it down on the table and left.

The meeting was over.

Garrett wasn't quite sure how to react. He knew he had made a strategic mistake, but enough was enough or was it? Those old Millsport feelings were there and he couldn't deny it. *The woman is a catalyst for the memories of my youth.*

Then for the first time he allowed himself to actually accept a thought in very clear terms that had been fleeting around his head for a while. He realized he had serious feelings for Anne Mills. He was very attracted to her.

My God, he thought, *Anne Mills, the progeny of Millsport provincials, those bastards who caused much pain in my youth. She is the first woman I've been attracted to since my wife left. Is this me being neurotic or just plain nuts? The only thing we have in common is we both come from Millsport and not another damn thing. Where am I supposed to go from here? I really pissed her off. OK, you find her really attractive. Maybe this is about nothing more than something I could never have, or maybe the old moth and flame nonsense. Well, not in Millsport for sure. Put it out of your mind and get back to business.* A myriad of these kinds of thoughts kept running through Garrett's mind for the next half hour. Garrett finally paid the bill, got up and left. As he was walking out of the building into the small park in front of the café, to his surprise, he saw Anne sitting on one of the park benches. He felt her gaze as if they were physically connected.

I got a little carried away back there and I'm truly sorry. This whole thing is getting to me. Let me buy you a drink or something - a little peace offering. We're supposed to be working together to find a way out of this mess, not fighting."

"OK, you can buy me dinner," and they spent the next few hours together in a nearby restaurant trying to talk about business but it wasn't working. Something personal and serious was going on between them. They both felt it, but too many things were in the way to work it out. Certainly, neither one could deny that there were powerful feelings afoot.

CHAPTER 43 GREAT MINDS MEET

They were all gathered. The place was chosen by the lawyers. The neighborhood was obscure, neutral, unexpected, uncomfortable ... perfect. One of the lawyers had rented a motel suite in Queens not far from the old New York World's Fair grounds. It was old and dreary and smelled of the familiar and unpleasant odor of overuse. The result of chemicals and soaps used to hide and mask the history of the bodies, their excrements, and cigarettes that had passed through the rooms.

The attendees ... mostly gloomy faces.

Jersey and Garrett were there to represent themselves with their own lawyer, Nap Hendricks.

Mike Levin and his assistant were present, representing the former, or current, Pristinimatic stockholders.

Jim Gale, his COO, CFO and their old and new Company lawyers, Del Patterson and his assistant.

And finally, Anne Mills and Bob Roberts with their council team, Levi Goldbart and two junior partners, representing ACS.

Coffee, water, and doughnuts were on a small side table and yellow tablets and ballpoint pens in the center of the meeting table. The chairs were well used metal folding types in different maudlin colors and were, for the most part, quite uncomfortable.

Garrett counted eight lawyers and seven clients representing four separate interests. *The lawyers are raking it in from the money pit today - eight sharks and seven fish. Baloney, this is no pit, it's a pool. It's filled with fresh meat and cold-blooded predators. Maybe, I'm overdoing it a bit,* he thought ..... *Nah!*

Mike Levin got up at the front of the table and peering almost amusingly at the attendees, "Ladies and gentlemen ... and my fellow lawyers," he laughed at his little joke. "We are gathered here to find a workable solution to our very nasty common problem. The Marquis of Queensbury rules are in effect and no low blows will be tolerated. We all are well aware of the angst, frustrations and anger collectively present in this group. I wish to thank all present for agreeing to attend this meeting and I urge all to work for a solution in the spirit of your enlightened self-interests. Please hear me – your enlightened self-interests, ladies and gentlemen, as opposed to only self-interest."

"Because of the cantankerous environment of this meeting all councils have agreed to accept a moderator to manage our discussions and debate. I do not personally know Judge Abraham Smith, but some of you do either through the courts or as students at Columbia where he lectures from time to time. The Judge, who has graciously agreed to perform this thorny, and dare I say,

146

egregious task, will be here in fifteen minutes and then we will get started immediately. The final thing I would like to say is that there can be no one winner to achieve a win. That will not work. Everyone must win by the successful merging of the two companies. We must find a solution through compromise that provides a collective win. We are here to preserve an extremely valuable asset. In the meantime, enjoy the coffee and doughnuts."

Each party quickly gathered into their small groups, having coffee and doughnuts. There were whispers and some implied unpleasantness as suggested by body language.

The Judge entered the room and was introduced to everyone by Mike Levin. Some knew the Judge and the others knew him by reputation. Levin had promoted the idea of using the Judge as a sort of Ombudsman to manage this difficult group with their conflicting goals. Much to Levin's surprise everybody had quickly agreed to the agenda which included the Judge's fee.

The Judge asked all to take their places and presented his concept of how the meeting would be organized.

"As I've come to understand by reading the documentation supplied by your lawyers, you have collectively found yourselves in a very nasty predicament. Apparently someone has managed to corrupt your entire software infrastructure. This has resulted in what you believe – again I use the word 'collectively' - the following:

If this is not fixed within a few days, it will be necessary to announce this publically and that must be preceded by informing the SEC.

This announcement will cause the current price of the stock to lose its value significantly, possibly worse.

The culprit who caused this must be found, and if possible, have him cure the problem.

There is apparently a candidate for culprit, but the alleged culprit has vanished.

I believe you all are in approximate agreement concerning these."

There was nodding of heads or quiet yes's from the group.

The Judge continued, "Let's hear positions from each of the group starting on my right. I want no interruptions, or noise of any sort. Everybody will have their turn. This is not a courtroom, but I expect all to behave professionally. Ms. Mills, Mr. Roberts, I believe, it's your turn. Would you or your council please begin?"

Anne Mills and Bob Roberts with their council team, Levi Goldbart leading and two junior partners backing him up, sat stone-faced.

Levi Goldbart was a middle aged graduate of an Ivy League law school who had begun his career as a Navy Lawyer. Although he had been out of the Navy for almost twenty years he still sounded, presented, and appeared as if he was military; everything about him projected the illusion of precision.

Goldbart began, "My clients, ACS, were responsible for suggesting, negotiating, underwriting, and organizing the Merger between the two companies, Pristinimatic and Photo Symbology. At no time whatsoever (he hesitated to make his point) did my client have anything to do with, or in any way interfere with, the operations of the predecessor companies or the Merger. Whatever went wrong occurred within the operations of the new Company well after ACS was completely through with its responsibilities. We have no accountability in this matter and are only here to protect ACS from any unwarranted liability that may be directed at us for another party's strategic and tactical purposes. If there is the least hint of such from anyone, we will bring suit against any and all who appear, to be part of such an action. And I assure all, it will be incredibly costly." Levi Goldbart nodded to the Judge that he was through.

Judge Smith nodded back, "Thank you Levi, for those kind words."

There was a wave of suppressed laughter from the group including Anne Mills and Bob Roberts.

"Mr. Gale," said the Judge directing, "You're next."

Jim Gale, his COO, CFO and their old and new Company lawyers, Del Patterson and his assistant, sat in readiness.

Jim Gale turned and said, "Del Patterson will be representing us."

Del Patterson was a fairly young star of one of the biggest law firms in New York. He was an overweight blond with a crew cut, who had once been a successful college athlete. He looked powerful and had the voice and elocution of a Broadway actor.

"Well," he began, "My clients entered into this Merger in good faith and with great optimism. They, above all, trusted that all aspects of Pristinimatic and its systems, including the, all important, 'Torpedo' software they received and depended upon as part of the Merger. They further believed and depended upon the representations from Pristinimatic that the software was exactly and precisely as represented. This, of course, included the integrity of the personnel from Pristinimatic, who agreed to join the Merger. The Pristinimatic software, 'Torpedo' was considered so good by the other partner - Photo Symbology - that it was immediately adapted and integrated into the standard systems of the Merger. Trust, incredible trust, on the part of Photo Symbology couldn't have been higher or more complimentary to the Pristinimatic group than to totally embrace the Pristinimatic 'Torpedo' software."

Garrett thought to himself, *what a crock of shit. They took our systems because theirs were terrible.*

Patterson continued, "Apparently there were problems that were hidden from the other partner in the Merger. These were problems so serious, that the entire future of the new Company - the Merger - is most surely in danger of total collapse. Under these circumstances, my clients feel they have been seriously damaged and there are indications that the damage is irreversible. We are investigating the possibility of criminal activity associated with these matters. The behavior and ethics of the Pristinimatic group would seem to indicate there was never good faith or good intent on the part of management.

148

It was fortunate that the Pristinimatic CEO and COO were not chosen to remain with the Company by a majority of the new stockholders but, unfortunately, this did not include Mr. Brian Goldberg, the CTO."

"We certainly understand these rejections had to be difficult for Smart and Carlssen. We also understand as well, that the apparently unstable Brian Goldberg, having lost his relationship with those two individuals - Smart and Carlssen - a relationship that had protected him all those years as Pristinimatic was being built, ultimately and naturally led to great anger and resentment. But, as a result, of apparently other very unseemly events occurring, disenchantment and a strong sense of betrayal on the part of the CTO occurred. Betrayal is one of the deepest and most hurtful of emotions that humans can suffer – 'Et tu, Brute?' These two men, Smart and Carlssen, for reasons we have only recently discovered, were the hatchet men bent on destroying a man who was always close to the edge of ethical and mental collapse."

What in hell is he talking about? Garrett thought.

Continuing, "The result of their collective actions has deeply injured the Merger transaction. The failure of the former Pristinimatic top management team above all, and I'm speaking of those two individuals sitting at this table, to reveal the delicate state and nature of the CTO, Mr. Brian Goldberg, was incredibly and maliciously irresponsible. They, knowing all this, allowed him ... permitted him, to continue in his role as the chief technologist of the Merger. This was at the very least not only irresponsible, but practically and morally reckless, but more condemning and frightening, dishonest and rotten to the core. Certainly, the action of the majority stockholders in rejecting these executives from any further involvement in the new Company was wise and perceptive, but, unfortunately, not timely in understanding the depth of their mischief. If we, at Photo Symbology, only knew what we know now, this could have been prevented. We now must consider the possibility of a total destruct ... ashes, Ladies and Gentleman, nothing but ashes, and good careers of good men destroyed for life in the name of greed, avarice, hubris, and dishonesty." Then he stopped.

The Judge looked at him, "You through ... with your indictment, councilor?"

"For the moment," Dell Patterson responded.

Jersey and Garrett's lawyer, Nap Hendricks, quickly jotted down a note and passed it to them. "Don't flinch; this is not a courtroom - just opening noise, and nothing more."

Judge Abraham indicated that Mike Levins was next.

Mike Levins began, "This Merger was built upon the concept that these two companies, involved in the same business, represented the best of their mutual market sector providers. Bringing them together would create the ability to dominate, something that they could not do separately, or, at least, certainly not in the foreseeable future. From a business perspective, it was, and is, an excellent idea, and so it came about with the co-operation of all parties in this room. Each one of you benefitted. Then, unexpectedly, something went wrong. Ladies and Gentlemen, the truth of the matter is that at this time, nobody, ... nobody knows what caused the problem to occur. There exists no evidence that I am aware of, nor do I believe anyone in this room is aware of, that would indicate otherwise. All we've heard is nothing more than conjecture. All concerned parties in this room will suffer the consequences if we together, can't repair and manage this problem responsibly, and honestly. To believe there can be separation is to deny reality. We all stand to win or all stand to lose. We all must act within the spirit of enlightened self-interest, not just self-interest. What went wrong can be fixed. It is not without pain or expense, but is doable. We need to plan and cooperate for the worst, and execute for the best.

Levin was finished and it was Nap Hendricks' turn.

Hendricks began, "I'm only here to observe as a personal representative of Jersey Smart and Garrett Carlssen and have nothing to say at this time."

"Well, Ladies and Gentlemen, we've all heard from each faction," the Judge continued, "Now I'd like to ask some questions."

For the rest of the morning, the Judge carefully interrogated every side. His questions were penetrating and to the point. As his questioning proceeded it became more apparent that there was very little innocence in the room, and what really had happened had yet to be revealed. Much was being hidden and the Judge, with his years in the courtroom, could smell it. Finally, the Judge announced that it was time to eat lunch and the meeting would resume in one and a half hours.

When the meeting was resumed there was a lot of talking but nothing was resolved, nothing! Jim Gale reported that the computer experts that had been hired to solve the problem were hard at work, but nothing had been found or cured so far. They agreed to meet in the same place, same time, the next day.

CHAPTER 44 IMPULSE

Garrett returned home in a disgusted mood. Sallie Kate was busy doing her homework and gave her father a 'grunt greeting acknowledgment' of his arrival. Garrett went to the kitchen and poured himself a drink and settled onto a kitchen's stool. Although he didn't want to, he reviewed the day's happenings in between fleeting thoughts of Anne. Finally, he went into the living room where Sallie Kate was and asked her about dinner. She responded she had eaten when she got home and wasn't hungry.

Back to the kitchen and an impulsive wave swept over Garrett. He called Anne Mills. She answered almost immediately.

"Hi Anne, this is Garrett."

"I recognize your voice by now and I know your number," she replied. "What can I do for you?"

"Have dinner with me now," came out of Garrett, almost without thinking.

"Why?" asked Anne. "It got pretty tense the last time we met alone. You really want to continue with something from that wonderful meeting we had in Queens this afternoon?"

"No, absolutely no! No business. I'm hungry and I don't feel like eating alone. I don't know why I said that. Anne, I really want to have dinner with you. It's that simple," sort of confessed Garrett.

There was a long pause on Anne's part ...

"It's just dinner Anne," argued Garrett.

"Why would you want to do that, Garrett?" Anne to her surprise was teasing. "Where?" asked Anne.

"Your call, but I suggest the French restaurant we went to in the Village."

"That food was quite good. Sold! Give me the address I'll take a cab. What time?"

"In an hour."

"See you then."

Garrett was feeling something he couldn't quite describe. He was amazed he had made that call, that he had been so quick and direct and that she had accepted so quickly. One thing was for sure, he wasn't sure.

As an afterthought Garrett called Henri's and made a reservation. Henri informed him he was very busy but would find a way to fit them in. "I assume it's the same lady I met?"

"Yesssss," hissed Garrett.

"Hmmmm, very good," replied Henri approvingly.

Garrett walked over to Henri's and arrived a half hour ahead of time. Henri was amused. "I detect you could use a bit of a drink to calm your obvious anxiety. Are you going to propose?"

"Ye gods, no! To tell you the truth, I don't have the slightest idea of what I'm doing," admitted Garrett.

Henri laughed, "I do."

"What?" demanded Garrett.

"Some other time, old friend, here comes your date. I recommend the Cassoulet," uttered Henri quietly.

Anne walked over to where they were standing. Henri greeted Anne with "Delighted to see you again and gave her the restaurateur's best kiss. Then he led them to a table that had been squeezed into a corner. Garrett had watched them do it when he came in. He felt mildly important.

"I'm here Garrett," she said with a pensive smile as they sat down.

"I'm hungry," was all Garrett good say. "Henry recommends the Cassoulet."

"Then let's have Cassoulet. What's a Cassoulet?" asked Anne.

"It's very good. It's a French peasant dish from Southern France. It's a collection of well cooked meats with white beans in some kind of delicious stock. Be patient, and you'll see. If you don't like it, I'll get you something else ... promise," reassured Garrett.

Henri walked over and placed some hors d'oeuvres on the table followed by a waiter who brought a bottle of wine Henri had chosen. "My treat, it's an excellent Bordeaux."

They began with the wine and it was Garrett's turn to speak and he said nothing.

Finally, Anne spoke, "Why did you really want to meet me for dinner? Have you learned something?"

"I think, I've fallen in love with you," came out of Garrett's mouth.

"What did you say?" replied a startled Anne.

Garrett shrugged his shoulders, "I think I'm in love with you." There was a long silence. "I know it makes no sense. We've nothing in common but Millsport and the Merger and those are hardly anything to build a relationship on."

"This is ridiculous. You and I ... no way. Come to your senses. Our backgrounds are much too different. You're a nice guy with a nice daughter, but we have nothing in common. And further, I have no intention of getting involved with anybody romantically. And if I did, it wouldn't be with a ... ," she stopped short when it came to saying Jew. "God, I can't believe I almost said that. That was my Mother talking. I apologize."

"Accepted, I agree with you. It makes no sense, but every time I'm with you I've got this feeling that I haven't felt for years, and I like it. It just comes down to a simple feeling; I want to be with you. Stop with the Jew thing, get over it. We're .just a man and a woman with all kinds of complexities in our lives and that's just one more damn complexity in the mix that defines us. If my parents were alive they would object, sure. And that Mother of yours would do the same. But, they're no longer an issue."

"Wrong!" interrupted Anne, "My Mother is alive, very old, very alert and very well and hasn't changed one little bit."

"I'll be damned," exclaimed Garrett, "She still packing her six guns?"

"I'm afraid, yes."

"C'mon Anne, you're too grown up to be run by her."

"I suppose you're right. I know you're right, but what about everything else as you so cutely stated, 'our complexities'? I'll admit I like you, Garrett. I like you a lot. And that's quite unexpected. But beyond that, probably nothing," informed Anne. "My 'complexities,' as you named them, are very complex and you might not like all of them, to say the least." She was thinking primarily at this time of her actions in the Pristinimatic /Photo Symbology deal.

Garrett pondered for a moment and then said, "Look, Anne, feelings, attractions between people happen in spite of those complexities. I'll admit I'm no great expert with my track record - I guess - my failed marriage, but I've grown a lot over the years and I've learned to trust my feelings and instincts, and I'm not careless nor am I irresponsible. I've had to raise a daughter by myself. Once I accepted that reality, with those myriad of implications, it became obvious to me that I had to grow and become a very responsible human being, a Dad. I think I got that right. What I'm trying to say is that I know what I'm feeling is right and I know it's good. And I'll just have to deal with your ... complexities."

Anne took a deep breath, "I haven't the slightest idea if I could feel the same way about you... I think? Figuring that out could really be difficult. My suggestion to you is, get over it. Don't complicate the nice life you have right now. Continue enjoying bringing up your daughter. She's terrific and will bring you all kinds of good things. I think, I know, I would bring you all kinds of aggravation."

Anne grew quiet. It occurred to her for the first time that she had some feelings about Garrett that were quite unexpected. It also was painfully clear to her that the obstacles, the 'complexities,' were too great to even consider any serious relationship.

After a few minutes, Garrett gently took her hand. She didn't pull back, to her surprise. "I didn't plan to say what I said to you, Anne. It just came out. But I'm glad it happened. For the first time, I've honestly admitted to myself how I feel about you and I let it all come out. You know my feelings, but you have no obligations to me. Let it go at that and for the moment let's enjoy Henri's dinner. Enjoy the fact that I'm for you Anne, and if nothing else, a friend. I'm hungry. Let's eat."

They did, and quite pleasurably. But everything had changed. Anne saw Garrett as if he was an entirely different person. She felt pleasure, and then she felt pain.

CHAPTER 45 TACTICS AND CONFESSION

It was time again to meet with the ominous crew in the Queen's motel. As Jersey was arriving at the meeting, he was getting more apprehensive. How could he stop Gale? The meeting began with another round of threats and intimidations. Jersey looked for an opening, an idea. Then an idea he had been considering ever since he had his last session with O'Ryan began to take shape. As the session went on he paid little attention to the meeting's dialog, but rather spent the time considering and reconsidering his idea. He examined its strengths and its weaknesses. He kept molding and remolding the plan. As the day went on he became more confident. By the middle of the afternoon session, he was committed. He knew there was risk, big risk, but he had to do something. He thought to himself, *I've taken risks before and I've usually won. I've always used my intelligence to think through the moves. There was always risk associated with every one of them, but I mostly prevailed. And I've got balls that most people don't. I got careless with the Merger because of my damn greed. It blurred my vision. That was a mistake. I will not let that happen again.*

A late afternoon phone call to the Company revealed that nothing special had been accomplished. The outside software engineers that had been brought in to find, and hopefully fix the problem, were busy at work, but again had nothing meaningful to report.

Nobody was feeling any relief, and tensions were growing in all quarters. Everybody was frustrated and worried. It was the lack of action that was particularly so frustrating. Even Gales team, who were all playing for a better piece of the Merger were in a funk. Gale strangely was not. Garrett seemed to notice a quiet confidence.

It was difficult to see a painless way out of the mess. ACS, with their attempts to isolate themselves, was beginning to have thoughts of a disaster. It was interesting how a few days of no progress was creating a sea of collective impotence. Impotence breeds rage and God knows what else bad would result from this … and Garrett, swimming in his strange sea of ambivalence, was in love.

After a meaningless meeting Anne went to Sam's Deli to have some coffee and a bite. *She really looks stressed,* thought Sam as he sat down at her table with his own cup of coffee. "You don't look very happy. Am I talking to the soldier or the woman?" Sam asked pensively.

"Sam I'm not really sure anymore," Anne replied wistfully. "Things have gotten out of control. It's everything; the office, the Merger that we're working on and, strangely and unexpectedly, my personal life."

"You want to talk about it, I've got time," said Sam as he stirred some milk and sugar into his coffee.

Anne looked away from Sam's warm stare.

"Anne, you're not the first human being who has, as you say, lost control. We all reach points like that in our lives. Tell me Anne, what's bothering you so much that it is causing so much pain. I will assume you haven't killed anybody," suggested Sam with a bit of humor in an attempt to lighten the mood.

"Sam are you sure you really want to listen to me complain about my life?" asked Anne seriously. *Am I really thinking of talking to this old guy who I only know over coffee, eggs, and deli sandwiches? He somehow seems to know some things about me that I don't quite know about myself. I really like Sam and he seems to really like me. Why? I can't begin to imagine. I have not been a very likable person. He reminds me of the kind of person I used to think about knowing, but never met. Maybe this old guy is like the father I would have liked to have grown up with. Get Serious Anne, he's nothing like what my father would have been. That's just a hole in my upbringing that can never be filled. I believe Sam's just a kind old man who, I guess, sees the fraud I am. What do I have to lose? I have to talk to somebody. I need some kind of advice and Sam's volunteering.*

"I guess it depends on how you define killing," began Anne. "I live in a world where material gain is everything. Nothing, nothing is more important than achieving that goal. In my world, one soon learns that nothing is sacred if it prevents the achievement of that goal ...nothing Sam. The only reason we generally don't commit murder is that the penalty is too severe if we get caught, or at the very least, too expensive and time consuming to defend, let alone embarrassing. Frankly Sam, I've been amazed how little it costs to manipulate and purchase most people. The politicians are the easiest. They're commodities. They merely require that we bid for their services.

My specialty Sam has been creating conditions at little cost to my company to achieve gains. I'm a star in that arena, a rare talent. I have an aptitude for understanding the soft bellies of the human psyche. I create situations, illusions, misapprehensions, that make people do things they probably don't really want to do. They rarely are aware of the actual implications for themselves, nor what they are doing to others. They focus almost entirely on their financial gain. They are voluntarily blinded, and they rationalize the risk. But, and this is the big, but, their actions, the ones I script for them, create rich material gain for me, and for my company. That's all that's bothering me Sam, just that little item." Anne took a deep breath and declared, "I don't seem to like me, and I've come to the realization that I don't want to do this anymore."

Sam sipped his coffee and said, "Would you like a Danish? They're fresh - strawberry or cheese?"

Anne was not quite sure how to respond. She had just unloaded her dirty wash for the first time she could recall and he was asking her about dessert. She just stared at Sam. She didn't know whether to be bewildered, embarrassed, or mad.

Sam looked at her and gently said, "After all that, you need something sweet - strawberry or cheese?"

Anne finally uttered, "Strawberry."

Sam asked the nearest counterman to bring over two strawberry Danishes. They sat in silence as the Danishes were delivered.

Eventually, Sam spoke, "There once was a man who lived in a forest. He made his living from firm old trees that he would cut down and turn into good wood planks and beams. He would only sell his wood to people who would, hands on, physically build their own homes. He would never sell to contractors or builders, as we would refer to them today - no exceptions. He charged very reasonable prices.

He was asked many times, "Why do you limit your sales only to people who build their own homes?" They suggested, "You could be very rich if you would sell to anybody who needed good strong wood."

He would always answer the same, "Balance." He would smile and say nothing else. Eventually, a great storm came along and lightning struck the forest causing a great fire that burned many trees before it had ended. People immediately assumed the man had lost his supply of trees and his business was gone. But to their surprise, the next family wanting to build a house that would be their home was visited by the man with an offer to supply the wood they required.

'We thought your business was finished because of the forest fire. How is it you survived?' the Father asked.

"Balance."

The Father asked pointedly, "Whatever do you mean when you say Balance?"

One of the younger children, a little girl spoke, "I know what he means, Daddy."

"You do?" responded her Father.

She smiled at the man and he smiled back, "Your child is very wise. You're a lucky man." Then he left.

Anne looked at Sam and smiled softly, "That could have meant many things, Sam."

Sam leaned over and placed his hands gently on Anne's hands, "I'm quite fond of you Anne."

CHAPTER 46 A FRIENDLY CHAT

Jersey decided it was time to have his 'one on one' conversation with Jim. Gale. He now knew things that might change, or influence Jim Gale's behavior. At least mitigate some of that arrogance and possibly more. Maybe, if the idea he had in mind worked, it would be enough to keep him off his ass. If he did it right - his best performance ever - he just might solve his most pressing problem. The pressure of the potential situation, and dark thoughts that haunted him, had convinced him he had to try.

Jersey made his call and after an initial refusal and some hard selling on his part Gale reluctantly accepted the invitation. Jersey had found out that Jim Gale loved expensive cigars, thus at Jersey's suggestion they arranged to meet at an uptown Cigar Bar.

The Cuban Island Gold Club was perfect. He'd never been there, but had heard it was one of the ultimate New York spots for cigar aficionados. He found out a $1000 fee would immediately make you a member in good standing. He was banking on the notion that Gale would be tempted to meet just to experience the Club. *The $1000 gamble is worth a shot,* he convinced himself.

Jersey arrived quite early and introduced himself to the staff and requested that they give him a quiet spot for his meeting with a guest that would be arriving in approximately two hours. Further, he requested no disruptions of any kind or greetings to him as a new member - just the normal service as quiet and discrete as possible. To make sure things went well and keep the manager happy he gave him a $100 tip. Jersey spent the next hour familiarizing himself with the Club, visiting the humidor rooms – there were three such humidor rooms. Further, he visited the lushly stocked bar, the wine cellar, and the men's room.

The Cuban Island Gold Club had a collection of rich, dark wood panel walls topped with narrow stained glass windows, softly lit paintings of pre-Castro Cuba, an unbelievable array of sipping liquors, and just about any good cigar you could want, including rare old Cuban's available at outrageous prices. It amazed Jersey that cigars if properly stored, could last for decades. He was seated in a corner of the room in an overstuffed wingback chair next to a French Rocco coffee table. Next to that, at a comfortable angle for chatting and enjoying the adornments of the Club, another similar overstuffed wingback chair.

Gale arrived as the day was ending. The sun's last rays were striking the stained glass windows casting colored highlights randomly throughout the room. The staff greeted him and brought him over to Jersey.

158

They shook hands and Gale sat down. "Well, Jersey, I'm here. Whatever do you want?"

"Relax, Jim, we are in a very nice place. Let's enjoy it a bit and then we'll talk, if that's all right with you," requested Jersey. "There's nothing but the best available in this Club. Participate, old friend."

"We're not old friends, were adversaries," barked Jim.

"True, but the cigars and whiskey will taste just as good," replied Jersey. With that, he signaled to the staff for service.

A small handsome, impeccably dressed gentleman with a Latin accent came over to them along with a lovely young woman wearing a very revealing black sequined dress. She was carrying a large tray filled with an array of different cigars.

The gentleman proceeded to ask, "Were there any particular cigars you wished to have or would you care to hear some suggestions concerning our newest arrivals". After a few minutes of conversation and descriptions, choices were made. The gentleman went on to suggest the appropriate sipping whiskeys for their choices. They both chose Aniversarios Rum from South America, and in few minutes the rum, cigars, and cigar tools arrived. Soon the first puffs and sips commenced.

"Adversaries, what a nice word, Jim; we really are dedicated enemies," said Jersey leaning back as he blew some smoke almost straight up towards the ceiling. "But we share some common interest in preserving value. Don't you agree?"

Gale begrudgingly nodded yes.

"Now you seem to be using this unfortunate event to improve your position. And I suppose, if I were you, I would probably do the same," Jersey went on, "But, upon quiet reflection, you know that stepping back and carefully, unemotionally considering everything, I would, from my experience in life and business try to take a longer view and consider all other possible implications. What one might call it ... ahhh 'unintended consequences' I believe".

Jim Gale, squinting a bit, after enjoying a sip of the incredible rum they had chosen and a satisfying puff of his delicious cigar said, "Just what are you getting at?"

"Oh, nothing specific, but there are a myriad of possibilities," replied Jersey, as he rubbed his lip with his forefinger. "We are human creatures with all sorts of tastes in our makeup. One person loves oysters, another detests them. Some like Russian novels, others are bored by them. Haven't you noticed that human beings have a spectrum of tastes that they present to all, but have a narrower set of tastes they present to a few, and still a narrower set, only to themselves?" He deliberately stopped at that point and signaled for the waiter and ordered some mineral water. Then he turned to Gale, studying him carefully, looking for signs of discomfort and/or tension, "Don't you agree?"

Gale casually nodded in agreement, "So what?"

159

"As the pressure builds up adversaries will seek more granular information about their enemies. They do this in order to manipulate an adversary as well as for defending themselves. You must admit, this is a nasty little mess we are all involved in, lots of adversaries, lots of enemies. You and I are members of the group. We are both enemies and, using your word, adversaries. ACS is not going to be easy. In fact, they might be the most difficult. They will be extremely granular in their pursuit of information," suggested Jersey.

"What do you mean by granular?" asked a slightly uncomfortable Gale.

"Oh, granular, what do I mean by granular?" Jersey said with a deliberate chuckle. "That I guess is my term for those little obscure details of stuff. The more granular, one could say, the more intimate, and of course ...the lessor known. This is the kind of stuff that defines companies, partnerships, relationships, or, of course ... and particularly, individuals. You know what I mean? Now you take our situation, you and your people are looking for those 'granulars' to use in order to improve your position. We're doing the same." Jersey took another puff of his cigar and smiling asked again pejoratively, "You know what I mean?"

Gale didn't respond.

Jersey thought his silence was a good sign and he smiled and took another puff and sip. Jersey continued, "We're hunters in this game. We also hire folks to help us find these 'granulars' hoping they will get something that will help our cause; something that will make a difference. You know what I mean, Jim. But, that is not what I called you here for"

A slightly surprised Gale asked, "What did you call me here for? Certainly it wasn't for cigars and fine whiskies."

"You're wrong Jim, that's exactly what I called you here for. In this bastion of luxury and pleasure, I wanted to remind you how good you have it. How sweet your life is and can be, that is, if you don't push too far in our current conflict. I know, you damn well know I had nothing to do with the 'Torpedo' software problem. Sure I was, and still am, a pissed off unit over losing my position, but I remain a very substantial stockholder. The success of the Company is of prime importance to me and my future. I'll admit I was a damn fool not seeing where ACS was taking the deal and screwing me. I'll get over it, but that is if I'm not pushed too far ... unreasonably. Jim, I'm sure you now understand what I mean."

Then with a sigh and a smile, Jersey got up, excused himself, and went to the men's room, entered a stall, took off his suit jacket, took off his tie, and proceeded to throw up. The cigar he had been smoking was the first cigar he had ever smoked in his life. When he returned Jim Gale was nowhere to be found, apparently he had left. *Just as well*, thought Jersey, *our business was finished.*

CHAPTER 47 BUSINESS ON THE STREET

Anne Mills entered her office with a coffee in one hand and a confidential memo in the other. It was in a sealed envelope which was unusual for ACS. She decided to drink her coffee first. A moment of peace before the Memo had a shot at ruining her day. It reminded her of letters that would come from her Mother when she was in College. They were, almost without exception, unpleasant as she knew they would be without even opening the envelope. At times, she would purposely not open them, sometimes for days, to avoid the pain. They were filled with advice as to what to wear and what not to wear, who to befriend, who not to socialize with, complaints about where the Country was going, a constant harangue about the "decay" of Millsport and its community values. But the most painful of all was her disappointment in Anne's development and her social failures. "Why aren't you dating? Why didn't you pledge a sorority? Why aren't you going to the Junior League dance?" and on and on.

She thought to herself, one *of us got the wrong relation, Mother.*

With the coffee finished she opened the envelope and read the Memo. The contents were ....

Dear Ms. Mills,

We have carefully considered the events that have led to the present situation concerning the Pristinimatic/Photo Symbology Merger and have concluded the following:

1. You were given the responsibility to form and execute a plan to achieve the Merger.

2. Management believes you created and executed a plan without, as required, informing management of the details. The resulting plan was not consistent with the values, ethics, or traditions of Ashton, Cooper and Smith.

3. In particular you have exceeded ethical standards that are, and have been, the watchword of this firm since its formation. Further, you might have approached, or possibly exceeded legal boundaries which would make this a criminal event.

4. Your conduct in this matter is completely unacceptable to this firm.

5. Therefore, we are, as of this date, terminating your relationship as an employee of ACS, and as a consultant to any of our subsidiaries.

6. Further, under the circumstances concerning your actions in this matter, ACS will not compensate you for any aspects of the Merger, and demand you return the partial success fees you have already received. This is to done immediately.

Signed,
Ibrahim Sahid, Chairman
Joseph Taglaferri, CEO

Anne threw her empty coffee cup across the room and it smashed into a spray of little shapes and pieces. *You sons of bitches, you're throwing me to the dogs, you bastards!* She thought. At that, she stormed out of her office and walked right past the executive receptionist and barged into Sahid's office. Taglaferri was with him sitting on the couch smoking his morning cigar.

She glared at them! They glared at her, but with an edge of anger. Ibrahim began by, uncharacteristically raising his voice, "How dare you .. "

Anne ignored him and cut him off with an even louder voice, "Do you think you are really going to pull off that pack of lies you put in that Memo and throw me to the dogs? I've been here for a number of years engineering your various plots with great success, and now that some unanticipated problem has arisen, you are making me the sacrificial lamb. No damn way is this going to happen," all this, at the top of her voice.

This was a first. They had never seen or heard this kind of behavior from Anne before.

Joe quickly stepped forward and raising his palms, calmly asked Anne to be quiet for a moment. She stopped. "Anne, this is no place to have this discussion. Please, let you, me, and Ibrahim leave the office this moment. We will go downstairs and take a table in the Atrium and discuss the situation ... calmly."

She gave in, actually embarrassed at her loss of control, and nodded in agreement. They immediately left for the elevators. Nobody said anything. An elevator door opened and the three of them entered. They were alone and the tension was unbearable. The elevator quickly descended and they walked out into the crowded lobby towards the entrance to the Atrium. As they were about halfway there, a woman carrying a large pocketbook and sporting a climber's vest looked straight at Ibrahim and said something to him. The next thing Anne would remember was a burst of bright color and an enormous pressure. Sometime later she woke up and could see nothing.

About an hour later Judge Smith was convening the morning meeting in the Queens Motel when the ACS legal representative, Dell Patterson asked the Judge to make an announcement. His demeanor was quite noticeably tense.

Dell Paterson spoke, "As you might have noticed, the ACS team is not present, only me." The news I have is quite incomplete and I'm not sure of my facts, but this is what I've been told. Apparently, there was some kind of incident in the lobby of the Broadway headquarters of ACS. It was an explosion of some kind that killed and injured some people. According to what my people have learned it somehow involved the Chairman and CEO of ACS, and for some undetermined reason, Anne Mills. According to the text I was just reading all three of them were killed."

Now there followed a wave of shock. Most of the attendees started looking at their phones for more information. Judge Smith looked at the group and said, "That's god awful. I believe under the circumstances, I must suspend the meeting for today."

A shaken group quickly left the premises.

No one was more upset than Garrett Carlssen. *My god,* he thought, *this nightmare gets worse.* He drove back to his Manhattan apartment listening to scattered reports on the radio which were filled with unanswered questions and conflicting suppositions. An overall sense of loss and pain overcame him. *Anne is gone, just like that, Anne is gone.*

CHAPTER 48   THE PHONE RINGS AND RINGS

A very upset Garrett had been home trying to rationalize the morning happenings while surfing the TV channels for updated information.

Then the phone rang ...

"Hello," Garrett picked up the wireless home phone.

"Hi Garrett," said a familiar voice, "I've been watching CNN and saw what happened on Wall St. this morning. Some of the ACS people we were working with for the Merger, apparently were killed in a terrorist bombing. That woman who was managing the deal for ACS was one of the victims according to the reports. What's going on?"

"Jesus Christ! Is that you Brian?" asked an incredulous Garrett. *Boy, when the wheels come off, they really come off*, he thought to himself.

"Of course," replied Brian.

"Where the hell have you been?" demanded Garrett.

"I went to Easter Island, and I'm still in Easter Island, Chile."

"What in hell are you doing in Easter Island?" asked an exasperated Brian.

"It's quite simple, when everything went to pieces I decided to drop everything and get away completely, far away from everything. Obviously that is no longer possible with things like CNN. I needed to try and put my head back together. Chile was far away and it seemed like a very good idea, Easter Island is even further away. You probably don't know this, but I have always been a mountain bike rider and that's what I've been doing in Easter Island ... riding my bike and thinking."

"Do you have any idea of what's been going on up here with the Merger?" asked Garrett.

"No, but I imagine they're pretty pissed off at me for leaving,"

"Pissed off is a kind way to express it, they think you are a master criminal out to take revenge," continued Garrett.

"Jesus, Garrett, I'm not that valuable," declared Brian. "What's the 'master criminal' stuff about?"

"I'll explain what's going on," suggested Garrett. "Brian make sure you're sitting down. Garrett devoted the next quarter of an hour laying out what had occurred over the past days and the common perception of Brian's guilt in the affair.

"My god, that's all bullshit. I never touched 'Torpedo,'" protested Brian.

"Can you prove it?"

"I think I can do even better than that."

"What are you talking about?" demanded Garrett.

Brian paused ..., "I'm coming home as soon as possible. I'll let you know."

"Brian, I know this will sound pretty crazy to you, but no emails, no texting, just call me as quickly as possible. Don't fly into New York. Jim Gale has probably got people watching for you at those airports. Let me see ... fly into Montreal. Let me know when by phone. Say nothing about where, but only the date and time. I'll figure out the rest. I'll come and pick you up. Are you really sure you can prove your innocence?" asked Garrett.

"Yes," replied Brian.

"Don't tell me how until you see me," ordered Garrett.

"This all sounds like a bad movie."

"Worse, much worse," replied Garrett. "Ciao!" The Brian phone went silent.

Then the phone rang again ...

A horse voice spoke quietly, "Garrett, this is Anne."

"Anne ...?" Garrett stopped and took a breath and then another very deep breath slowly expelling a precious breath of renewal. "Is that really you? Are you all right?" He paused again enduring the crazy array of emotions bombarding him. It all felt surreal. "The TV said you were killed in a terrorist attack."

"No, I wasn't killed, obviously," whispered Anne. "I need to talk to someone, a friendly voice. This is horrible. Would you mind coming over?"

"Where are you?" asked Garrett. "I'll come right over to wherever you are."

"Lenox Hill Hospital," replied Anne. "I'm surrounded by police. Be patient, they're going to give you a hard time."

"Anne, I can't tell you how incredibly glad I am that you're alive and all right," said Garrett. "I'll see you soon." He put the phone back in the cradle.

He thought to himself, *how, in God's name, do you rationalize a day like this?"*

Bob Roberts was discussing the reorganization of the Company with every senior person he could pull in. His cell phone began playing the beginning of a Bach fugue – his phone "bell." He thought he had turned it off. As the tune unwound, it occurred to him that a fugue, with its interweaving themes, was quite appropriate for all those events that had unfolded in the past week and a half. He saw it was Jim Gale and hit the answer button, "Hello Jim."

"Hello Bob," spoke an obviously tense Jim Gale.

"What can I do for you?" Bob asked coldly, not that he ever was very warm to anybody. It seemed at times that everybody, without exception, was an annoyance to Bob Roberts.

Jim began, "Frankly, considering all that has happened, I think it would be appropriate for you and me to meet and review the situation. Where do we go from here? Is there any reason to change our positions? Has this changed anything or everything? Frankly, I don't know. Too much has happened too quickly. I know you fired Anne Mills and that bitch was killed."

166

Bob Roberts, immediately interjected, "You're wrong! Anne survived. Haven't you been watching the news this morning?"

"You're kidding! She survived?" Jim blurted out. "How the hell did she manage that?"

"Apparently both Ibrahim and Joe were in front of her. They acted as walls of armor, a bomb shelter for her. She was amazingly lucky," he commented. "I'm in the middle of a meeting and can't talk now. I'll call you on your cell in about two hours," informed Bob Roberts and hung up.

The ACS meeting lasted a few hours more than Bob Roberts expected. Some of the staff that had been through similar events before, were quite apprehensive. To his surprise the newer staff, those that had not had such experiences were much calmer. *Ahh*, he thought to himself, *ignorance is indeed bliss*. Finally, Bob Roberts was able to calm and reorganize the emergency management structure. Roberts was only acting as the temporary head of the Company. He had been authorized by the Board of Directors to take charge. They knew he knew the Company inside and out and was quite capable of temporarily running and reorganizing whatever matters had to be dealt with under such an agonizing environment. They didn't like him and he didn't like them, but under the circumstances that was irrelevant. They knew they were lucky to have him for such a crisis. Eventually, he dismissed everybody but their top legal representative, Levi Goldbart, and the analyst Alan DeSocio.

He began, "It would appear that Ibrahim was the target of the assassination. Also, we can assume that Joe and Anne were in the wrong place at the wrong time. I can only presume at this time that the bombing had nothing to do with the firm, and, therefore, act on that assumption only. Life will be quite complex around here for some time. But ...but we have business before us that can't wait. There is too much at stake. Obviously, one of the most important matters I'm referring to is the recent Merger. There are some other matters, but they are quite under control. First, I think Ibrahim and Joe acted hastily when they fired Anne. Was that your advice, Levi?"

"Hell no!" abruptly answered Levi.

"Ohhhh," hissed Bob Roberts. "Then why did they do it? Anne's now a victim, and I must assume an ACS enemy. Frankly, I never particularly liked her, but she's very smart and quite ruthless."

Levi, rubbing his nose, looked over his reading glasses, and commented, "Bob, I never noticed anybody that you have ever liked in particular. I agree she is very smart and I'll take your word about the ruthless part."

Ignoring Levi, Bob Roberts went on, "Anne Mills knows all the details of all the mechanisms we used to accomplish our goals with the Pristinimatic/Photo Symbology deal and many other deals going back seven years plus."

Levi interrupted again, "Mechanisms? What exactly do you mean by mechanisms?"

"Later," Bob said, overriding Levi's question. "I don't believe we can ignore her but, we've got to do something to neutralize her. I've been thinking about it and …"

Levi interrupted once again, "Whoa, what kind of 'mechanisms' did you use in this deal? I'm here, as you damn well know, to protect this firm and you're referring to something that I don't know about. And I'm beginning to assume you don't really want to talk about it. It sounds to me like you've crossed some kind of line that you shouldn't have. Am I getting this correctly? Eliminate any bullshit. What in hell is going on?"

There was silence in the room. DeSocio and Bob Roberts looked at each other. DeSocio rubbing the back of his neck, "Tell him already."

The next 15 minutes or so was devoted to explaining to Levi what "mechanisms" were used in making the Merger happen. This was followed by a penetrating cross-examination and diligent note taking by Levi Goldbart. By the end of the exercise, Levi knew just about everything. "Well, you guys have broken all kinds of ethical precedents, but that's standard operating procedure for the street, however the shit you pulled with the Pristinimatic engineer and the stock manipulation, that's another matter. It goes beyond SEC rules and could be considered criminal by the government and the local DA. Got it guys, criminal! But that's subject to the SEC, a DA's judgment, and then a court. But there are civil matters that could fry your collective asses and the firm's treasury. First, the Pristinimatic guys could own you and the firm, for the crap you pulled – it was an illegal conspiracy – plain and simple. Jesus!" shaking his head.

"Next, one of your conspirators, this Anne Mills gets thrown out of the firm, and I'm assuming she's to be the 'patsy.' One must assume that she will turn state evidence to save her ass. Then she turns around and sues you guys for breach of contract and a dozen other things. If I were her lawyer, I would advise her to sue your individual and collective asses off. That leads me to the question, why would Ibrahim and Joe fire her without consulting legal? What was the rush? Ibrahim has always been so careful and deliberate."

"We don't really know," answered Bob Roberts. "Ibrahim never was comfortable with Anne. There were always sparks. It might have something to do with his background. He grew up in the Middle East. Powerful and smart women are not generally accepted in that culture. On the other hand, he attended a private school in England as a teenager and graduated from the University of Pennsylvania and the Wharton School for his MBA with further graduate work at the London School of Economics. He became a citizen of the US ten/fifteen years ago and did a three year stint in the US military - the Army. Nobody else around here seems to have any idea of why they fired her, and further, why so quickly."

Levi then asked, "How long has Anne been associated with the firm?"

"Almost eight years," responded Alan DeSocio.

"Well," asked Bob Roberts, "What should we do?"

"Right now," answered Levi, "I don't know, but I want to discuss this with one of my partners who are very creative in these situations ...the hopeless ones ... .and I'll get back to you tomorrow. In the meantime do nothing. Share this with no one

CHAPTER 49 A VISIT

It had been two days since the explosion and Garrett was finally able to convince the officials to let him visit Anne. She was a mess. She had one eye almost swollen shut and contusions all over her face and arms. Under the hospital gown and bed sheets the rest of her body had the same black and blue marks and cuts. Her hair had the messy look that hospital patient's usually only exhibit after a procedure such as an operation. Patients in this condition, obviously, don't feel good enough to care about their appearance. Garrett wondered, *what was the level of her physical pain? I guess the contusions were everywhere? Was anything broken?*

"Hi Anne," spoke Garrett to a resting Anne with her one good eye closed. The other injured eye was distracting. She turned her head, opened the good eye, and focused on Garrett.

She sort of smiled. "Thanks for coming."

"You knew I would come. Do you want to talk about it?"

Anne was quiet for a bit and finally said, "I have to, whether I want to or not."

"Why?"

"I don't know if I'm ready to tell you all the reasons why, but take my word, I have to tell you some of the reasons, at the very least, for my sanity and for legal purposes. You and I still have to figure out what happened to the Merger. That hasn't gone away and the bombing hasn't changed that one little bit. There's more, but that can wait."

"Before you go on, Anne, how's your physical condition? Are you all right? Is anything broken?" asked a very concerned Garrett.

"I know I look terrible, and I've got the cuts and bruises that you can see on my face and arms. It's the same all over my body, but no bones are broken, and they told me this morning that they think there are no internal injuries. My doctor tells me I'm going to be fine physically, but it will take a few weeks. He wants me to see a shrink because of the traumatic issues. We'll see about that. I got used to mental abuse from my family many years ago and I'm pretty strong in that department."

"My god Anne, you almost got killed in some kind of deliberate incident, a little loving mental care might be a good idea," suggested Garrett.

"We'll see," replied Anne. "It's too early to decide anything and there's work to be done. What you don't know and nobody else knows, I think, and I need your absolute assurance that what I'm about to tell you will go no further." She looked straight at him, "Well?"

"Absolutely."

170

"The morning of the explosion, I was fired."

"You've got to be kidding?"

"Absolutely not!" replied Anne. "The bastards fired me."

"Then why is there work to be done?"

"Think about it, nothing has really changed," Anne went on, "Whether I'm employed by them or not, I'm still part of the Merger. I was the principal manager of the transaction and I can't walk away from that reality nor can ACS. Ibrahim and Joe were probably trying to make me the patsy, but they cannot be separated from this deal with clean hands. And under the new circumstances, instead of protecting my Company, my former Company that is, I've got to protect myself."

Garrett raised his hands abruptly to stop Anne talking and put his forefinger to his lips. "Shhhhh." She stopped and tilted her head on the pillow with an expression of curiosity and surprise. Garrett began, "Have you watched TV or read a newspaper?"

"God no," she answered with impatience.

Garrett continued, "I'm not quite sure how to tell you this, but here goes. Both Ibrahim and Joe were killed."

"Oh my god!" said a startled Anne. "I didn't know. Nobody told me. Give me a few minutes."

She remained quiet. Finally, she asked Garrett for a glass of water. Then, she asked Garrett to bring her up to date, which he did for the most part. Then they both remained silent for a long time.

It was her turn. She related all the events of the morning that led to the explosion. "They would have never been in the lobby if I weren't so overwrought. I literally was screaming my head off, I was so angry. They wanted me out of the office as quickly as they could manage it and suggested we go down to the Atrium to talk things over. I agreed ...and they died."

"So did you almost die," interrupted Garrett.

"I guess, one of those crazy accidents we call fate," continued Anne. "Everything in my world seems to be coming apart. I can't make any sense out of it. You said it was a very small bomb, not the usual terrorist thing. What do you think the woman had in mind? Oh, that's silly. Who knows what she had in mind."

"At this point Anne, there is no theory, that I'm aware of, that explains what and who was the reason for the attack."

Neither one of them spoke for a few minutes. Then Anne said, "I saw the woman quite well. She was only a few feet from me. From the expression on her face, I'm sure she knew Ibrahim and I'm sure he knew her. She said something to him several times before the explosion. I heard it clearly, but I couldn't understand it. It sounded something like 'catar', whatever that means. I guess it was Arabic. '"

"Are you sure?"

"Yes, my impression goes further. She was angry and surprised when she saw him. In fact, I would say I had the impression that she was outraged," said Anne.

"Are you saying this was personal?"

"Look, I know body english and I know the facial expressions. I've made my living being good at this. Whatever was going on between those two, and I'm sure they knew each other, she was hostile and somehow it involved Ibrahim. Ibrahim said something back to her in Arabic. I couldn't understand or remember it. I don't know that she meant to kill him, but evidentially she meant to kill somebody, maybe herself," explained Anne, "but I'm sure about that word she kept repeating – 'catar.'

"She didn't die until this morning," informed Garrett.

"What?"

"She actually survived the bomb blast but as you might expect she was not in very good shape. She's in this same hospital and was in a coma, with all kinds of complications," said Garrett. "She died early this morning. By the way, no one organization has claimed responsibility so far. If she had lived, we might have found out what this really was all about."

"I'm sure it has something to do with that word 'catar'" suggested Anne. "Do you have any more surprises for me?" asked an exasperated Anne.

"I don't think so, but I'm not guaranteeing it."

"Where do I go from here?"

"You focus on recovery and I'm available to help wherever, I can."

They looked at each other and no one spoke. Garrett went over to Anne and gently put his hand on her cheek. Then he went to the window and looked out at the cluster of buildings that were so characteristic of New York City. It occurred to him that so many people living and working so closely together, created an unimaginable volume of human dramas. Farmers definitely had it simpler. Without looking at her, Garrett spoke slowly and softly, "I love you Anne."

Anne took a deep breath, "Don't go there, please. We're impossible for so many reasons. You said you would be my friend. I need your friendship now for this terrible moment. Please leave it at that."

Garrett said nothing more, "I've got to go now. I'll come back tomorrow. If you need me, my phone will be on, day or night."

Anne called out, "Please do me a favor, there's a Deli man in my neighborhood who's my best friend. His name is Sam Axinov. I want him to know I'm all right, please. Tell Sam I will come to the deli as soon as I can for the best breakfast and nicest person to visit within this entire city. Garrett, I will be adding you to that list."

Garrett nodded yes, "Sure I'll be glad to do that." Then he wrinkled his brow, "Your best friend is a deli man? I assume by his name he is not a friend of your Mother's?"

172

She sheepishly nodded yes, and told him the name and address of the deli which he recorded in his phone.

"I'll be damned," and then he left.

CHAPTER 50 AN IMPORTANT MEETING

The group that had been meeting in Queens got together as usual, but they made no progress. In the meantime, Jim Gale called his people together for what he was describing as an important meeting. Although he was outraged at what Jersey had done at the Cigar Club meeting, he was still determined to take advantage of the situation but, and he had to admit to himself, it had changed his plans a bit. He wasn't sure of what Jersey had learned about him. He also had to admit to himself that Jersey's never bringing up any kind of direct or remote concrete fact, but just the most distant hints – what did he call them – "granulars" - was extremely clever along with reminding him of the good life he now enjoyed. Jim was left to imagine the worst.

Jim Gale, Del Patterson - the Company lawyer - and his assistant, along with some of his senior staff were in the conference room.

He began, "I've spent much time over the past few days considering what should be done about our grievous problem. There is no doubt we have been the victim of a Pristinimatic generated scheme and we must be compensated. But we must accomplish this with a minimum of disturbance to the Company's future. There is no longer any doubt that we will be announcing our problem to the public by the beginning of next week. At the same time, we will announce a recovery program which is being put together by engineering as we meet. They tell me that we should be past our worst within the next quarter, if not completely recovered. They have been able to find data in the Pristinimatic desk and laptop computers that parallel pieces of the main system that they believe will provide great help, therefore, saving us much time and effort."

At this point one of the senior managers asked, "How is that recovery team doing that we hired? They won't talk to anybody but you."

An annoyed Jim Gale continued, "They're doing what I told them to do. They have made some progress, but we have to assume the worst. We must act on the premise that they will not be successful.

Now let me return to what I was speaking about: We shall manage the near future of this Company with the goal of achieving our deserved increased compensation. This Merger took place based on the theory that there was great value in putting the two companies together. There were management problems on the Pristinimatic side, but they are gone. The one hole that has to be filled is the role of the Chief Technical Officer, the missing Mr. Brian Goldberg. We are not completely aware of why he did it, but it appears it was revenge. He created the crisis, as a result of personal problems that arose

174

between the Pristinimatic CEO and COO. Fortunately those two are gone, but they must pay. This Goldberg has disappeared into thin air. But having said that, I believe a quiet and orderly settlement is in the best interests of our Company going forward. We do not want to get involved in a protracted legal fight. In the end that will cost too much money and will hurt our market image that can spill out in many different directions, all of them negative. Therefore, Del, his team, and I have decided to proceed as follows:

We will request that both the CEO, Jersey Smart, and the COO, Garrett Carlssen, give back to the Merger one half each of their equity shares in the Merger, and forego any further peripheral compensation such as medical insurance, etc.

They will agree to never work in our industry, and/or its related fields for the rest of their lives.

With their equity shares being reduced collectively to less than 5% of the Merger's outstanding capitalization they will agree, by contract, to be "silent stockholders"

In return, we will grant them a clean separation and release agreement."

"That's pretty generous in my opinion," said an outspoken senior manager.

"I agree," Said Jim Gale, "But we have to consider the Company's future and suppress our anger. The reason we exist is ultimately to make money for our stockholders, not satisfy our anger. This path is prudent in my opinion, and, therefore, serves the Company's interest best."

"They should be prosecuted," somebody in the group muttered.

"The most egregious villain in the bunch is Goldberg," pronounced Jim Gale. "We have an interesting possibility regarding Mr. Goldberg. It seems in the New York Courts there was a civil case similar to ours – something called Willis vs. Caldor Enterprises – that allowed the plaintiff to recover the defendant's entire equity position based on the harm to the corporation that had been maliciously committed. In this case the defendant, like Mr. Goldberg, had vanished. It will take time, but we will pursue the same path. Since he's gone, there's nothing else we can do."

Jim Gale paused and looked over the group for any reaction. There was nothing unusual to note.

"Meeting over," pronounced Jim.

Everybody left except the lawyers. Del Patterson spoke, "You made that sound like a walk in the woods, Jim. They aren't going to fold that easily. Levin will represent them. He's no longer our legal counsel so he's free to represent them. I would expect, after a lot of squabbling, there will be some kind symbolic agreement, but nowhere close to what you indicated. We have absolutely no evidence that they did anything wrong."

"We're paying you a lot of money for your services. Find something they did wrong or I get another firm to provide the services I want," barked Jim Gale.

"Well, I'll think about it. But you might just have to get another firm," responded Del Patterson angrily. "I, nor my firm, are going to create evidence. You think about that." He and his assistant got up and left.

Patterson looked at his assistant as they were exiting the building, "Do you believe that shit? He wants us to commit a crime or he will get somebody else to commit it for him. Not me, Ms. Heding, and not our firm. We can be sons-of-bitches when we have to, but never crooked sons-of-bitches."

The next day Jim Gale hired new counsel.

CHAPTER 51 COFFEE AND DANISH

Garrett found Sam's Deli and spotted Sam. It was easy. Sam was the boss, and one of those folks who are quite approachable. *What is it about people that they somehow emit those kinds of signals?* Garrett wondered. Garrett had, for some reason, been reticent about approaching Sam Axinov before he saw Sam. It had something to do with his feelings for Anne and what he might stir up in Sam. Sam was Anne's best friend according to Anne. It occurred to him, *I wonder if he knows anything about me. If Anne, indeed, had ever mentioned me to Sam - was I a good guy or a bad guy?*

"Are you Sam Axinov?" asked Garrett.

"Yes, I am for sure, Sam Axinov. What kind of trouble am I in? Do I owe you money? Ahhh, have I've won the lottery?" Sam laughed warmly, "What can I do for you?"

"My name is Garrett Carlssen and I am a friend of Anne Mills.

"Oh, my god!" declared Sam looking very sad.

"Anne asked me to bring you a message."

"She's OK? Oh, my god - please," responded Sam with obviously great concern.

"Although she was hurt, and was first reported killed, she is all right."

Sam sat down and took a deep breath and said nothing for a minute, "You have no idea how happy I am to hear that. Thank God. What kind of condition is she in?"

Garrett continued, "She suffered many bruises and cuts. Apparently she is covered with them. Fortunately there appears to be nothing serious. She told me to tell you that she will recover - good as new. She also told me to tell you, that as soon as she can, she will come to the deli for the best breakfast in town, and to be with the nicest person in all of New York City. She didn't tell me to give you a kiss, but I think she wanted to."

"That is very, very good news to hear. How nice of her to send that message. Other than the physical, is she all right in the head?" asked a very concerned Sam.

"Yes I think so, but it's complicated," replied Garrett who immediately thought to himself, why *in hell did you say that? You talk too much.*

"Do you drink coffee?" asked Sam

Garrett nodded yes.

"Let's sit down and have some good hot coffee and Danish - the best. Sam led them to a table in the rear of the deli and had coffee and an assortment of Danish brought to the table. "Tell me, who you are."

"That's a long story, Sam. Do you mind if I call you Sam?" asked Garrett politely.

"Of course not, please ... what's your name again, and, again who are you?"

"My name is Garrett Carlssen. I'm a scientist, a technocrat, who with a group of peers founded a technology company called Pristinimatic. Anne, as you probably know, is an investment banker who works for the banking firm, Ashton, Cooper, and Smith - ACS. Anne along with some of her colleagues cooked up a Merger involving our company, or should I say our former company, with our major competitor, a company that was called Photo Symbology. Anne was the manager of this project. As a result of the plans engineered by Anne and her team, the Merger went forward, and ... I ended up getting fired. And also, as a result of all this and some unexpected complications, I got to know Anne. We unexpectedly ended up spending much time together. And finally ..."

Sam raised his hand and gently interrupted, "You've got serious feelings for Anne, correct?"

"Apparently ...yes, I do. I'm totally smitten," confessed Garrett.

"Hmmm, interesting, tell me about you. Where do you come from? A little personal history, please?" requested Sam.

"Why do you want to know?"

Sam answered, "It's simple. I have become very fond of Anne over the past couple of years. She started coming in here for meals and somehow we became friends. We talk. We've come to know each other. I'm her friend, and I think one of her very few friends. I care very much what happens to her."

He had the distinct feeling that if he was ever to make any progress with Anne, Sam Axinov had to be on his side – not against him. Having walked through that door, Garrett, obviously a bit reluctantly, proceeded to tell Sam a short, but complete version of his life. It included his education, career, the history of his failed marriage, bringing up his daughter, his being brought up in Millsport, and his feelings about the Mills family. When he had finished, he was amazed how much he divulged to this stranger.

Sam commented, "That's some story. Who ends up loving who is one of the great mysteries of human beings. Thanks, you told me a lot. You really are in love with Anne. Don't worry, I will never, never repeat any of this."

They spent the better part of an hour discussing all kinds of things that Sam was soliciting ever so gently. It was obvious that he was trying to get the measure of Garrett. Sam also told him a little about his history. As the conversation went on he had a feeling that Sam was some kind of surrogate father for Anne. One thing was clear; he was really very, very fond of Anne and extremely protective. *Amazing,* he thought, *this Jewish deli man from the holocaust has become the Mill's daughter's protector. It's almost as ridiculous as Don Quixote. These tiny, almost invisible, threads that form meaningful connections within our lives are often the best of what we are, and support the best of what we can become. My, my, Garrett,* he thought, *you're becoming quite philosophic. But again,* he thought, *it explains some of the things going on with Anne and me. I really like Sam.*

"Tell me Garrett," asked Sam, "When I asked you about Anne's condition you answered 'all right, but 'complicated.' What means 'complicated'?"

Garrett answered, "First let me explain that, as you know, she was almost killed. But because the two men that were killed were lined up in front of her at the exact moment of the explosion, they were in effect, a wall that protected her. They saved her from the worst of the damage. As fate would have it, had the explosion been detonated a few seconds before, or a few seconds later, the positions of those two men who were directly in front of her would have changed because all three of them were walking together at the same time. Fate is an indifferent bitch."

"What was she doing there with those men?" asked Sam.

"Well Sam, that's one of the complications I was referring to," said Garrett. "I would be breaking a promise that I made to Anne to tell you why she was there with those two. As you probably are aware from the news, they were the CEO and COO of her Company."

"Am I to assume that there was something unusual about the three of them being where they were when the explosion went off," stated Sam. "Am I warm?"

"Yes, let it go at that. Let me just say there was a heated argument going on between them," informed Garrett.

CHAPTER 52 CANADA

There was Brian Goldberg floating down the exit escalator at Montreal International Airport looking very fit and sunburned. Garrett was standing some distance from the escalator as Brian continued to float down to the baggage floor. Garrett had driven up the New York State Thruway the night before and was waiting at the correct time for his arrival. They spotted each other.

"Brian Goldberg, you son-of-bitch, do you have any idea of the trouble you've caused by disappearing. Not available, I mean gone, poof, invisible, and/or non-existent! Even, a damn telephone number would have made one hell of a difference. Jesus, you look great, Brian. Just what in the hell have you really been doing on Easter Island?" finally asked Garrett.

Brian looked at Garrett and shrugged his shoulders, "Riding my bike as I told you, period. Oh, and doing a lot of thinking as I also told you, and nothing else. I had to get away. Too many things went haywire. I screwed up with Yvette. Jersey was somehow mixed up in all this and you know how I feel about him. I really didn't like my new situation. Frankly, it was either accept that or shoot myself or something worse. I decided to do the bicycle thing on Easter Island. It is a place like no other. I really did get away. I managed to clear my head a bit. I've actually returned to some level of sanity."

"Why Easter Island of all places on this earth?" asked a curious Garrett.

"To be perfectly frank, it just popped up in an ad and it seemed like a very good idea at the time, and it was."

They got in Garrett's car and started driving back to New York City. Garrett brought Brian up to date with every detail he could recall with the exception of his feelings for Anne Mills. Then Garrett anxiously asked, "You said you could prove that you did not corrupt 'Torpedo' - how?"

"I have a complete copy of all the 'Torpedo' software - from A to Z - in two separate places that they probably don't know about."

"You do?" responded a surprised Garrett.

"You all probably forgot the details of a step that I took late last year to protect us in case of an emergency. Like any responsible business dependent upon software, we have always had data and software redundancy by backing up everything in a remote protected location. You know one of those services that locate their servers three or four stories underground and won't let anybody enter without all kinds of security checks, etc. The way we were growing I decided we needed more redundancy and security so I added two other similar services. You guys approved it, but paid little attention. I, for security purposes, decided to call it a general expense in the ledger as a line item as opposed to the main backup service expense we normally charge to security expenses. Also, to reduce the profile of these services, I had the Company pay for them yearly rather than monthly. If I remember correctly we're probably only six months into the yearly payment. Sooner or later the Merger guys will discover the 'hidden' backup services and probably cancel them. I'm the only one who has the entry codes to one of the services. I gave the other to you. Remember?" asked Brian with a big smile on his face.

"Oh my god," responded Garrett. "Nobody has asked me for the codes, and frankly I thought whatever had to be transferred to the Merger was transferred. I guess sooner or later they would realize that the extra backup services were operating and ask for the codes. Was it really that hidden?"

Brian went on, "Well, sort of, I went out of my way to hide it from everybody. I don't think anybody in engineering knew the service was operating. I did it as a precaution because of all the recent thievery in our industry. You guys always thought I was overly cautious, but went along with it without really delving into it. It's not very expensive for a Company our size."

"OK, but how do you use it to clear your name?" asked Garrett. "Oh … you switch to one of the backups in a neutral server environment and demonstrate everything works correctly. If you meant to destroy 'Torpedo,' the backup would be corrupted or eliminated. But how do you explain that the regular backup is also corrupted?"

"Simple," answered Brian. "When I left impulsively, I had not taken the time to switch the hidden backup services to the Merger. I really didn't give a damn about anything at that time. For all intents and purposes, they were removed from the system that day. Therefore, we have, or I believe, we have a clean version to demonstrate.

"I'll be damned," remarked Garrett. "How will we know?"

"As soon as I can get to a computer with a decent firewall, I'll enter the backup and test the system. I could have done it in Easter Island, but there was no security possible. After talking to you, you scared the hell out of me and I decided I had to wait. I have a hacker buddy who is properly equipped for the test," informed Brian.

They drove on for a while saying nothing. Finally, Garrett spoke, "I don't know what happened between you and Yvette, but I'll swear on a stack of bibles that Jersey never had anything to do with her. Jersey can be a real prick, but he and your wife, no way. That doesn't add up! I don't know Yvette well, but Jersey Smart could only be revolting to her. I know Jersey with women. He does not have a trace of subtlety, charm, or frankly, smarts in that department. He's crude, insensitive, and incredibly selfish. He has always purchased whatever he wants or needs, one way or another. What in hell made you go over the line?"

"The picture."

"I've heard about that picture, but I've never seen it. What's in it?" asked Garrett.

Brian was quiet for some time before he finally spoke, "It was very sensuous. Yvette seemed to be looking at somebody - it must have been Jersey. What really got to me was the way she was looking at him."

"What special way was she looking at him?" queried Garrett.

"In a way she never had looked at me," commented Brian sadly.

"Oh ...," responded Garrett.

"I just couldn't deal with it. I went haywire. I accused her of betraying me. She never said yea or nay, she just walked out. She took nothing and I've never heard from her since," explained Brian.

"Just like that; no fight, no words, wow," responded Garrett. "And I assume you left for Easter Island after that."

"That's about it," confirmed Brian.

"What are you going to do?"

"I really don't know, but my bike ride helped a lot. I was a total mess when I went down there feeling like shit. But I feel better and I've got to get along with my life. Garrett, you probably know me better than anybody else and you know the crazy family I come from. I've always been screwed up inside. No denying that. Yvette is a very odd person, but I really love her and somehow we found a life together, and it kind of worked. I guess I'm going to try to find her and see if I can repair the damage."

"And if you can't find her ...then what?"

"I don't really know. I haven't got that far. But I will tell you one thing I've made my mind up about. Once this software thing is fixed I will have nothing to do with the Merger. I'm out of there for good. I never could stand Jersey, but hung in there partly because of my relationship with you. There were some good guys on the team and the work was very interesting. But this new crew and Jim Gale are not my cup of tea. I need a better situation and better people to work with every day. I'm no corporate player. I got involved in territory I know nothing about and I don't like it," explained Brian.

"What will you do?"

"I'll offer to consult for a few months and then find something else, but that's absolutely it. I'll leave and find something else." I know I acted like a jerk with Yvette, but I think if the Merger had never occurred, none of my problems with my marriage would have occurred. Maybe that's too strong, and just wishful thinking. Then again, maybe something would have happened, but it would be something I could have possibly worked out. What happened was like a bomb. I admit our relationship was delicate, but it worked in some kind of odd way. We really liked to do the same things. We were never social, as you know, so that was no problem. We never talked about the kind of things married couples should talk about. I wanted a kid, but I never brought it up. I always had the feeling that Yvette was not interested. Can you believe, I never even asked. Frankly, I was afraid," confessed Brian."

"Afraid of what?"

"I'm not sure ...maybe she'd leave me," replied Brian. "What do you think?"

"I think you're in love with Yvette and you think you've got to take a shot to find her and try to work it out. Look, Brian, I know you, maybe not super well, but well enough and I think I've got a picture of Yvette. You're both hurting units who somehow found each other. You made a stupid mistake buying into the Jersey stuff. I'll say it again; I don't believe it ever happened. I'm beginning to believe it was some kind of nasty game that was an ACS plan. They wanted to blow your mind – to really piss you off. Having accomplished that successfully would lead to a conflict in our group, which it certainly did. I believe that you, old buddy, were set up. You became the tool to break up our voting bloc. You went for it hook, line and sinker. It worked. The end result was to provide Jim Gale's group with control. Whether that's true or not, we might never know."

"Getting back to your marriage, try and find Yvette and get down on your knees and ask forgiveness. If she lets you in, both of you have got to open up and be honest with each other. You can't sustain a relationship holding everything in. I watched you two together, and in spite of your problems and hers, I believe she's got feelings for you and she trusted you, something that was, and I'm guessing, very rare in her life. Your accusation, or implication, shattered that trust. I think she's very delicate and was highly dependent upon that trust. Get it. You broke an already delicate glass. I don't know if it broke into a thousand or just a few pieces. Get my metaphor, Brian. If it's just a few pieces, it can probably be fixed; a thousand, no way. I suspect the few pieces theory is true. I think she really needs you, just as much as you need her. That's my best guess, today."

"What am I to make of the picture?" pleaded Brian.

"Hey, software honcho of honcho's, this is the age of Photoshop. Pictures lie, for Christ's sake. A good Photoshop technician could make Joe Stalin look like a pretty girl," reminded Garrett.

"That's true," nodded Brian in agreement. I still have the picture, maybe I should look at it more carefully. My god, what's wrong with me? I know exactly what to look for. Jesus!"

They proceeded along the highway in silence for the next hour. Garrett wiggled a bit in his seat and asked Brian, "How about a cup of coffee?"

Brian answered, "Yes."

They pulled over to the next service area and Brian volunteered to go and get the coffee.

Garrett began to go over some of the things he had said to Brian. He was quite surprised that he had a complete theory about the setup with the picture. It occurred to him that he had never put it all together before. He'd only thought about it in bits and pieces, now suddenly in speaking to Brian, he was conveying a complete concept of the scam, and he was speaking about it as if he had this idea in his head for a while; funny how the human mind works.

Who would do this thing? Who would put a plan together to drive Brian's marriage apart, or maybe they thought just a marriage brawl would result, and that would get the job done. Whatever it was, it was a terrible thing to do. Whoever had done this had to have done a lot of homework. They had to know the personalities. They had to figure out Brian's insecurities; what would make him go bonkers. How'd that picture get under the table in Jersey's office? It was Jersey's damn jelly beans spilling on the floor that caused Brian to go under the table where he found the picture. Then it came to him .. Fuck!

Jersey deliberately knocked those jelly beans over. I didn't actually see him do that, but it makes some kind of crazy sense. Son-of-a-bitch! It was Jersey, who put the picture there. It had to be him. But why would he want to? How would it serve him? He got fired just like me. Keep thinking; keep thinking, but his mind wandered to Millsport and the ease with which stupid, regretful things could occur. Garrett remembered when he was young and did just one of those things – a life-long incident of pain and regret.

Millsport was located in a valley that was formed by a Branch of the Susquehanna River. The river was formidable and wide. It often flooded in the spring, submerging the town in ten to twelve feet of water and those flood waters painted everything in their way with thick brown mud. It was also that same flooding mud that made wonderful vegetable farms along the banks of the river. Therefore, not everybody was unhappy with the floods. It always seemed to Garrett that most of the people treated the floods as a terrible inconvenience, but never as a tragedy. It was just one of those things you put up with if you lived in that part of the Susquehanna Valley. On occasion, somebody drowned, and that was very sad. But, when the waters receded, everybody, expending a great deal of energy, pitched in and cleaned up the mess, and that was mainly what there was to it. It would make the local paper and there would be news reported on the local radio and TV stations about how high the water had gotten and the cleanup problems. It certainly was not reported on national TV in those days. Things were much more local. It was somehow a smaller event than it would be today with the internet and cable.

Garrett, whose family fortunately lived up on a hill overlooking the valley, was not directly affected. Garrett remembered hiking up with friends to the Town Cemetery, which provided an excellent view of the flooded downtown area. It was always a high point if a spring flood occurred. The boys often brought hot dogs and hamburgers for a cookout. The Town Cemetery consisted of a large, extremely beautiful campus. The graves were not tightly crowded like in big city graveyards but generously spaced. It was always a great place to play. All day Capture-The-Flag games, organized by kids, were often held in the Cemetery. They rarely got chased. The only rule was stay far away from funerals. It wasn't that hard because the place was so big, unusually big for the size of the city. There were even a couple of very old mausoleums where the locks had broken or eroded that made terrific hiding places. Yeah, it was a bit scary, but not that scary. As the kids grew older they often drove their cars to park with their girlfriends to "make out" in various out-of-the-way places within the Cemetery. Nobody ever seemed to be "spooked out." It was commonly said that the Town Cemetery was a place that you ended up in as well as a place where you probably began.

He painfully remembered a railroad bridge that ran across the River. It was one of those old rusty girder bridges that were once so common in America when railroads dominated. It had the look that if you just touched it would make you filthy, and it would do just that if you touched it. It had two tracks running across it where dirty engines pulling dirty freight trains once crossed it many times daily. They hauled dirty coal cars to cities and towns that were once populated with houses containing dirty coal bins. The coal bins housed the dirty coal for the furnaces that once heated those houses. It no longer serviced any rail traffic because coal had been replaced by oil. The steam engine was gone, the railroads had changed and had contracted, and coal went elsewhere. The thing he remembered had to do with that abandoned railroad bridge.

The bridge rested on great cement stanchions filled with rust stains that came from exposed girders dripping water from their unpainted surfaces. There were at least six piers crossing that river supporting that bridge as best as he could recall. The bridge ran over an embankment on the Town side of the river and continued over Riverside Street, eventually bending to the west as it met the land. The top of the embankment came very close to the bridge undercarriage. Running under the bridge was an attached pipe that ran the full length of the structure. From the top of the embankment to the first pier was probably a distance of seventy-five yards or so.

Directly under the bridge on the river side of Front Street were the Arches, a plain old fashion Pennsylvania vintage beer joint. It opened in the morning and closed officially at 12:00am complying with the Pennsylvania Blue Laws, but Grady O'Shea, the crusty old bastard that ran the place, kept it going past the Blue Law time limits by making it a private club which any person, eighteen years old or older, could join for a buck. This provided O'Shea with the legal ability to serve any "club member" well beyond midnight under the laws granted to a private club.

The Arch was once somebody's house that had been converted into a beer parlor. It had two floors and a large back balcony that overlooked the river and the underside of the bridge. The balcony was a perfect place to sit, smoke, and drink, and of course talk. Grady had not painted it in years and it had turned into some kind of indescribable peeling gray paint mess. Lined up on one side, were a group of garbage cans, some with and some without, lids. Stacked sloppily on both sides of the building were wooden bottle cases housing the empties. There was often a dog or a cat scavenging for a snack. The Arches catered to a rough crowd at night time, and anytime to old burnt out alcoholics – true "barflies." The place always smelled of sour beer.

For some damn reason that Garrett never knew, and particularly on warm afternoons, some of the Arches' customers, sitting on the Arches' balcony, would be willing to pay teenage boys fifty cents to watch them transport themselves along a pipe that ran from under the bridge to the shore embankment where the pipe and railroad tracks met. The pipe was easily reached at the embankment but from there extended about 75 yards to the first cement stanchion. As the pipe progressed towards the stanchion from the shore the ground quickly fell away. About at the midpoint it was over the water at a good 75 feet or better above the surface. To and from the shore to the stanchion was approximately a hundred and fifty yard haul. The technique that was to be employed was known in Millsport as the "monkey craw." It consisted of hanging by your hands from the pipe and sliding one hand forward at a time, or for the real athletes, moving alternately one hand over the other. If you tired and swung your legs up to the pipe so that you were hanging by both your arms and legs, you were disqualified; consequently no fifty cents. Occasionally there would be "monkey craw" races. The racer with the fastest time would receive half the pot that had been waged by the balcony participants. Not exactly a gentleman's sport, but never-the-less a sport.

Now came the scary part. The Susquehanna River is a very dynamic body of water. Some days it had a lot of water running in it and on other days it would be very low. The "monkey craw" pipe spanned a part of the river that had once been a canal, but had been abandoned three-quarters of a century before. The river with its many moods had filled in the canal with mud and rocks. A 75 foot drop was quite tolerable if there was a lot of water in the river, but very risky when the waters were low. You could never tell, most of the time, where the water would be. The Susquehanna River is a very long body of water, and the local weather was not necessarily an indication of how much water was running in the river at Millsport at any given time.

Garrett was with a kid he knew, Daryl Curchoe. Daryl was a tough kid he had known since first grade. They had had a number of fist fights over the years but somehow, the way kids can do, got past it. Daryl lived in the town flood zone and knew the river better than Garrett. Daryl had taken Garrett to see where the new city storm water runoff pumping station entered the river. They were getting hungry, but between them they only had seven cents. Daryl suggested that they go to the Arches and see if they could make some "monkey craw" money. Garrett had done it a few times, but it really scared him. Daryl claimed it was no big deal and if there were some takers it would be quick money for food. Garrett didn't want to tell Daryl he was scared so he went along with the idea. They arrived at the Arches about a half hour later. Sure enough, the balcony was filled with the usual collection of beer drinkers and particularly the familiar 'barflies' that seemed to be always at the Arches. It was indeed a beautiful June 26th noon by the beautiful Susquehanna River. Garrett thought to himself, *I will remember that date, and I almost never remember any other dates.* Daryl called up to the balcony, "Anybody for a "Monkey Craw" race?

Immediately hanging over the balcony was one Slocum Utz, plastered as usual. He was, as always, attired in dirty clothes and sporting an unshaved face. To complete his presence was his shitty grin highlighted by his missing teeth.

If you got too close to Slocum, you would never forget his aroma. "I'll ask the crew if their interested," replied Slocum. "I, myself, got no extra money for your 'shabangon.'"

Garrett thought to himself, *I never did find out what that word really meant.*

The balcony crew chatted amongst themselves for a few minutes and then Slocum hung out over the balcony rail again. "This is the way it is if you kids will go together – one after the other – make it back and forth inside of six minutes, we'll give you two bucks." He stood straight up, stretched out his arms and waved in each hand a one dollar bill between each thumb and forefinger, laughing like hell. "Well boys, heavy duty money. Are you game or chicken shit?"

Daryl and Garrett looked up at Slocum waving the money and then at each other. Daryl then exclaimed, "Wow! That's enough for lunch, for sure, let's do it."

Garrett couldn't figure a way to get out of it without losing face so he agreed and they started climbing up the embankment. As he got to the top, he could feel his heart racing, but he was committed, scared or not. Daryl didn't hesitate for a moment. He put his hands around the pipe. Garrett did the same immediately behind him. Then Daryl hollered at Slocum, "We're ready, give us the count!"

Slocum, at the top of lungs, counted off One, Two, and Three – GO!

Daryl was faster than Garrett, and Garrett could see him, hand over hand, moving along with his body swinging from side to side. He could hear him grunting with each movement. Garrett was doing the same thing physically but trying not to swing as much. He was convinced the swings increased the danger. On they went as the stanchion got closer and closer, and finally Daryl landed where the pipe first terminated at the top of the cement stanchion. Garrett arrived ten or fifteen seconds later. Taking a few deep breaths they turned around and were on their way back, but Garrett could feel himself tiring. It was harder and harder to hold on. They were now about two thirds back when Garrett began to give in to the idea of scissoring his legs up around the pipe to rest when a bird that had been nesting in one of the lower girders apparently got spooked and took off. The bird somehow hit Daryl, just a little bit, scaring him. He lost his concentration; perhaps just for a moment, but enough to lose his grip and fall. Garrett saw it all very clearly as he was scissoring his legs around the pipe. Hanging from the pipe and looking down, he saw Daryl's body with blood running from his head. He had landed at the water's edge hitting a rock. Daryl Curchoe died that evening. June the 26th would always be there.

Brian returned with the coffee and some junk food. Two hours later they were approaching New York City and Brian had fallen asleep. Garrett woke him up. "Brian," Garrett asked, "When can you have your proof ready? We really don't have much time. So far the Merger has not announced its problem publically. Even the SEC has not been informed. I don't know how much more time we can hold off. If you're right, there is no problem. It will go away as a business problem overnight, but, on the other hand, there will be some collateral damage. Too many people have shown their hand. I guess we'll all have to live with that until the wood-be crisis has passed. In the meantime, Jersey and I got canned and you quit. That's a loss of a lot of horsepower. Where do you want me to drop you off?"

"In the East Village, around Forth St; I'll be going to a hacker who shall remain anonymous, and where she resides is secret," informed Brian. "I've already made arrangements before you picked me up. I'm expected."

"Is the hacker a she?" asked Garrett. "I've always believed that hackers are fat guys who need a shave and haircut, and who wear tee shirts with extremely offensive slogans printed on them."

"This one is a pretty good looking woman, but you're right she needs a haircut and a shave. The last time I saw her, the tee shirt she was wearing would offend all of the members of our collective families."

"I didn't know you had a sense of humor Brian," exclaimed Garrett. "That's the first time I ever heard you make a joke. Did you pick up a sense of humor on Easter Island?"

CHAPTER 53 WORDS

Garrett went straight to the hospital in the late afternoon after arriving back in New York. Much to his surprise Anne was no longer there. She had checked out earlier that day. He called her apartment, but there was no answer. Then it occurred to him, *I'll bet she went to Sam. Best I keep out of that.* He was right.

Anne came walking into Sam's Deli an hour after the dinner rush. Sam looked at Anne and gave her a gentle hug. "Anne," Sam stepped back, "Are you OK? Your friend Garrett came in and told me you were physically all right, but he wasn't so sure about the rest."

Inhaling deeply and nodding her head, "I guess that sums it up pretty well, Sam,"

"You got a lot of cuts and bruises. Do you hurt much?"

"Yes, but nothing that aspirin can't handle," she replied. "I know I don't look too pretty."

"Does your family know you're all right?"

"Hardly," answered Anne.

"Ohh, you've got some problems there?"

"Sam, my Mother and I don't get along very well," she said. "You wouldn't like her, and she wouldn't like or approve of you."

"Me, I'm a simple deli owner. We serve quality food and we treat people nice. She got prejudices?" asked Sam then nodding his head. "I'm a little too .. Jewish for her - that it?"

"My family, I have three brothers, and with one exception, they're not very nice. My father died when I was a young child. I grew up in, what you call today, a dysfunctional family. "We were and still are a mess.""

"That's too bad. I'm sorry Anne," commented Sam. "So to the present - you've had quite an experience. You want something to eat?"

"Coffee, please, nothing else," requested Anne.

"I'll join you with some coffee also," said Sam. They sat down at a rear table.

Finally, looking very carefully at Anne, Sam said "Soldiers live dangerous lives, Anne,"

"It worse than that Sam, it goes beyond the ... ah ...battlefield," stated Anne. "You were right, I am a soldier, I kill people, or at least I have been part of ruining their lives, or at least a couple of lives. I've done this for money. I guess that makes me a mercenary – or a kind of dishonorable soldier."

Sam looked at a very devastated Anne. He had never seen her so down. He gently and quietly said, "Anne, I know you, and you are not the beast you are painting, but I believe you are in the wrong profession. You are misusing your skills."

Anne protested, "Sam, how can you really know me? Because we've had coffee; together; shared some Danish; because I come into your deli to eat?" Then she smiled, "I guess I have to admit we have talked a lot over the years."

"No Anne," spoke Sam, "That is not how people get to know each other. It's so much more. It also includes those moments that they see, and feel another person's presence. Call it whatever you want, it is a collection of a thousand gestures; the movement of the hands; the expression of the eyes; the tilt of the head, this way and that way, and so many more ways that people communicate with one another and sooner or later they show, they reveal, who they really are.

Now let me tell you a little more about me than I ever have. As I once told you, I spent some time in a concentration camp when I was very young. As that part of my life unfolded, and so many events both good and bad unraveled, I appreciated more and more the many ways we communicate. I had to! For instance, much is said by what we don't say. In order to survive I had to hone these skills because, if an opportunity arose by some chance, I might be able to slip through some tiny crack in the camp where I was surviving. Eventually, as luck would have, it I did escape. I admit I was very lucky, but those skills helped me. Understanding my tormentors, their excitement, their anger, their boredom, even their humor, and of course, my fellow inmates, even though I was so young, provided me with the ability to see the opportunities that saved me from .. extinction. To want to survive, to feel I deserved to survive, became the thing that drove me to learn and embrace these things, even at my very young age."

"Now I've told you something about me that I rarely talk about, or care even to think about these days. I told you this for several reasons, Anne. If we are really to speak, it must be a two-way street. I believe I have understood who you are and I have always seen your pain. Listen, very carefully, I know from my own experiences that healing is possible. I didn't believe that for a long time, but I was wrong. Of course, there will always be scar tissue, but .. you can live with that."

Sam paused. Anne was moved, "God Sam, you lived through all that horror. Your family?"

Sam replied with a sad smile, "They're gone, not one of them survived.

Anne spoke sadly, "I'm so sorry Sam."

"That's history, but using the current popular parlance – I think that is the proper word – 'I was born again' in this beautiful country. I shall die sad for my first life, but happy for my second life; now enough of me, back to you."

"Sam, do you really know who I am? I've done some terrible things."

"Anne, you don't really know what terrible is, but you have apparently done some unethical things, and I detect that those things got out of control. I'm correct, right?" asked Sam.

190

Anne nodded yes.

"I think it will help for you to speak about these things ... just between you and me only," Sam reassured her.

Anne was quiet. The coffee cups were refilled. Ann contemplated whether she should open up to this man who was so different from the people in her family or career experiences. *Should I trust him? Can I trust him? I really am very fond of Sam and he seems to be very fond of me.* Then it occurred to her, as the careful researcher she had always been in her profession, to know more about Sam Axinov. Who was this man that was asking her to reveal her secrets?

Anne, the professional, began, "How'd you ever get here, Sam?"

Sam's mind drifted to his WWII survival and his return to his hometown, Dresden, Germany. "OK Anne, I understand, but this too is only between you and me – right?"

Anne nodded yes.

Sam began, "What life was really like in a Nazi concentration camp is indescribable. My vocabulary, and probably anybody else's vocabulary, is inadequate to explain it. I can only say it was not like anything I'd ever known or imagined – an infinitely foreign feeling every minute awake or asleep. There are no tears or agony that can explain it. Death, deception, abandonment, submission, filth, pain – these are just convenient words, not the reality. So all I can really tell you is that I survived. And this you must understand. I was lucky, and I wanted and felt, I deserved to survive. I can tell you no more that would improve your understanding of that experience."

Sam continued, "I escaped from the camp and eventually stumbled into, to my amazement, a group of Polish Jewish resistance fighters. They were a very rough bunch who didn't believe or trust me, even though, and particularly because, I still was a young kid at the time. At first they wanted to kill me believing I was a Nazi plant or simply if caught, would give them away. The truth was, I wasn't a Nazi plant, but I surely would have given them away if caught. The leader, a man named Dov, I'm guessing, saw the pain and history in my young face. I knew, and they knew, if any one of them were caught, they to a man, would also give the group way. Dov sort of became my protector having convinced the group that I could be very useful because of my youth. My innocent appearance and I was unusually innocent looking under the circumstances, could be put to good use for their activities. Also, the reality was that I was quite mature beyond my years because of the camp experiences, and certainly suffered from no traces of naivety. I had seen human beings at their worst and survived. He decided over many objections to let me live and be useful. We never spoke about it after that day and I completely understood the terms."

"The war ended, most of the group was dead, and the few that were left drifted off. Dov had been killed three days before it was over, and I was still alive, and I was on my own again in the great confusion of the war ending. Unfortunately, I was in the Russian sector. Because I was so young and starving,

191

the Soviet authorities paid no attention to me. I lived like so many; behaving like an animal with the foraging skills that I had learned living with the resistance fighters. I wandered for almost a year and eventually went back to my home town in Germany - Dresden."

"My great-grandfather, running from the nineteenth century pogroms of Russia, immigrated to Germany where he married a Rabbi's daughter and started a business making eyeglasses. By the turn of the century, the business had expanded into making lenses for cameras. After World War I, where some of the family members fought for the Kaiser, the Company had expanded into precision optics that would eventually be used in quantity by the German military. As Hitler built up his forces, the family optical business was a key supplier for ever more sophisticated optical products. The Company had achieved a worldwide reputation as one of the best precision optical suppliers in the business. Such capabilities were rare and not easy to re-create. The Axinov Optical business had become vital to the Nazi war effort. It was because of this that the Axinov family was not deported to the concentration camps until early in 1942."

"I soon found out that Dresden, in February 1945, was subjected to four allied air raids that consisted of 3600 planes and the delivery of an unbelievable amount of bombs and napalm. The result was that the center of the city became a firestorm wiping out almost everything within fifteen square miles."

"My decision to return to Dresden was something out of desperation and a fantasy that I might find some family, or at least something familiar. It was a long hard cold walk, but I was young, and somehow I made it."

"In my travels I'd seen, over and over, the massive destruction that wars leave in their dirty path. Dresden was in a new class for me. It was so completely obliterated I saw it only as the remains of a giant fire pit. I could find nothing of my home or the homes of my relatives - nothing. I found myself more disconnected than ever. It touched everything that defined my existence, but still ...I was alive. I continued to wander through this graveyard because I couldn't think of anything else to do. There were many other people like me. To complicate matters, the brutal Russian military had to be avoided. The people all seemed to be distant and not interested in anything but surviving. I foraged, stole, and begged and somehow, endured. Eventual futility so dominated my brain that I accepted the reality. I had to leave Dresden; I would go west. Maybe I could find my way into West Germany in spite of the Russians, and there maybe, things would go better."

"The day I departed was a cool brilliant spring day. As I left the City's remains I slowly re-entered a living world. The first thing I noticed were weeds poking up in the cracks of the road, and I thought for the first time in my life, *how beautiful weeds are.* Then scattered foliage began to appear, then trees with young green leaves, and then fields of growing vegetation. It was beautiful, the most beautiful thing I had ever seen. I thought, *I have to be like that, I must begin growing again.* As I continued I spotted a building at some distance that seemed

192

to be intact. As I slowly got closer, I realized it was not damaged. Then, as the road turned, I could see the front of the building. It was the Axinov Optical Works!"

"Even as a very young child, I visited the factory often and had been introduced to the staff. I had shown early interest in scientific things and loved to go to the Works. I, on occasion, would go to the factory with my father who headed up the Company. I was seen by my family, and the Company employees, as the Axinov child who would one day be the head of the Company."

"I approached the front of the building and there were a few cars and many bicycles in the parking lot. Could it be the Company *was operating?* I wondered. I was suddenly very scared. I wondered whether I should go in. I suddenly became aware of my appearance. I realized that my appearance was something I had not thought of for years. It was not like my upbringing in a household where appearance was fundamental. Concentration Camps are filled only with the colors of despair and death. It paints everything and everyone. The trick is not to appear but blend, not to be noticed. This is an important and delicate survival skill. It was just the opposite of the way I was brought up. Living with resistance fighters was in many ways the same. It included despair and death as well as expressing rage.

I realized I had been dirty and disheveled for the past four years of my life, and I had never thought about it once. I looked like what I was, a lost survivor who appeared and acted like the scoundrel I had become. That was my reality. That was how I survived. Nothing or no one reached out to help – to help me with restoration. My dilemma became quite apparent. *Was there something in that building that could change my condition? Something that could improve my life? Probably not,* I realized. Then it occurred to me, *I, me, I own that business, don't I?* Then reality surfaced. I realized how wrong I was. A year in Poland and East Germany had educated me; *the Russians or the East Germans own it.* Still I was curious. *This was part of my family history!*

I entered the lobby. Nothing had changed but the addition of an East German flag hanging from the wall and some pictures of Joseph Stalin, Vladimir Lenin, and some officials I did not recognize. The woman sitting at the reception desk looked at me dimly, "What are you doing in here, boy?"

"Just looking, my father used to work here and so did some of my uncles," he replied.

The woman looked at me, "Well, they don't anymore, get out or I'll have you thrown out."

Anne it was eerie "I remembered who she was and that was that and I knew there would be no going back."

There was silence from Anne. Then, shaking her head, "My god, Sam."

Starring at Sam for a few more minutes and contemplating, "Sam, it's my turn. I will tell you my story from the beginning," Anne went all the way back to when she got the idea for the Merger and the initial meetings with the

Pristinimatic and Photo Symbology executives. She divulged her research and how she had put the entire plan together, and then executed it. She explained the roles of the various people who were part of the Merger and even went into detail regarding the 'Torpedo' software failure, and her relationship with Bob Roberts, Ibrahim Sahid, and Joseph Taglaferri. And finally, how and why she was fired, and how she came to be in the lobby when they were together and she was injured and why she was not killed.

"That's quite a story and that's Wall Street? That's how it works?" asked Sam with a look of disgust.

"Yes, that's how it often works," replied Anne.

"You've been doing this for over seven years?"

"Yes, and five years at another firm – twelve, almost thirteen altogether."

"That's a long time soldiering," responded Sam. "I think maybe it's too long. You've had some adventure. Not all adventures are good. I know. Tell me Anne, a lot of things happened, but what troubles you most?"

"That's easy Sam," said Anne with a big sigh. "I destroyed a marriage that involved two people I don't even know. It's unforgivable."

"Maybe, maybe not, tell me some more details about this, about them."

"I don't really know a lot, but apparently when the Chief Technical Officer, Goldberg, who worked for Pristinimatic, confronted his wife with his suspicions based on the picture that I had arranged for him to find - she just left, disappeared," informed Anne.

"Just like that?"

"That's what I've been told."

Sam commented, "Hmmm, there must have been some other problems between those two. To leave so quickly, to disappear, would leave one to believe that there had been other troubles between them before you meddled in their affairs. Anne, you had no right to do what you did, but I suspect you are over estimating your power in this marriage breakup. So to speak, your timing was a tipping point event – a bad phrase I admit, but as a soldier ... you got lucky. The time was ripe and along you came. You've told me what troubles you most, but that's not all, what's next?"

Anne went on, "That was the worst, but Sam, it's what I see in the mirror, what I've become, I do whatever is required to make things happen in business. I now see I've been ruthless, I'm somebody who is capable of being destructive to achieve a business goal without caring what I do to people. The goal is always money, and more money. Sam it disgusts me."

Anne stopped speaking, took a deep breath, "My god Sam, I beginning to believe I'm a sociopath and further, that's who I work with - a bunch of sociopaths. My work has resulted in two of the founders of Pristinimatic getting fired. What's even worse, they are more talented than the new executives running the Merger."

"Why did that happen?" asked a rather bewildered Sam.

"Prejudices and egos," responded Anne. "Those weren't my choices. But I created the circumstances that made it possible."

Sam spent the next hour coaxing Anne to answer all sorts of questions about her life and her history in the business. Anne, to her surprise, held little back. This was the first time she ever could remember opening up like this. She had to admit to herself It helped. She trusted Sam in a way she had never trusted anybody before. In reality, she had no personal life, and she could not remember discussing any of this with anybody but, on very rare occasions, she would relate small unimportant snippets concerning business with the one brother she remained in contact with. Those were rare occasions indeed. Finally, Sam asked her about her family, which did not go so well. It was getting close to the closing hour and Sam had to get back to the final chores of the work day.

"Anne, thank you for sharing your thoughts with me and telling me all those things I know you need to talk about. I know it hurts, but you just can't keep things like this inside forever.

Anne looked at Sam with an expression of agony, "There's no excuse for some of the things I've done. I honestly just can't do this anymore. I've got to find another way to live my life. I've revealed things to you I've never revealed to any other soul. I will understand if you don't want to be my friend."

"Anne, friends are friends in spite of, not because of," responded Sam. "Friends help friends, not judge them. We love in spite of, not because of. Human beings are complex. We arrive at places in life that are barely in our control in spite of the popular nonsense we tell ourselves. But Anne, we can control our sensitivities, our responses and above all, our integrity. The most important integrity is that which is within us. I believe you have opened that door. That's, in my opinion, what's going on. This is good. It is also painful. I also know you haven't told me some other things that I think you need to talk about."

"Like what?" asked a slightly startled Anne?

"Oh, amongst other things, that gentleman that you sent over to carry your message to me from the hospital ... Garrett is his name," replied Sam with a slight smile and a tilt of the head.

"Ohhhh," Anne stood up, gave Sam a kiss on the cheek and whispered, "Thank you Sam." Then she hesitated for a moment and then left.

CHAPTER 54 A BUSINESS PLAN

As Garrett entered his apartment Sallie Kate was on the phone writing down a message. She stopped when she heard her father and said, "My God Dad, it's for you. It's Brian Goldberg!"

Sallie Kate, knowing much of what had been going on, was amazed. Wide-eyed, she sat down next to her Father listening intently to the conversation.

"Hi Brian, how'd you make out?" asked Garrett.

"I did really well," replied Brian. "I think I found out something more. Let's not talk about it over the phone. You've got me thinking like I'm in a bad movie. Should I come to your place, or meet you somewhere?"

"You are in a bad movie. Let's continue to be careful," stated Garrett. "Let me see. Every once and awhile we would go out for a beer. Do you remember?"

"Yes, I remember," informed Brian.

"It was always around the same time. Do you remember that?"

"Yup, absolutely."

"See you there later, same time, same place."

As Garrett hung up the phone, Sallie Kate excitingly asked, "Where did he come from?"

"Easter Island," Garrett responded. "Don't tell anyone under any circumstances that he's back. It's very good. I'll tell you all about it later – promise." She nodded her head yes. "I've got to go."

Across town, in the office of the just newly hired legal representatives for Photo Symbology, Jim Gale and several of his senior executives were having a meeting with the new lawyers. They had been at it for hours. The meeting could only be described as extremely contentious. Finally, Gale got up and directed counsel to leave the room and they did.

Jim went on, "We heard enough of this bullshit from everybody and it's now time to make a decision and move on. Please be reminded that we have very little time left to do this. Once this goes public, we will have lost leverage."

Gale's second in command Rheine Gutly, spoke, "Jesus, Jim, I've gone along with you from day one on this deal, but I am really worried that this is a bridge too far. If you can pull it off, we win. That I admit. If you're wrong and your plan doesn't work out almost exactly the way you're planning it, everything, and I mean everything, will come apart. Jim, it's too damn risky. But the risk aside, the ethics of it are shit. You're pushing into regions that shouldn't be touched. Even our new lawyers are warning you not to do this."

Jim interrupted "Fuck the lawyers, new or not. Lawyers get paid all kinds of money for their advice. I asked them how to safely walk through this minefield and the damn lawyers told us how to walk around it. My grandmother could have given me that advice, and she would have charged me nothing. They're just as useless as our old lawyers. The time has come for a bold move. I'm running this Company and we're going to do it exactly as I described it to you! If you don't agree with me, and this goes for everybody, get the fuck out now!"

The room was quiet, very quiet. You couldn't cut through the tension with a chain saw. Finally, after a few minutes, Rheine Gutly looked at Jim Gale and with a frown and a shake of the head said, "You're the boss. Do what you have to, but I'm out. I'll send you my resignation by email." He got up and left. Everyone else stayed.

As Gutly was walking out, Jim hurled a last thought, "Gutly, you'll never lead a company. You don't have the balls!"

Gutly thought to himself as he walked down to his office for the last time, *Gale, you son-of- a-bitch, you're really a crook. I'm out'a here.*

The idea that Jim Gale had put together was not the high road. He would immediately bring a criminal complaint and civil action against Jersey, Garrett, and Brian. Further, he had already retained a public relations firm who specialized in spreading garbage to the media, who were ready to go as soon as he gave the green light. Their purpose was to make Gale's version of the whole affair as public as possible. The story that would be manufactured would be that Jersey and Garrett were let go because of implied, but not revealed, criminal and civil violations.

Brian would be seen as a victim who was enraged, as a result, of Jersey's and Garrett's greed. They were the driving force that drove Brian to engineer the software corruption. Eventually, having realized what he had actually done, Brian had run away to avoid prosecution.

Gail's purpose, of course, was simply to destroy their reputations and nothing else. He knew full well there was nothing that would ever stick in a court action. Further, to raise the ante even higher, he would bring Garrett's daughter, Sallie Kate, into the story. She would be part of the media fairy-tale by implying Garrett's motives were tied to problems with his daughter, she being an irresponsible teenager who had been improperly brought up in by a negligent bastard of a father. Pictures of both of them were to be included as part of the publicity.

Jim Gale had done the homework for his plan utilizing the good services of Sean O'Ryan's firm. The purpose was to learn personal facts pertaining to Jersey, Garrett, and Brian. Having learned of Garrett's being a single father and of his devotion to Sallie Kate, had opened the door to applying more pressure on Garrett. He doubted that Jersey really gave a damn about Sallie Kate. Engineering Garrett's feelings regarding the protection of his daughter's reputation and welfare would make his plan even more likely to work out.

It all came down to this, with all his weapons, "locked and loaded" he would meet with Jersey and Garrett. He would present his demands, which were the total sale to him of all their remaining holdings in the Merger, along with a completely written release granted to him as well as to the Merger. This would eliminate all possibilities of any legal action in the future regarding the transaction or personal liability. Also, included in the contract, was an agreement never to discuss the transaction or release any kind of details regarding him, the Merger, and/or his staff. The sale of equity would be paid for on the spot. The transaction was to be at an extremely low price and would be in the form of checks made out to each of them along with the appropriate contracts and releases for signature, thus eliminating any future legal actions against Jersey and Garrett. Further, if all was complied with, he - Jim Gale - would take no action regarding Brian.

Now it was time to meet with Jersey and Garrett. This was the moment to present his demands in exquisite detail, emphasizing that he would unleash an ugly publicity campaign with all its pain if they rejected his terms. Jim Gale would make it un-mistakably clear that he could instantly cause all hell to break loose then and there. He anticipated they would have no option but to comply. To further emphasize the immediacy of his power to execute the plan, he would have his cell phone in his hand ready to send a "green light" to the PR firm, with but a mere click and a quick chat, and the process would start in full force.

It is beautiful, he thought; *a masterpiece of the business game. This will be a brilliantly engineered terrible moment of choice.* While he wasn't quite sure of Jersey, he was confident that Garrett would protect his daughter at all personal cost. He knew that they knew it was all untrue, but there would be nothing they could do about it until it was too late. He was sure, in the end, they would both give in because Garrett would do what he had to do to get Jersey to comply. He dismissed his remaining staff and called the lawyers back in. They went to work. He gave them twenty-four hours to get it all done and he put calls into Jersey and Garrett.

CHAPTER 55 A BATH AND A CHAT

Anne Mills had returned to her apartment and spent the rest of the day trying to figure out what she should do. The FBI and Department of Home Security had left messages, both wanting further interviews. *My god,* she thought, *I'm getting hit from all sides. I'll return their calls tomorrow. I need some quiet time.* She had spent hours with them in the hospital going over the little that she really knew. She was at the wrong place at the wrong time, and that was all there was to it. Anne finally decided it would be a good idea to take a warm bath. In fact, her doctors had advised that it would be good for her to take a lot of warm baths. Her external contusions were superficial, but a lot of muscles and joints were still quite painful.

She had been in the bathtub for some time with a glass of wine and the Jacuzzi massaging her body and had fallen into a pleasant shallow sleep. She awakened with the question, *why did Sam ask me about Garrett? He was implying there is something between us. OK, Garrett has declared his feelings for me. Apparently he has also related his feelings about me to Sam. I wish he hadn't done that. There is no way we can ever be anything more than friends, and when Garrett finds out what I've really been up to, even that will end. I wonder who will tell him. I guess it's possible that it will never come out ... unless I tell him. How can we ever really be friends if I'm not completely open and honest with him? I have to admit it's too bad this has happened the way it has ... I really do like him - strange. What a mess!* She slowly fell into a shallow sleep again. She began to dream at the edge of consciousness.

She was in a dark place and she was afraid, terribly afraid. She began to run, but couldn't see where she was running to, only that she had to keep running. It was obvious she was running away from something or someone - something terrible; something that would hurt her. Then she appeared in her dream - Anne - against an extremely bright light ... It was the decimating brightness of the setting sun falling directly into her eyes as it entered the bathroom window. She was quite awake and could feel her heart racing. The mellowness and comfort of the bath disappeared and she couldn't wait to get out. The bath was repelling. Suddenly everything made her uncomfortable.

As she was drying herself, the phone rang. The caller ID identified it was Garrett. She let it ring. It was time for another glass of wine.

Jim Gale was in his apartment having a quick dinner with his live-in. He was feeling the satisfaction of somebody who had made a decision and was acting on it. He was a fighter who was about to enter the ring and was sure he knew how and why he would win. He glowed with confidence. *I know their weaknesses,* he thought. *Damn, I know their weaknesses! Garrett's daughter, he'll fold like a cheap suit — perfect, and Jersey's arrogance, thinking I give a damn about some of my bad habits. He's in no position to throw rocks, and I'm going to remind that son-of-a-bitch of that. I'll play his game right back to him, and better.*

The live-in remarked, "You're in one hell of a good mood. I haven't seen you like this for months. What's going on?"

Jim replied with a smile, "Yes, I am in a very good mood. I figured out how to win the game?"

"Which of the many games you play are you talking about?" the live-in asked.

"Business, of course," he answered. "I won't talk about it now, but maybe I'll let you know about it after tomorrow."

I assume that it depends on a successful outcome," responded the live-in with a smirk.

Jim responded with a nasty sneer, "Don't worry about it and don't nag me. I'm not going to discuss it under any circumstances. Shut the hell up. Do we understand each other?"

Garrett and Brian met at an old time bar in the East Village. The place had been in business since the Civil War, and as of then, still made its own beer. As usual the place was filled and noisy, but, as taverns go, it was delightful. They found a quiet table located outside in the rear patio.

"It's been a few years since we've been here," commented Garrett.

"Yes, too long," replied Brian. "Whatever happens, I've got to live my life a little different from now on. Before we begin, I want to apologize for my behavior that screwed up the deal and evidently got you fired. I wasn't thinking past my nose and I know that's no excuse. It was wrong and incredibly inconsiderate. I think I handled everything about as badly as I possibly could. My best decision was to go bike riding out of the country. I calmed down and amongst other things, I began to realize what I had done to you. You have always been a true friend to me and it is unforgivable. I'll do anything you want me to do to make it up to you. I don't want to lose your friendship, but I can understand if you tell me to go to hell forever. It was wrong, so darn wrong."

Garrett looked at Brian, "Oh, you certainly screwed up, but the real damage was to yourself. I'll get over this, and to be quite frank, the Company wasn't fun anymore. Life, as well as work, has to be pleasurable; something you look forward to most days. Pristinimatic had lost that shine for me. My career coming to an end at the Company was not tragic. I admit I have tolerated Jersey for too many years. We both started our careers at a think tank on exactly the same day. We worked well and productively together for years. As we flourished Jersey became more and more difficult. Some of the things he's done recently have exceeded my standards of behavior – I guess you'd call those ethics. I was brought up as a small town kid with very clear definitions of right and wrong. I was coming to the point of changing things, maybe even leaving the Company. I wasn't quite there, but events accelerated that little detail. As far as you and me, Brian, I was really pissed off at you and that was for damn sure. But now I'm no longer mad. I guess my feelings were mitigated by other

200

events that seemed in a strange sort of way to put your actions in perspective, and knowing what I know now, the anger is gone. Old buddy, we're all right and I always believed where you were coming from. But, you, you have got to do some personal fixing. But, before any of that can happen we have our immediate problem to deal with. Whatcha' got?"

Brian began, "Garrett, you will be amazed at what I found. Using an old movie metaphor, 'sit down and fasten your safety belt,' this will be like being launched off an aircraft carrier. First, I was only able to get to one of the back-ups. It appears to be without fault. There is nothing wrong with it. We're in excellent condition here. It includes every bit of 'Torpedo' and data from the day we began the Company to the day I turned it over to the Merger's engineers and accounting department. I had my hacker friend, and I guarantee she's as good as they get, check the files over and over for any problems. She found nothing. Everything could be fixed at the Merger in a matter of a few days. So we've got the cure. I went a bit further and had her download my back-up into her computers to make sure there was another back-up of the back-up. I know I'm beginning to sound like a paranoid inmate."

Brian continued, "Second, we hacked into the Merger's computers which wasn't such a big deal, since I designed and authored so much of it. Together we examined the corrupted software. It's corrupted all right. It's a complete mess. Now this is interesting, my hacker friend thinks the damage was done by a "Visitor" or a "Spider" virus. These viruses, developed in Romania several years ago, were designed not only to destroy software but also cause hardware damage. They possess a unique capability. After causing their mischief, they eliminate all traces of ever having been in the computer. No fingerprints, no traces, nothing. Now, I know that sounds devastating but the anti-virus people have known about them for quite a while and found that they were very easy to detect before they entered a computer and caused their turmoil. Also, they found they were relatively simple to eradicate. Now there's a potential "fly in this ointment." If the virus was introduced from within the Company, on the unprotected side of the anti-virus software the virus was quite free to do its thing. Under those circumstances, the virus protection that would normally prevent them ever entering would be impotent."

"Whoa!" barked Garrett, "If there's no trace that a virus was in the system, how can you support such a conclusion?"

"I can't, but hold on," countered Brian. "You remember that I told you about my having two separate back-ups with two different companies. Yes?"

Garrett nodded in agreement.

"I also told you that I did this independently because of my general paranoia in and around our kind of business, including not telling anybody but accounts payable, and that in a rather routine way. And further, I had them pay the bill a year ahead of time, but I knew sooner or later what I had done would surface."

Brian continued, "Now this is the interesting part. The first back-up service was called Software Vault Back-Up Corp. - a company obviously in the back-up business. The second back-up service is called the Tech Insurance, Inc. Unless you looked carefully you would think they were some kind of insurance company, but there is no hint in that name revealing what they do for a living. They're just a small service located in Canada. Somebody from the Merger called up Software Vault and cancelled the contract and had the back-up transferred to a Belgium back-up service. In order to cancel and do such a transfer requires certain specific paperwork and signed orders from a top executive, usually the CEO. They received what they required. Amongst everything, they received a signed letter from Jim Gale granting them permission to release the 'Torpedo' software and data to the Belgium Company as well as ordering them to do the transfer immediately. Further, it ordered that all software and data belonging to Pristinimatic that might be residing in their servers be destroyed after the transfer. Nothing unusual here, but all of this was done in handwritten form. Nothing was done electronically."

"How the hell do you know about this?" asked Garrett.

"Ahhh, serendipity," stated Brian. "It gets better. It appears that the Software Vault people decided to scan the handwritten material and put the file in their Company data files. My computer maven hacked it, and we have a copy. How do you like them apples?"

"My god, that son-of-a-bitch Jim Gale has had the fix all along." That greedy bastard will stop at nothing. He cooked this whole damn thing up when 'Torpedo' crashed." Then Garrett stopped, took a deep breath, hesitated, then exploded by bringing his fist down hard on the table cursing – "son-of a bitch!" This caused their beer mugs to hop, spilling beer all over the table and scattering the free popcorn that came with the drinks. Brian flinched. Some people sitting near them were startled and glared at Garrett. A big tough waiter came over and asked if there something wrong. Garrett apologized for his outburst and ordered some more beer and handed the waiter a ten dollar bill. The waiter cheerfully cleaned up the mess and left.

Garrett looked at Brian, "Jim gale planted the virus."

"You're probably right, but we can't prove it, but we have enough to stop him," stated Brian.

"Jim could not have done all of this by himself. He needed help. He's no software engineer," said Garrett.

"Gutly, his right hand man is, and I think a pretty good one," remarked Brian.

"It fits, but there are still missing pieces," stated Garrett. "Who was behind the picture business? Was getting rid of us the first step in some grand plan, and the virus the second step? Let's get out of here. I need to take a walk and do some thinking." They left and began walking west from the East Village where they had been. It was a warm night and the streets were filled with people and stores offering a wonderful variety of stuff - clothing, antiques, art, food,

202

and some objects that defied description. This was Greenwich Village, a place where such a conglomeration of goodies and treats are only found in special areas in cities like New York.

After walking for some time they ended up in Washington Square Park and found an empty bench to sit on.

Finally, Garrett began, "This is important, when did Jim cancel Software Vault?"

"I don't know," responded Brian. "Why?"

"It matters," stated Garrett. "If he cancelled before the software crash occurred it makes him, or rather implicates him as being the guy that caused the crash. If he cancelled after the crash occurred, it kind of says he wasn't the 'Torpedo' crash villain. Further, it suggests that the reason the Merger found out about Software Vault so early was, as a result, of all the investigation they were probably conducting after the crash."

"Where are you going with this?" asked Brian.

"There are missing pieces as I said to you before. When you think about it, from Gale's perspective, the crash would never be a good thing for him to pull off unless he absolutely knew he had a fix in hand from the very beginning. Think about it, the mess and risk of a crash, or really any other devastating software occurrence, would be much too risky a game, no matter how greedy he was. The guy had just won the Merger battle and he was in the driver's seat. Why risk it? On the other hand, the crash occurs unexpectedly, the Chief Technical Officer disappears, and Gale discovers, post-crash, he has a software fix and nobody else knows about it.

"Ahhhhh, our boy says an opportunity has presented itself! He sees a chance to get more – a gift! He knows the risk is minimal. Makes sense, in my opinion."

"So you're saying if Jim Gale found the backup after the crash occurred, he didn't cause the crash, right?"

"You got it," continued Garrett. "Somebody else was responsible or it could have just been a virus from a third party, but I doubt it. The experts that the Merger hired would have sniffed that out by now. Somehow this is tied to the picture business. Getting rid of us didn't free up more equity. We still have the percentage we agreed to when the Merger occurred. But the crash and the accusation against you opens up matters for negotiation, which, if we can't defend ourselves adequately, will translate into, one way or another, a significant or complete equity giveback to the Merger or somebody. Gale's trying to beat them to the punch. Is there anybody who would gain from this beside the Merger or Gale? I can't see it. You got any ideas?"

"No," replied Brian. "I better find out the date of Jim Gales' order to Software Vault damn quick. I'll call my hacker friend and see if she can give us that information right now." Brian got up and walked away from where they were sitting and made the call.

CHAPTER 56 LOVE AND INTELLIGENCE

Garrett decided he needed a little time to think about the next move and went back to his apartment. Both Garrett and Brian agreed that Brian should not reveal his presence back in the States yet. It was a matter of catching the bad guy, or bad guys, unaware before he or she or they had time to react. But at this time they didn't have a plan of how best to use their surprise.

Garrett entered his apartment and Sallie Kate was with one of her girlfriends watching some teenage stuff on TV. "Any calls?" asked Garrett. No answer. A second time louder, "Sallie Kate, were there any calls for me?"

She turned her head towards her Father and shook her head no.

Garrett walked into his home office and sat down at his desk and started doodling on a notepad. Then he decided he was hungry. The only thing he'd eaten since breakfast was the complimentary popcorn with the beers that he and Brian had consumed in the old tavern. He walked into the kitchen and made himself a sandwich. As he was eating he decided to try to call Anne. *Maybe she'll talk to me now,* he hoped.

He called and got her voice mail. *Damn it!* He thought. Then he left a voice mail message. The message said it was quite important regarding a business development, and further, there was nothing personal. About ten minutes later she called.

"Hello, Anne," picking up the phone and responding to the message.

"Garrett, what's so important?" asked Anne.

"There's something I want to inform you of, but not over the phone," stated Garrett.

"I don't mean to be rude, but are you trying to see me?"

"I'm always trying to see you, but this is not what this is about," explained Garrett. "Even though you've been fired, you're hardly out of harm's way in this situation and what I have to tell you will be meaningful."

"I'm quite aware that my being fired has not remedied my situation but, possibly, has even made it worse," she said. "Before we go on, please Garrett, I want to make it very clear that there is no possibility of you and me .. a relationship."

It didn't feel good to hear that but .., "Look Anne, I told you that this call is about business and not my feelings for you and yours for me. Will you meet me?" asked Garrett.

There was a pause. "I don't feel very well as I'm sure you know. Is this absolutely necessary?" asked a worn sounding Anne.

"Yes, absolutely yes."

"Where do you want to meet and when?"

"Now ... your apartment?" suggested Garrett.

"I don't think that's a good idea."

Garrett thought for a moment. "How about Sam's Deli in a half hour?"

"All right, Sam's in a half hour."

Garrett walked into Sam's Deli looking for Anne. Sam, seeing Garrett, gestured with his head towards a booth where she was sitting. Garrett found her wearing sweat pants, a Yankee Baseball Shirt, a Yankee Cap, and sunglasses. This was the first time he had ever seen her in such casual attire, thinking about it further, it was sloppy attire – something he could not imagine happening before this meeting. Even when they went bike riding together, she was carefully and fashionably dressed – always appropriate for the occasion – vintage Anne.

"Is that you under that Yankee uniform?" he asked as his opening greeting.

"It fits the way I feel and my mood," she answered. "Now please, what's so important that you insisted on this meeting?"

Garrett sat down opposite Anne and requested she take off the sunglasses.

"Why?" she demanded.

"I want to see your eyes!" retorted Garrett.

She complied.

He looked directly into her the eyes, "Anne, I know you feel something for me. I've seen it before, and can see it in your eyes now," declared Garrett.

"Ye gods, you're terrible! Go have your eyes and your head examined. You promised nothing personal."

"I guess I lied," responded Garrett with a smirk.

"One thing I'm learning about you, Garrett, you're a hopeless romantic. Tell me what you want to tell me, please. I want to get out of here and go home and rest."

"OK, then to business only. Anne, I need to have your word that, what I'm about to tell you will not be repeated to anybody. Do I have your word on this?"

She hesitated for a minute, "Look if this is so important that it be kept secret, please don't tell me."

"Anne, stop busting my chops," barked Garrett

"OK, you have my word," responded Anne.

Garrett began, "A lot of things have happened in the past forty-eight hours. The net of it is this ... I have a fix. By fix I mean that I can get all the 'Torpedo' software operating again, no ifs, ands, or buts! Everything that's dead, all those ones and zeros brought back to life in complete health."

"Are you sure?" asked an astounded Anne.

"Absolutely!" responded Garrett with a reassuring smile.

"How did …. Ohhhh, you're not going to tell me. You can't tell me anything? Why, if you trust me enough to tell me this much, why not everything?" asked a perplexed and always clever Anne.

"Look Anne, I've pushed this as far as I can because of .. well, damn it, it's my personal feelings for you whether you like it or not. I don't want to see you get hurt more than you are. You need some good news and I just gave it to you and let it go at that," declared Garrett.

Anne began to feel guilty. *This guy is sticking his neck out for me because of his feelings for me. He hasn't the slightest idea who I really am and what I've really done.* "How are you going to present this to everybody?" she asked.

Garrett responded, "That's my little secret, but there are other things to figure out. As things have unfolded, like the six sides of a box you can never see all sides at the same time unless you can unfold it. Unfolding it the right way will answer some unanswered questions."

"Like what?" she asked.

"Who cooked this up? Who was responsible for the picture under Jersey's desk? Why does Jim Gale feel he can be so damn aggressive in this deal? Why does he think he's so entitled to increase his equity? He projects he is without sin, and we are swimming in sin. Strange, I've got the fix, and it still provides few if any answers to those questions," stated Garrett.

Anne was overwhelmed to the point of pain by the first two questions. She knew the answers to some of those only too well. Sam had suggested confession or something like that. There could be no lies. She wasn't quite beyond that for the moment. She just couldn't do it. *If everything is fixed, let it die there,* she thought. Suddenly and quietly, she felt her eyes tighten and tears began to flow. She bowed her head and covered her face with her hands. After a few minutes, she regained control. Garrett was staring at her intently. She returned the stare. "I've got to go. Thank you Garrett. You really are one hell of a nice guy."

Garrett could not hold back, "I love you."

She looked at him sweetly. That was an expression that Garrett had never seen before. She sighed, "I hope you're wrong for your sake." She quickly got up and left.

When she left Sam came over to the table, "Anne didn't look too happy Garrett. Something bad happen?"

Garrett replied, "It's funny Sam, I brought her good news and it seemed to make things worse."

"You really do care about her - love and other maladies are things that we must learn to live with. That goes for both of you."

Garrett bit his lip and nodded his head, "Yep, I'm in love with her, Sam. I think she's got some feelings for me, but she denies it vehemently. I'll admit she's the last person in this world I would have thought I would ever fall in love with. No, that's dishonest. Even when I was a young man we once unexpectedly met at a party and danced together for a few minutes. I know as sure as I'm here talking to you, that we both felt the magic. Bet you didn't know that."

Sam nodded, conceding he had no idea.

Garrett continued, "Sure we both come from the same town. She was who she was and I was what I was. We were oil and water or some damn unmixable combination for that time, for that town. That's the way we were brought up. But we're not in that town anymore and those rules are just memories, and even those rules have changed. I believe we're no longer the same kind of oil or the same kind of water. Sam, she accuses me of being a hopeless romantic. Perhaps I am, but I've been guilty of worse, and my feelings are undeniably real."

"The two of you are caught between the cultural shifts of the baby boomers age. Those rules - walls - you refer to are not made of brick and mortar but of emotions from your past."

"Sam is it that clear?" asked Garrett.

Sam continued, "Garrett, I have a suggestion. But first, I want to tell you something I believe. Anne is a Wall Street soldier who has attacked her enemies as soldiers are required to do. Enemies on Wall Street are almost everywhere. She's been very good at it, but it has come with a price - the terrible scars of combat. I've told her this. I know - and hear me carefully - she does not want to be that soldier anymore. She believes she's a sociopath surrounded by sociopaths. She wants out. That can be your opening. I too suspect she's got the same kind of feelings for you that you have for her, but she has a lot of ground to cover before she can admit it. It won't be easy Garrett, but I think it's more than worth a try."

CHAPTER 57 SOMETHING THAT NEVER HAPPENED

Jim Gale had made calls to Garrett and Jersey for the purpose of setting up a meeting with them early the next day. Jersey said yes immediately thinking Gale was somehow ready to meet a better set of terms, as a result, of his Cuban Cigar Club meeting.

Garrett felt he wasn't completely ready for Gale and resisted. But after a conversation with Brian, they both realized they had no choice but to move quickly and, therefore, the meeting was accepted. The main issue was 'do they reveal the 'fix' at this time or hold off for a better moment'? Then there was the fact that a 'big' meeting of all parties was scheduled for later that day. The Judge would be presiding, which raised another issue – should they inform the Judge ahead of time of the 'fix' and of Brian's return, or not telling the Judge ahead of time would put themselves at a disadvantage.

They decided, under no circumstances, would Brian's return be revealed to Jim Gale or anybody, including Jersey, for the moment, and they would take their chances with the Judge. Therefore, with only Garrett and Jersey attending Jim Gales' meeting, Garrett would play the revelation of the fix by "ear." It would be driven by whatever Gale was up to with the meeting.

They agreed to meet at a hotel room near Times Square, which Gale had rented specifically for that purpose. Garrett had seen this kind of move before. It was usually done for absolute privacy and usually it meant things would be discussed that were to be very confidential. Garrett assumed, knowing Gale, that whatever he had in mind would not be particularly nice – but, whatever.

It was an overcast morning with scattered thunderstorms. Times Square was blurry and wet as seen through Garrett's windshield - *Ahh, appropriate weather for setting the mood of the meeting,* he thought.

Jersey met Garrett in the lobby with coffee and a bag of bagels. *My, my,* Garrett thought, *Jersey must be feeling good. Other than jelly beans, this is unusually generous. He never does anything munificent like that. Hmmm?*

Jersey and Garrett entered the hotel room located on the 25th floor. The three of them sat down at the table next to a window providing a spectacular view of Times Square. It was a front row seat for the next arriving thunder shower. All three of them had their own agendas. There were no warm greetings, no handshakes, or no exchange of polite niceties.

"Well Jim, you called us here, your turn," stated Garrett. "Help yourself to a bagel and coffee."

"I'm here to talk, not eat." Jim Gale reached into his pocket and took out his cell phone and tapped in a few clicks and laid it on the table for all to see. "I'm going to make this very simple. I've retained a public relations firm and had them prepare an ambitious information campaign. They are ready to go as soon as I send a message with a mere click which will translate to a 'yes' on this phone."

"Ohhh," Garrett commented, "and why are you telling us about your information campaign?"

"It's simple, as I said," stated Jim. "You and Jersey and that Brian Goldberg have almost completely destroyed the Company that is, or should I say was to be, the product of our Merger. I will have to spend enormous resources building it back up if that is really possible. Further, you have managed to put me in a position where I will be humiliated in our industry and embarrassed on Wall Street, probably beyond repair. And finally, you are well aware that I will have to go before the SEC, probably on my knees." He paused.

"And ... ," insisted Garrett.

"I want compensation, and I want it now!"

"And what exactly is the compensation you want .. now?"

"I insist that you sell me all your remaining holdings in the Merger now - this morning - along with a complete legal release covering me and the Merger. I also want you to sign an agreement that guarantees complete confidentiality regarding our transaction. I will pay you a dime on the dollar for your equity."

"Oh, that much!" interrupted Garrett sarcastically.

"Yessss ...," hissed Jim Gale.

"Well, in that case please go on if there is more," encouraged Garrett.

"Listen very, very carefully, gentlemen. This is the deal, if you don't comply with my demands, I will immediately, with merely a tap on my cell, initiate a criminal complaint and civil action against the two of you and, of course, the phantom, Brian Goldberg. Next, using the best PR methods available I will make the whole affair as public as possible. I will tell the world you were fired because we found out about your criminal activities and civil violations. Brian Goldberg, will be portrayed as a victim as well as a perpetrator of your irresponsible behavior - a sacrifice to your collective greed. The world will know that it was Brian who was directly responsible for engineering the software corruption. Then, because he realized what he had done, he ran away to avoid prosecution. I will absolutely destroy your reputations before you can do a damn thing about it. I don't need to do anything else. Of course, I admit, if you don't comply with my demands there will eventually be a court fight which will be a mess for everybody, and in the end, you will settle to preserve some of your remaining equity and the cash flow it implies," stated a confident Jim Gale.

Jersey barked, "You are one low life bastard."

"Quiet Jersey, please, I don't think he's finished," insisted Garrett.

"Don't give me your shit, Smart, you threatened to screw me over big-time." This is payback," retorted Jim Gale. "Now, just to make sure I've got your co-operation, Garrett, and this will be a test for your very good friendship with your buddy, Mr. Jersey not-so-god-damn Smart, we will bring your daughter - Sallie Kate is her name I believe - into the festivities."

"What in the hell are you talking about?" demanded an alarmed Garrett.

Jim Gale continued, "She will be a major part of the story. It's simple and common amongst your class. It was part of your motive along with your obvious greed. What I'm talking about are your massive problems with your "sweet" Sallie Kate. She is an irresponsible, very troubled teenager who has been improperly brought up in your dysfunctional family. You are a negligent bastard of a father - you, Mr. Garrett Carlssen — and you need lots of money to keep her out of trouble and support your irresponsible lifestyle. The PR people have pictures of you both and they are not very complimentary. The media will get to show them even this very day. That's the deal. It's up to you gentlemen to decide right now."

Garrett was in a rage. He could feel his entire body tense to the point of breaking. He wanted to hit Jim Gale with every cell in his body, but somehow he held himself back. Unlike so many examples in life of what happens when you lose control and pay the price, he would not, could not, make that mistake at this crucial point. Fortunately, he knew he had weapons to obliterate Jim Gale, but he had to act immediately. There was no longer a timing decision to be made. He had to act before Gale let loose this disgusting scheme of his making. Fix or no fix, if the Gale PR campaign got started, even for a few hours, the havoc it would reap would be overwhelming even though every last bit of it was false. He took a deep breath and said, "That's quite a plan you've put together. I need to spend a few minutes alone with Jersey to consider your offer."

Then Jersey spoke, "If we agree to your terms, is that the absolute end of this for us personally?"

Jim Gale replied, "Yes, it will be completely over with. There is paperwork here to cover that."

It struck Garrett, that Jersey's response was odd under the circumstances. He thought i*t would appear that Jersey is willing to pay this price without any further negotiation in order to end it now and without further conflict. That's not the Jersey I know.* Then it occurred to him, *Jersey apparently doesn't want this to go any further. He wants to end it immediately. He's willing to pay the price. Hmmmm, he's hiding something, by god.*

Jim Gale stood up, picked up his cell phone, holding it in one hand and with a finger pointing at it with the other hand and announced, "I'll go for a walk around the hotel. Get some coffee. You guys have a half hour. See you then," and left.

Garrett commented sarcastically, "That was interesting."

Jersey commented, "What a low-life son-of-a-bitch!"

Garrett went on, "We've got to stop Gale from initiating his PR campaign. The damage would be much too great for everybody. He knows that, of course, and he is giving us a way out at great personal financial cost. I can't let Sallie Kate get hurt and he knows that. If I've ever come close to violence with anybody, it was in the past five minutes. How do you feel about all this, Jersey?"

Jersey looking more passive than his usual body signals and, shrugging his shoulders, "I guess we have no choice."

"Jersey," responded Garrett, "just like that, you're giving in? I know you Jersey; you would normally be coming up with multiple strategies in this type of situation at a 100mph pace. What in hell is going on with you? Has this low-life son-of-a-bitch done you in?"

"I'm tired. I need to get away from this shit," answered Jersey.

"Bullshit! You were very energized when I met you this morning. No sign of tired. C'mon Jersey, what's going on?" demanded Garrett.

Jersey blustered and then hesitated, and then finally said, "We can't let Sallie Kate get hurt - right?"

"No 'we' can't. I'm not buying it, Jersey. You're not telling me something."

"Fuck you Garrett, there are some personal things here, and I'm going to keep them personal," stated Jersey. "Just be happy I'm willing to take his rotten deal, but I guess we should try to negotiate."

Garrett sat quietly for a few minutes and then he said, "Jersey, I can stop him right now!"

"You can? How?" demanded Jersey.

Garrett pulled his laptop out of his carrying bag and turned it on. He typed in some instructions and directed Jersey to read the display.

Jersey read it and then asked, "How in the hell did you get this?"

Garrett waved a finger back and forth indicating "no," "Don't ask. You don't need to know and I will never tell you. Just enjoy the gift horse we've gotten."

"This indicates that Gale had a way out of the 'Torpedo' software problem from the very beginning. I guess this was an extra back-up of the system we were unaware of – right? This has to have been Brian's work, right?" demanded Jersey.

"Yup!" answered Garrett.

"That's typical Brian, putting a Band-Aid on a Band-Aid on a Band-Aid. I guess there were three back-ups" stated Jersey. "We thought there were only two. Why didn't we know about number three?"

"Because Brian didn't trust us – sound logical?" responded Garrett with raised eyebrows.

"It occurs to me that this lets Brian off the hook. Then who is the villain that corrupted 'Torpedo'? Was it Jim Gale? He couldn't have done it by himself. That's not his skill set. This was not a simple attack. It was much too sophisticated. He needed help, big time. An amateur would be too easily traced," stated Jersey.

212

"I don't know who or how it happened. The experts who Gale hired should, sooner or later, shed some light on the problem. I did some due diligence on those guys and they came up very clean."

"It doesn't make sense that Gale hires good guys to find out he is the villain. Somebody else did it. I guess Gale took advantage of it."

"So it would appear. In the meantime, we've got to stop him. I don't know what's between you two, but there's something, something beyond the obvious. Let me handle him," requested Garrett.

Jersey nodded in agreement. They waited.

Jim Gale returned at exactly the appointed time, "Well, what have you two decided?" and placed his cell phone on the table.

Garrett without warning grabbed Jim Gale's phone and smashed it into pieces by driving it into the edge of the table. Both Jersey and Jim Gale were aghast and surprised at this action.

Before Jim Gale could say anything, Garrett, raising his voice said, "Relax Jim, just buying a little time."

Gale, visibly shaken, responded, "It won't stop a fuckin' thing! I'll make the call on the room phone or somewhere else."

Then Garrett turned his laptop around and pushed it in front of Jim Gale, "Read that!"

It was Gales' handwritten note to the Software Vault people cancelling the back-up service and the order for the immediate destruction of all data and the 'Torpedo' software. Jim Gale turned white and said nothing.

Garrett then said, "See you at this afternoon's meeting. This meeting never happened.

CHAPTER 58 SOME THINGS THAT DID HAPPEN

Bob Roberts was sitting in the Board Room waiting for the management team and the Board of Directors to take their seats and begin the meeting. He was well aware of their dislike of him. He was quite aware that as soon as the crisis was over he would be back to his old position, or perhaps, maybe worse. It occurred to him that he was the oldest person in the room. It also occurred to him that they were the younger guys who ran the Street these days and they were just as greedy and ruthless as his generation, but they were short term thinkers. They did not have the wisdom associated with patience. They wanted the money all right, but they wanted it fast. Their weaknesses included, as far as Bob Roberts could perceive, no regard whatsoever for tradition. They did not regard building a foundation for protecting against the unexpected. *They're wrong, so wrong, and it will eventually take them down.*

Bob Roberts began, "Ladies and gentlemen, let's call this meeting to order." Once the formalities had been addressed Bob Roberts informed them of the latest information he now possessed.

"This is early, of course, but this is what I have been informed of by the government through Homeland Security and some other information services we have retained to try to understand the attack. We are, of course, particularly concerned regarding our future. For instance, are we on some terrorist's target list? Apparently, and might I add fortunately, the woman who committed the violence was, they believe, what they call a "lone wolf." Also, she knew Ibrahim and there was some kind of relationship in their past. I know none of the details regarding that relationship. Her name was Inaya Al-Fulan. She was a British citizen who was educated at the London School of Economics, the same school that Ibrahim attended. She was a Palestinian whose family still lives in Lebanon. She had worked for two Wall Street firms, both small and unimportant. I was also informed that the bomb she carried was very crude and not up to the usual standards of that genre. Certainly it killed Ibrahim and Joe and injured eleven people, but as you all know the physical damage was modest as these things go. For those of you who don't know, she passed away this morning. The authorities think she was after Ibrahim as the specific target. It was just a crazy coincidence he was there when she was in the lobby. They speculate she was on her way to see Ibrahim in his office and it was very personal. It appears that she had said something to him repeatedly before she triggered the explosion. It was an Arab word – something like 'kater'. They think she was saying KHATARA. It means betray. This is an early speculation in my opinion;

214

therefore, take it for what it's worth. Wall Street is upset as hell, as you all know, and this will have to work its way through the various news cycles. We can really do nothing about it other than communicate with the press through our lawyers and our PR people. Prudence must be the watchword, and I stress and urge all of you to leak nothing. It can only hurt us.

"Now to the other business at hand, and that is the Pristinimatic/Photo Symbology Merger problem and Anne Mills. As you all know by now, Anne Mills was fired by Ibrahim and Joe the morning of the bombing. Neither he, nor Joe, told me why they decided to fire her, but I can guess. Simply put, since she was the named manager of the Merger project, they naturally blamed her for any problems that occurred. In order to protect ACS they would probably have announced to the public that once they became aware of 'the problems,' there was no choice but to fire her and probably they would have started legal action for malfeasance and recovery of her bonus and success fees."

At this point, one of the Board members, J.T. Kot, Jr., the Chairman of a public Company involved with heavy equipment manufacturing, KOT Industries, interrupted, "Bob, are you in agreement with what they did?"

"No," answered Bob Roberts, "They, in my opinion, acted too hastily."

"Ohhhhh, then what would you have done?" asked J.T. Kot, Jr.

Bob Roberts hesitated, and then replied, "Frankly, I would have tried to put her in a publically exposed position where she would look very bad. I would have used our PR people to get the maximum effect. Then I would, with the Board's support, very publically have fired her."

"Yes, it's exactly what I would have bet you would have done, Bob," stated J.T. Kot, Jr. with a disgusted look on his face. This drew a modest laugh from the room.

Continuing, "Now Bob, what exactly did Madame Mills do to deserve this action? It's quite unclear to me, and I would assume I'm speaking for other members of the Board.

At this point, Bob Roberts knew he had to be very careful or he might implicate himself. "Well, as I have come to know some of the details, she, Anne Mills, apparently found a way to upset one Brian Goldberg the Chief Technology Officer and a Pristinimatic partner.

"Upset? And I assume you have just recently learned the details?" sarcastically queried J.T. Kot, Jr.

Bob Roberts replied, "As I understand it, she knew that the Pristinimatic insiders, the founders of the Company, were a solid voting bloc. The CTO, Brian Goldberg, who was considered by the group to be honorable and extremely fair, controlled, on behalf of the group, a voting trust. Besides his vote, the trust also consisted of some original outside investors. This made it possible for the 'group' to control their Company and, more importantly, would have given them control of the Merger. Anne knew if she could find a way to break up the 'group's' voting as a bloc, that would open the door to providing

Photo Symbology the voting power, along with the votes we controlled through the public market, to manage the future of the Merger."

Bob Roberts continued, "We did not want the Pristinimatic management to run the Merger. We preferred the Photo Symbology management."

"Why?" demanded J.T. Kot, Jr.

"We didn't think the Pristinimatic people were that good."

"That's interesting," commented J.T. Kot, Jr. "I've reviewed both Company's books and spent time researching their histories. The Pristinimatic people built a better Company. They are obviously more advanced technically and it would appear overall, a better managed organization. Why they agreed to the Merger doesn't really make sense to me, but whatever. Now Bob, cut the god damn crap, why did you get rid of the Pristinimatic management?"

"I didn't, Anne did," retorted Bob Roberts.

"Sure, you had nothing to do with it. And I believe in the good fairy and the good sweet will of Wall Street," barked J.T. Kot, Jr. with a sarcastic laugh. "I've known you for over twenty years, Bob, and the classic son-of-a-bitch you are. I know better, and so does everybody in this room, and we all know, as sure as shit, you also had your hand in this. Now, stop playing games with us, why did you all get rid of the Pristinimatic management?"

Bob Roberts was angry, worried, and embarrassed, but there was nothing he could do about it. J.T. Kot, Jr., had always been difficult and uncooperative. Why Ibrahim and Joe had tolerated him was something he could never understand.

Finally, with no way to avoid it, he spoke, "They were not our kind of people. They would be very difficult to control. The Photo Symbology management are more our kind of people. They will respond much better to the plans we have for their future. It's that simple."

J.T. Kot, Jr., responded. "It's interesting, here you have a solid emerging Company with what appears to be excellent management, at least for this phase of their development, and you decide, based on your antiquated petty prejudices that the management must go. You, the ACS management, in its grand wisdom about technology companies, decides you will control the Merger by putting weaker management in place - you being the grand puppeteer. What a perfectly brilliant decision, installing weaker management. I'm amazed. Now that we understand that brilliant strategy, what exactly did Anne Mills do to make this all happen?"

Bob Roberts was having problems controlling himself, but he had no choice. He thought, *I'll find a way to get back at that arrogant bastard someday.* "She found a way to split Goldberg apart from the group, and he voted with Photo Symbology and, we got control!"

"And how was that? What in hell was her 'way'?" asked J.T. Kot, Jr.

"I'm not entirely sure, "replied Bob Roberts, "I think she convinced Goldberg that the CEO of Pristinimatic, Jersey Smart, was having an affair with Goldberg's wife."

216

"How nice, but what did that accomplish?" demanded J.T. Kot, Jr.

"Apparently, he became incredibly upset and that led to his voting with Photo Symbology, and I assume that led to his corrupting the Pristinimatic 'Torpedo' software along with the Mergers entire database. Then he disappeared."

"Let's go back a step. How exactly did Anne Mills convince Goldberg that such an affair was taking place?" demanded J.T. Kot, Jr.

"I don't really know," replied Bob Roberts.

"Frankly Bob, I don't believe you; I think you really know, but you don't want to admit it. You're trying to protect yourself under these potentially treacherous circumstances. Don't bother denying it again, let's move on," suggested J.T. Kot, Jr. "More important for the moment, what does this mean to the firm? Let us understand what the corrupted software will do to ACS."

Bob Roberts was so upset he was actually considering giving in to his anger, resigning and walking out. But, then again, a lifetime of controlling himself kicked in and he continued on. He took a deep breath and replied, "Simply put, the Merger can't operate with all its software not working - it's a business paralysis. The biggest problem, if we can't figure a fast way out, will be the SEC investigation. Second on the list, would be losses from fines and a class action lawsuit. Beginning estimates are somewhere in the $300MM range. Insurance would cover two-thirds of it. So the real loss would be around $100MM. In terms of cash flow, I'm sure we can easily stretch the payout to at least three years. Our reputation would take some hits, but if we handle the PR correctly we could quickly overcome that. Using the public sympathy created from the bombing will help. Ladies and Gentlemen, simply put, we need a patsy. Anne Mills will fill that requirement."

"Just how do you intend to handle Ms. Mills, since it would appear she was fired before anyone really had investigated anything about the Merger problems, and I would assume she must surely have retained council intending to countersue. I assume my conclusion about this is correct?" asked J.T. Kot Jr.

"Yes," answered Bob Roberts.

"Well, again I'm asking, how are you going to handle Mills?" demanded J.T. Kot, Jr.

"The best way we can under the circumstances," barked Bob Roberts.

"Come, come Bob, you must have something in mind," coaxed J.T. Kot, Jr.

"We are digging into her private life to see if there is some distracting material there. There usually is with this kind of woman. Then the PR guys will do their work."

"Jesus, that's not going to accomplish anything for the firm," commented J.T. Kot, Jr. "So the public will scorn her as a classic bitch, and nobody will hire her for a while. But with the success of her track record on Wall Street she'll eventually get hired, probably at a better salary, I'll guarantee it. We need to know if she did anything illegal. Making her the patsy for what was basically a mismanaged project isn't going to get the job done."

Now it was the rest of the Board's turn to ask questions and comment. They spent the better part of an hour and a half at it. JT Kot, Jr. said or asked nothing further. Finally, J.T. Kot, Jr. spoke, "Well Bob, you've got a meeting with all the parties this afternoon. What do you intend to do?"

"Nothing, just listen."

"Finally, an intelligent answer!" stated J.T. Kot, Jr.

Anne realized that there was no way she could avoid the meeting that had been called for that afternoon, and further she had to get an attorney to represent her. She was very familiar with the practice of one Ann Bladen a very good and very tough lawyer. She contacted her and spent much time on the phone explaining her situation and the upcoming meeting. She was lucky because Ann Bladen cleared her schedule and agreed to represent her. The meeting was scheduled for noon. Anne Mills and Ann Bladen met at a restaurant in walking distance from where the 4:00 afternoon meeting was to be held. They would go over all matters and discuss strategy.

Ann Bladen was a 35 year veteran of the corporate wars. She was called the 'Blade' and for good reason. She had successfully sliced up a vast army of legal opponents in her career history. The "Blade" was a first rate corporate commando. If there was a school for lawyers similar to a Navy Seals school for her kind of work, she would have graduated Summa Cum Laude. She was a slightly overweight woman with steel gray hair who always wore black suits and had deep set brilliant blue eyes that exuded intelligence. The surprise of knowing her was the softness of her voice and decorum. This extremely tough lawyer was easy to like, maybe too easy to like.

She began, "Anne, you've told me many things, but you haven't told me everything. Now, what exactly did you do that you shouldn't have done .. in your opinion, of course?"

Anne hesitated, she was embarrassed, she realized that what she really was feeling was shame, a feeling she had evaded for years. Somehow she found herself experiencing the discomfort of being that teenage daughter being chastised by her Mother. *This woman is not my Mother, she's my lawyer,* she thought, *get over it!* This made her very angry and she wanted to express the rage she had been suppressing. She didn't. Ann Bladen could see all the emotions bubbling within Anne but could not read them. Then Anne finally spoke, "I'm not sure I want to tell you everything."

"My god," Ann Bladen responded, "How am I to help you get through this if I don't know what's going on?"

"There's something I can't really tell you because I gave my word not to tell anybody."

"I'm not anybody," responded Ann Bladen, "I'm your lawyer!"

Anne hesitated for a minute then said very carefully, "I will tell you this much, I became aware within the last twenty-four hours that a "cure" for the

218

software problem exists and that the problem may disappear. That's all I will tell you."

"Then why did you call me in such a panic?" asked an annoyed Anne Bladen.

Anne answered, "Because, the information I just related to you may be wrong. This whole affair has never been clear and has been filled with odd events. I've really never had a feeling as to where it's actually going. I've participated in many projects with their ups and downs, but usually had a pretty good understanding of where they could and couldn't go. What people on Wall Street like to call the "thirty thousand foot view." This project has me baffled. I called you because I know I'm in some kind of trouble and I guess, for the first time I can remember, I panicked."

Ann Bladen looked at Anne and shook her head, "OK, for the moment, I don't have to know about the 'cure.' It's good enough to know that it might be coming, but if it's to come when will it occur?"

"I think," Anne answered, "It could be this afternoon at the meeting I told you about in Queens."

"If that happens, what do you think it means for you?" asked Ann Bladen.

"First, it would mean there are no problems for ACS as a firm. No regulatory issues to deal with, business as usual," stated Anne. "But for me, the firm has already fired me. Further, they have threatened me with serious civil litigation and a criminal complaint. They, as you know, are demanding that I return the success fees I have received and give up the fees I have earned, but not yet received. Regarding the Merger, if the software problems are fixed, there are no problems that would directly affect me, but there is a lot of peace to make within the Merger."

"Tell me about that," insisted Ann Bladen.

"I don't really know the details, but the head of the Merger, Jim Gale, who used to be the head of Photo Symbology, has been on a tear regarding the CTO, who was the former CTO of Pristinimatic. He has accused him of causing the software problem and then disappearing out of guilt. There are many pieces to this that I really don't know anything about. ACS has put me in a terrible position by firing me.

"Look, if you want me to help you you've got to tell me exactly what you did that you are so worried about," stated Ann Bladen.

Taking a deep breath, Anne quietly responded, "I didn't do anything that was overtly criminal. I orchestrated an event that caused a conflict to occur between the Pristinimatic partners, and I did it with the co-operation of one of those partners to achieve that goal. I've told you all this. It was sneaky, obnoxious, and thoughtless. Frankly Ann, I'm ashamed that I did it. It was on the level of a teenager acting without any consideration of the human consequences. That's it. I'm through telling any more about it. Please let's move on to this afternoon's meeting."

"Hmmm, you said it wasn't overtly criminal," stated Anne Bladen. "Overt means openness, obvious, something you can view. Are you telling me that if I look carefully I might see a criminal event? We lawyers occasionally must deal with an inchoate crime – an incomplete crime - usually a first amendment issue. In medieval times, there were countries that made laws regarding inchoate crimes. A typical inchoate crime was wishing the King was dead. Nothing occurred, other than a thought. Eventually, some countries made laws concerning these types of crimes accompanied by severe punishments. The way the prosecutors made their case was to torture the violator who would under terrible duress, eventually confess in order to stop the pain, whether they were guilty or not. With the confession, the conviction followed and, of course, the punishment – usually the removal of one's head or worse. Are we in this type of territory, Anne?"

"I don't know," answered Anne. "Are you going to help me this afternoon?"

A meeting was taking place in midtown Manhattan at Mike Levin's office. Jersey, Garrett, and Mike Levins were present.

The meeting was focused on planning an overall strategy for the 4:00pm Queens meeting. It agreed that Mike would lead their discussion and start moderately avoiding any tactical traps. Jersey, who was aware of the software fix, thought it should be introduced quickly. Mike convinced him it was best to see where everybody was coming from before any revelation occurred.

Garrett had had an earlier conversation with Mike Levins divulging the return of Brian Goldberg and the software 'fix' Brian had revealed and Jim Gale's manipulation plan. One of the topics of the conversation was about Jersey. Garrett was now becoming quite suspicious of Jersey's participation in the whole mess. He admitted he had nothing to confirm his opinion, but he was damn sure Jersey's hand was in there somewhere. "We're going to a very important meeting this afternoon, Mike; do we tell Jersey about Brian? He knows about the 'fix', but nothing about Brian."

Mike asked, "Do you trust Jersey?"

Garrett simply replied, "No!"

"Then in my opinion," Mike advised, "We don't tell anybody about Brian until the appropriate moment in the meeting. We get Brian to stay out of sight, in some near-by hotel room, someplace close to where the meeting is being held. We'll call him by cell phone when we need him to appear. We tell nobody about him. The way I would like to play the meeting is to get the right moment when we have everybody's rapt attention, fearing that they will be stripped naked, and then blow them out of the water – defenseless."

"Sounds great to me, I'll get to Brian and get him moving. He'll love it. He's pretty pissed off."

He quickly called Brian and got an immediate response. "I'll let you know what and where as soon as I know, Garrett."

CHAPTER 59 COME TO JESUS TIME

Garrett looked around the table and saw each of the players. It was interesting to see everybody's game face. There was a lot of worry in that room. It was tense, very tense. A few were trying to fake it, but not really succeeding. Mike Levin and an associate of his were representing Garrett, Jersey, and now for the first time, the currently un-revealed Brian, and possibly the former stockholders of Pristinimatic.

Garrett understood his feelings, but wondered what fears drove each of the other participants. He was well aware that Jim Gale had had the wind taken out of his sails a few hours earlier. It will be interesting to observe and to learn, perhaps even educational, how much Gale has related to his folks; in fact, if nothing else, fascinating. Garrett suspected that he had not revealed much, or at best – a highly edited version. Probably his fears were focused on what else could emerge in this meeting that could hurt him, particularly from Garrett.

The ACS people were looking at all kinds of corporate trouble. They had eliminated or increased their team by adding new lawyers from yet another law firm. Sitting across from him was Anne. Her still quite bruised face consisted of minute expressions of worry and anxiety, quite unusual for that fine face. She was busy making notes that she was showing to a woman sitting next to her. Garrett assumed the woman was her lawyer. Garrett looked at Anne seeking eye contact - nothing. Finally, sitting at the head of the table, was Judge, Abraham Smith.

The Judge began, "Ladies and Gentlemen let us start. Since there are some new faces in the room, I want everyone to introduce themselves again."

Around the room went the introductions until Anne's lawyer, Ann Bladen, introduced herself. Then there was some detectable fidgeting within the ACS crew.

The Judge then asked, "Who would like to start?"

There were no volunteers.

"If no one wants to begin this process, I will choose who starts. But first I wish to remind you all that you have much at stake, and it is now time to find a reasonable path forward that will first, and I mean first, protect the stockholders of the Merger, then second, and I mean second, help all the participants in this room work out their problems in the least painful way," stated the Judge who looked at each person sitting at the table eyeball to eyeball. "ACS, you begin."

222

With Bob Roberts sitting at his side, the ACS lawyer, Levi Goldbart, rose and asked the Judge for permission to transmit some slides to each of the laptops in the room. Everybody, including the Judge, was digitally armed. Apparently, the ACS people had gotten everybody's email addresses in their system in preparation for the meeting.

The Judge nodded yes.

The first slide was a carefully laid out graphic history of the deal with dates, stock distribution, and finances. The second slide was a graphic display of ACS's roll, and financial participation. The third slide was a presentation of the personnel involved with descriptions of their roles and responsibilities. It quite simply pointed at Anne Mills as the guilty party.

Bob Robert's thought, *So much for J.T. Kot, Jr's advice.* Then again he pondered, *I wonder where this is really all going.*

Goldbart made an excellent verbal presentation with each of the slides and a final compelling declaration of ACS's innocence and Anne's irresponsible behavior.

"One would think you're in a courtroom, councilor, with that presentation, but we are here to negotiate a solution not a conviction," barked the Judge. "Levin, it's your turn."

Mike Levin stood up and rubbed his hands together and brought them almost to a praying position just touching his mouth. With his head bowed, looking over the tops of his glasses, he began, "The assumptions, ladies and Gentlemen and your Honor, have been as follows:

One, the all-important software, 'you folks call 'Torpedo,' that is used to run this newly merged Company apparently failed completely because it was corrupted.

Two, the backup systems that were in place to prevent such an occurrence also failed – again failed completely because they too, were corrupted.

Three, the failure was a malicious act of revenge by the Chief Technical Officer of the Merger, who also had been the Chief Technical Officer of Pristinimatic before the Merger occurred.

Four, the Chief Technical Officer disappeared, as a result, of his malicious act to avoid prosecution. His motivations were personal but nevertheless, effective."

Mike paused, "Do I have it correct? Does anyone wish to add to these ... assumptions? No? Then I will assume there are no other assumptions we have to deal with."

The room was intense but extremely quiet, with no volunteers offering to add to the 'assumptions.'

"There are guilty parties in this room," then he paused and looked at everyone deliberately and carefully. "They know who they are, and they should be incredibly uncomfortable at this moment because - all - hell - is - about - to - come - down - upon - them!" stated Mike Levin using a deliberate staccato delivery - then, another long pause.

"Well, councilor, deliver the hell you've promised even though this is not a courtroom," insisted the Judge, who was equally interested to find out what Levin was talking about.

"I'll begin with a witness, your Honor," informed Mike Levin, who picked up his cell phone and made a call. Mike looked at the Judge and asked for a few minutes time to get the witness, who was waiting close by, to be called in.

The Judge granted the request.

Brian had been waiting in the neighborhood. The room's occupants were hushed, nervously waiting. A few minutes passed, the door opened, and then there was a moment comparable to a meteor dropping into the middle of a baseball game, as Brian entered the room."

There was a wave of Jesus's, my gods, and some other common surprise noises including 'Who's that?'

"Who is this?" demanded the Judge looking at Levins. "No, let me guess," looking at Brian, "I suspect ... you, sir, are the missing suspect, one Brian Goldberg, the prodigal Chief Technical Officer?"

Looking directly at the Judge, "Yes," responded Brian with a slight smile.

Jim Gale looked terrible. Anne was amazed. ACS was shocked. The Judge was amused.

The Judge waved his hand at Mike Levins to continue.

Mike continued, "We've been told that the software was corrupted, corrupted by Brian Goldberg. Further, Mr. Goldberg has been accused of allegedly corrupting the back-up."

Continuing, "The common preventative measure to stop such mischief is, as you all know, a back-up service. It is usually a remotely located back-up service supplied by an outside third party that is extremely secure and permanent. There is always an in-house back-up system which we also know was corrupted. These are the methods normally used by responsible management in responsible companies for the purpose of protecting against bad occurrences."

Then he paused, on purpose, for at least a deliberately painful minute for effect, and then, continued. "There was, and always has been, a healthy third party back-up in existence." Then looking directly at Jim Gale, "and Jim Gale knew it and always knew it, and knows it now!"

"Now a fascinating wrinkle, Brian established another third party back-up before the Merger occurred, providing ...complete redundancy. Now another surprise; neither Jim Gale, nor his management team, were aware of its existence. Why, is a discussion for another time."

"Everybody pay particular attention to what I'm about to tell you. Jim Gale personally - and we can absolutely prove this - cancelled the primary third party back-up when he became CEO and had all healthy uncorrupted data transferred to another third party back-up service. This was purposely never, never revealed by Gale - he kept this from everyone, but possibly a few members of his senior management team. The implication was, though never

224

investigated, that the back-up service - the one he cancelled - was also corrupted. It was not! I repeat; it was not! This all had happened before the corruption occurred. Therefore, in fact, he has had a good back-up in hand from day one. None of this that we all have gone through was necessary!" At this point, Levins stopped speaking and let it sink in for a long moment.

Then he continued, "Ladies and Gentlemen, we don't need Jim's back-up because Brian also possesses a perfectly good back-up - it's alive and well with no problems. Hear me carefully; the "Torpedo' software problem that is the basis of all this trouble can absolutely be eliminated within the next twenty-four hours to forty-eight hours. So folks ... the problems are gone."

"But the problem of Jim Gales' actions still exists," Mike Levins stated ever so clearly. "Mr., Gale, of course, knew all about the existence of a third party back-up that he had established; he knew that it had no problems and that it, therefore, could be used to restore the software at any time. But, he was not aware of the fact that the original service that he had cancelled had taken their own precautions. Such services keep emergency back-ups of cancelled files for a certain period of time to protect their clients, as well as themselves, from problems that might arise from any data transfers or service cancellations. Read the fine print next time Mr. Gales. This is necessary for them to be able to aid a client with lost data, or more important to the back-up service, prove there was no problem in case a client accuses and/or sues them, claiming the back-up service was flawed and/or irresponsible. Back-up services exist to prevent the problems the Merger is experiencing. Well, Mr. Gale, what do you have to say about this?" demanded Mike Levins loudly.

There was rapt attention while everyone waited for that answer.

Mike Levins turned towards Jim Gale, "It's either here, or in court under oath, you'll have to answer that question."

Gale's lawyer immediately stopped Jim Gale from saying anything.

Mike Levins sighed, "Yes, I admit, that's a different problem which will have to be worked out in a different venue."

Judge Smith looked at Mike Levins, "So you're saying, the problem could have been solved at any time by the Merger management because an uncorrupted back-up was in their possession at all times as led by Mr. Gale. And further, as of today Mr. Goldberg also has within his control a solution to the critical problem we are trying to solve and it is ...for all practical purposes solvable by tomorrow or the at the very least the next day. Is that correct?"

"Yes to both, Judge,"

At that point, Brian handed the Judge a large package he was carrying. "Your Honor, that contains all that is necessary to restore the Merger software. There is more than one copy of this in existence as well as a back-up service I commissioned."

The Judge, looking at Gale and shaking his head, "Then I would expect that ACS has no further problems with the Merger as a public entity, but must now reconsider certain aspects of its relationship with the Merger management, but that is not a problem for this gathering. Regarding Ms. Mills and her participation in this gathering, that too is no longer an issue. You, Ms. Mills, and your, I believe, former Company will have to mutually work out your collective problems. The group that Mike Levins represents, which frankly is a little confusing to me, would appear to have no further issues that are a concern for this meeting. Brian Goldberg and the Merger will have to work out their quite thorny issues elsewhere. And finally, it would appear that the Merger Board and the Merger management have some interesting personnel problems to solve. I will submit a report to all within a week. Apparently there is no further purpose for this gathering. Therefore, this meeting is ended and there are no further reasons to meet."

The Judge stopped Mike Levins on the way out, "Mike, I have rarely seen anybody verbally convicted so quickly and effectively in my courtroom, and obviously, Mr. Gale never answered your question. I suspect he never will."

Mike smiled, "Thanks for the compliment! Actually, it wasn't that hard Judge, under the circumstances. I was relatively easy on him, there is much more."

"Oh! I'm still wondering what you were trying to get Gale to answer. You never really quite asked the question," stated the Judge.

"Well, it's a kind of 'smoking gun,'" said Mike Levins knowing damn well that the hacked document could never be presented in a courtroom.

As the participants were getting into their cars, Levi Goldbart started waving his hands and shouting for everybody to gather around. He had an announcement to make. The group surrounded him including the Judge.

Goldbart spoke, "I have an announcement to make. I've just heard from the Merger. The team they hired to find and fix the software problem was successful in finding the cause of the problem, which apparently was a virus/hardware issue, whatever the hell that means. In other words, although they do not have a way to fix the software, they know how everything was corrupted. They declared the damage was the result of some kind of virus. They called it a "visitor" virus. I then told them of our development and that we have a complete and healthy version of 'Torpedo' available. They said it would probably take a couple of days to get new servers working, maybe even sooner, but that's the worst of it."

Garrett looked at Jim Gale and shook his head in disgust, "What in god's name were you thinking?"

Gale simply responded by giving him the finger!

Garrett retorted with, "That's the best you can do?"

Brian fuming uncharacteristically accosted Jim Gale, "Do you have any idea of the damage you've done to me? What you've done to my life?"

Gale froze for a moment with Brian casting a stare of complete contempt.

Then Jim Gale shrugged his shoulders and turned away. As he was turning away, Brian slapped him as hard as he could across his face, knocking him down.

226

Garrett grabbed Brian and quickly pulled away, "Are you crazy? That could only lead to more trouble. I don't blame you, but it will solve nothing."

"It felt so damn good," Brian replied almost whispering.

Jim Gale was shocked at the slap and picked himself up looking even worse than he did when Mike Levins went after him at the meeting. ACS showed no emotion. Anne just put her hand up to her mouth, shaking her head. Then, out of nowhere, Garrett found the incident funny. Maybe it was because he would never have expected Brian to hit anybody. Maybe it was the release of tension, but he began to laugh uncontrollably. It became contagious and Jersey and Brian joined him. They were laughing like kids who couldn't contain themselves. Gale was aghast.

Finally, Gale hollered directly at Brian, "I'm gonna' sue your ass off buddy!"

The Judge stunned, but also amused at all that had occurred, declared, "Amazing!"

Brian still laughing and waving his hand in disgust just said, "Yeah, yeah, yeah ..

The Judge spoke again, "I would be careful Mr. Gale, you have a lot to account for.

CHAPTER 60 TRUTH AND ...

Anne Mills and her lawyer drove back into the city. They said nothing for a while then Bladen spoke, "This is a new one for me. The trouble was the result of a software/hardware fault caused by some mysterious virus ... they think. It then became a random opportunity that was seized on by a crook – allegedly; I'm speaking of Mr. Gale. Apparently, Mr. Gale saw a way that he could have some kind of advantage, providing a capitalization gain by putting these unrelated events together to create a story of corporate mischief complete with corporate villains. It turned out to be nothing more than a fairytale. We never heard what exactly he was after, but that doesn't take too much imagination to assume it was some kind of means of getting more for himself, and maybe the Merger. His biggest mistake was assuming that Brian Goldberg would be gone permanently or at least for some longer time, certainly much longer than he actually did. Since Mr. Gale had the fix in his hands from day one, he knew, innocent or not, Goldberg was not the key to restoration. He always possessed a safe system back up, one that would achieve normal and healthy operation. Amazing, this whole episode is only a couple of weeks old - from feast to famine, then back to feast, and a terrorist act thrown in that has absolutely nothing to do with the monkey business, but regardless, affects the players. Unfortunately, that was real and resulted in injury and death. It is fascinating how these apparently unrelated events came together to create this drama. It reminds me of a line from Shakespeare's The Tempest .."

"These actors (As I foretold you) were all spirits and melted into thin air ... leave not a rack behind."

She continued, "I love those lines. It describes the foolishness of created illusion – lies - and the resulting behavior.

Well, Anne how does one put this all together emotionally? Time will help, but complete understanding, perhaps, never. This was indeed an amazing display of confluent events that were not related to one another. There will be one hell of a management blow-out at the Merger. I wonder how that will be handled considering the makeup of the new Merger management. Oh well, they'll find some way to spin it and life will go on. Some of the story will leak. I would suppose Mr. Gale and some of his management team will have to find new opportunities for employment, but who knows. Mr. Gale really should be criminally and civilly prosecuted, but it probably won't happen because it would damage the Merger. Brian Goldberg will have his day in court suing Mr. Gale, then again, thinking about it, maybe not. His reputation was not harmed at the end of the day, and he did jump ship without telling anybody."

The two remained quiet as they drove down the Eastside Highway. Ann Bladen broke the silence as they were turning west leaving the Highway, "Anne you have some significant issues to deal with concerning your former employer. They accused you of wrongdoing and fired you for cause. The problem, in their eyes, was the negative outcome of certain matters that you created and thus, were responsible for. You were bringing shame, disgrace, and financial losses to the firm, therefore, in their eyes, you have to be blamed, exposed, and punished. But, in the wink of an eye the problem evaporated. There has to be a resolution to what they started. Obviously from the presentation Goldbart made, you were the target of all that was bad. Now how does ACS proceed and how do we respond? I need more information from you - no editing, everything."

Anne replied, "I need some time to think this over. I know they threw me to the dogs, but I'm not without guilt. Frankly, I think I'm in shock."

Ann Bladen responded, "How much time? We've got to move quickly. Each day delayed improves their side. ACS is a big rich Company and you can't get into a pissing contest with an elephant."

"One day," was Anne's response.

"One day, so be it. Be in my office the next working day at 9:00am."

Anne returned to her apartment, opened a very good bottle of wine, poured a generous amount into a wine glass, retreated to a hot bath, and settled into the foam topped delight of warm bubbling waters with their sweet fragrance. It began to release some of the agonizing tensions of the past days. Sometime in that pleasantness she drifted off into a sweet nap.

The next day Mike Levins, Garrett, and Jersey agreed to meet at a nearby bar that Levins knew of for a couple of drinks. Brian was invited but declined.

They sat down and said nothing for a few minutes then Jersey asked "What do you think will happen to Jim Gale?"

Garrett answered, "He'll get fired, but there will be some bullshit story supporting a resignation tale. But at the end of the day, the devil will avoid his due."

Levins nodded in agreement.

Garrett had been churning big time for the past couple of days regarding Jersey's part in all this mischief. He knew Jersey so well and Jersey's normal responses had been absent of their usual swagger during this whole episode. It was time to confront him! He waited until Jersey was a little loose. Garrett knew Jersey didn't need much alcohol to feel a buzz.

As the second round of drinks arrived Garrett struck, "Jersey, as this whole episode unfolded, and even before, I've been noticing you, your attitude, the way you've responded to events – not the usual Jersey Smart behavior. I've known you for many years and, damn it, I think you're hiding something. I know you, and I've lived with a great deal of your bullshit. I know you can be a son-of-bitch and it doesn't bother you for one god damn little moment. But something went down that you have been ... worried about, or concerned over, or possibly ...... exposed. What in the hell is going on?"

Jersey responded angrily, "I lost my job, I got kicked out. How the fuck would you expect me to act?"

"I don't buy it. The Jersey I'm familiar with would be on fire, looking to get back - burn the place down. Instead, you've been something much quieter - a suppressed something, maybe ... guilt. I'm unfamiliar with that side of your personality. You remind me of somebody ready to duck. That certainly is not vintage Jersey." Garrett drilled into Jersey with stainless steel conviction, "I've suffered the same outcome as you. I know what I lost and I feel the same humiliation and anger. So don't cry on my shoulder. I'll come right to the point. I'm convinced that you played a part in what happened. The picture on the floor in your office was no accident. That becomes more obvious with each day. But why would you do it? What did you have to gain? You got thrown out."

Levins was watching all this with some amusement and some trepidation. The Garrett he was used to was usually relatively cool and rarely showed his temper. He had never seen these two in a confrontation.

Then Garrett looking straight at Jersey, "You bastard, you low life bastard, you made a deal. They came to you and promised you something if you broke up our voting bloc. Of course, they told you that you would be the CEO, ... didn't they? C'mon! They screwed you instead, and you couldn't do a damn thing about it. You got them the voting control they wanted. You gave them the gift on a silver platter. Magnificent - a double, double cross! If you complained or took any action, you would be exposed and subject to all kinds of legal crap. Jersey, they had you for lunch. You threw Brian to the dogs, but you didn't anticipate how far that was going to go. Jesus, after all these years with our crew, our days at NASA, the struggles to start Pristinimatic, how in the hell could you do it?" Garrett stopped and shook his head and then looked up at the ceiling and then at Jersey, "Don't say a thing, I know, you once told me, 'It's your nature.' It sure as hell is!"

Jersey, now exposed and furious and red faced as hell, stood up and barked, "Fuck you Garrett, that broad you have the 'hots' for, set the whole thing up!" and then he walked out.

Both Mike Levins and Garrett were astounded. Then Levins commented, "I'll be damned, he admitted it. He screwed everybody and then ACS and Gale screwed him. There's a certain poetic justice in that scenario. What woman is he talking about?"

"Anne Mills," Garrett answered, raising his voice to almost a scream. "God damn it! That puts the whole thing together. Anne screwed me to the wall! Anne, how could you?"

"You have feelings for that woman?" Mike Levins asked rather incredulously.

230

Garrett nodding his head yes, "Right now, I want to kill her. Yeah, but strangely, I have those feelings …… Mike, I'm in love with her."

"Oh my God, how in the hell did that happen?" queried an astounded Mike Levins.

"It's an odd story," Garrett continued. "Actually, I knew her as a child in my hometown. We were on different sides of the social order in a very provincial place and would never have gotten together, particularly in that town. But, Wall Street brought us together as opponents and …I found her irresistible. I just knew. She knows how I feel and proclaims our relationship is impossible and has turned me down flat. I choose not to believe her and I think she feels the same way I do. How's that for confidence, or possibly, I admit, total idiocy? Love is indeed blind, etc, etc. A lot of poets have created beautiful sonnets proclaiming the same. I wonder if any of them knew what they were talking about."

"Ye gods, Garrett, she's the real villain according to Jersey," proclaimed Mike Levins.

"Apparently," replied Garrett. "But I don't think it's that simple. I'm not saying she doesn't have blood on her hands, but I've come to believe there is real contrition. I have reason, perhaps it's my intuition, to believe this is a person in transition. I sincerely believe she does not want to do those things anymore. I believe she is carrying a very heavy load. I think these are feelings covered by a veil she has never removed and now, time and circumstances have obliterated the veil. I understand only too well where she came from, and the scars and emotional depravity of her upbringing. I honestly feel she's a good person. And then again, I might be completely deceiving myself."

Shaking his head, and with a sad smile, Garrett looked at Mike and said, "I'm incredibly drawn to this woman. It's complicated, but so are human emotions. We are creatures composed of so many layers. To perceive the dark sides and bright sides that make up the texture of a person requires more than simply about what is seen or heard. It requires communication on some deeper level, and I'm not sure of what that really is, but somehow I feel it; pretty weird, Mike? But then again, maybe not. Maybe this is the most significant part of the way we learn how to know folks, and we never realize that is exactly what is actually happening. Perhaps this is the path to what we call intuition"

"Garrett, what are you smoking? Anne Mills is Wall Street. There's no room for good or nice or guilt. Wake-up you're dreaming," retorted Mike Levins. "I'll admit she's very good looking, but ….. ,"

"I know," said Garrett, "You're generally right and I may be out of my mind, but we are connected, and I'm not a naïve kid. I swear I was able to look into Anne's innermost core and what I saw was good and … I want her. There's nothing blinder than love, I guess. I also saw the pain, the guilt, the barriers, and the struggle. Curiously, what Jersey revealed, his shot at me, explains much of the puzzle surrounding Anne. It was meant to hurt, to be son-of-a-bitch mean, but instead, it actually helps. It explains things I didn't understand before."

"Mike Levins responded, "I hope you know what you're doing."

"So do I," answered Garrett. "So do I."

The next day, late in the afternoon the building intercom sounded, "Ms. Mills, there was a messenger here who just left an envelope for you." Her respite was shattered.

A few minutes later Anne sat down at her kitchen table and nervously opened the envelope. Anne was still at her kitchen table several minutes later staring at the simple note that had been delivered in the envelope. She was overwhelmed with a burst of feelings, some good, some bad, some terrible, and some not even identifiable. She had never expected this. A door had opened, or had it closed, she only knew that things had changed. Her imagination ran ferally with possibilities. Did this mean she was free of the burden of confession?

The note simply said ...

Anne,

I know everything. We must talk.

Garrett

CHAPTER 61 A HUNT FOR CONTRITION

I wonder how this will end, Garrett mused. It had been several days since the Judge had ended the meeting. Garrett was finally gathering the snippets of his thoughts to re-establish his dialog with Anne. He could feel the weight of its importance and, of course, his unremitting desire. After all, and there was no denying this, it was about the future. All these thoughts were contaminated with so much anger, as a result, of the recent revelations. The guessing was gone. The picture was clearly in focus.

He remembered other calls in his life he probably should have made, but didn't. There are so many would've, could've, and should've items that make up a life. Anne was complexity personified for Garrett. He knew she had done some bad things. He didn't know the exact details, but apparently it was her idea to plant the picture with Jersey's co-operation. And there was no doubt that it tore Brian to pieces. Brian was back and he seemed all right for the present. Maybe the all right was connected with his official removal from corporate villainy. It would be completely naïve to believe his pain was gone. Of course, there was much work to be done there, but it was good to see that Brian was apparently together. He thought, *Will Brian try to find Yvette? I wonder.*

Garrett was looking at his phone. He had to call Anne, reconnect, but he was pensive as well as just plain afraid. There were so many emotions he was feeling. Garrett stalled for another few minutes. *Sam said it was worth a try. I think he's a pretty smart guy. I sent the note. I can't back out now and I don't want to back out now. Anne may be a terrible mistake for me and perhaps, me for Anne. I just can't deny what I feel. Make the damn call already!* And he did.

Anne, not surprisingly, gave him a very hard time. She made it clear that there was no purpose for their getting together. "I have no special feelings for you," she repeated many times during their phone conversation.

Garrett, ever the optimist, thought, *you've told that to me too many times.*

Finally, she gave in and agreed to meet.

They sat in Sam's at the rear of the deli. Anne looked disheveled. Once again, the normally very carefully coifed business woman was dressed sloppily in jeans and a tee shirt - no make-up, nothing. Her hair was even carelessly combed. The strains of all the recent events were quite visible along with some remaining scabs and fading black and blue marks from the bombing. They sat opposite one another, having cups of coffee. Their respective territories on the table were separated by a bowl of pickles and another bowl containing pickled tomatoes and of course, salt and pepper shakers.

Leaning on her elbows and with her chin resting in her hands looking directly at Garrett, Anne asked, "Who told you?" Then running her hands through her hair and bending her head, stared at the table.

"Is that important?" responded Garrett.

"No, I guess not," said Anne. "I assume it was Jersey Smart."

Garrett acknowledged it with a nod of his head. "Who are you Anne? No, that's not the right question. Who do you want to be?"

With her hand in front of her mouth and a suspicious expression she said, "That's a strange question. I am who I am."

"And who is that Anne Mills?" asked Garrett.

"Someone, that I'm not too comfortable with these days! Maybe I never was comfortable with me on any day, come to think of it," mused Anne.

"Guilt, is that what I detect? The arousal of conscience? Anne, how could you?" asked Garrett not really expecting an answer.

"Is that why you got me here? To berate me for my actions?" responded Anne. "I know I've behaved terribly, but that's what I'm expected to do. They pay me a lot of money if I do it well. Sam says I'm a soldier - a Wall Street soldier. As a soldier, I do whatever it takes to win."

"Is winning that important?" demanded Garrett.

"On Wall street it is. That's everything!"

There was silence for a few minutes. Anne couldn't look at Garrett. It was becoming very painful. Garrett stared at her. "Anne, I don't know what to do with you. I'm furious. I couldn't be more pissed-off. I know what you did and …… I'm still in love with you. Good or bad, that's the way it is for me."

Anne looked directly at Garrett, "Get over it. It's amazing, where your head is at - the romantic. Where's the scientist? Where's the logic? This isn't Millsport and I'm certainly not your dream girl. Go find a nice girl to fall in love with. I'm truly sorry for what I did, that I swear. I'll never do that or anything like it again."

"Damn it Anne, Why the change?" demanded Garrett.

"Simply, I can't handle it anymore. I'm not sure why now, after all these years, but I just can't handle it or want to handle it ever again," stated Anne.

"Maybe you've changed, and are no longer the same angry kid you once were," suggested Garrett, "but you must be very lonely."

"How would you know about me as a kid? We probably saw each other a dozen times and never said anything but hello or goodbye or a grunt," said Anne. "Oh, we danced once and I admit it was very pleasant."

"True! But c'mon Anne, I saw how your family was," replied Garrett. "Body english goes a long way. I know what a prick your big brother Grahm was, and probably still is. Everybody in town knew that. And your Mother was as subtle as an outhouse. I knew how she felt about us; everybody in my community knew that. It must kill her that she can't keep some of my brethren out of the country club. Times change, we all have to adjust, or something like that."

234

"What is this tirade about, Garrett? This can't be the only reason you called me down here."

"No, but it came out nevertheless," answered Garrett. "Of course I'm angry. Think of what happened."

"I'm through, get it! It won't happen ever again. Let's put an end to this, please. I want to go home," pleaded Anne. She stood up and said, "Goodbye. I must admit I would have liked to have known your daughter better. Somehow, I think we connected."

"I think she feels the same."

"Really?" responded Anne.

"That makes two of us who are interested," replied Garrett smiling for the first time. It suddenly occurred to him; *a possible crack in the veneer*. "Go home, Anne" ... and she did.

CHAPTER 62 RE-ARRANGEMENTS

The day was steamy hot, as Anne Mills and her lawyer Ann Bladen, were approaching the ACS building. As they entered, Anne was amazed to see that there were no traces of the bombing event in the lobby - they'd repaired it and scrubbed it clean. It had only been a few weeks since it happened, but there was now an entirely different security system and more guards present. Fifteen minutes later they entered a conference room. Bob Roberts and two lawyers were present. Anne recognized Levi Goldbart but not the other lawyer. Roberts introduced him as Goldbart's assistant. Also in the room was a Court Stenographer sitting apart from the conference table with her steno equipment ready to record all the spoken events that were about to take place.

Anne Bladen spoke looking directly to Levi Goldbart, "I see you have a Court Steno present."

"You have a problem with that Ms. Bladen?" queried Levi Goldbart.

"No, I think it is a good idea."

Then another person entered the room. It was obvious that Bob Roberts was surprised. "Hello, J.T. You're joining us?" asked a concerned Bob Roberts. The gentleman nodded yes. Bob Roberts continued, "Everybody, I'd like you to meet a member of our Board, J.T. Kot, Jr., the Chairman and CEO of KOT Industries."

J.T. Kot Jr. did not join either group at the conference table, but rather sat at the unoccupied end.

After the introductions Levi Goldbart began, "As you all know, ACS has made some serious allegations about the irresponsible actions of Ms. Mills regarding the recent Pristinimatic/Photo Symbology Merger. There are criminal as well as civil matters involved. There have been discussions with Ms. Mills' lawyer, Ms. Ann Bladen, to see if there was a way to settle matters out of court. I'm sorry to say we have made no progress in that area. Therefore, as of today we are prepared to bring this matter to the District Attorney as well as initiate a civil proceeding. I've called this meeting as a last chance to see if Ms. Mills will change her position and we can avoid the worst."

Ann Bladen interrupted with a sardonic smile on her face, "Why would you do that Mr. Goldbart?"

An obviously annoyed Levi Goldbart hesitated then replied, "We recognize her seven years of employment, and therefore we would like to avoid the most severe punishment under the circumstances."

Ann Bladen continued, "It's interesting that you recognize her seven years of employment where she made a fortune for ACS with her talents - the same talents that made the Merger successful. That's a long time on Wall Street. Let me be blunt, Gentlemen. If her hands are dirty in this affair, your hands are just as dirty – possibly, dirtier."

"Hardly," responded Levi Goldbart. "But ignoring that for the moment, let me state what we require, to avoid litigation and the criminal issues. We want a written sworn statement from Ms. Mills regarding all her actions in this matter. ACS will keep this statement confidential as long as Ms. Mills keeps all matters involving ACS and the Merger confidential. With regard to this, there is to be a signed statement guaranteeing secrecy. There is to be a return of all income associated with this project along with a signed release of any and all financial obligations, as well as a guarantee that there will be no litigation under any circumstances in the future. Further, Ms. Mills is to turn in her Series 7 license, therefore, leaving the profession permanently. And finally, she is to return all her ACS stock and stock options."

Ann Bladen began, "As I understand, it was the recently diseased Joseph Taglaferri and Ibrahim Sahid who did the firing. Is that true?"

"Yes," answered Levi Goldbart.

Looking at Bob Roberts, Anne Bladen asked, "Mr. Roberts, is that true?"

Roberts responded, "You just got your answer from Levi."

"I want it from you," insisted Ann Bladen looking directly at Bob Roberts.

Levi Goldbart responded, "Where is this going? We're not in court yet!"

"I want the current head of the Company to acknowledge who did the firing, not the Company lawyer," demanded Anne Bladen.

Levi Goldbart quickly gave Bob Roberts an instruction not to answer.

"Interesting Mr. Goldbart, nobody has been sworn in. This isn't a deposition," stated Ann Bladen. "Let us move on."

"Now there are some other questions I need to have answered. Who was my client's boss? Who did she report to?" asked Ann Bladen.

Levi Goldbart burst forth, "Ms. Bladen we are here to negotiate. It was you who just made it clear that this is not a deposition and we are not in court."

"So, why not answer the question? You will have to answer them in Court as sworn testimony," stated Ann Bladen.

"I'm well aware of what occurs in the Court Room," responded an annoyed Levi Goldbart.

At this point, J.T. Kot Jr. chimed in, "I want an answer to that question and the question before. Who the hell did the firing and who did she report to?"

Goldbart, not happy with where this was going, stood up and began to walk towards J.T. Kot, Jr. as if he wanted to say something to him in private.

J.T. Kot Jr spoke, "Stay where you are Levi. You work for me. I want to hear those answers, now!"

Levi Goldbart retreated, "Answer her Bob."

Bob Roberts spoke, "She was fired by Joe and Ibrahim. I was completely unaware of it until the next day. She reported to Joe, Ibrahim, and me on the project."

"Oh," responded Ann Bladen. "As I understand it, she generally reported to you and rarely to them. On those occasions that my client would see them, you, Bob Roberts, were always present. Those occasions were to discuss tactical and strategic moves and to hear reports concerning the status of the project. The exception that I'm aware of is the day that she was fired. Come to think of it, you might have been killed or injured if you had participated in the firing. Be careful Mr. Roberts, there are witnesses and records."

At this declaration, Anne wondered whatever and wherever her lawyer was going.

"Where are you going with this?" Levi Goldbart demanded.

Ann continued, "Where I'm going is the following. Joseph Taglaferri and Ibrahim Sahid fired my client because they were informed of the Merger problems by Anne's boss, Mr. Bob Roberts, who made damn sure my client got all the blame."

Looking directly at Bob Roberts, "you scared the 'bejesus' out of them and they apparently panicked and proceeded with the firing. Anne was to be the sole villain. Mr. Roberts, you did so to cover your ass! It's just that simple. You're as much a part of this as you are accusing my client of being. Nice try Roberts, would you like to try it out in a courtroom? To add to all of this was the rotten luck that led to the deaths of management along with physical and traumatic injury to my client and, of course, the injuries to innocent bystanders."

Anne now realized how deliberate her lawyer's message was, 'fuck with us and we'll bloody you.' They bantered back and forth for next 30 minutes or so.

With some pauses, the lawyer battering was getting more intense. Suddenly J.T. Kot Jr. interrupted, raising his voice and slamming the table with his hand, "Stop!" They stopped.

Then he said, "I've listened to this for going onto almost an hour and I want it ended now. Both lawyers, there's nothing more for either of you to contribute, so please, shut up. I've made a decision on behalf of the Board, which has empowered me to settle this matter. Now, between the two advisories in this matter, Roberts and Mills and probably some others who have not surfaced at this time, there is no doubt that both of you were responsible for the conduct in the Merger that was unacceptable. As it has fortunately worked out, ACS has not been harmed. This is not a result of any efforts on either of your parts. That apparently was a matter of good luck and nothing else."

He continued, "Bob Roberts, you tried to bullshit us regarding your role in this affair. You're a liar and the Board knows it. Therefore, we are letting you go.

He let that hang in the air for a long minute.

"We'll honor your contract and pay you out on condition of a release of any further obligation on the part of ACS and a guarantee of confidentiality. Please submit a resignation letter by the end of this day. I'm sure you will get a lawyer and try to start something, but you would be best advised to accept our decision. Frankly, we should have dismissed you years ago. Go find employment somewhere else or retire. Some advice: Spend some quiet time thinking about your recent conduct and the other things you have done over the years that should remain un-revealed. Goodbye."

J.T. Kot Jr. motioned towards the door for Bob Roberts to leave. Bob Roberts hesitated, as if about to say something. He was humiliated and flustered. He wanted to say something, but could not find the words. He waited for another minute, staring with disdain at J.T. Kot, Jr. He finally took a deep breath, picked up his belongings, and without any other comment left the room.

Everybody was shocked and quite surprised and it showed on their faces. Only the Court Stenographer was unmoved. J.T. Kot Jr. thanked and dismissed her. He then turned to Levi Goldbart, "Levi your business is done here, thank you. I wish to have a private conversation with Ms. Mills and her lawyer."

Levi Goldbart left as ordered and J.T. Kot Jr. turned his attention to Anne Mills and Ann Bladen, "Ms. Bladen refrain from lawyering for the next few minutes. Ms. Mills, may I call you Anne?"

Anne replied, "Of course, yes."

"Anne, you have been a puzzle to me at times regarding this affair. You're hard to read. I have reviewed all your reports and emails as well as looked back at previous projects that you were involved with. I began by believing you were a ruthless bitch, but a very smart and effective one. And I still believe you probably were all that. You made a great deal of money for this firm, and that, in my book, counts. You've been extremely successful in this Wall Street dirt. But the woman I see here is contrite. You've said nothing, but I'm reading it none the less. I'm very good at that. I'll admit, in front of your lawyer, that your firing was a mistake, but you were fired, and that's the reality. Anne, contrition and Wall Street don't mix, and that's a reality also. I think you should apply your vast talents elsewhere. Therefore, what we are offering is the following:

One, we'll accept a backdated letter of resignation and there will be no firing on your record.

Two, we will honor your contract and you will receive all your Merger success fees and your ACS stock and options will stay in effect and whole.

Three, you will sign a separation agreement with all the confidentiality caveats.

And finally, four, there will be no litigation matters pursued by us or you.

If that is acceptable, this meeting is concluded. Ms. Bladen, are we finished?"

Ann Bladen looked to her client smiling and without conferring with Anne replied, "We are in agreement and the meeting is finished."

As the two women left the ACS building, Ann Bladen commented, "Kot likes you and respects you. He saw your pain. Anne, he looked at more than your emails and reports. He probably knows your history all the way back to when you were a kid. He made it plain as hell. He's absolutely correct in my opinion. Get away from Wall Street and get on with your life doing something that makes you feel good."

They left the ACS building and caught a cab going uptown.

As the cab was slowly working its way through traffic Anne began to drift. She re-called how she felt as a child with the fate of her father - the ultimate emptiness, the cold unrecoverable reality, and the constant fright. Her Father was her protector. She was always safe when he was there - safe from her Mother, safe from her brothers. That wasn't really fair regarding all her brothers; it was brother Grahm who was so terrible. Her middle brother, Webster, was weak and followed Grahm. If there had been no Grahm she guessed it would have been easier, but there still was Mother. Grahm probably frightened Webster and he probably followed him to protect himself. Her youngest brother August never hurt her. If there was anyone she could still love in the family it was August, August with his problems, but maybe not so many today. Fortunately, he seems to have married well.

Darkness came early on the December night she remembered, and would always remember. There had been two snowstorms in a row and about two feet of snow had covered everything. Anne remembered the view from her bedroom window. It included snow covered bushes, snow banks from street plowing, shoveled paths and sidewalks, and snow drifts manufactured by the wind. Her view went all the way to the Abraham Lincoln Elementary School yard. She remembered particularly how beautiful it all was. It was very close to Christmas and many houses were already decorated. There were wreaths, colored lights, Christmas trees, and the signs of holiday anticipation everywhere. As six o'clock approached the Mills family sat down for dinner. Her brothers and her Father, the Judge, ate heartily. The Judge had been in court from early morning to well past five and was very hungry. After dinner, he put on his boots and an old Pea Jacket he still had from his days in the Navy and took their dog, Lady, for an evening walk. It was a few minutes to seven when the Judge left the house. Anne went into her room to do her homework. The Judge usually took a half hour for, as he called it, "his and Lady's evening constitutional." Sometimes it was longer because he would run into somebody and chat. He loved neighborhood gossip.

Eight o'clock came and the Judge had not returned. At eight fifteen, her Mother sent her brothers out to look for their Father. By this time Anne had become aware of the goings on. By twenty-five minutes to nine, nothing. Her Mother called the Police. Anne, dressed for the winter cold and without asking permission, slipped out the kitchen door and proceeded to go on her own search. She knew better than any members of the family where her Father would wander for his many constitutionals because she often accompanied him so often. She was worried that he had somehow hurt himself and couldn't get back. Maybe he'd broken a leg. She knew her brothers would search the streets but probably not a certain path through the woods in back of the school. This was sort of a secret place she and her Father liked to go when they walked together. It was their place.

A full Moon was out illuminating the fresh snowfall as she approached the path. She was struck by the beauty of the evening and the sharp shadows of the leafless trees as they painted the white surfaces with their black images. This familiar place was completely changed with the snow and the full Moon; nothing was familiar, but quite alien on this beautiful cold evening. She became frightened. She saw footsteps and paw prints that were probably from her Father and the dog. Then she saw Lady standing and suddenly wagging her tail as she detected Anne's presence. As she got closer, she saw Lady's leash stretched tightly down into the snow, keeping the dog from running to her. Her father was lying down in the snow face, eyes open. "Daddy, are you all right?" She bent down on her knees and saw her Fathers face illuminated by the moonlight. It was a mask she had never seen before. She took his very cold hand and held it tightly. "Don't go Daddy, I love you," she whispered. "I can't let you go." The police found her with her dead Father a half hour later whispering to herself something they could not understand.

Later she learned that her Father had a heart attack. From that day on, she seemed to be alone and afraid. Reflecting, as she sat riding in the cab remembering it so clearly, it was that terrible moment of abandonment that had defined her life, and in so many ways, apparently, her professional conduct. She knew she was smart, smarter than most, and she applied that gift to protect her from those pains and find a way to win at whatever she chose to pursue.

She continued with her thoughts. *My family is remote. I rarely see them or want to. In spite of all my combat on Wall Street, my brother Grahm still scares me. I know a lot of people, but strangely I only really have one friend in this world, Sam Axinov. How unlikely that Sam is my one friend. It amazes me. Somehow Sam really sees me, understands me. He knows me for the fraud I am. He knows I'm the frightened girl who never got past the loss of Daddy. He doesn't know the specific details, but it makes no difference, he sees who I am and feels my history.* Then it occurred to her she always felt better when she was with Sam. *I haven't known that feeling since Daddy died. My God, at this point in my life, I have stumbled into ..... a father. I don't know how he does it, but he understands.* She realized for the first time how deeply she cared for Sam. Then once again the new thing happened to her, tears came. Then thoughts of Garrett arose, *I wonder if he could ever forgive me.*

Ann Bladen spotted them, but said nothing. Later she would bring it up and ask, "Why the tears? You've had a really good day."

She answered, "A reverie and a realization."

"Oh, what reverie and what realization?"

"It was all about how I got to be me.

CHAPTER 63 ADVICE

The day was once again hot and Garrett was trying to decide whether it was worth it to go bike riding. The phone rang and it was Brian. After polite greetings Brian asked, "Garrett, I would like to talk to you. Have you got any time this afternoon?"

Garrett replied, "Sure, I'm going for a bike ride now, but c'mon up for lunch I'll give you a superb tuna fish sandwich and a beer and we'll chat."

Brian arrived at noon and announced, "You probably don't know this yet, but the Merger Board has decided to retain Jim Gale as head of the Company."

"You've got to be kidding! After all the shit he pulled they want him. It doesn't seem to make sense. All right, tell me how this scam was accomplished," said an exasperated Garrett.

"Yeah," replied Brian. "Somehow he has convinced them that what he was doing would have benefitted the Company, and in some crazy damn way he is taking credit for gaining control of the vote that enabled Photo Symbology to dominate."

"My god, that's fucking disgusting," commented Garrett. "I need a beer. You ready?"

"Sure, that sounds good. There's more news. They offered me my old position back with a big fat raise."

"Are you going to take it?"

"Nope, that's a bridge too far."

"So what are going to do?"

"Look for Yvette."

"That's it, nothing professionally?"

"Not for a while," informed Brian. "Look Garrett, I've been doing a lot of thinking and I owed you a heads up as this whole thing unraveled, and frankly it probably would have come out different if I had spent some time discussing it with you. Obviously, I couldn't care less about Jersey, but you, you have always been a good friend. What I would like you to consider is, if you can forgive me, that is. I would like you and me, once again, to do something professionally together. I know I'm asking a lot, but, as a result, of all that I've been through, I think I actually grew a little. I don't think I would ever do such stupid and inconsiderate things like that ever again."

"I know you as well as anybody knows you, Brian," said Garrett. "I understand what happened. You certainly screwed up big time. You bought into some real bullshit. You've paid a big price for that and now you're living with the pain. Yeah, who knows if I could have talked you out of it? That's water way under the bridge. Let's start over in a little while. I need some time

242

to get some other things worked out and you need time to work on your Yvette quest. When you come to a resolution of that matter, either pro or con, if you still want to get together, I'll be glad to."

"Thank you Garrett. I really appreciate that more than you can imagine," responded Brian.

"Before you get too comfortable, there's something else you need to know," informed Garrett. "Anne Mills was the person who cooked up the picture bit with Jersey. She probably had help from Bob Roberts."

"I know most of or it or guessed it," said Brian. "So what's the problem?"

"I don't know an easy way to tell you this, but here goes. I'm in love with Anne Mills," stated Garrett.

"Heh, ... doesn't that beat all? However did that happen?" asked Brian. "You've really fallen for the devil."

Garrett answered, "It's not that simple. It's a long story. We both come from the same town and neighborhood and I knew her as a kid. It gets very complicated. Without going into the details, we spent time together as the Merger was evolving. When it got into trouble, once again we spent time together and somewhere along the way, it just happened. I believe she deeply regrets what she did and will never do it again."

"She feels the same way about you?" asked Brian.

"Frankly, she says no and has clearly told me to get lost," stated Garrett.

"I don't get it," stated Brian.

"Well, I don't believe her ... I really think there's something very meaningful between us," said Garrett. "Sound like an idiot, don't I?"

Brian nodded yes, "But of all people, I'm in no position to judge such things."

Garrett changed the subject, "Tell me Brian, how are going to find Yvette? Got any ideas where she is? Do you want to talk about why she left?"

Brian became quiet. A few minutes passed. "To be quite frank, I never have had a girlfriend and I never was really good at dating. I guess you know that. When I met Yvette, it was under weird circumstances. It was watching her in a club where I rarely if ever went. I was completely; I guess you might say, enchanted. We then met accidentally on a train, would you believe? I, unlike anything I had ever done before with any woman, pursued her. After that unexpected meet on the train somehow, I was able to break down some of her walls and she eventually agreed to marry me. We have had a very odd relationship as a married couple. There were no written rules, but nevertheless there were rules - very ridged rules. They just kind of quickly evolved as we lived together. To tell you the truth it was cold, there was no real intimacy. We expressed all our feelings through gardening, food, the way we arranged the house, etc. Garrett, I'm deeply in love with her, but I don't have the slightest idea how she feels about me. I was always terrified to confront her with such questions. We did everything together – gardening, cooking, and a million things but ...we never ever slept together." There was a pause.

Brian continued, "We never really had a real personal conversation. I don't know a thing about her past. She never said a thing and I knew she did not want to share it with me. One of those rules I spoke of. Crazy, huh? You're probably wondering how I put up with it. It's simple; I took what I could get and accepted what I couldn't get. It's pathetic, I know, but I love her. What should I do now?"

"Wow!" commented Garrett. "Do you want to hear the truth or do you want me to bullshit you?"

"It's time for the truth, that's why I'm here asking for advice. Go ahead, tell me what you really think."

Garrett answered, "What I really think is that it's time for you to grow up. You've been acting like a sixteen year old kid. I know your character well. I know how crazy your family was and probably still is. You're, and I know what I'm talking about, really a very good person and it's time you recognize that and start to treat yourself as a good guy you are. You deserve better than Yvette. Oh, I know how beautiful she is, but she's not capable of warmth and the love you need. I would guess you were some kind of safe haven for her, but never a real husband. That requires being friends, lovers, advisors, advisories, admirers, judges, critics, and people who trust each other completely. Does any of this apply to your relationship?"

"It's not that simple!" barked Brian.

"The hell it's not!" retorted Garrett. "It's time to move on. You need a real relationship, not the constricted conundrum you've been living. She completely disappears the moment you make a stupid mistake. She had every right to be angry, but in a real relationship, you work it out. There was no betrayal here, only your insecurity. Considering your arrangement, the least she could have done was reassured you. The way you describe living with Yvette was like living in a minefield. One wrong move, this way or that way, and boom! And you made a wrong move. My friend, it's time. No more minefields. That's my advice."

Brian said little. It was obvious he was in pain. Finally, he said, "I need some time to think about all that," and he left.

Garrett thought to himself, *Oh Brian give yourself a break!*

CHAPTER 64 AN OFFER

After the last meeting with Anne at Sam's, he realized he had accomplished nothing but some personal venting. Somehow he had to get past that and see if he could find a way to break through the wall that Anne was using to hide her true feelings for him. He was basing this all the premise of Anne's admission about her feelings for Sallie Kate. It was a thread, admittedly a very slender thread, which he was depending on to finally connect. A few days later he made a call to Anne and asked to meet her once more. She immediately refused, but he managed to negotiate an arrangement. He used the idea - guilt - that she owed him something more under the circumstances and made an agreement that this would be the last meeting. She finally agreed. They would once again meet at the Modern Museum of Art – the MoMA.

Anne had come to the point of facing the fact that real personal confrontation was something she had always feared for reasons that had haunted her all her life and probably would not ever go away. She entered MoMA looking for Garrett and spotted him immediately. "Hello Garrett," she said. "Let's have coffee and finish this once and for all."

Garrett said nothing and they walked into the coffee shop, sat down, and ordered.

Anne began, "This obsession you have is based on things that cannot be. We come from such different places. I was brought up to be something very specific - a member of the social elite. We are not supposed to be social equals. I realize how damn silly that sounds, but it is the basis of a lifetime of thinking and habits. Coming from the incredibly dysfunctional family that I'm part of, I never developed a good capability for personal relationships."

She continued, "Garrett, I was never loved by anybody but my father, and he died when I was very young. I forgot how to love or I never learned - it's that simple. Please accept it."

"For crying out loud, Anne, you do know how to love, your father taught you," remarked Garrett. "You just shut down to protect yourself. Stop talking about yourself as a child. You're a grown woman and it's time to open that door and love, and allow yourself to be loved."

"You come from an ethnic family I know nothing about, but I know it is very different from mine," protested Anne.

"Oh, and that relationship that you have with Sam, whose ethnic as hell, how do you explain that?" demanded Garrett. "He loves you and I think you love him. Stop with the nonsense, people are people, some are good, some are bad, and some are irrelevant. Get past it, as apparently you have with Sam. Trash the social bullshit you're hanging on to."

"But nevertheless, I have treated you in business terribly, and I'm ashamed. I think you are a very nice person and you have a lovely daughter. Let's end this now, please," pleaded Anne.

Garrett responded, "All I really heard you say is that you were brought up miserably after your father died and you don't feel worthy of love. The rest is a bunch of crap. Don't bother answering. I want you to try something. I want you to take a risk. You have nothing to lose but a little time."

Anne asked, "What are you talking about?"

"I have a new sailboat that I keep in Maine in a beautiful place called Southwest Harbor," said Garrett. "Sallie Kate and I are going there for two weeks starting at the end of the month. I want you to join us sailing around the beautiful Maine Coast. The worst that could happen is you get a pretty tour of Penobscot Bay and some other wonderful places. If, after spending that time with us, you feel the same, I'll drive you back to City and that will be that - we're done."

"You don't give up easily, Garrett," responded Anne. "I think your idea is ridiculous. I just finished telling you how I feel and you want me to agree to spend two weeks cooped up in some boat with you. Are you expecting some kind of miracle?"

"No, but I want to get you somewhere where you can see the horizon," replied Garrett.

"I don't understand," queried Anne.

"I know you don't. I think you've got to find out before you can forgive yourself and maybe accept the thing you are terribly afraid of."

"And exactly what is that?" demanded Anne.

"Christ, Anne, what have you got to lose but a couple of weeks of time," asked Garrett. "And god knows you need a break."

"I don't know what you're talking about, Garrett," said Anne. "And what about the things I did?"

"For some reason, that is no longer important to me. It's over and it's time to begin a new chapter," stated Garrett.

"That's amazing to me. The last time I saw you, you were very, very angry with me," responded Anne. "How can you have changed?"

"Anne, I was very angry and I had to express it. Damn it, that's healthy. There will be no pretense, no hiding anything, but I'm not going to stay angry. What I really want you to know is that I will not let that anger rule my life. It sounds, I know, too simple, but that's the way that it is, and I know exactly what I'm doing. Back to the boat trip, look at it this way, you will be with someone who claims he loves you, and my daughter who you like and who likes and admires you. It's very safe. If nothing else, it will be a vacation from what you've been experiencing," answered Garrett. "And there is this possibility, after spending two weeks with you, I might find I'm wrong about my feelings for you, and that too is important."

"That's interesting, but back to the horizon," demanded Anne. "What is this horizon business you're talking about?"

Garrett chuckled slightly, "Anne, the only way you will find out is to come sailing with us. I believe you will find it quite worthwhile - take a chance. I could be wrong, but I'm betting I'm right."

Anne responded, "Thank you for the invitation Garrett. It's very nice on your part and I know you mean well, but the answer is no. Think again about what I did to you and the trouble I caused for so many people."

"I have," responded Garrett, "I was extremely disappointed, but I really believe you are contrite about that and those other things you've been doing for ACS. I honestly believe, and I admit I want to believe, that you no longer want to be that person who was capable of such behavior. I see it in your face and body. I also admit I'm not objective, but I believe I see the real person you are. It's that simple. I'm ready to take the chance that I'm right. Admittedly, it's a gamble, but so is life. Strange, I think I fell in love with you those many years ago when we danced. And I think something happened to you also."

"It's still got to be no. It's very sweet of you to make such an offer and I'm truly touched. I will not ever forget how nice you are being. I'll try to figure out the horizon thing myself." She stood up and bent over and kissed Garrett gently and said goodbye and left.

A very disappointed Garrett also left. *How am I ever going to get through to her,* he thought. *Perhaps never.*

CHAPTER 65 THE VISIT

Two days later Anne received a phone call from her brother August. He informed her that their Mother had died and the funeral was in two days. Early the next morning she was driving to Millsport and remembering and remembering. The thoughts were unpleasant. She could not recall a pleasant or loving thing about her Mother. She could see that severe upswept hair, the tight lips, the disapproving eyes, and hear her cold voice. Then also, there was Grahm, once again, to contend with. It all was dark. The more she thought, the more she wondered why she was even going to her Mother's funeral, although she knew that was not how she was raised. Her Father would certainly have expected her to attend her Mother's funeral.

By the time she was crossing the river entering Millsport she was tense, depressed and admittedly anxious. She drove up Main Street passing the old drug store that was now a deli. She passed the massive grey stone Evangelical Church she had walked by so many times in her youth. It was an imposing building with great columns and a myriad of stained glass windows with a great statue of the Christ on the front lawn. It struck her odd that she had never been in that beautiful church or any other church other than the one her family attended. *I wonder why that happens. I guess there are walls. It's never about God, but about those walls that we build to guard and maintain the ridiculous concepts we think is our proper place in this world and, of course, our security.*

As she continued, she passed house after house that were so familiar and depressing. She was surprised as she got closer to her Mother's house how many little details of the houses she passed she remembered. It was almost like time had stood still as commanded by her Mother. Some parts of the town were acting as if they had been ordered by her Mother to comply. *Indeed,* she thought, *Mother was so good at making time stand still. Mother was always the same as she was at her beginning. But now time had finally caught up with Mother. Now she would change. She was now like everybody else, a collection of molecules that would return to the earth and become a plethora of organisms and/or elements. Isn't it wonderful,* she thought, *eventually we all become equal in the ground or in the fire.*

She entered the driveway and saw the house with all its Tudor angles and ivy. There were many cars where usually there were none. She parked and knew, anxious or not, she could not do anything but enter.

As she entered the front door, she was surprised to be greeted by an unfamiliar man. He introduced himself as the funeral director and asked, "Was she a member of the family or a friend?"

To her surprise she was amused by his question. She simply answered, "Something like that."

He didn't know what to do with that answer so he led her to a table, had her sign an attendance book, and directed her through the door that led to the living room.

She entered the room and the first thing she saw was that it was filled with people she did not know. The next thing she saw was her Mother.

The casket was where the piano usually was. The piano had been moved to the opposite corner to make room for funeral viewing. Funeral flowers covered the piano and occupied the floor beneath. There was also, a surplusage of flowers surrounding the casket. A painting of her mother as a young woman was displayed on an easel next to the casket and there was a variety of organization awards she had received. It was all beautiful, superfluous, and Anne regarded it as incredibly hypocritical. *There are no real tears for this woman,* she thought. She approached the casket. *Mother, you look the same as always, cold, un-giving, and coiffed to the hilt. Death has not managed to change your appearance ... so far. You can't hurt me anymore, Mother. The damage is done; there will be no further damage - it's over.*

Then August came over to her and put his arm around her - she flinched and looked to see who it was. She was relieved to see it was August.

"What a cold lady our dear Mother was," said August. "Hello sister."

"Hello August, how have you been?"

"Oh, just wonderful, actually, a little better under the circumstances. I'm not quite sure why I'm here," said August.

Ann volunteered, "That makes two of us."

She looked around the room to see if she knew anybody. Then she saw Grahm and Webster. Webster motioned for her to come over. She and August walked over and Grahm quickly spoke, "Let's go upstairs there are some issues we have to discuss."

"Jesus, Grahm, can't this wait? Anne just got here," pleaded August.

"Absolutely not!" replied Grahm. So upstairs they went into Anne's old bedroom which had been completely redecorated as a guest room.

"Grahm, what can't wait?" asked a suspicious Anne.

Grahm began, "Let's get this very clear, Anne. Several years ago you walked out on Mother and me. As a result Mother, properly in my opinion, disowned you. Therefore, you will inherit nothing. From that moment on you were no longer considered a member of this family. You are nothing but an embarrassment to the Mills family. I am aware of your recent parting from ACS. Mother also was aware of it. She was not surprised. The only reason you are here today is August took it upon himself to call you before I could stop him. I tried, but you apparently had left and left your cell off. You are not wanted here - just leave now."

"For God's sake, Grahm, regardless of anything, she was Anne's Mother. Can't this wait until after the funeral?" demanded August.

Anne interrupted at this point, "Apparently not." Then she commented, "It's very hot in here. When I lived here I always kept the windows open, even in the wintertime."

The room had two dormers facing the side of the house and two dormers facing the front of the house. As her brothers watched quizzically, Anne proceeded to open the side windows and then each of the front windows. The last window wouldn't open. There was a vase sitting on a shelf next to the window which she calmly picked up and hurled it through the window smashing both the window and the storm window, sending shards of glass all over the roof and down to the driveway. She now had her brother's full attention.

Grahm yelled, "What in god damn hell do you think you are doing?"

Anne calmly answered, "Obviously, cooling the room."

"I don't know what you think you're up to, but get the fuck out of this house before I physically throw you out!" Grahm barked.

Anne responded, "I don't know everything that makes you so damn mean, but you are. You have always been a cruel bastard of a brother. You've managed to intimidate Webster into being your lapdog. You have managed to isolate August and demeaned his accomplishments. Oh, you have always had a partner and leader in that project, our dear Mother."

"Grahm, all the way back from my earliest memories you bullied me and have always bullied me. You did terrible things to me as a young child." Looking at August and Webster, "This bastard, your brother, raped me once because he could get away with it. He threatened me physically if I ever told anybody about it. Well Grahm, I'm telling it now to anybody who will listen. This is your last chance to hurt me. Well?"

She stopped for a moment and stared at Grahm. "You won't lift a finger to hurt me because for the first time in my life I realize, I no longer fear you. Your strength and ally are dead, Mother. It occurred to me, as I was coming up the steps, that it was her that made you the bastard you are. She's gone and you're on your own, and Grahm you're not complete - mommy's not there anymore. I suppose you think the money will compensate. It won't. Where I worked all these years, I really came to understand what money can do and what money can't do. The damn inheritance you want, relax, I don't want any of it under any circumstances. August, I will always love you and I want you and me to keep in touch. Stay away from your brothers. Webster, save yourself and get away from Grahm. Grahm, never, never ever cross my doorstep again or I will destroy you. Believe me, I know how. I've been well schooled in these matters."

Grahm said nothing; he didn't know what to say. She had turned the tables on him.

And with that, Anne left the room and went downstairs into the living room, directly to the casket. Once again she took in the entire scene with its style and symbols. *There is little or no truth here except that Mother is dead.*

250

She moved to the bar that was set up in the connecting sunroom. She ordered a double bourbon on the rocks. She quickly drank it down and immediately ordered another. By this time, she was beginning to attract a bit of attention. She walked back into the living room over to the casket and looked down at her Mother. She then turned around facing everyone in the room.

"Ladies and Gentlemen," and turning to look at her Mother's body declared, "A last toast to a cold, mean, and rejecting woman, my dear Mother. A final toast from your only daughter – 'May, you burn in hell, lady.'" Then she raised her glass, "On the other hand, I really don't believe in any of that superstitious bullshit - too bad. I'll just have to be satisfied that you are gone and can do no further damage."

Then Anne slowly proceeded to pour the double bourbon complete with the ice cubes on her Mother's face and chest, "Goodbye Mother." She gave a wave to the crowd and walked out of the house. Everyone who watched and heard her toast was shocked. Her Mother, of course, was not.

Anne got in her car and looked back at the front door entrance as if she was expecting someone to follow. Then it occurred to her, after that performance, no one would want to follow. She started her car, backed out of the driveway, took one last look at the house, and said out loud, "Anne, old girl, it's time to leave this town and family for good", and she did.

CHAPTER 66 CHICKEN SOUP AND CORN BEEF

Anne returned to New York that evening and went directly to Sam's deli. She arrived late, but Sam was still there. She sat down and Sam, seeing her, came over to the table and said, "Anne, how are you?"

Anne looked at Sam and smiled, "I'm better."

"And why are you better?" asked Sam.

She paused and took a deep breath, "Sam, what I'm about to tell you may shock you, but it's the honest to God truth. Reality, the path to truth, has become my best friend lately, for a change, might I add."

She paused and took another deep breath, "I just came from my home town expecting to attend my Mother's funeral. She died two days ago. As soon as I arrived things immediately got a little sticky. In a meeting with my brothers, I was reminded that I had permanently been kicked out of the family by my older brother, and my Mother some time ago. It was the official announcement in some crazy way. I will inherit nothing and I am not welcome, ever. It sounds terrible, but strangely and wonderfully, it isn't. The whole experience was an epiphany for me. It freed me. I should have left years ago. The awful reality is that my Mother did not like me; in fact, she never liked or loved me. I always was a complete failure for her, even as a child. She treated me terribly. It's odd, but I could never be the person she wanted me to be for any aspect of my life. No accomplishments of mine were ever good enough. I don't know why this was, but it was. She was a small minded racist bigot, who tolerated nothing if it wasn't exactly like her. I, in her eyes, failed her completely. My older brother, Grahm, somehow became her surrogate. Sam, he was, and remains a complete son-of-a-bitch. Somehow I now see the whole thing clearly, and I understand it. More important, I accept it. Sam, I really accept it. It's what's real, like it or not. It hurts, of course, and I'm sure it will always hurt, but for the first time in my life I'm not afraid, and, therefore, I'm not going to let it influence my behavior anymore, with all of life's bumps, cuts, and bruises and the rest of the metaphors."

Sam looked at her and gently nodded approval and then he said, "Anne, this will take lots of down time spent thinking for it all to settle in, but I think you are on your way."

Sam, I'm hungry, very hungry. What is still hot?"

An amused Sam replied, "Chicken Soup and Corn Beef."

"Please, bring them on with some good hot coffee."

Anne said nothing for a few minutes. The food was served and she began eating the chicken soup. Then she stopped and began to cry, gently at first, and then a burst of heavy emotion. Sam had never seen such raw feeling exposed by Anne before. *This is good,* he thought. *It's about time.* The bus boy and dishwasher were peeking out from the kitchen at this display. Sam waved them back into the kitchen.

After a few minutes, she calmed down, "It's all true, Sam. I'm not exaggerating. There comes a time when you have to accept the way things really are and live your life within that reality. How's that for growing up? Sam, you've been right, I have been a soldier and I've quit for good, I'm out, I will never to re-enlist. I want to be something else. I do not want to ever inflict damage on anybody. I will defend myself, but I never ever want to plan and initiate harm again. I could tell you all the stories of my family, but I've told you all that counts."

Anne then related all the things that had happened over the past few weeks including, and finally, the invitation from Garrett as she finished her meal.

"So you turned him down," said Sam. "Do you think that was a good idea?"

"I thought so at the time."

"You've changed your mind?"

She said nothing, smiled, and announced it was time to go. As she departed the deli she gave Sam a hug and a kiss and said, "I really love you, Sam."

Sam reached out and gently took both her hands and replied, "I love you too, Anne."

Walking down the street Anne took out her cell phone and called Garrett.

Garrett answered, "Hello Anne .. are you OK?"

Anne responded, "I think so." There was silence for a moment. "Garrett, I'd like to go sailing."

THE END

ACKNOWLEDGEMENTS

This is not the first book I've written, I've written some children's books for my grandchildren, but it is my first novel. And it's the first experience I've had with an editor. Marni Greenberg put me through literary boot camp and I will be ever grateful for her many corrections, do's, don'ts, and suggestions. What an interesting experience that turned out to be. However, if you, as a reader, enjoy this book, Marni was responsible for making it more enjoyable. Thank you, Marni!

I wish to thank Liz Davis, the first person other than my wife Margie, who read the first draft of the book and said keep going; I think you've got something or words to that effect. I must thank my dear friend Arnold Grubin, an author of many books that he refuses to publish – a mistake in my opinion – for his critique and good advice on how you manage such a project. He read, he commented, poured vinegar on some of my ideas, and told me what he liked. As usual Arn, Thanks! Thanks go to my friend Bill Hebel, who was my Wall Street authority, making sure I got the Street right. Much appreciated, Bill.

I would like to extend my appreciation to Lis Sowerbutts of Bookformatter.com of New Zealand for providing the technical help necessary to comply with the many parameters and idiosyncrasies required for digital publishing.

And finally, with deep appreciation and love to my wife Margie, who read chapter after chapter as they were written, and commented and critiqued, using her superb intelligence and sensitivity. Thank you for being you.

THE AUTHOR

 Alex or "Zandy" as he was called growing up, was born and raised in the town of Williamsport, Pennsylvania, birthplace of Little League Baseball. He currently resides in the Catskill Mountains in New York with his wife of more than 50 years where he enjoys playing one of his favorite roles as "dad" and "grandpa".

Professionally, Alex is known for his work as an entrepreneur and technologist. He graduated from Muhlenberg College with a degree in Natural Science and has worked as an applied physicist, holding over 90 patents in some of the most widely used products. He began his career at Razdow Labs, a think tank devoted to NASA projects. Alex is considered the 'Father' of Monolithic Switch Technology which is used globally in products such as microwave ovens, telephones, mobile phones, cash registers and more. He conceived and developed the first machine to print bar code masters and was an essential part of the team that developed the first portable bar code scanner. Alex has been a founder and member of the executive leadership of 5 companies of which 4 were acquired or taken public. He is the recipient of a Special Congressional Recognition Award for his entrepreneurial work and has received numerous other accolades.

deceit-PODv8